P9-DMY-840

Praise for
Leaving Carolina

"Tamara Leigh always manages to wrap biblical truth in a fun, light-hearted package. *Leaving Carolina* reminds us that the good stuff may require a little digging. This wonderful romance does not disappoint."

—KRISTIN BILLERBECK, author of *What a Girl Wants*

"Want to be drawn into a story rather than just reading it? Then allow me to suggest Tamara Leigh's *Leaving Carolina* as your next 'gotta have it' story—because this is more than just a novel. It's an adventure. It's entertainment. It's why you turn off the TV and pick up a really good book!"

—EVA MARIE EVERSON, author of *Things Left Unspoken*

"Tamara Leigh is a must-read for laugh-out-loud humor and soul-bearing honesty! And *Leaving Carolina* is classic Tamara Leigh, with quirky Southern characters, feel-good giggles, and many deep truths to ponder. Come spend some delightful hours in Pickwick, North Carolina, and see why *Leaving Carolina* has a bright spot on my keeper shelf."

—AMY WALLACE, author of *Enduring Justice,* Book 3 in
the Defenders of Hope series

"This is definitely a book I would recommend to my friends. Piper Pickwick is charming!"

—ERYNN MANGUM, author of *Miss Match*

"Of all Tamara Leigh's novels, this one is my favorite so far! The colorful characters in Pickwick invited me to sit down to Sunday brunch and dig into the biscuits and gravy! A fun novel not to be missed!"

—CAMY TANG, author of *Single Sashimi* and *Deadly Intent*

"*Leaving Carolina* is a soul-stirring sip of inspiration. With a Southern twist, Leigh draws us back to core values sweetened with a hint of romance. Good to the last drop!"

—LOIS RICHER, author of *A Ring and a Promise*

"*Leaving Carolina* is the first book in Tamara Leigh's Southern Discomfort Series, and I can't wait to get my hands on the next one! Leigh's cast of eccentric down-home characters, her warm-hearted and harried protagonist, and her charming Southern style provide readers with a story that is warm, witty, and wise."

—MARTA PERRY, author of *Twice in a Lifetime* and *Leah's Choice*

"*Leaving Carolina* was a joy to read. It is delightfully funny, heart tugging, and honest. Tamara has a unique voice, a wonderful way with words, and has created a memorable story with great characters. I loved it, and I am looking forward to her next book."

—PATRICIA H. RUSHFORD, author, speaker, and OCW Summer Conference Director

Leaving
Carolina

Leaving Carolina

a novel

Tamara Leigh

MULTNOMAH
BOOKS

Leaving Carolina
Published by Multnomah Books
12265 Oracle Boulevard, Suite 200
Colorado Springs, Colorado 80921

All Scripture quotations and paraphrases are taken from the Holy Bible, New International
Version®. NIV®. Copyright © 1973, 1978, 1984 by International Bible Society. Used by
permission of Zondervan Publishing House. All rights reserved.

The characters and events in this book are fictional, and any resemblance to actual persons
or events is coincidental.

ISBN 978-1-60142-166-1
ISBN 978-1-60142-236-1 (electronic)

Copyright © 2009 by Tammy Schmanski

Published in association with the literary agency of Alive Communications Inc., 7680 Goddard
Street, Suite 200, Colorado Springs, CO 80920, www.alivecommunications.com.

All rights reserved. No part of this book may be reproduced or transmitted in any form or
by any means, electronic or mechanical, including photocopying and recording, or by any
information storage and retrieval system, without permission in writing from the publisher.

Published in the United States by WaterBrook Multnomah, an imprint of the Crown
Publishing Group, a division of Random House Inc., New York.

Multnomah and its mountain colophon are registered trademarks of Random House Inc.

Library of Congress Cataloging-in-Publication Data
Leigh, Tamara.
    Leaving Carolina : a novel / Tamara Leigh. — 1st ed.
      p. cm. — (The Southern discomfort series ; bk. 1)
    ISBN 978-1-60142-166-1 — ISBN 978-1-60142-236-1 (electronic)
  1. Women public relations personnel—Fiction. 2. Family secrets—Fiction. 3. North
Carolina—Fiction. I. Title.
    PS3612.E3575L43 2009
    813'.6—dc22

                            2009014681

Printed in the United States of America
2009

10 9 8 7 6 5 4 3 2

*To my mother, Zola Mae, who gave me my Southern roots,
pouring out love, wisdom, and discipline in her silky Southern
drawl and serving up pickled corn, biscuits and gravy, and tomato
and mayonnaise sandwiches straight out of her mama's kitchen.*

*Yes, Mom, I always wear clean you-know-whats in case of
an accident; I work at remembering that if a lady can't say anything
nice, she shouldn't say anything at all; and I haven't forgotten my
"Yes ma'ams" and "No ma'ams." I hope I've made you proud.*

He who conceals his sins does not prosper,
but whoever confesses and renounces them finds mercy.

—PROVERBS 28:13

*F*amily is rarely convenient. Case in point: Uncle Obadiah Horace Pickwick. Despite his summons to discuss his will, likely brought on by hospitalization for chest pains, I won't be flying to Pickwick, North Carolina. As I explained to his ancient attorney before he put me on hold, as much as I like my uncle, I can't get out from under my work load on such short notice.

Of course, neither am I ready to return to the town I escaped twelve years ago.

Staring at the phone on my desk, I will Artemis Bleeker to return to the line, but the music continues to drone from the speakerphone. *Whine, whine.* "Oh ma darlin'…" *Groan, groan.* "You left me standin' here…" *Wah, wah.* "Left me starin' after you."

"Yeah, yeah." I flop back in my chair. "Cry me a river."

"Well, ma dear"—the nasal voice drops several octaves—"I'm back."

I roll my eyes. "Nice lyrics."

"What'd ya say, Piper?"

It's him! I grab the receiver. "Mr. Bleeker—"

"You're no longer a little girl, Piper Pickwick. Do address me by ma first name."

As he had asked me to do when I took his call, after which I politely informed him I had dropped the "Pick" part of my name. Though he spluttered over my "butcherin'" of the family name, I didn't defend myself. But had I, my defense would have been based more on the Pickwicks' scandalous reputation than on the nursery-rhyme alliteration that plagued me through my school years.

Piper *Wick* clears her throat. "Thank you, Artemis. I'll try to remember that. So you said the doctors are running more tests to determine the cause of Uncle Obe's chest pains."

"They are, but your uncle is certain it's heart failure. And a man knows his own body. Um-hmm."

"But so far the tests have come back negative."

"These things can be elusive."

Especially when it's simply indigestion. Certain that has to be it, I'm relieved. I spent little time in my uncle's presence, but he was never unkind to me, unlike the other Pickwicks.

You are over that. It's Uncle Obe we're talking about—a black sheep like you.

True, not only did he increasingly shun society the older he got, even forgoing marriage, but unlike his three brothers, he was always upstanding. Not a smidgen of inappropriate behavior—at least in the "criminal" sense. Now in the "odd" sense…

"Uh, what was Uncle Obe doing when he started having chest pains?"

"Just sittin' in his hospital bed watchin' a rerun—"

"He was in the hospital when he *started* to have chest pains?"

"What?" Artemis barks. "Ya think a man his age survives such a terrible accident without payin' a price?"

Where is Scripture when I need it? Not committed to memory

like I encourage my Christian clients. Fortunately, something of an alternative exists, Band-Aid strength though it may be: close eyes, breathe slowly through the nose, exhale slowly from the mouth…

"Piper! Did I lose ya?"

I clap a hand to my chest. Was Artemis booming when Uncle Obe's chest pains started? "I'm just wondering why you didn't say anything about an accident."

"'Course I did."

He's old. Very old. And should have retired from practicing law years ago! "I'm sorry, but would you go over it again?"

He sighs. "Your uncle was in a head-on."

Dear Lord!

"He was thrown clear but sustained cuts and bruises and messed up his knee. Unfortunately, it didn't go so well for Roy. He had to be put down."

"What?"

"Cryin' shame. Of course, he wasn't much use, what with them cataracts and that incontinence problem."

Hold up. This is Pickwick, North Carolina. All is not as it seems. "Is Roy a…dog?"

"Ya all right, Piper? You're not into drugs like all them folks out there in Hollywood, are ya?"

I will not bang my head. "It's been a long day. So Uncle Obe hit a dog with his car."

"Ya don't listen too well, do ya? He hit the dog with his *golf cart.*"

Right.

"Musta been goin' fifteen miles an hour. Traumatized your

uncle, it did. The good news is, if he has to undergo heart surgery, the prognosis is good."

I throw my hands up. "How can it be good if the doctors don't know what's causing the chest pain?"

"Why, he's in good health."

Sighing, I pull my desk calendar forward, and in the middle of June 3, I jot a note to send flowers. "I'm glad the prognosis is good."

"For the surgery. But as for his will…ain't nobody can talk him out of it. Nobody but you, maybe."

Here we go again. "Talk him out of what?"

"The changes to his will. Your family is up in arms."

Family. Hardly. "I assume it affects them monetarily."

"It does."

"Then he's cutting them out of his will?"

"'Course not! He means to provide for his Pickwick kin, but he's got it in his head to make provision for others."

Up in arms is putting it mildly. "Uncle Obe's money is his to do with as he sees fit, so even if I could influence him, it's not my business."

"If the changes to his will become public knowledge—and they will once he passes away—it's gonna be as much your business as your kin's."

Public knowledge gives me pause. But then, in light of the business I'm in and that the words were spoken in the context of the Pickwicks, they should. "Go on."

"Even if the integrity of your inheritance don't mean nothin' to ya, I'm sure your reputation does."

My reputation? Considering how far I've distanced myself from my family, that doesn't seem possible, and yet… What have they done now? More, how might this affect Grant? Recently, a columnist noted that I'm the first woman he's seen regularly in a while. "Business," Grant had assured everyone. And it's true. Grant hired my PR firm to aid in his reelection, resulting in trips between our office in L.A. and his headquarters in Denver. But now there's a personal component to my relationship with U.S. Congressman Grant Spangler.

I look at the photo on my desk that shows us at a fund-raiser months back. We stood before a dozen of his supporters—well, nearly so. The woman in the crooked blond wig (chemo, she said) asked some tough questions, her New England accent setting her apart from the others. Though she warmed to Grant, her body language said she wasn't convinced. But you can't make all the people happy all the time.

"Did ya hear me, Piper?"

"I heard you." I slide my gaze to Grant. At five foot ten, he stood lean and erect beside me. At five foot three, I stood passably fit beside him, curves contained by regular exercise and close monitoring of calories, jaunty red hair limp, smile tired. *To Piper,* Grant scrawled across the bottom of the photo. *We make a good team.*

"All right, Artemis, tell me about the will."

"Well, see, the changes are confessional in nature."

My uncle has something to confess? Whatever it is—watering his garden during the hottest part of the day or breaking up a family of earthworms to plant a rosebush—it can't be scandal worthy. "What does Uncle Obe have to confess?"

"Vandalism."

So he ran over a road marker with his golf cart.

"Cheatin'."

Probably skim-read a novel.

"Tax evasion."

Bought Girl Scout cookies and believes he should have paid tax.

"Theft."

Took a fund-raising mint at the cash register thinking it was free.

"Illegitimate children."

I cannot have heard right. "Surely you're not saying that the one irreproachable son of Gentry Pickwick fathered children out of wedlock?"

"I am. Your uncle has a daughter and a son not much older than you."

Oh, dear. "So there's something to these confessions? And Uncle Obe is responsible?"

"Yes and no. They're serious wrongs, but he ain't responsible for them all. For instance, the cheatin' was done by your great-grand-daddy when he won that big piece of land from the Calhouns back in the early 1900s."

"That was just an ugly rumor."

"Your Uncle Obadiah believes different. And if he provides for the Calhoun descendants in his will, it's gonna be seen as true. Just as it's gonna be believed your daddy conned Widow Stanley into investing her life savings in a shrimp farm that didn't exist. As for the town square statue that went missing all those years ago…"

"That was a Pickwick?"

"Yep, and it's somewhere at the bottom of Pickwick Lake."

This could be bad. "Is Uncle Obe doing this because of his heart scare?"

"That brought it to a head, but I'd say it goes back two years to when his godson came to town."

Godson? Since when?

"Ya see, this feller is one of them 'near-death experience' Christians—nearly died and decided it was time to join the club. The more time your uncle spent with this young man, the more I noticed a change in him. Obe started payin' attention to sermons, and I can't tell you how many times I've caught him with his Bible open."

The shame of it! "I didn't know Uncle Obe had a godson."

"'Course you didn't—was a surprise to all the Pickwicks when he showed up."

So my uncle is in the clutches of a con man.

"Now don't be thinkin' Obadiah is a bad sort—"

"Obadiah? Uncle Obe's godson is named after him?" Must be ingratiation since no one in his or her right mind names a kid that. Take the Pickwicks, for example. *Not* in their right minds.

"That's his name, but like I said, Obadiah Smith has given me no cause to believe he's manipulatin' your uncle."

I write *Obadiah Smith* in my planner. "Besides changing his will to make amends to those wronged by the Pickwicks, is Uncle Obe altering it in any other way?"

"No."

"Then he's not leaving anything to Obadiah Smith?"

"He most certainly is!"

I thrust a hand through my chin-length red hair. "Then obviously—"

"I see where you're goin', but this godson has been an heir since I drafted the first will twenty years ago, and his portion of the inheritance will be reduced by the same amount as the Pickwick heirs in order to provide for the new beneficiaries."

Talk about naive! This guy shows up on the doorstep of a godfather he probably never met, then uses Christianity to lay a guilt trip on an old man to get him to right long-ago wrongs? He's probably in cahoots with the new beneficiaries. Well, maybe not the IRS…

Ugh. Tax evasion could make for *really* bad press. Or, as we say here at the firm, "There will be headlines to pay." "If Uncle Obe truly wants to make amends, why wait until he passes away?"

"Though there's millions in the estate, much of it's material— the mansion, its contents, the land, etcetera."

"Uncle Obe has gone through his money?" Or someone did. Obadiah Smith?

"Your uncle has enough to keep up the estate in an acceptable manner, but not to make the kind of restitution he'd like. That will happen when his assets are liquidated followin' his death."

"But he could liquidate now and make amends quietly. Call the restitution a gift."

"True, but the thought of standin' by as the family estate is turned into a tourist attraction or mown down for some fancy development just kills him."

"What about his illegitimate children?"

"That there is a sticky situation, Piper, one I'm not at liberty to discuss further."

Just enough to make me bite. "What role am I expected to play?"

"As I suggested to your relations, there are two possibilities. The first is as the favored niece. Ya know, he always liked ya best."

Considering he doesn't much like anyone, that carries little weight.

"So he might listen to ya more than your cousins. Failing that, ya put on that PR hat I understand ya wear so well."

I'm surprised he knows my line of work. Of course, my work with some of Hollywood's biggest names was recently mentioned in an entertainment magazine.

"Who better to explain the consequences of this 'tell all' will," Artemis continues, "than someone who devotes her life to helping people out of nasty scrapes?"

Then it's on me to get the Pickwicks out of this? Piper *Wick*? Not! While I don't care to be exposed as "one of those Pickwicks," it's not likely to affect my career or my relationship with Grant, especially since my only crime is being born into a family I've completely avoided for twelve years.

"I had nothing to do with anything Uncle Obe wants to make restitution for."

"Ya think?" Artemis rustles some papers. "Before I let ya go, I ought to tell ya that your uncle wants to include Trinity Templeton in his will."

The name conjures remembrance of a girl who the meaner kids called Trinity *Simpleton*. "Why Trinity?"

"Your uncle believes she took the fall for a prank of Pickwick proportions, namely what happened at the Fourth of July parade the night before your mother and you up and left Pickwick."

An invisible hand slams me back in my chair.

"Caused quite a stir, what with Hugh Lawrence capturing it on his video camera. Made the nightly news and quite a few papers. Ya recall?"

I rub a hand over my face. "Everyone thinks it was Trinity?"

"That's right, though I hold with your uncle that it was one of his nieces. Problem is, y'all were accounted for."

All?

"Maggie had given birth a few days before to little Devyn."

Her illegitimate child that she refused to put up for adoption.

"Bridget was handin' out them tree-huggin', animal-lovin' fliers up and down the street. And her sister, Bonnie, made a right spectacle of herself throwin' that other girl off the float." He smacks his lips. "So that leaves you. And everyone knows Piper Pickwick would never do somethin' like that."

Innocent by reputation, but Uncle Obe doesn't believe it and neither does Artemis. "How is it that Trinity took the blame?"

"There was no accountin' for her that night, she's the right build, and everyone knows she don't fire on all cylinders. Then, when rumors started circulatin' that it might have been her, she didn't deny it."

"Why not? I mean, if it wasn't her." Er, right…

He snorts. "Like I said, she ain't all there."

Oh, Trinity… "What happened to her, Artemis?"

"Her grandparents who raised her decided that anyone who would do such a shameful thing couldn't be trusted to run the family business—ya know, the knittin' shop near the Piggly Wiggly. It went out of business years ago, but your uncle says that don't absolve the Pickwicks of wrongdoing."

"What became of Trinity?"

"Oh, she's around. So ya see, though I don't fault your uncle for wantin' to right family wrongs, this could be bad for the Pickwicks."

And me. *Relax. You were eighteen. It was a teenage stunt.* But one the future fiancée of a conservative politician will have a hard time explaining if it gets out. And it could if the will is changed. I feel the pitter-patter of a headache and rub my forehead.

"One other solution is bein' whispered about."

"Yes?"

"Ya remember your cousin Luc?"

That no-good, Easter egg–thieving— "I do."

"A mutual acquaintance told me that, if need be, Luc will have your uncle declared mentally incompetent to prevent him from changin' his will."

I feel split down the middle—one side relieved at a relatively simple answer to my problem, the other appalled that I'd consider it. *Selfish, Piper. You ought to be ashamed of yourself.* I am. Unless… "*Is* Uncle Obe mentally incompetent?"

Artemis harrumphs. "Your uncle is a different duck, but he knows what he's doin'."

"But how together can he be if he's letting himself be influenced by this *Obadiah* Smith?"

"I told ya, your uncle's godson is a fine young man, if overly Christian. Though he influences your uncle, it ain't in a bad way. Just inconvenient—for the Pickwicks."

I sigh. "Where do you stand in all this?"

"As your uncle's attorney, I stand with him. However, I believe he's makin' a mistake tryin' to right them wrongs. Ya know, time was, the Pickwicks were well regarded, but your dad and his brothers messed that up with their gamblin', drugs, scams, and shady politics. Now, just as respectability is returnin' to the family—"

It is?

"—your uncle decides to hang out the dirty laundry. Um, um, um."

I picture Artemis shaking his head, neck and jowls reddened by the rubbing against his starched collar.

"So ya gonna do right by your family? Now I know the town of Pickwick wasn't kind to your mother and you, but things have changed. Forgive and forget, I say, as does the Good Book. Uh-huh."

Forgive, yes. But forget? That would be like taking a leisurely stroll in front of a firing squad.

"Of course, the one thing ya shouldn't forget is the kindness your uncle showed your mother and you."

He *was* good to us. And my relationship with Grant could be on the line. "Okay."

A piercing clap makes me jump, and I imagine him slapping a big, beefy thigh. "Glad to hear you're comin' home. That is, providin' ya ain't anglin' to have your uncle declared mentally incompetent."

"No. If Uncle Obe is as you say, that would be wrong."

"I was hopin' ya felt that way, being God-fearin' and all. Though it's a cryin' shame that your church attendance is down."

How does he know that? I haven't contacted anyone in Pickwick since we left.

"Why, your moth—" Artemis clears his throat.

Uh-huh. "What about my mother?"

"Whatever do ya mean?"

"Have you or Uncle Obe been talking to her?"

"That falls under attorney-client privilege, Piper Pickwick."

Which answers my question. "Wick."

"Pardon me—*Wick*. By the way, what happened to your pretty drawl? Ya sound kinda flat."

Gone the same way as the *Pick*. "I left the South a long time ago, Artemis." There *is* more to my drawl's demise, but that's explanation enough.

"Yep, went and traded us for the big city."

I look across my office to the windows that would offer an impressive view of the skyline if not for today's tiramisu-layered smog. Ah, L.A.—hub and tailpipe of life, giver and taker of dreams, shining star and black hole of the universe.

"'Course, I imagine Los Angeles is gettin' old."

Someone has *definitely* been talking to Mom. Did she reveal the incident from two years ago that precipitated our talks of trading L.A. for something tamer? The memory crawls up the back of my neck. A deserted parking garage, a soft tread behind me—

I grit my teeth. No, I'm not as happy here as I'd like to be, but I'm trying. "Actually, L.A. has been good to me."

"Careerwise, but"—Artemis chuckles—"you're what—thirty? And single?"

True, but once Grant is reelected…and after a suitable period of settling back into office…and when the timing is right, he will propose. "I don't believe in rushing into something as important as marriage."

"Um-hmm. So when can we expect ya? Tomorrow?"

Is he trying to be funny? "I'll have to check my—"

"Sorry, ma dear. I've got someone on the other line. Bye."

Lovely. As I lower the handset and reach for my planner, my headache goes from a patter to a pound. *Lord, keeping in mind that I am God-fearing, even though work continues to get in the way of church—help me get in and out of this mess as quickly as possible.*

Unfortunately, I'm booked through June and my schedule doesn't lighten up until the first week of July, which would put me in Pickwick during the Fourth of July parade and bring me full circle to *that* night. With a growl, I flip back to June.

"You okay?" my assistant asks as she appears in my office doorway.

I meet Celine's gaze. "Peachy."

She narrows her lids. "Ask a stupid question, get a stupid answer."

Typical Celine. Though I resisted her attempts to befriend me when she came to the firm five years ago, her upbeat attitude and gentle but unabashed Christianity won me over. I don't always listen to her when my moral rudder goes askew, but she doesn't preach or criticize. And when I sit on my pride long enough to ask for advice, she delivers.

"Family crisis," I say.

She frowns, but then her eyes pop wide, and she steps in and closes the door. "The Pickwicks?"

She's the only one I've told about my connection to them, and while I kicked myself following that moment of weakness, I don't regret it. "Yes."

"Do you want to talk about it? Over an early dinner before book club?"

I'd forgotten about book club. Half the time I don't get around to finishing the books, but when I'm able to attend meetings, I enjoy the discussion and diverse group of women. "Dinner, yes. Book club, no."

"Okay."

No pressure. "So, what did you need to talk to me about?"

She startles. "Oh! I just got word that the Lears are in the building."

Why am I not surprised? I consider telling her to turn away the young Hollywood couple who begged me to squeeze them in. After all the shuffling it took to accommodate them, they didn't show. Now, an hour and a half later, they waltz in here as if they're my only clients.

"You do have a half hour before Mr. Gibbs's appointment."

Unlike the millions of women who adore Justin Lear and the millions of men who adore his wife, Celine hopes the "perfect couple" will stay a couple despite the revelation that Justin strayed. The good news is that they're working to save their marriage. The bad news is that Cootchie's self-confidence is in the toilet. That's where I come in: coaching the actress on the art of appearances and arranging opportunities for her and Justin to look to all the world as if their love can overcome a never-to-be-repeated indiscretion.

"Send them in?" Celine asks.

"Yes, but make them wait ten minutes." A slap on the wrist, but it's something.

I continue to search my planner, but no matter how far out I go, I don't have time to deal with a Pickwick pickle. "Thanks a lot, Uncle Obe," I mutter, only to be struck by a memory of him in his garden, loosening a vine from a sapling as my ten-year-old self peers over his shoulder.

I gasp. "Why, that's poison ivy, Uncle Obe. You shouldn't be touchin' it with your bare hands."

"Not to worry. Its oils don't bother me. Want to see if you're also immune?" He turns. "Here, touch it."

And let that vicious blister-causin' plant do to me what it did to my cousin Bart? I retreat a step. "Mama said to stay away from it."

He shrugs. "Well, then, I guess you'll have to find out the hard way."

Or not at all. I cross my arms over my chest. "You should use weed killer."

"Oh no." He strokes a leaf. "This here is God's creation. Once I free it, I'll replant it in the woods."

Mama's right. Uncle Obe may be churchgoin', tolerant of children, kind to animals and plants, and make the best pickled corn in the county, but he is a little nuts.

Shrugging off the memory, I narrow my gaze on the name written in my planner. Who is this godson? And why is he messing with my life? I underline the name.

"Just wait until I get my hands on you, *Obadiah* Number Two!"

2

The Pickwick estate.

Gripping the bars of the gate, I look between them at the driveway and rolling acreage illuminated by the headlights at my back. At the top of that long, winding driveway, at the top of that hill, sits the mansion. I'm only able to pick it out against the dark sky because I know it's there and because the enormous white columns frame the entryway against the gray stone.

What happened to the lights? And the gate ought to have been left open—or at least unlocked! I shake the iron bars.

"Some welcome." And some day—a tractor-trailer accident on the highway causing me to miss my flight, two hours waiting for a seat on another plane, my late arrival in Asheville making me miss Uncle Obe's hospital visitation hour, driving to Pickwick in a rental car that made strange noises throughout, missing the new downtown Pickwick exit and having to take the old Pickwick Pike. And now I'm on the wrong side of a locked gate without a battering ram. Hmm…

I peer over my shoulder at the car's front bumper. It seems sturdy—

No, crashing the gate would not be a good idea.

I did purchase the optional insurance—

That would be wrong.

So I'll have to drive into town and get a room as I'd planned before I received Artemis's message yesterday. I thought it strange that, considering my uncle's privacy issues, he wanted me to stay at the mansion, but I agreed. And now this.

I size up the gate. I'm fit enough to climb it despite a few pounds I've put on over the last couple of months (stress eating). But there's one problem—my linen pantsuit, new and specifically chosen for my meeting with Artemis. A meeting that didn't take place because when I called to tell him I would be four hours late, he refused to budge on his office hours.

"A man's gotta get his sleep, Piper Pickwick. Pardon me, *Wick*. I'll see ya Monday mornin'."

"But that's three days away!"

"Well, God may have set aside one day a week for rest, but I always take two, especially now that I'm nearin' eighty. A man's gotta be good to himself. Uh-huh."

Frustrated at having dropped everything to fly out two days after his call, I reminded him of the urgency of the situation. He informed me that though Uncle Obe is still hospitalized, there's no cause to worry, as Artemis has been able to drag out the process of changing the will. He then said he would leave a key under the welcome mat. Too bad he didn't leave the gate open.

I smooth my waist-length jacket and consider its fate. I'll just have to be careful. I return to the car and cut the lights, and night rushes into the spaces and corners I'd briefly ruled.

My scalp prickles. *It's just darkness. No one's there.* I'm far from alone out here in the middle of what once was next to nowhere. My companion, the working-late-woman's best friend, sits at the bottom of my oversized Rebecca Minkoff purse.

Fondling it through the leather, I lock and close the door, then cross to the gate. The iron fence surrounding the estate is eight feet tall beside the arched nine-foot gate, but the latter is the obvious choice due to foot- and handholds courtesy of bottom, middle, and top rails and the spear points projecting from each.

I remove my two-inch heels, shove them into my purse, place a foot between the spear points on the bottom rail, and begin my ascent. Piece of cake. Unfortunately, it gets tricky once I reach the top. While the spear points are decorative, they could still cause me a world of hurt.

Oops. A Southern thought. It's a good thing I won't be staying long. The last thing I need is to return to L.A. walking and talking Southern—especially talking, since I don't have time for further voice coaching. Get In, Get Out must be my motto.

I grip the top rail, then heave myself onto my arms to get a leg over, but there is only enough space between the spear points for my hands. Maybe they aren't purely decorative after all.

I return my feet to the middle rail and peer at the iron fence to the left. No spear points mean a resting place. Holding onto the gate, I sidestep, boost to the top of the fence, and swing a leg over. After a brief pause, I twist, drag the other leg over, and reach a toe to the gate's middle rail. Contact.

"Good job," I say as I transition back to the gate. I'm overstating my accomplishment, but it's been a rough day. Fortunately, it's looking up.

"Don't move!"

The barked command rattles me so deeply I lose my grip. The burst of light makes me startle so hard my foot slips. Then the weathered bars slip through my hands as I slide down the gate toward the concrete driveway. Impact. Or not.

My progress arrested, I stare wide eyed through the bars. I'm still vertical—thanks to a belt loop caught on a middle rail spear, meaning I'm hanging like a Christmas wreath months past its use-by date. That explains the discomfort between my legs, but what about the guy at my back? Why is he creeping around at night on private property? It can't be Artemis because *this* voice is twangless.

Not again. But this time I'm prepared. Pulse pounding in my ears, I uncurl my right hand, then reach for my purse and my faithful companion within.

"I said, don't move!"

Lord, please help me reason with him, or at least distract him.

I draw a long, slow breath, then gaze over my shoulder and narrow my lids against the light beyond which I glimpse a shadowed figure—on the tall side and broad. "Look, if you don't mind—"

The sound of tearing fabric is followed by a lurch, then my bare feet hit concrete and I fall backward.

The light jerks and swings, and I hear a clatter as a hand closes on my arm and yanks me up. I get my feet under me, but my back slams into a wall of muscle and bone. Meanwhile, my heart starts making plans to relocate without me.

Oh no! This can't be happening—

Hysteria will not get you out of this. Easy does it.

I track the beam of light that illuminates the lower half of the gate back to its source—my assailant's dropped flashlight. He doesn't have that advantage anymore, and soon he'll find out that muscle and bone aren't much of an advantage either. *Oh please, Lord.*

"Are you all right?" His gruff voice is so near I practically seize up.

I ease my free arm up my side, then touch the bulge at the bottom of my purse as I glance over my shoulder into his shadowed face. "I…"

He could be kin to a Neanderthal! I lurch forward, breaking his grip on me, plunge a hand in my purse, and pull out the pistol. Amazed at how light it feels—must be the adrenaline—I whip around and point it at my assailant.

Oh my, I'm aiming, and not at a paper target. The guy has to be scared to pieces, but why isn't he running?

"That looks dangerous." He sounds as if he might laugh. The sicko!

"It is dangerous, so don't think I won't use it."

"You must be Piper."

He knows me? I strain to pick out his features, but the flashlight on the driveway points opposite and provides only enough light to confirm that my imagination is not in overdrive. He *is* big, buff, and hairy. "Who are you?"

"The name's Axel."

Dangerous name.

"I'm the gardener."

Unlikely occupation.

"I live here."

He does? Though Uncle Obe always employed groundskeepers, they never lived on the estate. "Where?"

"In the guesthouse."

I blink as memories of the cottage arise. On more than one occasion, Mom and I accepted Uncle Obe's offer of a place to live. We never stayed long, but it was a comfort to have somewhere to go when things got rough.

"Now that we've established that neither of us is trespassing, you can put your shoe away."

I startle. "What?"

"I commend you on your resourcefulness." He steps past me in the direction of the flashlight. "I certainly never saw *that* coming."

I lower my gaze. Despite the dim light, even I can see it's not a pistol I'm clutching. No trigger—how did I miss that? No barrel—how did I mistake a two-inch heel for a piece of deadly steel?

My cheeks warm, and suddenly I'm grateful for the dark. But does this Axel not realize how close he came to being on the receiving end of a bullet-firing weapon? I'm pretty sure he does, but it's hard to believe he would then walk away. Of course, he did establish who I am. The problem is, I have only his word as to who he is.

The flashlight's beam crisscrossing me as he returns, I dig out my other shoe. That's when I notice my scraped fingers and palms, courtesy of my slide down the gate. Which reminds me… A whimper escapes me as I take in the snags and rust marks on my jacket. Then there's the torn belt loop. Lovely.

"You messed up your clothes," Axel says, reminding me there are worse things than a ruined outfit, like letting one's guard down in front of a dangerous stranger.

I shove my shoes beneath an arm, plunge a hand into my purse, and grip—

Oh no, not making that mistake again. I release the spine of the go-anywhere Bible I tossed in this morning, then finally lay a hand to the cold steel that snuggles alongside God's Word. (There's something not right about that.) But I don't pull out the pistol. After all, it's not as if I couldn't shoot through my purse as they do in movies.

I release the safety (didn't think to do that with the shoe). "How do I know you are who you say you are?"

His stride falters…falters again… Did he twist an ankle when he snatched me from my fall?

He halts three feet from me. "Obviously Artemis neglected to mention me."

He knows Uncle Obe's attorney. I peer closely at him. The angle with which he holds the flashlight reveals more of his features, and I'm relieved he isn't as frightening as he first appeared. Still big, buff, and hairy, but his resemblance to a Neanderthal was overimagined. In fact, he might be all-right looking.

He tilts his goateed, long-haired head. "Neither did he inform me of your arrival."

I frown. "He didn't tell you I was coming?"

"He did. He didn't say when."

"But he's known for two days."

Axel shrugs. "Artemis is getting up there in years."

And this man is just the gardener.

Just the gardener? Somehow that doesn't fit him, particularly in light of Uncle Obe's past hires, who were more often old and doddering. I would be surprised if this man is much past thirty-five. "How long have you worked here?"

"A couple of years."

I wait for him to elaborate, but he seems content to let the silence play out. I'm not. He may not be the missing link, but he's still a stranger. "What about the lights? Uncle Obe always kept the house and driveway lit."

"Which I've continued to do since his hospitalization. However, when I returned from town a while ago, the power was out. I was attempting to determine if it was intentional when I saw your headlights."

A chill skitters through me. "Intentional?"

He hesitates. "Once I've determined the cause of the outage, we'll continue this conversation up at the house."

He thinks I'm going to invite him in? Just the two of us? "Let's continue it here."

"All right, but is the safety on?"

I knew he knew. I thumb the lever and consider returning it to its "safe" position. After all, he hasn't made an untoward move.

"A spooked woman with her finger on a trigger makes me uneasy, especially when the barrel is aimed at me."

I stand taller. "What makes you think I'm spooked?"

"That would be the shoe I was staring down the heel of a short while ago."

He has a point. Keeping my finger on the trigger, I put the safety on.

"Thank you."

He heard that? *I* barely heard it. "Explain 'intentional.'"

"Since your uncle was hospitalized, we've had some uninvited visitors."

Another chill. "Burglars?"

"If so"—there's a derisive edge to his voice—"not your garden variety."

The chill dissolves. "Which Pickwick?"

"The first time it was your cousin Bart. He broke the lock on a side door and had just entered when I showed up."

Good ol' Bart, who never met a stimulant he didn't like.

"After I ran him off, Artemis asked me to keep a closer eye on the estate."

"Then you aren't *just* a gardener."

"I suppose not. I also ran off your cousin Luc."

The only surprise is that Luc was caught. He was always too clever for his victims' good. "So that's why the gate is locked."

"One of the reasons. Of course, it won't keep people out, as you know firsthand, but it will slow them down."

In other words, whatever they're hoping to take out of Uncle Obe's home won't be removed by the truckload.

"And the intercom system allows your uncle to verify his visitors' identities and admit them without leaving the house—when the power is on."

"Intercom system?" There wasn't anything like that in use twelve years ago. And there wouldn't have been since the gate was never locked.

"You didn't see it when you drove up?"

"No."

"Hard to miss." Axel turns toward the gate. "Let's get your car inside, Miss Pickwick—"

"The name is Wick."

He looks around. "I did hear that about you."

I bristle. "Heard what?"

"Your embarrassment over the family name and that you dropped the first part of it after you and your mother left Pickwick."

Artemis must have told him. With a toss of my jaw-skimming hair, I lift my chin. "You wouldn't understand."

He stares at me, and despite the darkness, it makes me uncomfortable.

"How are we going to get my car inside with the power out?"

"I have a key for rare occasions like this." His flashlight illuminates posts on either side of the gate—the intercom system—and he walks away with that hitch.

He seems harmless, at least as harmless as a broad, five-foot-tenish, undergroomed man can be. I lower the pistol to the bottom of my purse and step into my heels. "When did Uncle Obe have the system installed?"

"Several years ago, to keep out Pickwick's growing populace—a curious bunch intent on invading his privacy."

My own curiosity perks up. Because of the extensive arrangements required to leave L.A. on short notice, I had little time to research Pickwick's revitalization that has transformed it from the dying town I left into one of the fastest-growing communities in North Carolina. I wish I hadn't missed the downtown Pickwick exit, where I could have gauged the growth for myself.

"Why are they so interested in my uncle?"

Axel halts at the gate, and I hear the clink of keys. "They're drawn by the historical value of the Pickwick estate. Some believe it has the potential to become another Biltmore Estate—on a smaller scale—and attract tourist dollars."

"Not much chance of my uncle allowing that, wouldn't you—?" I shake my head. "Of course, how would you know?"

He doesn't comment. When he pushes the gate inward, his slightly uneven gait is more pronounced.

"Did I cause that?" I step forward.

"What?"

"Your limp."

"You?" He sounds incredulous.

"When I fell from the gate and you caught me."

Leaving the gate gaping, he follows me to my car. "It's an old injury, or will be given a few more years."

I pull the keys from my purse. Uncomfortably aware of my scraped palms and fingers, I unlock the door.

"Drive up to the house, but stay in the car until I get there. I still need to find out what's responsible for the power outage."

I resent the fear crawling up my back. Uncle Obe may be odd and not the best of hosts, but I never knew fear when I was here before. "Do you think someone's up there?"

"If the outage was intentional, whoever is responsible would be foolish to still be hanging around. Of course…"

…foolishness is not alien to the Pickwicks. But if a Pickwick *is* lurking up there, I have nothing to fear, other than embarrassment at having once shared a last name with the perpetrator.

"All right, I'll see you up there." As I slide into the car, he moves toward the gate, and I'm flushed with guilt at the thought of him walking up the hill, especially with that limp. He does know Artemis, has had run-ins with two of my male cousins (not a bad thing), and his behavior thus far has been aboveboard.

I close the door, start the engine, and switch on the headlights, causing the shadows around Axel to flee. I'm surprised by what I see. His long, sandy-colored hair isn't gnarled or knotted but falls back from his face, as if recently released from a ponytail. As for his facial hair, it isn't all that hairy—a connecting mustache and goatee. Though I can't tell what color his eyes are, they don't look crazed. In short, the guy is good looking, in a G.I.-Joe-action-figure way.

I lower the window as I pass through the gate. "Do you want a ride?"

He peers in. "That was easy."

"What?"

"To gain your trust. And you, a gun-toting woman from the big, bad city of Los Angeles."

He knows where I live—more evidence he's legit. If he hadn't just called me gullible, I'd feel even better about him. "I'll see you up there."

He steps back, and as the aggregate rumbles beneath my tires, my headlights pass over the estate's landscape—acres of lawn mown at light and dark angles, bushes and trees trimmed and mulched, and colorful flower beds set on either side of the driveway. Uncle Obe's gardener is no slacker.

At the crest of the hill, the grade is so steep that my headlights spotlight a stretch of roof before moving down the stone face of the house, its wide-eyed windows staring back at me from high above and on either side of massive carved doors. I brake on the incline to take in the magnificence of the place where my father and his three brothers were born. Uncle Obe may refer to it as a house, but it's nothing short of a mansion.

Gazing up at the enormous white columns, I'm swept with a sensation not unlike falling—but falling *up*. As I lower my eyes, I'm flooded with the expectation that my uncle will stick his head out the door and impatiently beckon me inside.

My throat tightens. I hardly know Uncle Obe—the only Pickwick worthy to carry on the family name, according to my grandfather—and yet memories fly at me. I shake my head, but the day of the Easter egg hunt when I was six seeps through me like water on parched earth.

3

I am happy. And Mama is tryin' to be happy too. I don't know why she isn't, 'cause last night when I couldn't sleep for waitin' for Daddy to come home, I found her prayin' a-side her bed. She said she was askin' God to hold back the rain so it wouldn't spoil the day, and today the sky is Blue blue. Yessir, I'm happy, 'cause when Mama prays, God listens. Even better, I got me a basket of Jesus eggs. And a mess of pink mallow bunnies in my pockets.

"Happy," I sing and poke another chocolate-eyed bunny in my mouth.

"Did you see that?" Aunt Adele starts up again with her chatter that always gives Mama an ache right a-tween her eyes. I think that's why she's helpin' in the kitchen, mixing up punch for us kids.

"I saw it," Aunt A-linda says, soundin' bored.

Suckin' sugar from my fingers, I look a ways up the hill from where I had to stop to catch my breath. Aunt A-linda and Aunt Adele are behind a table keepin' them plates of goodies filled up. My Aunt A-linda has pretty hair, all long and blond, and sometimes she smiles at me. I like her better than Aunt Adele. Mama says I ought not to say it, but she didn't say I couldn't think it.

"Her mother should set a better example," Aunt Adele says.

Who're they talkin' about? Trinity? I frown at the girl sittin' by

*herself on the bench across the way from my aunts. Stripey legs swingin',
she bites into a peeled egg. Nah, can't be her, 'cause a girl in our class says
she don't have a mama—or a daddy. Poor Trinity.*

*Not far off, my big cousin Luc is leanin' against an ol' tree near the
top of the hill. Glad he's not messin' with me, I look at the other kids all
over the lawn of Uncle Obe's big house. It sure was nice of him to invite
the whole town for an egg hunt. I'll bet there are a hun-derd of us.
Maybe two hun-derd.*

"Humph!" goes Aunt Adele. "Barely six and she's straining her seams."

*What does that mean? Rememberin' Mama sayin' not to worry that
my Easter outfit don't fit good—that she'd let out a seam—I look at my
apron dress. The zigzaggy pockets are bulgin' with bunnies. I think I'll
have another.*

*As I lick off the eyes, I catch sight of Aunt Adele again. Is she starin'
at me? Hopin' I didn't do nothin' wrong, I wave at her, but she don't
wave back. Must not be me she's lookin' at. I bite off the bunny's ears,
then its bitty feet.*

*"See there!" Aunt Adele sounds upset, like when she saw the grass
stains on my cousin's brand-new dress. Poor Maggie. Though she said I
couldn't play with her and her friends at school and was kinda mean,
Mama says we need to pray for her—that it's not right a little girl don't
have time to be little, what with all them beauty shows her mama puts
her in.*

*"Mark my words, Belinda," Aunt Adele says, "that girl is gonna
have a weight problem like her mother. Fat, I tell you."*

*That's a mean word. Aunt Adele ought not to talk ugly about other
people.*

"Well, certainly a little plump." Aunt A-linda nods.

"Her mother was a little plump two years ago. Now look at her. Believe you me, that girl is gonna be the same. No wonder her daddy didn't come."

Neither did mine. But Mama said he got in late last night and we shouldn't ask him to keep a promise that might make him sick. Still, I wish he was here so I could show him my Jesus eggs. Hey! If the plump girl is alone like me, she can show me her eggs and I can show her mine.

With my countin' finger, I count ten girls on the lawn who seem like they eat too much, but they aren't alone. They got somebody. Some got a couple somebodies—a mama and a daddy. I reach into my pocket and squeeze a bunny. Maybe one more...

"Oh, no you don't, missy," Aunt Adele says like she means business.

The air gets stuck in my throat, but it's not me she's talkin' to. It's Maggie.

A cookie in her hand, my cousin puts her chin up like she means business too, her red curls bouncin' like I wish my flat red hair would bounce. "Why?"

Aunt Adele points a finger past her. "See your cousin?"

Is she pointin' at me?

Maggie turns, and by the way her nose wrinkles up, I know she's lookin' at me where I stand a little ways down the hill.

"Do you want to look like Piper?"

The curls on my cousin's head swing. "No ma'am. Or talk funny like her."

I do not! I stopped sayin' "ain't" like Daddy told me to. And Mama stopped sayin' it too.

Aunt Adele snatches the cookie away. "Then you aren't to behave like her."

"Adele!" Aunt A-linda says. "I think the child heard you."

Aunt Adele's eyes pinch me hard like her boy, Luc, pinched me when I got to the rainbow egg a-fore him. "Somebody's gotta tell her the way it is. Her mama sure hasn't seen fit to."

It was my mama they were talkin' about. My mama Aunt Adele said is fat and what made my daddy not come. It feels like I got a real bunny in my throat. And there's a big hurt in my heart—like it done fell and broke and the sharp pieces are stickin' me.

"I'd best go talk to her," Aunt A-linda says, and I feel a piece come unstuck. Maybe she'll smile at me…pat my back…carry me inside so's if I cry, no one will see.

As she comes around the table, I step toward her.

"Mama!" Little Bart calls, his blond hair a mess and his bottom lip stuck out as he stomps toward Aunt A-linda. "Luc bite!"

And just like that, my pretty aunt turns from me to him. "See what your boy did, Adele! And with him ten years old and Bart only three! That Luc needs a whippin', and I've a mind to do it myself. There's something not right with him."

Aunt Adele puts her hands on her hips. "If your brat had stopped pesterin' Luc, it wouldn't have happened."

Poor Bart. Mean Luc. Sad Piper. The sharp pieces feel like they might cut right through me, and I pick up my basket. Why's it so light? I glance down at the shiny crinkle grass. No rainbow egg. No eggs at all.

I hear laughter, and when I look up, Luc is poking his red-haired head around the big ol' tree and sticking his tongue out. He laughs again and steps to the side to tilt his bucket. It's full. And that's a rainbow egg on top!

A cry jumps into my throat. It hurts—like it's too big to fit, but it's comin' through anyway. I turn and run a little ways down the hill and hunker behind a bush.

Still Luc is laughin', though he can't see me no more. I lift my skirt and wipe my runny eyes and nose, and some of my little pink bunnies fall outta my pockets and onto the grass. I grab 'em, but bits of yuck are stuck to 'em. They're not good for eatin' now. Aunt Adele would be happy.

But I am not happy. Not anymore. Is this why Mama has to try to be happy? 'Cause people say ugly things about her? I wish she would take me home and Daddy would speak nice to her and I'd sit a-tween them and they'd hug on me. I wish…I wish God hadn't listened to Mama's prayer. I wish it had rained!

I shake the sticky bunnies off my hands and jump up and stomp them into the ground until the pink mallow squishes out from a-neath my white shoes.

"What are you doin'?"

I jump back. Bart's big sister, older 'n me by two years, is standin' there like she went poof! I sniffle. "I—I didn't see you there."

Bridget makes a snorty sound. "My mother says you're in a world all your own."

Is that bad too? "My bunnies fell out of my pockets and got dirty."

She crosses her arms over her chest. "And you thought you'd teach them a lesson by grinding them into the ground and killing the grass, hmm?"

She's mad at me, and I don't think she's ever been a-fore. Usually she just ignores me.

"Why, I bet they ain't biodegradable."

Bio—? I don't know that word. But Daddy would say she sounds like a hick if he heard her use the "ain't" word. Pickwicks aren't supposed to do that or make one-syllable words into two or turn all them "-ings" into "-ins."

"That mess will probably get stuck in some poor bird's throat and kill him dead." Bridget shakes her head, and her thick blond braids swing pretty like Maggie's curls. "You're a litterbug, Piper."

And plump. Her mama said so. I start to cry again.

"Did you find out what's wrong with your cousin, Bridget?"

I peek a-tween my fingers at Uncle Obe comin' up the hill, his hair orangy red in the sunlight.

"All's I know is she's a litterbug." Bridget frowns. "And a crybaby."

"Did you hurt yourself, Piper?"

I shake my head, and Bridget says, "Litterbug!" and runs off.

As Uncle Obe comes near, I see a boy's with him, about Luc's age, with hair so short he's almost got none. He's starin' at me—not mean-like, though when he looks to where Luc is, his face gets kinda ugly.

Uncle Obe puts a hand on his shoulder and says somethin', and the boy stays put. My uncle comes over, squats down, sets his elbows on his knees, and lets his big hands flop a-tween them. "Did Luc take your eggs?"

I nod. "And the rainbow egg I was gonna give Mama."

His eyes look up the hill. "Your Aunt Adele and Aunt Belinda are makin' a right spectacle of themselves. Gonna give the town a lot to talk about."

"I wanna go home."

"All right, but not without your share of eggs." Uncle Obe gets up. "Come on."

I shake my head.

He puts on a thinkin' face that makes him seem old, like maybe *forty, and then holds out a hand. He never did that a-fore, him not likin' company. "Let's go talk to that floppy-eared rodent—the, uh, Easter bunny. He's in my garden."*

I wanna go home, but I wanna see the bunny, so I put my hand in his. As he walks me up the hill, I remember the boy. Maybe he wants to meet the Easter bunny too. But when I check over my shoulder, he's gone. "Who was that boy?"

"My friend's son, just here for today."

I wanna ask who his friend is, 'cause I don't know that he has any, but Aunt Adele calls to Uncle Obe. I hook my thumb around his thumb and hold tight so's she can't take him away like Bart took Aunt A-linda away.

But Uncle Obe turns aside like he don't wanna talk to her. "Was supposed to be a frog strangler today, but the sun came out and not a cloud in the sky."

I nod. "Mama prayed the rain away. God listens to my mama."

I think he smiles, but I can't be sure 'cause his mouth don't ever move much. "I'm sure everyone in Pickwick is grateful to her."

"I don't think they know, 'cause if they did, they'd be nicer, and maybe she could make her some friends. Maybe I could too."

Frownin', Uncle Obe leads me around the house to his garden. It's so pretty, even if only a few flowers have got back their color.

"Sit here." He lets go of my hand. "And cover your eyes while I have a speak with that rodent."

I wiggle onto the bench and set my basket on my lap. "I wanna see him."

"He won't allow little ones to see him on Easter day, so don't look or he won't leave you any more eggs."

I put my hands over my eyes as his feet crunch away. A while later, he's whisperin' and the bunny whispers back. I hope they hurry so's I can find Mama and tell her how much she sounds like the Easter bunny.

Finally I hear Uncle Obe's feet again. "More eggs have been delivered for you."

I drop my hands, and sure enough, there are colored eggs all over the garden. I run to him and hug his legs. "Thank you!"

He pats my head. "Go get 'em."

When I find the last one, Mama comes out the back door of the kitchen, wipin' her hands on a towel. I don't tell her about Luc or what Aunt Adele said 'cause she seems more happy now, and I don't want her to lose her happy face.

She holds my hand as we walk to the front lawn, and Uncle Obe follows. The kids are still there with their mamas and daddies, and I'm glad I got my mama. She leads me to a big patch blanket, and we sit on it.

Mama looks over her shoulder at where Uncle Obe is walkin' away. "Poor Obadiah," she says like she don't know anyone is listenin'. "I don't think life turned out the way he expected. I know the feelin'."

Poor Uncle Obe. Poor Mama. But not poor Piper, 'cause I got a basketful of Jesus eggs and I'm not gonna think about the ugly things Aunt Adele said. I just hope she and Luc don't bother us over here. "Mama?"

"Yes?" She smiles, and I want to kiss her smile, it's so pretty. So I do. And she laughs. I like it when she laughs.

"Would you say me a prayer?"

"What kind of prayer?"

"That everyone is nice, and anyone mean will go away so we can be happy."

Her eyes get wet like when she waits supper for Daddy and he don't come, and then she closes them and prays. Not more 'n a minute later, Aunt Adele is draggin' that Easter egg–thievin' cousin of mine after her, and he's got a hand over his face and is bellerin' like someone hit him. And Maggie is followin'. Then they're in their car and drivin' down the long driveway.

See, God does listen to my mama. Though I still got a hurt in me, I'm gonna try hard like her to be happy. "Happy…"

4

As the little girl's voice drifts away, I hear the woman she became whisper, "Happy…"

For fear of slipping into another memory, I squeeze the steering wheel hard and accelerate into the cobblestone parking area across from the entryway. I reach to cut the headlights but draw my hand back. They are the only lights on the estate, and I don't want Uncle Obe's gardener stumbling around in the dark, which could happen if, say, his flashlight dies.

The minutes tick by without a sign of Axel. Did something happen? He did say the outage could be intentional…

I pull my purse onto my lap. As I once more grip the pistol alongside the little Bible (I have got to rectify that), I scan the driveway. *Where are you?*

He likely has me worried for nothing. It probably *is* just an outage. I don't recall seeing any other house lights when I came down that winding mess of a road, better known as Pickwick Pike.

Correction. Bronson and Earla Biggs's lights were on—notable because some of the lights were of the Christmas variety. "Why take 'em down?" Bronson used to defend his right to leave them up year-round. "I'll just have to put 'em up again next year." So if the Biggs's lights were on…

Of course, they are a mile away, and the outage may not have extended that far. In fact, I'm certain nothing sinister is happening. It's just fear talking. I release the pistol, cut the lights, and open the door.

As if on cue, a half-dozen darkened windows light up. "Power outage." I sling my purse onto my shoulder and slam the door. A few moments later, I ascend the mountain of steps.

In spite of Artemis's forgetfulness, the key is under the welcome mat. I open the door, and the soft light within sweeps away the shadows surrounding me. At first look, the entryway appears as grand as ever with its far-flung walls and soaring ceiling. But at second look, it's tired like an old woman dressed in all her finery that, on closer inspection, reveals her shawl is pulled and yellowed, the folds of her skirt are rimmed with dust, and her slippers are worn. The twelve-foot ceiling is discolored, the iron-and-crystal chandelier is strung with cobwebs, the mirrors and marble-topped tables on either side are thick with dust, and the rug that stretches across the entryway is threadbare.

Disturbed by the disparity between the past and the present, I enter, close the door, then peer beyond the pillars that mark the end of the entryway and the beginning of the great hallway. Various rooms are set left and right, and at the farthest reach is the grand staircase. It appears to be in no better shape, and yet Artemis assured me Uncle Obe had enough money to keep up the estate in an acceptable manner. Obviously, our definitions of *acceptable* don't match.

So now I'm inside the Pickwick mansion and soon to be at the center of a Pickwick mess. I almost wish I had accepted Mom's offer to accompany me, which she made after I confronted her about her conversation with Artemis. She admitted to filling him in on our lives, which would be fine had she left out the reason I started carrying a pistol. None of his—or anyone's—business.

And that's why I turned down Mom's offer. She's not anyone's business either. L.A. may be big and scary at times, but it's more diverse and accepting than Pickwick. Mom has friends there, a well-paying job at an insurance company, and a good church. She's happy, not just *trying* to be happy. Thus, the town of Pickwick is going to stay in her past, and as soon as I'm done here, it will return to mine.

I venture deeper into the house, the only sound that of my heels as I transition from the rug to the wood floor—until I hear a creak from the direction of the library.

Probably the house settling. Still, I squeeze the pistol through my purse. *Or it could be Axel.* "Hello?"

Another creak, followed by a growl. Was that a dog? Some wild creature stalking the hallways, waiting for its next meal to show up? Might that be me?

I pull out the pistol and back away.

"Hey," a voice calls from the library, "is that you?"

That wasn't Axel.

The growl sounds again.

"Uh…" The one in the library clears his throat. "I could use a little help in here, cuz."

Surprise, surprise. I step forward, slide a hand around the doorway, and flip the light switch.

My "cuz" doesn't seem well, but the beast at the foot of the rolling ladder probably has something to do with that. If not for my pistol, I'd be scared sick too.

I move through the doorway and look from the blond man on the angled twelve-foot ladder to the dog, whose head is turned in an almost-casual manner toward me. As big and mangy as he is, he's kind of cute in a Benji-on-steroids way—until his eyes lock on my pistol. Then he whips around and growls. Not so cute.

"Hey," says my twang-infected cousin, "long time, no see."

Not long enough. "What are you doing up there, Bart?"

"Cowerin'. Have you seen the points on those teeth?"

"Let me rephrase that. What are you doing sneaking around Uncle Obe's home?"

The dog takes a predatory step toward me, and I catch my breath.

"He doesn't like the gun. Put it away."

Right. When all that stands between me and death or dismemberment is a bullet?

The dog shows more teeth, causing my trigger finger to tremble. He's going to force my hand. I don't have to shoot to kill, though, just to disable. "Don't make me do it." My final warning. "Back off!"

"Ah, Piper, you aren't gonna shoot the dog, are you? He's just doing his job."

That hadn't occurred to me. Does he belong to Uncle Obe? Did the gardener leave him inside to discourage intruders?

"And he's good at it." Bart chuckles. "Got me up a ladder."

My cousin, the intruder. "Speaking of which—"

The dog makes its move. I yelp and seek him in my sights.
Aim low.

"Errol! Halt!" A hand reaches from behind me, closes over my
gun arm, and swings it to the right.

Despite my thundering fear, I don't squeeze the trigger, and I
don't know why. Unless I'm just a pistol-toting wannabe who doesn't
have the guts to pull the trigger on anything beyond a paper target.
But in this case that might be a good thing. The growling, fang-
bearing beast has transformed into a tail-wagging mutt.

"Sit!" Axel continues to hold my arm with the pistol pointed at
the floor.

The dog obeys, ears perked and tongue lolling as it looks at the
man over my shoulder.

Warm air sweeps my ear, causing strange sensations to zip
through me. "I told you to wait in the car," Axel says with the stud-
ied patience of one speaking to a naughty child.

That does it—no more sensation. Just me and a man who has
no business touching me, especially since I'm practically spoken for.
I pop my head around to tell him to remove his paw, but when we
come face to face, he looks even better indoors, despite a clenched
jaw. It must be the eyes. None of that gray stuff people pass off as
blue—myself included. They're…well…capital-*B* Blue.

He continues to glare at me, and when I don't respond, his eyes
soften with questioning, but only for a moment. Then he steps from
behind and pulls the pistol from my hand. "You could have killed
Artemis's dog."

"Or your cousin," Bart says. "I told her to put down the gun,
Axel, but did she listen? No, just as unreasonable as ever."

Yanked back to my *unreasonable* self who, for one crazy moment, was attracted to Uncle Obe's gardener, I reach for my pistol. "Give me that."

He flicks on the safety, then slides my pistol into his waistband as he walks farther into the library.

"That's mine!" I hurry after him.

At the base of the rolling ladder that juts out from rows of cloth- and leather-bound tomes, Axel halts. And though I'm tempted to snatch the pistol from his pants, reason prevails. Curling sore fingers into sore palms, I follow his gaze up the ladder.

My cousin, his back to a jumbled shelf, smiles.

"Artemis told you what would happen if you were caught sneaking around the property again," Axel says.

Bart does surprise well—unless you know him. Then it's akin to crying wolf. His quirkily appealing face, which has gotten him out of trouble more times than he deserves, opens wide and innocent. "Why, I just dropped by to welcome my long-lost cousin home." He nods at me, as if seeking agreement.

Which he doesn't get.

"And, I suppose, that required turning off the power while I was in town?"

Bart's eyebrows shoot up. "I can't believe you're accusing me of something so underhanded."

"The switch was thrown on the main power box."

"And you think I did it?"

Axel lowers his gaze, then pointedly trails it up the ladder to where Bart perches near the ceiling. "You came in through a window."

"Appearances can be deceiving." My cousin considers the big dog in the doorway. "Is it safe to come down? I'm getting a cramp."

"That depends on whether someone wants to press charges for breaking and entering."

Bart chuckles. "You know my uncle won't do that."

"Your cousin might."

The eyes Bart turns on me are puppy-dog big. "You wouldn't, would you, cuz?"

I wish he wouldn't call me that. It tempts me *to* do a thing like that. But he is my cousin. "Far be it from me to fault you for welcoming me back in such a creative manner…*cuz.*"

Bart gives Axel a "ha!" look.

"However, in future, you'll need to present yourself at the front door when you come to call." Another Southern moment…

"Now that the element of surprise is no longer a consideration, it would be my pleasure." Bart descends and, to my dismay, falls on my neck. "Welcome home, Piper."

Home.

He pulls back. "You've changed—for the better."

Some compliments are best left unspoken. *And comebacks.*

"If Artemis hadn't said you were coming home, I wouldn't have recognized you." He takes a step back. "Well, I did what I came to do—"

Did he?

"—so I'll get going and let you settle in."

As Bart starts to turn away, I find my social skills. "How are Bridget and Bonnie?"

"Uh…still my sisters."

I bite back sarcasm. "I mean, what are they up to?"

"Oh." He frowns. "Bonbon got her degree, married her professor, and has twins. She doesn't visit often, what with all the research she and her husband are involved in. As for Bridge, she's still into her silly environmental causes—in seventh heaven with all this 'go green' movement. Oh, and she's widowed."

News to me, since the filter between L.A. and Pickwick became increasingly clogged with each passing year.

Bart shrugs again. "That's it in a nutshell."

I'll say. "I'm sorry Bridget lost her husband."

His face falls a degree. "Yeah, freak accident. Happens to the best of us."

O…kay. I glance at Axel, but his chin is down, and I'm certain that his interest in his shoes is a front. Back to Bart. "And I'm happy for Bonnie."

"Thanks." He tosses his hands up. "I'd better get going."

At Bart's approach, the dog stops thumping his tail, and when my cousin reaches a hand to him, he growls.

"I don't get it." Bart snatches his arm back. "I'm one of the most dog-savvy people I know, but I can't seem to connect with Errol."

"It's probably the Great Pyrenees in him." Axel smiles. "They're intelligent dogs."

Bart drops his jaw. "You wound me." He waits for a retraction, and when it isn't forthcoming, he skirts the dog. "Later, Piper."

"Just a warning," Axel says. "Artemis has placed Errol at Ms. Wick's disposal."

What? I am *not* having a big, stinky dog—

"Wick?" Bart's eyes pin me. "It's true. You *did* change your name."

I have nothing to be ashamed of, especially relative to the antics of my Pickwick relations, but I make an effort to soften what is perceived as an insult. "I abbreviated it."

"Why?"

"For one thing, Wick is short; for another, it's somewhat unique." Although not as unique as Pickwick, which, in these parts, is associated with dysfunction. "Thus, it's easy to remember and is a better fit with my first name." No more "Piper Pickwick picked a peck of pickled peppers," thank you very much.

"That's lame."

"It works for me."

Bart snorts. "Even if you threw out the 'Wick' with the 'Pick,' you'd still be a Pickwick." He thrusts his chest out. "It may make you feel better to pretend you're not someone you are, but I'm proud of who I am. Sure, I've done things I regret, but I'm working to better myself and restore integrity to our family name."

By cutting the power, breaking in, and sneaking around like a criminal? I glance at Axel, whose eyebrows are up, confirming we're on the same wavelength.

"Things may have been bad when you and your mom tore out of town," Bart continues, "but some of us learned from our mistakes and are trying to live godly lives."

Had I anything in my mouth, it would be all over him.

"That's right—godly." Bart responds to the disbelief I feel hanging from my face like a sign swinging by its last nail. "I am a changed man—"

A loud scrape is followed by a rumble at my back, and Axel calls out a warning. I leap forward and whip around to see the last of a dozen books hit the floor amid a cloud of dust. Only a few remain on the uppermost shelf, and one appears ready to throw itself overboard. But something is there that doesn't belong in any library. "What's that?"

My cousin drops his jaw. "Wow, what *is* that?"

"Night-vision goggles," Axel says dryly.

Bart jerks his head around. "You think?"

"I know."

So do I, though I've only seen them in spy movies. I scale the ladder and retrieve the binocular-eyed object from the dusty shelf. "Axel's right."

"Interesting," Bart murmurs.

I descend and cross to where he, Axel, and Errol stand in the library's arched doorway.

I expect Bart to reach for the goggles—they had to cost a small fortune—but he merely smiles. "Wouldn't you love to know why our reclusive uncle keeps such a high-tech piece of equipment lying around?"

"Perhaps in the event the power is shut off?" Axel says.

I exchange a knowing look with him, the depth of which surprises me given our brief acquaintance.

"Let me tell you, they would have come in handy tonight. I could barely see a hand in front of my face." Bart lifts one and wiggles his fingers.

It's halfway convincing. So either he's innocent, or Bart is good

at what he does, meaning he may have crossed the line between ha-
bitual lying and pathological lying.

Something slaps my hand, wetting it from fingertips to palm.
"Ugh!" I jump back, but the dog reaches again with his slimy
tongue.

"Errol, sit." Axel commands.

Errol lowers his rump as I wipe the drool on my once-favorite
pants. Disgusting!

"I'll see you around." Bart starts down the hallway.

"A changed man, hmm?" Axel murmurs as we hear the front
door open.

I don't know why I feel the need to defend my cousin, but I say,
"He may not have known about the goggles."

Axel opens his mouth and then closes it, as if realizing it isn't his
place to argue.

With a growl, Errol lunges into the hallway.

"Hey!" Bart halts a few feet from where the dog stands between
him and us. "It's just me."

"Down!" Axel says.

The dog whips his head around, and—I declare!—he looks
frustrated.

Axel shrugs. "I'd let you, boy, but Ms. Wick appears to be fond
of her cousin."

I am *not*!

"I was thinkin' "—Bart glances at the goggles—"Uncle Obe
would probably want me to have those."

I do a double take. "Oh?"

"For animal watching, a new interest of mine."

"And you need night vision for that?"

"For the ones that come out at night."

"Nocturnals."

"Right."

"I'm sure they would be useful, but I'm not at liberty to give away Uncle Obe's possessions without consulting him. However, when I visit him tomorrow, I'll ask on your behalf."

Though his wallet has to be pinching him, Bart says, "Nah, I'll ask him myself." He starts to turn away. "Of course, maybe I could just borrow them for a little while."

So he can return them to some unsuspecting merchant for a refund? "Sorry."

He sighs. " 'Night."

The front door closes, and I peer down the hallway to be certain Axel and I are truly alone. "So the goggles *are* his."

Axel extends a hand. "May I?"

I pass them to him, and our fingers touch. I did *not* feel that tingle. As I fold my arms over my chest, I recognize the gesture as defensive and drop them back to my sides. *Exude confidence—feet planted shoulder-width apart, arms loosely held at sides.*

Axel examines the eyepieces that project from beneath the headband. "Not military issue, but they'll do the job." He taps a small third eye. "Built-in infrared illuminator for total darkness. Relatively light so they can be worn for extended periods of time. Probably cost seven or eight hundred dollars."

How does he know so much about them? A fan of Tom Clancy novels?

"Good for caving and"—he gives a tweaked smile—"observing nocturnal wildlife."

I blow a breath up my face. "Okay, so my cousin used them to snoop around Uncle Obe's home. What I want to know is why it was necessary to turn off the power."

"If detected, he would have the advantage of night vision, unlike his pursuer. And, of course, he didn't want to set off the alarm."

When did Uncle Obe install an alarm? "But alarm systems have battery backup. At least mine does." Always a comfort when I come home after a twelve-hour workday.

"Obviously, your cousin didn't consider that. Not that it would have made a difference, just as it didn't matter that he turned off the main power." Axel returns the goggles to me. "The alarm system is not of the electrical sort. Errol is the alarm."

The big lug yawns, slides his paws forward, and stretches out.

"When Artemis warned Bart and Luc to stay off the property, he told them an alarm system had been installed. What he didn't say was that it was highly mobile and had a tendency to drool."

I smile. "Clever."

Axel smiles back, not only with his mouth but with those Blue eyes that act on me like a double boiler on chocolate. Not good, especially since one of these days I'm going to be engaged to Grant.

I step past him, set the goggles on a table beside a worn sofa, then survey the books that line every wall except the front, with its large-paned windows. "What do you think he was looking for in here?"

"He may not have been looking in here. Even if Errol was napping when your cousin broke in, I doubt Bart would have gotten as far as the library undetected. My guess is that Errol chased him in here, where he remained until you arrived. That would be when he tried to stash the evidence of his covert activity."

Covert… Perhaps Uncle Obe's gardener has a military background? I'd love to see his bare arms—*strictly* for confirmation. If he has served in the military, he's bound to have tattoos. Stereotypically speaking. "Do you know what he was after?"

His hesitation speaks volumes, though not in any language I understand. And when he says, "He's your family, not mine," it's obvious he has no intention of translating.

I rub my forehead. While my internal clock should be on L.A. time, it seems more in line with North Carolina's three-hour difference. "It's late, and I'd like to settle in."

Axel pulls my pistol from his waistband and extends it, barrel down. "I doubt you'll need this during your stay, but if it makes you feel safe…"

I snort as I take it. "Considering my night thus far, that's almost funny."

"You were never in any real danger."

"No, but in the two years since I received a permit to carry, I haven't felt the need to point my gun at a single living thing." I check the safety and return the pistol to my purse. "Now, I've pulled it twice in one night. Obviously Pickwick is a dangerous place for me."

His mouth curves in the space between mustache and goatee. "Perhaps, but I doubt a bullet could save you from its dangers."

Spoken like a true gleaner of Pickwick family gossip. Or not. The Pickwicks do "hang it all out there," and I'd guess they're still making news despite supposedly recouping some respectability.

"Of course, I'm sure a pistol makes a woman feel safer in the big city," Axel muses, "as it has probably made you feel safer since what-ever caused you to start carrying."

Memories of that event arise—another late night, a deserted parking garage, and the realization I was not alone that came almost too late. Almost. *Thank You, Lord.*

I blink and find Uncle Obe's gardener watching me. Naturally, embarrassment calls for indignation. "You assume more than you have a right to." As soon as the snooty words are out, I wish I could rewind. I sounded downright—

Downright. How many Southern moments will I have to suffer before I shake the Pickwick dust from my feet?

"You're right." Axel's lids lift. "I am just the gardener."

And I feel worse, even though he doesn't look humbled. In fact, going by the turn of his mouth, he's amused. "I'm sorry. It's been a long day and I'm tired."

"Then you should be in bed."

Before I can identify the double entendre in his eyes, which I've become accustomed to with male clients, he walks past me with Errol on his heels. "I'll get your luggage."

A few minutes later, he sets my bags inside the front doors. "I meant to ask how you got into the house."

"Artemis left a key under the welcome mat."

"He must have done that while I was in town." He looks at Errol. "Stay."

"You're leaving him?"

"That's Artemis's plan, and I have to agree about the need for se-curity, especially after what you walked into tonight." He inclines his head. "Good night, Ms. Wick."

That's it? Just like that I'm stuck with a stinky mutt? I follow Axel onto the landing. "But there's no need for a guard dog. I have a gun."

"And high heels."

Ah!

He moves outside of the light that falls through the open doorway and descends the steps. "I'm in the cottage if you need anything."

I glare at his back, then hurry inside and position myself behind Errol. I sink my hands into his matted fur, then push, shove, and grunt, but he doesn't budge. "You big lug!" I give one last thrust.

My feet slide out from under me, knees hit the rug, and I fall into the mutt. His ripe smell gagging me, I lurch upright only to discover I have been shed on. In addition to snags and rust stains, white and gray hair now defiles the formerly fine fabric of my designer jacket.

I point at Errol. "I am not your new best friend, so you had best give me a wide berth." *Best give me? You, Piper Wick, had* best *remember you are not Southern anymore.*

He drops and offers up his hairy belly.

"Yeah, right." I move around him and close the door more firmly than intended. In fact, it could be mistaken for a slam.

Pulling up the retractable handles on my luggage, I wince at my smarting palms. As I wheel past Errol, he pops up and follows me toward the staircase. I whip around. "What about 'wide berth' do you not understand?"

His furred eyebrows go up, but the rest of him lowers to the wood floor that is in dire need of refinishing.

"Glad we understand each other." Now to get back on task so I can put Pickwick behind me. This time forever.

The breath I draw through the sheets is warm and stale, and I wish I could squeeze my ears closed as easily as my eyes. But my iPhone is trilling.

I turn my head and open an eye. My shoulder comes into focus, the lightly freckled expanse broken by the strap of the camisole I slipped on before falling into bed last night. What time is it?

As I flip onto my back to glance at my watch, my cell phone quiets. "Six thirty…" Who was calling so early? And on a Saturday? I squint into the bright room, sunshine streaming through mullioned windows. Strange. I don't remember it being this light at six thirty—

"Oh!" I forgot to turn the time ahead to reflect the three-hour difference, meaning it's nine thirty. I toss the covers back and cool air sweeps my limbs, tempting me to go back under. I resist and, a few moments later, flex my tingling toes amid carpet that has seen better days.

In keeping with my morning routine, I should go running, but sometimes exceptions must be made. In this case, for the greater good of Get In, Get Out.

My iPhone beeps from the dresser, alerting me to a message. Grant responding to the one I left him last night?

As I hurry forward, my attention swerves to the go-anywhere Bible I set on the corner of the dresser last night after putting an end to the fraternizing at the bottom of my purse. Since the gun was there first…

The message is from my mom, and I'm a little disappointed. Of course, Grant is a busy man. Mom says she misses me and then passes on information from the agency I hired to look into Uncle Obe's godson. It turns out that Obadiah Smith—a.k.a. Obadiah Number Two—was honorably discharged from the army. Nothing shady so far, but the investigation is far from exhausted.

I glance up. "Think You could put a rush on this, Lord?" I wince. "I know I haven't been spending much time with You lately, but"—I zero in on the little go-anywhere and swipe it from the dresser—"I brought a Bible."

I open toward the back and land on the book of Luke, chapter nine. Of all the Scripture on the two pages, only the fifth verse stands out due to the stroke of my yellow highlighter. *If people do not welcome you, shake the dust off your feet when you leave their town, as a testimony against them.* Which I did twelve years ago when I left Pickwick. And will do again.

I close the Bible and set it on the dresser. My little venture into God's Word may barely register on the daily devotional scale, but it's a start.

I turn to my luggage at the foot of the bed. My favorite outfit sits on top, and the damage is worse than it appeared last night. Not only is the fabric soiled, snagged, and furry, but there's a tear above the jacket's right pocket, and the belt loop on the pants tore through the pleated material. At a retail price of twelve hundred dollars, it looks like a proper burial is in order.

Grumbling, I shake out the jacket, fold it, do the same with the pants, then lay the pieces in the wastebasket beside the bedroom door. "The price of family," I eulogize, which would be unconscionable if my credit card had born the burden. Fortunately, all the outfit cost was a trip to the showroom of a clothing designer whose reputation I helped restore following a DUI. Not only did she pay her bill in full, but she insisted that I choose a new wardrobe from her latest line. *I* insisted on just one outfit—a flattering two-piece that would serve me well for years. Too bad I didn't factor in Pickwick. Or my impulse to climb the gate.

Twenty minutes later, dressed in stylish cargo pants and a vibrant scoop-necked top, I brush my teeth in front of the window that overlooks the back of the property. Unlike the mansion's pitifully tired interior, Uncle Obe's beloved garden is trim and bursting with the beauty of late spring. Not that it boasts the grandeur depicted in the black-and-white photos taken in the early 1900s, when construction on the mansion and the surrounding grounds was completed, but it is lovely. Axel is certainly doing his job.

I gaze at the cottage in the distance that sits among trees on a hill. Despite the turmoil that often landed Mom and me at Uncle Obe's door, the tension eased the moment we entered the cottage.

Determinedly, I return to this day and the reason I'm here. Not as a child in need of sanctuary, but as a woman with a mission. However, food comes first, meaning I'll have to head into town. Further meaning that a little cover is called for, as Bart has surely informed others of my arrival. I retrieve a brown, velvet-trimmed baseball cap and tuck my short red hair beneath the band.

When I descend the stairs, that dog is waiting. Tail whipping, he turns, changes direction, and turns again. If I didn't know better, I'd say he's happy to see me, but he's probably in need of a sturdy bush.

As he bounds across the lawn to take care of his business, I slide into my rental car and toss my purse on the passenger seat. "Pickwick, here I come."

Houston, we have a Wal-Mart.

I slow on the four-lane road that was once two-lane and consider the block-and-mortar building. For all its simplicity, it sprawls almost regally where there used to be a field and a fruit-and-vegetable stand. In the foreground are a Chick-fil-A and a Cracker Barrel restaurant, and farther down the road I pass a shiny new gas station with multiple bays and a minimart.

"Progress," I murmur. Wide-eyed with the thrill of discovery that contrasts with pangs of familiarity—the high school (yuck), Martha's Meat and Three Eatery (yum)—I smile. There's a chain bookstore. A swanky hair salon and spa. A block of office suites that resemble a village. A large bank with a bubbling fountain. A boutique named Le Roco Roco. A billboard advertising a single-family home development on Pickwick Lake.

Ah, civilization. Maybe my stay won't be so bad after all.

My stomach reminds me of its need at the next light, so I make a U-turn and lock in on Martha's Meat and Three Eatery. As I near it, I change my mind to Cracker Barrel, where it's less likely I'll run into people from my past. And less likely I'll be fed, after being told to expect a thirty-minute wait.

The good thing about a wait at Cracker Barrel is the diversion provided by its old country store. Browsing among the shelves and tables, I catch the sound of familiar voices and peer around displays to identify a grouchy old neighbor lady, a high school classmate, the lazy-eyed barber who cut my father's hair, and the librarian who looks much as she did the last time I checked out a book.

Content to remain an outsider, not unlike when I was growing up here, I keep my distance and am relieved when "Wick, party of one" is called.

Shortly, a cup of coffee is set before me. Though I trained myself to drink it black—in the interest of projecting confidence and strength in a dog-eat-woman world—I'm tempted by the pitcher of cream left by the previous customer. This *is* Pickwick, and I don't need to impress anyone here.

The splash of white tumbles into my cup and comes up creamy brown, which begs the question of sweetener. I eye the multicolored packets but resist. The less retraining I have to do when I return to L.A., the better.

Wishing the five occupants at the table to my left were less boisterous, I go through two cups of coffee before my breakfast of eggs, bacon, and blueberry pancakes arrives. Excusing the overindulgence with the reminder that this is breakfast *and* lunch, I start in on the meal. Partway through, a man and woman are seated at a table to the left of the fivesome. What makes me look twice is the woman's hair. It's fiery red, like mine, but long and wavy.

"Maggie," I breathe as I push past the Easter memory that was so recently revived, only to be dumped back in high school where my cousin Magdalene was head cheerleader.

It's the first day of our freshman year, and it feels twice as long as a middle school day. Entering the cafeteria, I wince at the clamor of voices and falter at the sight of the hot-lunch line. By the time I get through it, I'll be lucky if I have ten minutes to eat. But at least I have something to pass the time. As I hurry forward, I open the battered copy of A Wrinkle in Time *I checked out from the school library. I've wanted to read it forever—*

Something slams into my shoulder, and I stumble back to find Maggie rubbing her own shoulder.

"Sheesh!" She scowls. "Do you need glasses?"

Her three friends, two pretty brunettes and a blonde, snicker, and then the taller of the brunettes says, "Well, that would certainly complete the picture." They exchange knowing looks.

"Sorry, Maggie," I say. "I wasn't watching where I was going."

She rolls her eyes. "Whatever." With a shake of red curls, she steps past me, and the others follow.

"There's no way she's your cousin," one of them says as I force my feet forward.

"She is." Maggie sounds fatalistic. "She has the hair."

As I bring up the rear of the hot-lunch line, I hear a snort and look around.

The four have claimed a nearby lunch table, and the blonde waves a hand in Maggie's face. "Hello, red hair isn't exclusive to the high-and-mighty Pickwicks."

"Yeah," says the brunette who is poking around her sack lunch. "Maybe her mom cheated on your uncle—you know, has a thing for red-headed guys."

My feet suddenly feel hot in my shoes, my hands hot on the book, my neck hot all the way up to my scalp.

Maggie in profile looks at the girl and then shrugs. Just shrugs.

And I hurt. Just hurt.

"Well…" The brunette wrinkles her nose as she carries a shiny red apple to her mouth. "That's what your mom said to my mom."

Aunt Adele said that?

Maggie peers into her sack lunch. "Then it must be true."

I'm not hungry anymore. And maybe I do need glasses, because my vision is blurry as I turn toward the cafeteria doors.

"Whoa! You okay, Piper?"

It's Trinity, and her voice carries.

"Yeah." I hurry past her and out the doors.

Though I didn't have much of a relationship with my Pickwick kin, from then on I made a concerted effort to dissociate myself from them. And the dissociation became more important when Maggie started hosting a different kind of popularity exclusive to boys. By her junior year, she was dating one guy after another, and word was that the relationships went beyond kissing. By her senior year, she was pregnant.

The last time I saw her was the day we graduated from high school. In alphabetical order, we sat side by side during the commencement, cousins who shared only a surname. And I was grateful, because the last thing I wanted was to be the one whose graduation gown was stretched over a basketball-sized bump. No matter how high Maggie held her head, she had further besmirched the family name.

"At least she didn't have an abortion," Mom said in her defense. This was to be expected, not only because of my mother's faith, but also because of the circumstances of my own conception.

I blink and am returned to Cracker Barrel just in time to see my cousin's head turn toward me. Quickly, I hunch over my plate.

Come on, Piper, you're oozing guilt. Sit up straight and pick up that fork!

I comply, and as I cut through the pancakes I turn off the self-talk and turn on the God-talk. *Lord, don't let me blow my cover. Give me a little more time before it starts raining Pickwicks.*

Chewing the pancakes with faux pleasure, I turn my chin and am relieved that Maggie's attention is once more on her companion.

Glad I wore the baseball cap, I allow myself to relax. This lasts until the table between us is vacated. I miss the human barrier and the noise that overrode the conversation at Maggie's table.

"No, Seth," she hisses.

Seth? Seth Peterson who dumped me in eleventh grade when he lost the glasses and braces and got a "hip" haircut that made Maggie take notice? Seth who crawled back to me when my cousin was finished with him (and whom I sent crawling back the way he had come)? It is, and while he once more wears glasses, they're fashionable on a face that has gotten better looking with age.

Maggie's shoulders rise with a deep breath—classic body language for "I'm trying to be patient." "I appreciate your offer," she says in her husky Southern belle voice, "but I can't accept."

"Why?"

I attack a piece of bacon, but it isn't crunchy enough to muffle my cousin's voice.

"My feelings haven't changed."

"And let me guess: they aren't going to now that you're coming into money."

She is? I look from Maggie's wide-eyed stare to Seth's reddening countenance.

Maggie leans across the table. "Who says I'm coming into money?"

"Your uncle's bad ticker, that's who. Once people start having problems with their hearts, it's only a matter of time."

Considering her chilly gaze, I'm surprised he isn't quaking. "This conversation is over."

"Then let's talk about the time and money I've put into our relationship."

She slaps the table. "That's enough!"

Assailed by the excitement that runs through the dining room at being witness to a Pickwick scrape, I'm relieved that, when it's over, I can slip away with none the wiser. But to be certain, I tuck errant strands of red hair beneath my baseball cap.

"I've been patient so far," Seth says, "but I'm getting tired of waiting—"

"Did I ask you to wait? I like you, although not much at the moment, but as I've told you repeatedly, I will never feel for you as you feel for me."

No one's pretending not to listen anymore. Except me. Where is my waitress? Or any waitress? Zooming in on a lanky woman bearing two plates, I raise a hand and she meets my gaze. My breath stops. It's Martha from Martha's Meat and Three Eatery.

I look away. Once more hunched over my plate, though my inner image consultant protests, I attack my breakfast and sigh when Martha passes without pause. All is well, until she sets the plates before my cousin and Seth and talks between them in a voice so hushed all I catch is her smoker's rasp. Translatable, though, is her nod over her shoulder. At me. Fortunately, my napkin slips to the floor (with a little help).

I duck under the table and make a show of straining to retrieve my napkin. All I wanted was to eat, and now I'm about to be pulled into my cousin's public display of Pickwickery. Having exhausted my fumbling, I pinch the napkin.

"It *is* you," a voice says, and I startle so hard my head knocks the underside of the table.

Wincing as the dishes clatter overhead, I look into Seth's slightly unfocused face where he's down on his haunches beside the table.

"Welcome home, Piper."

I frown a little, transition to surprise, and break into a smile, the intensity of which almost hurts considering the effort required. "Why, if it isn't—"

Should I forget his name? *Petty, Piper.*

"—Seth Peterson. How are you?"

"Good. Are you coming out from under there?"

Do I have a choice? I whip my head from beneath the table, and my bangs slide into my eyes. I left my cap behind. I dip down to retrieve it; however, it's not on the floor but stuck to the underside of the table. Yuck!

I tug it free, and several inches of gum follow before snapping. Looks like another proper burial is in order.

"My mom always told me not to play under tables." Seth rises. "Nasty stuff down there."

"Yeah." I push a hand through my hair and stand. I peer neither left nor right, but I know I've become a curiosity. Whatever it takes, I will maintain my dignity. Will *never* again be cause for gossip and sly asides.

"You know"—he shakes his head—"you got lots better lookin' with age."

I stiffen. Though my thoughts earlier ran the same course about him, it's not something I would have voiced, and I certainly wouldn't have used the qualifier "lots." Hmm. This *is* the perfect opening—

You're being overly sensitive. It's not as if he said, "Gosh, what happened to ugly?"

Not in so many words, but he dumped me for Maggie. I hate that it still hurts, a little. "You're very kind, Seth."

He hitches his chin over his shoulder. "Come over and say hi to Maggie."

"Sure. I haven't seen her in ages." To ensure that my cousin is my final stop on the way out, I remove my wallet and drop two fives on the table.

Most of the other diners have returned to their food, but it's a front for those who are longtime residents of Pickwick. So I make sure I'm in top form when I cross to the table where Martha stands alongside Maggie.

The older woman's mouth bows as she steps forward and lifts

my left hand from my side. "Piper, darlin', look at you—all sophisticated and prettier than ever."

I'd forgotten how much I liked her. I peck her cheek. "It's nice
to see you again."

Her smile turns rueful as I pull back. "Bet you didn't expect to
find me waitin' tables at a Cracker Barrel."

I can guess what happened, and had I paid closer attention, I
would have noticed the absence of cars at her eatery.

She glances around the dining room. "Atmosphere, good food,
and value for the money. Who can compete with that?"

It's said matter-of-factly, but it can't have been easy to accept the
progress that flattened her business. "I'm sorry."

She chuckles. "Actually, I'm happier—makin' a better livin', and
when I clock out for the day, what's left of it is mine."

I search her face to see if she's downplaying her loss, but she appears sincere.

"Hello, Piper," Maggie drawls as she unfolds her nearly six-foot
frame. As when I was younger, I wonder why God gave her the tall
gene and me the short, her the svelte gene and me the not-so-svelte.
Not that I want all of the eight inches she has over me. I'd be happy
with an equal distribution that would raise me and lower her to five
foot seven.

Maggie doesn't embrace me when Martha steps back, but she
smiles, and what surprises me is that her mouth doesn't tighten as it
did years ago when she was forced into my company. If anything,
there's discomfort in her smile. Because she knows I overheard her
argument with Seth?

She raises her eyebrows, and I realize I'm staring. "Lovely to see you again, Maggie."

"Hardly ideal circumstances, though Uncle Obe appears to be doing fine."

That can't be genuine concern. After all, her father went through his inheritance at about the same rate as mine, but he was able to supplement his dwindling assets with successful scams. Thus, Maggie's father had less reason to "make nice" with his brother Obadiah than my father and Bart's father. No, not genuine concern. Her inheritance is surely the issue—that Uncle Obe wants to spread the wealth around a bit more.

I consult my watch. "I meant to leave earlier for Asheville, and here I am jabbering."

"You're driving in to see Uncle Obe?"

"Yes."

Maggie's eyes brighten. "Maybe I'll see you there. I'm taking my daughter, Devyn, to visit after Seth and I finish our meal."

Lovely. Becoming reacquainted with my uncle is going to be uncomfortable enough without adding Maggie and Mini-Mag to the mix. *Think something happy…*

Grant. Once everything lines up, we'll be happy indeed. So why does my smile feel taut? "Well, if we miss each other, perhaps I can meet your daughter another time."

"Certainly. I know she'd like to meet you."

Oh, the pleasantries—people saying the opposite of what they feel. And Maggie has gotten better at it. I turn to Martha. "It was nice to see you again."

She nods. "Don't leave town this time without saying good-bye, hear?"

"I hear." With a wave at Maggie and Seth, I head opposite. When the grouchy old neighbor lady catches my eye, I smile. When the lazy-eyed barber beams at me, I beam back.

"You did it," I congratulate myself as I slide into my car. "Made it through the fire." Okay, I'm exaggerating, but there are bound to be fires to contend with in the days ahead. Where money is involved, the ugly side of humanity comes out to play. And since we're talking Pickwicks, it could get exceedingly ugly. Or ridiculous.

I turn the key in the ignition, but nothing happens. I try again. Nothing. And five minutes later, still nothing.

"Great!" I smack the steering wheel, but the engine isn't interested in solving our differences by violent means, leaving me with no recourse but to call the rental company. They apologize, but since they won't be able to send another car until tomorrow, I'll have to postpone my visit with Uncle Obe. Of course, that could be a good thing as I won't risk running into Maggie or Mini-Mag.

I brighten. Tomorrow *is* another day.

6

Sometimes I think I'd rather be plump. Then I could indulge in double-cheese pizza rather than low-fat-dressing-spritzed salad, heavy-on-the-cream ice cream rather than nonfat frozen yogurt, and lounging as opposed to running. I hate running. But here I am pounding the pavement and clenching my teeth as I strain to triumph over the driveway's wicked incline.

Yes, had I been born someone other than a Pickwick, I could be happy on the other side of slender. Once I accepted myself, it would be a done deal. No secret yearnings for the forbidden, no drooling over another person's meal, no torture to burn off excess calories. But God made me a Pickwick, and "plump" is not in the personal vocabulary of the body-conscious Pickwicks. It is, however, in my genes—*and* my jeans when I overindulge. As much as anything else, it sets me apart from the other Pickwicks.

It couldn't have been easy for my attractive father, especially once Mom started seeking comfort in food, but he was never really cruel. Just absent as he followed his wandering eye. Thus, I remained one sturdy Pickwick until my senior year, when I gained control over my eating, which led to the teenage stunt that has come back to haunt me.

My calves burn deeper as I lengthen my stride, and I return my thoughts to my father. I have forgiven him for not loving Mom and me, but I'm grateful I won't be running into him during my stay, since he's out of the country. Permanently. Jeremiah Pickwick resides in Mexico, where our justice system decided to leave him rather than extradite. That also goes for Uncle Jonah, Luc and Maggie's father, though I doubt the brothers have much to do with one another in their adopted country, having run dirty campaigns in their joint bid for the job of Pickwick's mayor.

I remember the headlines that ushered in my second year of high school, the snickers and sly glances that took the long way around Maggie to crash land on me. I shake my head. And pitch forward when my shoe catches on the uneven aggregate. I throw my hands up and follow through with the opposite foot. Close one.

Leaning forward, I grip my thighs and heave breath up my face. "Don't lose…your focus. Get in…get out."

"Are you all right?" a twangless voice calls.

I snap my chin up and see Axel twenty feet to the left alongside the commercial mower that was beneath the hundred-and-some-year-old tree when I left for my run. This afternoon, his sandy hair is in a ponytail, eyes are obscured by sunglasses, and jeans and T-shirt are streaked with the soil of his trade. But for all that, he really is nice looking and has a physique to fit.

And your brain is overheated. Note: ponytail, mustache, goatee, outdoorsy, probably tattooed, and is that a wrench he's holding?

I walk my hands up my thighs. "I'm fine. Is something wrong with the mower?"

He sets the wrench down and heads toward me, his limp less noticeable today. "A cracked hose, but I'll have it replaced and the machine running shortly." He halts at the edge of the lawn. "I didn't realize you had returned from town."

"My rental car broke down, so I took a taxi."

He glances at his watch. "You didn't make it to Asheville to see your uncle?"

"No, I'll see him tomorrow."

"Do you need a ride?"

Is he offering? I mean, I hardly know him beyond having aimed a high-heel shoe at him. "No, thank you. The rental company is delivering another car in the morning."

He nods. "What did you think of Pickwick?"

"A lot has changed."

"Your uncle told me you've been gone twelve years."

"About that."

"Considering you spent the better part of your life in the South—"

The *better* part?

"—I'm surprised you don't have the slightest drawl."

Thanks to all those voice lessons at the university I attended. For two years, I participated in a study to test a new method for helping those with distinctive accents subdue them. I was one of the success stories, but I was motivated. A Southern drawl, particularly one as pronounced as mine, is not a good way to stand out in the "fast lane" that is L.A. It leaves the wrong impression—as in slow and gullible.

"You don't have a drawl either," I point out.

His mouth tilts. "I wasn't raised in the South."

"Where are you from?"

"My dad was a marine, so that pretty much covers everywhere."

"That must have been hard."

"Mostly it was uncertain, which is why I'm inclined to stay in Pickwick." He graduates to a smile. "It's a good place to settle down."

"I'm sure it's a fit for some." I grimace. "Now that it has a Wal-Mart, it can hardly be called 'small town' anymore."

"Most of the changes are for the better."

Though overall I approve, I can't help but think of Martha. Yes, she said she's happier at Cracker Barrel, but I hate that one of the few good things about Pickwick is gone. "Some of the changes aren't for the better."

Axel pulls off his sunglasses and crosses his arms over his chest. Someone not trained in body language, who doesn't know to factor in context and other nonverbal cues (raised eyebrows and lids, curved mouth), might say his stance is defensive, but I'm a professional. He's simply settling in to the conversation. Not good.

"The way I understand it," he says, "ten years ago Pickwick's population was declining and businesses were struggling or closing, including the old mill."

The textile mill Grandpa Pickwick left to Bart's father when he passed away and which I understand closed down when Uncle Bartholomew's get-richer-quicker stab at the stock market failed.

"What turned it around," Axel continues, "is the new highway exit that provides easier access to Pickwick, as well as the town's commitment to renewal and preservation of its heritage."

Heritage? I never stepped inside a Wal-Mart until I shook the Pickwick dust from my feet.

"The population has nearly tripled, and it's not only newcomers who are responsible, but those who left and have returned to be with their families."

That last tempts me toward "warm and fuzzy," but I have no interest in Pickwick. Once I convince Uncle Obe to let bygones be bygones, I'm out of here. "I'm happy that Pickwick is thriving."

Axel's Blue eyes narrow. "But it has nothing to do with you."

Am I that transparent? Piper Wick who specializes in advising high-profile personalities on the use of body language and the well-chosen word? Of course, I have little to lose by revealing my true feelings to this stranger. "You're right. It has nothing to do with me."

The press of his lips is so fleeting I'm not sure if it's from disappointment or disapproval. I wish it were neither since it makes me feel like a snob.

Axel starts to turn away. "I need to fix the mower."

On impulse—what has come over me?—I hurry forward and touch his arm. "I'm sorry. That sounded…" The muscles beneath my fingers are warm and firm and the golden hair is ticklish, but I don't snatch my hand back. That could be read as "bothered," which I'm not. "I didn't mean to sound cold."

His eyes slide to mine, reengaging me and providing the excuse to return my hand to my side. Not bothered at all.

"It's just that I never intended to come back to Pickwick. Yet…here I am."

He returns the sunglasses to his face. "Sounds inconvenient."

He said it, not me. "Family calls."

"You didn't have to answer."

And let Uncle Obe wreak havoc with his tell-all will? I almost say it aloud, but no one outside the family need know about this matter.

"Unless you're worried about how the changes to the will could affect you."

A gasp sends saliva down the wrong tube. Though I struggle to preserve my dignity, the instinct for survival is stronger, and I bend forward and hack.

Axel's soiled boots come into view, and he thumps my back. "Better?"

My, he's close. "Yes, thank you." As I straighten to peer into his darkened lenses, he removes his hand from my back. "You know about my uncle's will?"

An eyebrow pops up above his left lens. "I have lived here for two years."

"But you're just the—" *You are getting dangerously close to sounding like a snob.* "What I mean is that Uncle Obe is a loner and intensely private. I'm surprised he confided in you."

Something plays about Axel's mouth. "I am also something of a companion."

"How so?"

He nods across his shoulder. "Mind if we talk over the mower? There's a job in town I need to get to."

"A job in town?"

"I have a landscaping business on the side."

"Then there isn't enough work here to keep you busy?"

His brow bunches at the disbelief I should have kept from my voice. "It's a big estate and could easily employ several gardeners, but it's too expensive to maintain all of it. My job is to keep up the immediate surroundings. Beyond that, it's my time, and I use it to build my business."

I make a face. "I didn't mean that to sound…" *You're doing it again.* "I'm sorry."

He nods and starts back across the lawn.

I'm tempted to return to the mansion and call various clients, but Axel's relationship with my uncle is still in question. As I follow Axel to the mower, it occurs to me that I haven't seen the dog since I returned from town. "Is Errol tied up?"

"No, I took him to town for grooming so he won't offend you when he's inside."

I'm equal parts surprise and dismay. "That's considerate, but it isn't necessary for him to patrol the house." I halt beneath the massive tree that shades the machine and an iron bench and wait for him to speak. But he starts poking around the mower. "So about your relationship with my uncle…?"

He glances at me. "Obe often comes by the cottage to talk, and sometimes we have dinner together. Maggie and Bridget drop by occasionally, but he's still lonely."

Maggie and Bridget who?

Ugly, Piper. Some people change.

But Pickwicks?

You're a Pickwick.

In name only—and not even that now.

Like I said—UGLY.

But I'm not the one who stole other girls' boyfriends—including her cousin's—snubbed those deemed beneath her, and became pregnant at seventeen. As for Bridget, I'm not the one who pulled the great crop circle hoax—

No, you *pulled the Fourth of July stunt.*

"Luc and Bart are scarcer," Axel continues, "but they do come around."

"You mean other than when they break locks and slip in through windows?"

A smile appears in the middle of his mustache and goatee. Whatever made me think he looked like a Neanderthal? Of course, a Neanderthal is on the extreme end of masculinity, and Axel is *very* masculine. Nothing soft or faintly pretty about him.

As he continues to train his dark lenses on me, his smile slips. Surely he isn't reading something in my stare that isn't there? "Er, anyone else stop by to visit Uncle Obe?"

"Bonnie came by once when she was in town. And Miss Adele."

Maggie and Luc's mother remained in Pickwick when her husband fled to Mexico. Though she and my mother finally had something in common, it gave Adele another reason to disdain Dory Pickwick. According to my aunt, if my father hadn't run a dirty campaign, her husband wouldn't have felt compelled to retaliate in kind.

Jolted by Axel's voice, I look to where he has come around the mower. "I'm sorry. What did you say?"

The sunglasses come off again. "You look upset."

Oh, Piper, take your own advice: be in the here, be in the now. I shrug. "My uncle *is* ill. If not for that, I wouldn't have returned to Pickwick."

"Then you can't wait to get back to Los Angeles."

"I'm a busy woman."

"I'm sure." His smile reappears.

Hmm. Kissing a man with facial hair must be a different experience altogether, and not without a hazard or two. Yes, Axel's is closely trimmed, but those coarse hairs could cause a rash on sensitive skin like mine—

I did *not* think that! "I'll let you get back to your hose problem."

"It's fixed."

That was quick. "Well, I—"

"Miss Wick."

This is where I should invite him to use my first name, but his drop in pitch bothers me. "Yes?"

He gestures to the bench. "Have a seat."

"Is there something we need to discuss?"

"Yes."

I lower to the bench, and when he settles on the opposite end, I kick myself for not sitting in the middle, which would have sent the message that I don't care to share.

"You're damage control, aren't you?"

I blink. "Excuse me?"

"You didn't return to Pickwick out of concern for your uncle. You're here to convince him to leave the family skeletons in the closet."

I stare at him as I struggle to contain the knee-jerk response common to many of my clients—telling the person to mind his own business and stomping off.

"I understand there is little love lost between you and the other Pickwicks, so my guess is that one or more of those skeletons belong to you."

I surge upright. "I have no idea what possessed my uncle to take you into his confidence, Mr…" What is his last name? "My reason for returning to Pickwick is no one's business, so I am not going to discuss it with you, Mr.…" *And you call yourself an image consultant.*

Axel rises from the bench. And smiles. "Smith. Mr. Smith."

Whatever he finds amusing, he can keep to himself. I have other things to ponder. *Like what just happened here?* Thank goodness he has no idea what I do for a living. Or maybe he does.

"I apologize for overstepping the bounds, Miss Wick."

As well he should. "I have work to do." I head toward the mansion and the phone calls I need to make, among them one to the agency that's investigating—

I whip around. "Since you seem to know everyone's business, perhaps you can tell me where to find my uncle's godson."

His eyes widen. "Obadiah Smith?"

A.k.a. Obadiah Number Two. "Yeah, named after my uncle—a matter of ingratiation, I'm sure."

His brow lowers. "Actually, it had nothing to do with ingratiation and everything to do with honoring a friend."

Is there anything my uncle *didn't* tell him? "Where can I find him?"

He strides forward with that increasingly familiar hitch. "This is probably the wrong time for a formal introduction"—he extends a hand—"but I'm Obadiah Smith. Obadiah *Axel* Smith."

7

I stare at the hand, taking in the sturdy, grease-streaked fingers and wide, calloused palm of one Obadiah Axel *Smith*. How could I not have—?

Common name. And, honestly, who expects Obadiah of the Old Testament to be paired with a name usually associated with Axl of Guns N' Roses bad-boy fame?

Still, I feel stupid. And more so when the other pieces fit. Last night, after the incident with Bart and the night-vision goggles, it occurred to me that Axel might have a military background. Then the message from the investigative agency mentioned Obadiah Smith was in the army…

Actually, I feel *really* stupid. And "meanspirited," as my mother would call someone who said what I did about Axel's name being a matter of ingratiation.

Continuing to stare at his hand, vastly different from Grant's smooth and well-manicured version, I draw a slow breath. *Yes, your comment reflects poorly on you. Yes, it was ugly. But simply apologize and—*

Hold it! *This* is the man responsible for my return to Pickwick. If not for him, Uncle Obe wouldn't be wanting to change his will. Obadiah Number Two is a meddler—and quite possibly a con man.

"I suspected you didn't know." He lowers his hand. "I should have said something sooner."

"Why didn't you?"

"It was one of those rare opportunities you know you should pass on—"

"What opportunity?"

"To better understand the big-city woman who bears little resemblance to the girl her uncle talks about."

As if I want to be understood! And what did Uncle Obe tell him about me? That Axel would know me by my obscure appearance? sturdy build? lack of fashion sense?

Now, now, what would Piper advise? No huffing and puffing and big, bad wolfing, as I advised Cootchie Lear after she slammed her purse upside the head of a reporter who asked her the odds of her husband cheating on her again.

I take a step back. "Who knows that you're my uncle's godson?"

"Most everyone."

"Including my relatives?"

"Of course."

"Then you didn't attempt to hide your identity from them as you did from me?"

His eyebrows lower, casting a shadow over his eyes. "Until a short while ago, I thought Artemis had filled you in."

"Well, he didn't. And neither did Bart last night or Maggie when I ran into her this morning."

"They must have assumed you knew."

I tilt my chin up. "Thanks to Artemis, there seems to be a lot of that going on. He should have told me that my uncle's godson is also his gardener."

"I'm sure he just forgot."

"I'd call it selective memory—the better to manipulate me."

"The man's almost eighty." The serious set of Axel's face lightens slightly. "Recently, your uncle told me Artemis has started keeping extra pairs of shoes at the office for when he shows up in socks."

That *is* forgetful. I shake my head. "That may be some of it, but not all."

Axel looks away a moment, then says, "I'd hang most of the blame on forgetfulness, but it's true that he has an ornery streak."

A vision of next month's credit card statement flashes before my eyes. "One that's going to cost me a bundle to track down the very person who's been right under my nose."

Axel's jaw hardens. "Are you investigating me?"

I startle as my words play back, too clearly to have been mere thought.

"Are you?"

I sigh. "Yes, I hired an agency, but it was the responsible thing to do considering I'd never heard of you until Artemis called me in L.A."

He crosses his arms over his chest. "What did you find out?"

I cross my arms over my chest, intentionally mirroring him. "Only that you were honorably discharged from the army." In the next instant, another piece fits, and I lower my gaze to his right leg. "Because of your injury." An assumption, but I know it's right.

He frowns. "*That's* what you paid a bundle for?"

"It's just the initial findings."

He stares at me and then in a cool voice says, "Save your money, Ms. Wick. If there's anything you want to know about me, you only have to ask."

But will he be honest? "All right... So you're Obadiah Smith."

"I prefer Axel, though I doubt for the same reason you prefer Wick."

That arrow has my name on it. "Tell me this, Axel. How did you convince my uncle to change his will, and in such a way the Pickwicks will suffer further ridicule?"

He's so still that with a few smears of camouflage he might disappear into the landscape. "Despite what you think, your uncle isn't easily influenced. He's burdened, and if making amends to those hurt by your family relieves him, he has my support."

I feel a sarcastic "How noble of you" coming on but resist. I am not in a good place. As I advise my clients to do in difficult situations, it's time to extricate (live to fight another day). I drop my arms to my sides. "It's good to know where you stand, and now I need to get to work." Lots to do, and providing I don't have another Bart-in-the-library-with-night-vision-goggles encounter, it should be a productive day. Of course, there's no accounting for Pickwicks...

"Mr. Smith, I'd appreciate it if you would continue to keep unannounced visitors away. Guard the estate, if you will."

His lids lower, reducing his eyes to simply blue—nothing at all capital-*B* about them. "And, thereby, Piper Wick."

I resist the urge to put my hands on my hips. "I can take care of myself."

"Yes, I forgot about those lethal heels of yours."

Ack! He's not going to let me forget that, is he? I draw myself up. "I just want to avoid a repeat performance of Bart's welcome home."

"Between Errol and me, I'm sure we can accommodate you."

I grit my teeth. "Thank you. I'll see you later." I pivot.

"At Church on the Square tomorrow?"

That nearly stops me, not because of the sardonic edge to his voice, but because I can't imagine stepping foot inside the church of my youth. While Mom and I were more welcome there than most places, some of those who "amened" the loudest at Jesus's command to love one another were the quickest to shun us the following Monday.

"No, thank you," I call back. And he can take that however he likes.

My clients are happy, my partners at Budge, Biddle, Wells, and Wick are happy, and I'm happy. Well, trying to be, but as I haven't had an interruption since I returned from jogging hours ago, I'm definitely on the happy end of the spectrum.

I lower my iPhone to the counter and stretch my arms above my head. Long day, but before I go to bed, I plan on exploring the mansion, though not in any way that intrudes on Uncle Obe's privacy. Just a peek behind doors closed to me when I was growing up.

I turn on the stool to survey the kitchen—a room three times larger than any family needs to prepare meals. Of course, my great-grandparents entertained on a grand scale, so there was a time when the kitchen fit the need. Now it's just cavernously outdated.

"But functional," I murmur as my stomach groans. Earlier I was surprised when a look in the refrigerator and pantry revealed both were stocked. More surprising was that the contents weren't exclusively "Southern"—no chitlins, biscuits, or bacon drippings. I did notice a half-dozen jars of pickled corn on the uppermost shelf of the pantry…in the back corner…beyond a row of baked beans…behind the applesauce. Not that I went looking for them. Well, actually I did. While I dropped most Southern foods from my stomach's vocabulary due to their effect on my waistline, there is one I've missed—Uncle Obe's pickled corn that took Best in County every year.

Dare I open a jar? After all, once I return to L.A., the pickled-corn well will dry up, and I could be left with unanswered cravings. Far better to resist temptation than wallow in taste bud memories. So just the one jar.

I hop off the stool and cross to the walk-in pantry. From atop a creaky stepladder, I reach past the applesauce and snag a jar of pickled corn. I can almost taste the yellow kernels that press against the glass, as if looking out at me as eagerly as I look in at them. Hmm. Cold or fried in butter?

A loud rap from the kitchen causes me to whip my head around. Unbalanced by the sudden movement, I shift my weight opposite but overcompensate. With a high-pitched creak, the stool tilts floorward.

"No!" Not the pickled—

All ten fingers splay as I grab for something to keep the stool upright. I catch the lip of a shelf, but as the jar heads for the floor, the stool goes out from under me. I register a shriek, a crash, a spray of moisture, and a scent I was so looking forward to in a different context. A moment later my sandaled feet hit the floor, and I slam back against a shelf.

"Oh no." I survey the yellow mess splashed across the floor and lower shelves amid shards of glass.

"Miss Wick!"

I screech when *that* man appears in the doorway with *that* dog. And *that's* when I remember what caused this—Axel pounding on the back door!

"What are you doing here? And how did you get in?"

As Errol backs away (must be the pickled smell), Axel's eyes move over me, making me uncomfortably aware of my appearance. He shakes his head.

Is he laughing at me? at the mess *he* caused?

Sliding his hands into the pockets of his painter's pants, he leans a shoulder against the doorframe—an unnerving pose because it isn't a pose…because he isn't putting his best face forward…because he looks real and sturdy, like a man you could hold onto in a storm—

Ah! Grant is real. And sturdy. It's just that, as a public figure, he has to keep his guard up and put his best face forward—*GQ* style. I like *GQ* style.

I press my shoulders back. "I asked what you're doing here, Mr. Smith."

His smile reaches all the way to his eyes. "It's called knight-in-shining-armor syndrome. The knight hears screams, and rather than wait for the damsel to open the door, he rushes in to save her from fiends." He glances at the floor. "And the odd jar of pickled corn. Found your uncle's stash, I see."

I have no reason to feel guilty. I'm a guest, and Artemis said to make myself at home. Nor is there any reason to feel embarrassed. I step away from the shelf. "I was deciding what to make for dinner when your banging on the door made me lose my balance."

"So this is *my* fault."

I start to nod but am struck by the pettiness of trying to pin this on him. "No." I sigh. "But if there *were* a fiend in this twisted fairy tale, it would be you."

He chuckles. "Had I known you were risking your neck for pickled corn, I would have let myself in with the key."

He has a key? Of course he does. He got in last night, didn't he? And just in time to save Errol from my twitchy trigger finger. Once again, I feel vulnerable. Axel may be Uncle Obe's godson, and he may have made no untoward moves when we were alone last night, but he's still a stranger.

Not until he frowns and moves back from the doorway does a body language check reveal that my unease shows. Determinedly, I put my face in place, a snap in my back, and pep in my step as I trod over glass to emerge from the pantry.

"Would you like help cleaning up the mess?"

That would mean working side by side, and he rattles me too much as it is. "I can get it."

"Then since I've made my delivery, I'll get out of your way."

I look to the dog, whose shiny coat contrasts sharply with the matted one of last night. Once more he retreats, obviously offended by Eau de Pickled Piper. I narrow my gaze on Axel. "Is it too much to hope Errol isn't your delivery?"

"Groomed and ready to serve and protect."

"I don't need a dog."

"You'll have to take it up with Artemis."

"But I won't see him until Monday."

"He rarely misses church, so you can catch him there tomorrow."

Church on the Square? Nothing doing. Of course, I could intercept him on his way in. "Maybe I'll do that. Good night."

Axel's eyes lock on mine with an intensity that nearly makes me step back. "Are you always such a snob, or do I just bring out the worst in you?"

Me a snob? Compared to whom? Certainly not my relatives. Still, the question gets under my skin, and I go defensive. "It must be you."

Axel nods slowly. "I'll have to work on that."

Is he patronizing me? Hot breath fans my palm, and I snatch my hand up and glare at Errol, who seems to have overcome his aversion to pickled Piper. "You know"—I look back at Axel—"you could start by taking this dog with you."

"Like I said, talk to Artemis." He crosses to the door that leads out to the garden and inspects its splintered frame, courtesy of knight-in-shining-armor syndrome. "I'll fix it tomorrow, but you shouldn't have any worries with Errol inside." He walks out and closes the useless door behind him.

I smell bad. Unfortunately, before I can shower, I have a mess to clean up. Ignoring Errol, I tromp to the pantry. All I wanted was a little pickled corn and what did I get? A failed rescue attempt by a gardener-turned-knight who thinks I'm a snob. Ha! I know snobs, and Piper Wick is not one... Am I?

Not even twenty-four hours in Pickwick and I'm questioning myself. Yes, I was short with Axel—all right, *rude*—but it's hard not to be defensive with Pickwick wreaking havoc on my ordered world. I have to convince Uncle Obe to leave well enough alone. And as quickly as possible.

Turning back into the kitchen, I recall a Scripture that Mom often quoted after we left Pickwick: *"Forgetting what is behind...I press on toward the goal."*

There's more to the apostle Paul's words, but that puts me in the right frame of mind. "Get in, get out," I say. Before I do become a snob.

"Am I a snob, Celine?"

"What?"

Bless her disbelief. "Am I a snob?"

"No!"

Bless her lack of hesitation. "Are you sure?"

"Absolutely."

And bless her conviction. I switch the phone to the other ear and reach to turn off the light on the nightstand.

"Once people get to know you, Piper, they realize it's just a defense mechanism."

I snatch my hand back. "What?"

"You know, to keep from getting hurt."

I know what a defense mechanism is! "You're saying I come across as a snob?"

Now she hesitates. "Sometimes."

"Like when?"

She sighs. "Like when I tried to get to know you when I started at the firm. You were pleasant enough in the context of work, but try to chat with you or ask you a personal question? You didn't go there. But I'm persistent, and I can now say that you are one of my best friends. And I'm one of yours—don't deny it."

I can't. And wouldn't.

"So you are going to take this as constructive criticism, learn from it, and when you get back to L.A., buy me lunch to show your appreciation for my keen insight."

I'm not so sure I appreciate it, or agree with it, even if Axel backs it up. "Okay. Now how about an update on Grant's reelection campaign?"

"Aye, aye, cap'n."

Fifteen minutes later, Celine says she'll e-mail a detailed report of what we've discussed. I thank her, but as I start to say good-bye, she says, "One more thing."

"Hmm?"

"I got a call today from a woman who identified herself as a freelancer assigned to write an article about Hollywood's image makers. As you were recently talked up in a magazine, she thought she would start with you."

I hear the "but" in her voice. "What's wrong?"

"She wasn't forthcoming about the magazine she's writing for, and when I told her you were out of the office and asked for her number, she started buttering me up—complimenting me on my professionalism and saying what an asset I must be to you and the firm."

I hear the peal of an alarm that Celine obviously heard.

She chuckles. "All true, of course, but an obvious change of subject. I played along, and the next thing I knew, she asked if you were out of town. That's when *I* changed the subject, and back and forth we went until she asked if it was true that your relationship with Grant Spangler is more than professional."

Am I being investigated? Although my name change presents a bit of a barrier, with some work the "Pick" part will come out. "What's her name?"

"Janet Farr, or so she said, and she sounded like she was from New England."

New England… Why does that ring a bell?

"When an urgent call came through that I just had to take"— I hear the smile in her voice—"I hung up and did an Internet search."

"And no evidence of a freelance writer named Janet Farr."

"You got it."

I'm not naive. I knew if my relationship with Grant progressed to one of commitment, my ties to the Pickwicks would have to come out. But we're not even engaged. However, if we're ever going to be, Uncle Obe's will has to remain as is.

I sigh. "Thanks for the heads-up, Celine."

"No problem."

I flick off the light. I should get down to the business of sleeping, but it's the business of worrying that eats up the hours. And then there's Axel's belief that I'm a snob. Am not!

8

All right, I'm a snob, albeit reluctant. And it's not just Pickwick that's bringing out the worst in me, or Axel. It's me. Growing up here, I detested the dismissive way my mother and I were treated. But now, for fear of getting too close to something that could burn me again, I'm the one whose nose is in the air. After hours of wrestling with my pillow last night, first over Janet Farr and then over Axel, there was no other conclusion. And more than ever, I can relate to Jacob's nightlong wrestling match with God, right down to the pain in the hip.

"Great," I grumble, favoring my left side as I descend the stairs, "you're not only a snob, but a drama queen." I look up. "Sorry, God. I know I shouldn't compare that night to last night, but I'm worn out." I lower my gaze to Errol at the foot of the stairs, his tail acting as a dust mop on the wood floor. "And that dog is still here."

As I near, he starts in with his gotta-go-potty dance.

I walk wide around him, but he bounds in front of me, looking like a big sissy with all that prancing and sidestepping. "And to think you scared me that first night."

He bumps my knees and nearly knocks me over.

"You big lug!" Something warms my toes, and I glare at the wet spots spreading across my canvas shoes. "You peed on my Keds!"

And that's not all. The hardwood floors have been dribbled on. Despite my protesting hip, I bound forward and wrench open the front door. "Out!"

Excitement dampened, he slowly draws even with me and lowers to his haunches to consider me with big, wet eyes.

"Don't you look at me like that. I am *not* a dog person."

He pops his head to the side.

Muttering words just this side of a bar of soap, I cross the threshold, and he follows me to the steps where he once more looks at me. I wave a hand. "Go potty."

He races down the steps, and I hurry back inside and close the door. "Problem solved." Except for the dribbles. Is cleaning up messes—literal *and* metaphorical—to be my lot in Pickwick? I trudge to the kitchen and retrieve the mop I used to clean the pantry last night.

An hour later, dribbles eradicated, Keds soaking in the sink, and having prevailed over the gate's intercom system to allow for the delivery of my replacement car, I finish off a refrigerated bagel as I go out the door. Though I intended to head to Asheville to visit Uncle Obe, this morning's events necessitate a detour.

Shortly, surprised by further evidence of Pickwick's renewal that comes at me from every street I turn down, I pull into the town square and take in the buildings that bordered on shabby when last I was here—the Pickwick Arms Hotel, pharmacy, courthouse, old theater, antique shop. While they still retain the nostalgic look of years past, the paint is fresh and the windows bright. And the park in the center is manicured and inviting.

I snag a parking space near Church on the Square. The unob-

structed view across the park, courtesy of the missing statue supposedly at the bottom of Pickwick Lake, allows me to pick out Maggie from among those who converge on the church. Red hair
catching the early morning sun, my cousin chats with an older
woman. Between them walks a brown-headed, pigtailed girl with
her face stuck in a book. Maggie's daughter? When she lifts her head
to speak to the older woman, I have my answer. Even at a distance,
I can see she doesn't resemble Maggie. Too plain. And she wears
glasses, not to mention a dress entirely devoid of frills. No, Mini-
Mag will be just that—a miniature version of her mother.

Within minutes of Maggie ducking into the church, her
brother—my Easter egg–thievin' cousin—appears. It's a shock considering the only time I ever saw Luc in this setting was when his
parents dragged the family here for Christmas Mass and Easter service. Not so shockingly, a thin, big-bosomed, blond woman is on his
arm. As for Luc, despite his good looks and couture, he's as shifty
eyed as ever. And I don't need to see his eyes to know that. It's in his
carriage and the self-satisfied turn of his mouth.

I check my dashboard clock. It's only ten minutes until the service begins, so Artemis should be here soon. I nearly miss him when
I dismiss a sporty red Lexus that powers into a parking space halfway
between me and the church. It's his bulk emerging from the small
car that makes me look again. With that much mass and age, the
sports car doesn't fit. Old-age crisis?

I jump out of the car and call to him.

He jiggles an ear as he circles to the passenger side.

I call again, and he jiggles the other ear as he helps his wife out
of the car.

"Artemis!"

As Mrs. Bleeker ratchets upright, her husband looks around. "Is that you, Piper?"

I halt before him and run a hand through my hair. "It's me."

He breaks into a tobacco-stained grin. Ugh! I forgot he did snuff. "Well, lookie here, Mrs. Bleeker. It's Piper."

The old woman's creased eyes nearly disappear amid her frown. "Piper who?"

"Jeremiah Pickwick's daughter—the one who up and ran off with her mother."

"Ah"—Mrs. Bleeker shakes her head—"a shame. Your poor daddy."

Let it go. She probably doesn't remember that your "daddy" was long gone by the time you and your mother left.

"Well, you have some fence mending to do, but we Pickwickians are forgiving."

As Mrs. Bleeker pats my arm, I sink my teeth into my lower lip to keep from disputing the belief that my fences are in need of repair.

"Service is fixin' to start, Arty." Mrs. Bleeker squints up at her husband.

He urges her forward, closes the car door, and pulls her arm through his. "You're welcome to sit with us, Piper."

"Thank you, but I'm not attending the service."

His head comes around, his fleshy neck rubbing his collar. "Why ever not?"

"I'm"—I shift my weight side to side—"heading into Asheville to visit Uncle Obe."

"Humph. I'm sure your uncle can wait a couple hours to allow ya to renew your acquaintance with God."

Watch the body language! "Though it's true my church attendance is off"—*Thank you very much, Mom!*—"I have a pretty good relationship with God." *When you make time for Him.* True, but I am trying to get in the habit of a daily devotional. *Ah, like this morning when you pretended you didn't see your go-anywhere Bible on the dresser?* I clear my throat. "I just dropped by to catch you before you go in."

Mrs. Bleeker makes a sound of dissent. "Kids these days!"

"Yes, dear." Artemis kisses her forehead, then returns to me. "If you're wantin' to talk business, I remind ya that this is a day of rest."

"It's your dog I want to talk about."

"Errol?" Mrs. Bleeker's little figure stiffens. "Is something wrong with my big boy?" She catches her breath. "Come to think of it, I haven't seen him all morning. Or yesterday morning."

One look at Artemis confirms we are talking about the same dog, and his stern gaze warns me to zip my lip. "Errol is fine, dear. We'll see him when we get home—maybe throw him a stick or somethin'."

Only if they're planning on dropping by the Pickwick estate.

"And now Piper needs to get to Asheville to visit her uncle, don't ya?"

I curl my fingers into my palms. "Maybe after the service you could call me on my cell phone?"

"I said we'll talk tomorrow." He steps forward. A moment later they pause, and Artemis looks over his shoulder. "Tell your uncle I'll visit him tomorrow followin' his surgery."

My jaw drops. "Surgery? Then there is something seriously wrong with him?"

"Well, why else would he still be in the hospital?"

An ache starts in my chest. *Lord, it's not just indigestion.* I was certain this was a false alarm. Why didn't I make more of an effort to see him yesterday?

Artemis sighs heavily. "Ya didn't answer me last week when I asked if ya was doin' drugs, but if ya are, Piper Pickwick—pardon me, *Wick*—ya need to get help for it."

There goes my jaw again.

"Your cousin Bart did, and he's come a long way."

Right. Now he's just into breaking and entering.

"Who's doin' drugs?" Mrs. Bleeker asks.

I'm tempted to walk away, but if I don't set Artemis straight, a rumor might spread that could make my stay in Pickwick more uncomfortable. "I do not take drugs."

He shrugs. "Then it must be that Los Angeles smog gettin' to ya. Mutates them brain cells, I hear."

That has to be it, because it couldn't possibly be that Artemis forgot to update me on my uncle's condition. "Could be. Well, enjoy the service and I'll see you tomorrow."

"Or maybe the day after."

What?!

"I'll call ya."

I hold my breath as he guides his wife across the square, following their progress until a familiar figure at the church entrance captures my attention. Of course, why Axel should be familiar dressed in something other than soil-stained work clothes and boots is beyond me. Just as it's beyond me why I find myself admiring the way his button-up shirt conforms to his broad shoulders and tapers down to the waistband of his navy pleated pants. Maybe Axel does have a little *GQ* in him…

He raises a hand, and I groan. He's seen me. My first impulse is to turn away without acknowledging him, but his words from last night—*"Are you always such a snob?"*—play back.

With a tight smile, the best I can manage on short notice, I flash a hand and then hurry to my car. See? Not a snob.

9

*F*ore!" A woman trumpets in concert with a thump against the hospital room door.

Hand on the knob, I pull back to confirm that the nurse sent me to the right room. The dry erase board reads O. Pickwick.

"Hole in one," calls a gravelly male voice. "Ha!"

"Betcha can't do it again."

"How much?"

"A loaf of my flaxseed bread to a jar of your pickled corn."

"That's bold of you to put up that stuff you call bread against my pickled corn, but I'll take your bet."

Why doesn't my uncle sound like someone propped up in bed with needles and tubes sticking out all over the place?

I rap on the door and push. The lanky man standing before the window, wearing a purple robe over orange pajamas and gripping an upside-down cane, looks up. From beneath a thatch of seriously silvered hair, he smiles questioningly, causing deep grooves to angle from the corners of his mouth to the flare of his nostrils.

I stare. Despite the years that have had their way with his red hair, it's Uncle Obe. And he appears amazingly spry for someone about to undergo heart surgery.

I shift my regard to the woman placing a dinner roll atop a

yogurt cup on the floor. What is she doing? And what's with her hair? Not that I don't see dreadlocks in L.A., but it's out of place here.

"There!" With a bounce of blond dreadlocks, she straightens.

If I didn't know better, I'd say that's— It *is* her.

"Oh." The bowed mouth of the unapologetic perpetrator of "the great crop circle hoax" purses; however, in the next instant amusement pushes out her lower lip. "If it isn't my little cousin Piper."

Only *little* because I'm thirty years old to Bridget's thirty-two and five foot three to her five foot six.

She shakes her head. "If Bart hadn't told me he'd run into you, I wouldn't have recognized you."

Was that a slam? Or am I being overly sensitive? Regardless, I'm grateful that my clothes, hair, makeup, and weight are all fashionable. In fact, *far* more fashionable than Bridget with that ratty hair and those holey nondesigner jeans.

"Goodness!" Uncle Obe exclaims. "It *is* Piper."

Talk about a delayed reaction. Equally disconcerting is the enthusiasm that brightens his face. "Welcome home." He takes a jerky step toward me only to motion me aside. "Mind if we postpone this joyous homecoming? I have a…" He frowns. "…bet to win."

"We'll be with you in a sec," Bridget says.

This is too strange. Might it be a dream?

"Do you mind closing the door?"

I comply with my cousin's request, but as I walk toward the bed, where a rolling table and cafeteria tray sit, something crunches underfoot.

Bridget chuckles. "Still walking around in that haze of yours I see."

"Spacey"—that was what she christened me when no further opportunities to call me "crybaby" or "litterbug" came her way. I scoop up what was once edible. "It's not every day one finds one's self walking on dinner rolls." I deposit the remains on the cafeteria tray.

Nor is it every day one sees a roll teed off a yogurt cup. But that's what Uncle Obe prepares to do to the unfortunate twin of the one I trampled. To top it off, he gives a waggle as he lines up the handle of his cane with the roll. *Has* to be a dream.

A moment later he shouts, "Fore!" and the roll hits the door.

"Wahoo!" Bridget punches the air. "Missed the hook by a foot!"

That little thing on the door?

She gives Uncle Obe a thousand-candlepower smile that transforms her from a dreadlocked rag doll into the Barbie doll I remember. "That'll be one jar of pickled corn, you old geezer."

Yep, same old Bridget, tricks and name-calling and all. *Er, "pickled corn" and "old geezer" sounded affectionate as opposed to cruel.* Well, it starts somewhere. Tomorrow it could be his wallet and elder abuse.

Uncle Obe sighs. "That hurts, but at least I won't have to jaw that bark you call bread."

She wrinkles her nose and turns to me. "So you're back."

"As requested." *You sound like a martyr. Think before you speak!*

Bridget grimaces. "At least pretend to be happy to see us. Or aren't we good enough for you anymore?"

Now *that's* backward. As I flounder for a response, she steps forward and sticks out a hand. "Bygones be bygones and all that feel-good crud, hmm?"

I slide my hand into hers, then do her one better by pulling her in and hugging her, as modeled to clients in need of coaching in the art of demonstrations of acceptance and forgiveness. It's harder than I make it out to be.

Bridget pulls back and claps a hand to her chest. "I'll be! I could almost believe you like me."

Leaning heavily on the cane, Uncle Obe advances with a limp more pronounced than Axel's. "Now, Bridget, you don't go stirring up a cake after it's baked. If anything, you add a little…white stuff—frosting."

"Can't stand frosting," Bridget mutters, and when I look at her, she shrugs. "Let's just take it slow, okay?"

"I couldn't agree more." *Watch your tone!*

Uncle Obe halts alongside me, forcing me to tip my head back to see to the top of the extra foot he has over me. "Got a hug for your old uncle?"

Did he just wink at me? Has to be a dream. He may have been kind to Mom and me when we were in need, but he never displayed affection. And rarely conversed without reluctance.

The hug is awkward, and not just my side of it. Obviously, this dream stuff is still new to him.

"I have to go," Bridget says.

Uncle Obe pulls away and pats her shoulder. "Thank you for dropping by."

"I'll see you tomorrow."

"Before or after I go under the knife?" Despite his teasing tone, tension knits his words.

I start to reassure him, but Bridget says, "Don't you worry. Your doctor is the best in these parts, and this little ol' surgery is going to be over before you know it."

Little? We're talking about his heart. I'm all for reassurance, but that's a lie.

Uncle Obe sighs. "And the good Lord *is* watchin' over me."

Bridget tenses and, with a smile so forced it nearly slips, says, "There is that too."

That?

She grins. "Of course, if you don't pull through, your stash of pickled corn is mine."

If he doesn't…?! That is not something you tease about. I look to Uncle Obe, but he makes a closemouthed sound that thumps up from his chest and quivers his lopsided nostrils. Was that a chuckle? "Maybe I'll write that into my will."

Bridget's gaze pins me, and I'm reminded of the reason I'm here—a more pressing reason if Celine's suspicions about Janet Farr are correct.

Bridget looks back at our uncle. "I'd be forever beholden to you." She crosses to the door where I once more fall under her gaze. "I'll be by sometime this week to pick up my jar of pickled corn."

"In the pantry, Piper," Uncle Obe says, "on the highest shelf in the back, behind the baked beans and applesauce. Until I make up a new batch, I only have six left—"

Five.

"—so don't let her take more than one." This wink is so exaggerated there's no question that's what it is. "Have to keep an eye on my supply. Won't be any fresh-picked…corn for a little while yet."

Obviously, I have a lot to answer for. I look to the door and catch Bridget's raised hand as she slips into the corridor.

Uncle Obe sighs. "It sure is good to have you home, Piper."

"Thank you. Er, shouldn't you be lying down? I mean, considering you're having surgery tomorrow?"

"I'm tired of bein' on my back. Got boredom coming outta my ears."

Hence, the dinner roll debacle. "I'm sure the doctors want you to rest. You don't want your condition to worsen."

"They do say it could completely give out at any moment."

I stare. "But if it's that serious, why are they delaying surgery?"

"You've forgotten that things move slowly in the South." He gingerly lowers to the mattress. "Dr. Pernick had a golf tournament this weekend, so tomorrow is the earliest he could fit me in."

Golf takes precedence over heart surgery?

Uncle Obe frowns. "Are you all right?"

"No." I blink. "I mean, yes. I'm just concerned about you."

"I appreciate that, but it's a fairly open-and-shut surgery. They open me up, put a new one in, and close me up. Just like that."

What? No one said anything about a heart transplant! There's nothing open and shut about that. He could die!

"Goodness, Piper, if you go any whiter, they'll be throwin' a sheet over you long before they throw one over me."

I lay a hand on his arm. "Would you do me a favor?" I reach past him and plump the smushed pillow. "I'd feel better about our visit if you were resting."

He grimaces. "My back end gets mighty sore, but all right."

I pull the covers over him and draw a chair near.

"I truly am glad you're home. You were always a good girl." His eyebrows lower, and he mutters almost to himself, "If a bit odd."

Odd? Me?

"Of course, I'm hardly one to talk."

No, he isn't. In fact, in the short time I've been here, he's probably said more than I heard from him in all the years I lived in Pickwick.

He plucks at the blanket. "Artemis tells me you've made a name for yourself workin' with actors and politicians—polishin' them and cleanin' up their messes."

"I make a good living at it."

"Uh-huh." He looks at the ceiling. "How's your mother?"

"Well, thank you. We share a condo in L.A."

"I always liked her. I'm sorry Jeremiah wasn't a better husband and father."

"Me too." I would have loved to be loved by the first man in my life.

"Chalk it up to further evidence that God can turn bad into good. Just like He did when I went flyin' off the golf cart when I hit poor Roy." His eyes moisten. "For hours I lay on the driveway, my chest achin' somethin' mighty, certain I was about to die, and all I could think was that I'd never be able to make right all the things it was in my power to do somethin' about."

My throat tightens as I imagine the state of his conscience as he lay there.

"I promised God that if He spared me, I would no longer sit

around just thinkin' about making good on the wrongs committed by our family. And do you know, not two minutes later, Axel found me."

Too bad his timing wasn't better. A few minutes earlier, and I might not be here. Now, not only do I have to convince Uncle Obe not to change his will but to break his word to God. Of course, does God expect him to make good on a promise made under duress? And Uncle Obe couldn't have been in his right mind as he lay there waiting to die. And we mustn't forget he might not be in possession of a right mind even under the best circumstances…

"So here I am with a new purpose in life." He beams. "And it feels good."

I draw a deep breath. "I understand that you plan to rewrite your will."

"Though I know that doesn't sit right with some of the Pickwicks, my mind is made up."

"But—"

He waves a hand. "I'm more tired than I thought. If I'm goin' to go under the knife, I need my rest. Now how about I say a prayer so you can get on your way?"

I don't argue for fear it could push his heart over the edge. "All right."

As I set my cool palm into his warm one, he closes his eyes. "Lord, I thank You for bringin' Piper home. I know it couldn't have been easy for her after the way she and her mother were treated, but I'm grateful, even if she believes the only reason she's here is to convince me to leave my will alone."

My lids fly open, but Uncle Obe continues. "Your Word says

that in his heart a man plans his course, but the Lord determines his steps. I pray You will direct Piper as she renews her acquaintance with her family and that she will forgive them as You have forgiven her for all the mistakes she has surely made."

I close my eyes, not to join him in prayer, but to calm myself. I have forgiven the Pickwicks, but that doesn't mean I want a relationship with them. That would only set me up for further hurt. I came back to stop Uncle Obe from making a mistake. If I succeed, then not only will I have done myself a good turn, but my relatives, and that should suffice in the relationship department. Then it's dust-shaking time.

"Heal her hurts, Lord, and let her rest in knowin' that we Pickwicks get better with age. Well, most of us. I also ask that You open her eyes to my godson, Axel."

What?

"Not only is he a fine specimen of a man, but marriageable."

I open my eyes in time to catch him peeking at me before he closes his lids.

"They would sure make a handsome couple, and I know You would bless them with a mess of little ones."

Not on his life. In the next instant, the thought boomerangs. *On his life—nice one. If the transplant doesn't go well, it* could *be on his life! The least you can do is humor him.*

I close my eyes again, and as he continues to pray, I ask God to bring him through the surgery and for his healing to be swift and complete. Of course, it never hurts to ask for a miracle, so I add that if it's His will, He heal my uncle's heart without the need for surgery.

"And Lord…" Uncle Obe's voice trembles with emotion. "I can't thank You enough for releasing me from the terrible pain I was sufferin'."

That's a miracle in itself. After all, how many people about to undergo a heart transplant are able to engage in a game of golf, albeit with dinner rolls and a cane?

"More, I praise You for healin' my heart—a miracle, indeed."

I peek at him. He doesn't really believe he received healing and won't require surgery? He certainly looks earnest. Poor Uncle Obe.

"Now I know this is askin' a lot after all You've done for me, and I'll understand if Your answer is no, but I'd appreciate one more miracle before tomorrow's surgery."

Then he *doesn't* believe he was healed?

"Heal my knee, Lord."

His *knee*? Oh, right, the limp.

"It's feeling better, but if You could do for it what You did for my heart, I'd be grateful. Why, the thought of goin' under the knife…" He shudders.

Hold it! We're talking Pickwicks, meaning there is more to this than a couple of nuts rolling around in Uncle Obe's head.

"That's it for now, Lord. Amen and amen." He opens his eyes and his thin lips turn into a smile. "I never could stand to pray in front of others, but I'm gettin' it."

I slide my hand out of his. "Uncle Obe, I'm confused. I understood that tomorrow's surgery was for your heart, that you're receiving a transplant."

His head jerks. "Whatever gave you that idea?"

*What*ever gave me that idea? How about *who*ever, as in an ancient attorney and a nutty uncle! *Calm thyself, O angry one.* I slowly breathe out and in. "When Artemis asked me to return to Pickwick, he said you had been hospitalized for what appeared to be a heart attack."

"True. I was in a lot of pain, so much my heart felt as if it might pop."

"But now you're talking about *knee* surgery."

"Uh-huh. My right knee has been botherin' me for ages, and I keep puttin' off surgery. But when I flew off my cart and landed on the driveway…" He shrugs. "That's all she wrote."

Artemis did mention he had injured his knee. "But what about your heart?"

He snorts. "Why, it was a miracle. Didn't Art tell you?"

Let me think… "No."

"God healed me. The doctors call it 'broken heart syndrome,' but I call it God." His brow lowers. "Really, Piper, would I be playing golf if they were settin' to pluck my heart out? Use your head, girl."

Where's a thick pillow when you need a good scream? I asked for a miracle, but this is *not* how it works. "So there's nothing wrong with your heart?"

He pats his chest. "Like it never happened."

So I rushed back to Pickwick for *knee* surgery? I carefully fold my hands in my lap. "When did you take a turn for the better?"

He considers the ceiling. "Thursday night."

The day after Artemis convinced me of the urgency of returning to Pickwick and the day before I boarded the plane. But then what about Maggie and Seth at the Cracker Barrel yesterday? Was

Maggie as much in the dark about this turn of events, or did her anger keep her from sharing the good news with Seth?

"Yep, I was feelin' a bit better, and they ran more tests and came back with that ridiculous diagnosis."

I have heard of it, and while it can be deadly, most times it proves harmless as the person recovers quickly and fully. "Broken heart syndrome," I mutter.

"Right, though there's some fancy medical name for it. It mimics a heart attack and is usually brought on by a stressful event."

"Like your accident."

"Or the death of a loved one."

I lean forward. "How did you feel about Roy?"

His brow ripples. "I was partial to that old dog—always coming around beggin' for food—but I can't say as I loved him. Still, it wasn't easy lying there on the driveway and watching him struggle for his last breaths." He puts up a hand. "However, for all that, it wasn't broken heart syndrome that made my chest buck and burn. It was a good old-fashioned heart attack, and God healed me."

So knee surgery it is, which makes sense—now. After all, if heart surgery were in Uncle Obe's future, it's not likely Artemis could have convinced him to postpone the changes to his will. Had I known, I wouldn't have returned—

Actually, you would have. It was that stupid stunt of yours that brought you back to Pickwick, and heart surgery or not, your relationship with Grant is at stake.

"Now I understand why you looked so worried." Uncle Obe pats my shoulder. "I appreciate your concern."

I *was* concerned, even if that's not what brought me back.

"Regardless of the reason you came home—"

My body language must be telling on me.

"—I'm glad you did. Now I'd best rest up before the physical therapist puts me through my presurgery paces.

Dismissed. "I guess I'll see you tomorrow."

"My surgery is scheduled for the morning, so make it late afternoon or I might sleep through your visit."

I lean forward and kiss his forehead. "I'll be praying for you." I *will* make the time.

"Drive carefully. Oh! And give some thought to Axel." He smiles sheepishly. "I know it's presumptive to match you with someone you met only once when you were a little bitty girl, but—"

"I met Axel? You're confusing me again. Until two days ago, I'd never met him."

"You don't remember the Easter egg hunt at the big house, when your eggs were stolen?"

"Yes, but Luc stole them, not some miniature version of Axel."

"That's right, but Axel is the one who nearly busted Luc's jaw for taking them."

He was there? And he defended me? I search my memory, and the first time through I come up empty. But the second time...

Uncle Obe is walking up the hill, and there's a boy with him whose hair is so short, he's almost bald. He's staring at me, but not in a mean way. It's like he's sorry for me. Then he looks up and sees Luc laughing, and that's when the boy starts to look mean.

It was Axel. He's the one who made Luc and Aunt Adele and

Maggie leave the egg hunt in such a hurry. He defended me, though I don't remember hearing about it.

Uncle Obe chuckles. "And Axel younger than Luc. But, then, he was big for his age, and with his daddy in the military, he knew how to take care of himself. And had a keen sense of justice."

Obviously.

"Well, give him some thought."

Maybe I will— No, I won't! He may have defended me, but he probably doesn't remember it. Too, it surely had more to do with him being bored and looking for trouble.

"I should tell you that I'm seeing someone, Uncle Obe." *Who has yet to return one of your three calls.* It's reelection year and his campaign has to take precedence. *Oh, right, you're just the woman he asked to research how his engagement to you might impact his political career.* It *is* my job. *How romantic.*

"Are the two of you serious?"

"Uh…pretty serious."

"Engaged?"

Why did I mention it? "Possibly. I mean, eventually. When the timing is right. For him. And me. Careerwise. And otherwise." What has come over me?

Uncle Obe sighs. "I know all about waiting for the right time. And lettin' it pass by. Be careful you don't do the same."

The regret in his words is deep, and I'm twinged by his pain.

"I'll see you soon." He settles back against his pillow.

Five minutes later, I point my car east toward Pickwick and dial Grant. And leave another message.

"I miss you, Piper."

"I miss you too."

"You'll be happy to know that I went on another date."

One hand pressing the cell phone to my ear, the other on the doorframe Axel repaired while I was in Asheville, I freeze. "How did it go?"

"Better than good."

While part of me thrills, the other flinches. The date may have been at my urging, but what if it proves a mistake? "Define 'better than good.'"

"Four times is a charm. This time we hit it off. In fact, we—I probably shouldn't tell you, but we kissed."

I suck air. "Come again?"

"Now, Piper, it was just a little one." My mother giggles. "And chaste. Or nearly so. Lasted maybe five seconds…or ten."

I close the back door and lean against it. "So the two of you are going out again?"

"Oh yes."

I rub a hand down my face. "That's good. You need this."

"I certainly do. Not to say that it will lead to marriage, but it's nice to feel attractive and wanted."

Which she never felt in Pickwick.

"So how about you? Have you met anyone nice there?"

Axel has no business popping to mind! "Mom, not only is this Pickwick, but I'm taken."

Silence stretches that doesn't portend well. "I suppose you are. And Grant is a good, upstanding man…"

Here she goes again.

"…but it seems to me his career takes precedence over everything. And though I know you're fond of each other, neither of you is in love."

"Mom!"

"Don't take this wrong, but I think your lack of experience with men is why you're so eager to hitch your cart to Grant Spangler."

I'm grateful no one's here to see me blush. Not that I should be embarrassed at having never been with a man in the "being with a man" sense of the words, but in my world, most people think something is wrong with a mature woman who hasn't had sexual experience. There isn't. Still, it can be uncomfortable in the workplace, especially if one lets it slip that her virtue is virtually intact. (I kiss and have even succumbed to inappropriate touching a time or two.)

But one good thing came of my mistake in confiding to one of the partners who took me under her wing years ago—Grant, a politician who is cautious about who he works with, and who is as different from my father as anyone I've been able to find. Responsible, goal oriented, and ultraconservative.

"Besides," Mom continues, "if you were in love with Grant, you wouldn't encourage him to wait until after the election to seriously consider marriage."

"It's my job to advise him on what's best for his career."

"And if he were in love with you, he wouldn't listen. He would pop the question, and in a couple of years, I'd have grandchildren."

Puffing out my cheeks, I peer out into the dusky garden where, years ago, the Easter bunny delivered eggs to a little girl whose stash was stolen. "Mom, did you ever meet Uncle Obe's godson?"

"I don't think so."

"Uncle Obe says he was here the day Luc stole my Easter eggs—that Axel hit him in the jaw for taking them."

"I don't remember your uncle pointing him out, but Luc and another boy did tussle, and Luc got popped in the face. That was Axel Smith?"

"Apparently so."

"He can't be all bad, then."

I smile. "Well, it's getting dark, and I want to explore the mansion like I keep promising myself." Too, there's the devotional I have yet to make time for, unless I count the prayer time with Uncle Obe. Hmm. That was pretty intense. "Tell Rufus hi for me when you go out again."

"Of course. Good night, dear."

I disconnect and dial my voice mail. Still nothing from Grant, but that doesn't mean Mom is right about him. He's just busy.

Pushing thoughts of him aside, I embark on an exploration of the mansion. It's an adventure in dust and cobwebs and neglect and unexpectedly gives rise to a memory of when I was seven or so and Uncle Obe invited Mom and me to join him for Christmas Eve dinner. Every goose bump raised by the chill walk from the cottage melted when I saw who was waiting for me—Uncle Obe in Santa's clothing. Of course, at the time I was certain it was Santa, and I had further proof the next morning when I found Daddy under the Christmas tree. He took us home to be a family again, and I was so happy.

It didn't last long.

10

*E*rrol stands guard at the foot of the stairs again—the last place I expected to see him, since Axel didn't come knocking last night. Convinced that Artemis must have collected Mrs. Bleeker's "big boy," I went to bed happy to be rid of the dog. Obviously, Axel let him in. I want that key!

I descend the last steps and, as Errol dances around me, head for the front door. Sure enough, once I coax him outside, there are more dribbles to mop up. And I do, all the while promising myself that a housekeeper is in Uncle Obe's near future, especially considering what I found last night. Though most of the rooms are no longer in use, that's no reason not to take a vacuum and furniture polish to them from time to time.

I go the bagel route again, this time smearing it with peanut butter. Chewing thoroughly to give my pituitary gland time to alert me to the feeling of fullness, I open the back door. I walk out into the morning air, and I'm struck by the beauty of Uncle Obe's garden and the scents that wend toward me as if by way of a calligrapher's pen—the extravagant sweep of sweet lilac and spicy viburnum, the bold stroke of spring roses and glorious magnolias, and the subtle curlicues of spearmint and basil.

Guessing my heightened reaction has something to do with the twelve years I've put on since I was last here, I step to the path that lazily winds among clusters of blues and reds and yellows and oranges.

When I pause beneath a Bradford pear tree at the center of the garden, all that's left of my bagel is crumbs. I peer into the leafy branches and sweep back to an eight-year-old Piper clinging to limbs of smaller diameter. I shouldn't have been in Uncle Obe's garden, as Mom said the best way to show him gratitude for opening up the cottage to us was to honor his privacy. But I was bored and certain that what he didn't know wouldn't hurt him, as my father was fond of saying. If I hadn't panicked when a limb snapped underfoot, I could have been out of the tree and halfway back to the cottage before Uncle Obe made it down the path, but I froze.

"Piper Pickwick." He sighs. "I am particularly fond of that tree, and you're busting it up. Come down here."

"I can't."

"Why not?"

"I'll fall."

"Not if you come down the way you went up."

"I don't remember the way I came up."

"So you'll be sleeping up there tonight?"

Wishing he were normal like other kids' uncles who would have scaled the tree to bring their poor little niece down, I say, "No, I want to sleep in my own bed."

"Then you'll have to work out a way to get down." He turns and tosses over his shoulder, "Don't be breakin' any more branches."

I pray for my courage to return. It doesn't, but Uncle Obe does—

with a ladder. I scramble down, mumble my thanks, and run as fast as
my sturdy legs will carry me back to the cottage.

So long ago… I lay a hand on the trunk that is far rougher than
it was then. Even trees get wrinkles, deeply craggy wrinkles. Considering it's not much older than me, I should be grateful mine can
still be classified as "fine lines."

"I am not chasing you!" Axel's voice sounds from a distance.

Squinting against the rising sun, I scan the cottage, but he's
nowhere to be seen.

So who is he *not* chasing so early in the morning? Might he be
entertaining someone who spent the night? I hurry back onto the
garden path and shoo away any attempt by the beauty I pass to im-
pinge on my senses. Opening Uncle Obe's eyes to the kind of person he's allowing to influence him might not be so hard after all.

"I mean it," Axel calls. "You've worn me out."

I break into a run. If what's happening up there is what I think
it is, I could be winging back to L.A. before long.

"That's it, bring it here."

Bring what where?

As I hurry up the grassy rise, I mentally steel myself for the de-
bauchery to which I may be an unwitting—sort of—witness.

At the top of the hill sits the cottage. Seeing it up close makes
my heart tug, but I shake the sentiment. It's Axel and his shenani-
gans I need to focus on.

"Good boy!" he calls as I head around the side of the cottage.

Boy?

"Go get it!"

Rounding the corner, I glimpse Axel with his arm flung out

and a blur of fur hurtling toward me. Then something knocks me backward.

Black is my new favorite color…

"Piper?"

"Umm?"

"Open your eyes."

Why? I'm content, except for a pulsing above my right eye. Actually, it's more like a throb. And it stings.

I startle at two sharp pats to my cheek. "Open your eyes."

I let in just enough light to confirm the identity of the one whose face is directly above mine. "Did you just slap me?" And is that slurred voice mine?

Axel nods. "A necessary evil."

Evil, yes, but necessary? The throb above my right eye begins to pound, and I squeeze that lid closed to ease the pain. "What do you mean necessary?"

"The stick hit you straight on."

Peering at his wavering face through my watery left eye, I touch my swollen right temple. "That was a stick?" I would have said it was a lead pipe.

His mouth turns down. "A big one."

I consider my red-tinged fingers. "You threw a stick at me?"

From where he's down on his haunches, he leans nearer. And I have half a mind (that *is* possible under the circumstances) to push him away.

"Your pupils appear to be the same size." He draws back.

I lift my head, but the world tips on its edge. "What do my pupils have to do with you throwing a stick at me?"

"I didn't throw it *at* you. I threw it for Errol. You came around the side of the cottage as I released, and my throw knocked you out."

To say the least. I *am* bleeding and— "It was Errol you were talking to?"

He inclines his head. "I do live here alone and, besides your uncle, rarely have visitors."

I'm too muddled to recall exactly what I heard, but something tells me it should have made perfect sense that his one-sided conversation was with a dog. So relieved that he doesn't suspect what I suspected.

"Did you think I had a woman up here?"

What is with this guy? "I didn't say that."

"You don't have to." For a moment, he looks alarmingly severe, but then he grins. "And here I thought you dropped by to check on me like a good neighbor."

His mock disappointment tempts me to squirm. Or maybe it's his smile—not! I am merely incapacitated. And the sooner I distance myself, the better. I push up on my elbows, but darkness drags at me again.

"Easy!" Axel grips my shoulder.

"If everything would stop moving…"

"Lie back down."

"I'm all right." I sit up. My head feels like it's about to bust its seams. I probe the lump. "Do I need stitches?"

"Not likely. The cut isn't deep." Axel looks pointedly at my hand. "But if you keep that up, you might need antibiotics."

I pull my hand from my head and consider my dirty fingers. "Oh."

He stands, almost fluidly despite his bum leg, and reaches to me. "Let's get it iced and cleaned."

His arms are bare. My eyes travel up a thick wrist and forearm, across a defined tricep, and onto the solid deltoid that thrusts out from the armhole of his sleeveless T-shirt. He looks powerful, like a heavyweight boxer—

"Piper?"

There's a frown between his eyes, but in the depths of the Blue shines a glint of...interest.

Why are you gawking, Piper?! He is not your type. See any resemblance to Grant? None. This is a different breed of man—too broad, too rugged, and from his woodsy smell, he probably doesn't own a single bottle of cologne. In short, he's sophistication-challenged.

Right. Floundering for a way to explain my behavior, I blurt out, "No tattoos."

The interest in his eyes flickers. "Is that what you were looking for?"

"Of course." I nod, which makes my head hurt more. "I mean, what else? You were in the military, and military guys have tattoos."

"Standard issue, hmm?"

"Apparently not, because you don't appear to have any." Am I babbling? "Unless you keep yours hidden, which defeats the point of having a tattoo—you know, symbolic muscle flexing."

It's his mouth that flexes into a smile. "I don't have any tattoos." He reaches nearer. "Now let's take care of your cut."

I search his eyes, but the interest that was there is gone. Still, I should decline his offer, and I would if I weren't so shaky. I thrust a hand in his general direction, and his big, warm fingers close around mine, causing my pulse to speed—

It did not! If it's going to do any speeding because of a man's touch, it will be for Grant. I teeter as Axel pulls me upright, but he steps closer and slides his other arm around my waist. And there goes my pulse again.

"Lean on me."

And risk a speeding ticket?

"What's wrong?" Now his breath is in my ear.

I look around. Wow, his eyes are *really* Blue. "Er, what about your injury?"

His mouth constricts. "I assure you, I'm fully functional."

My first thought is to tell him I wasn't questioning his manhood, but my second is that I can't tell him the truth—that he's affecting me.

"Let's get you inside." Taking most of my weight, he walks forward.

"Inside?" I glance at the back door of the cottage.

"Would you prefer that I collect your pistol first?"

Actually, I would. Or am I being ridiculous? After all, if he had illicit designs, he could have done something before now. Not only have we been alone several times, but he has a key that allows him access when I'm at my most vulnerable.

"Well?"

And I could probably outrun him considering that hitch of his.

"Piper?"

And it's not as if he just rolled into town and has no history here.

"Piper!"

And Uncle Obe trusts him. "Ow!" I clap a hand to my cheek. "You slapped me again."

Axel raises his eyebrows. "That was a pat. And you looked dazed."

"I was thinking!"

"And in the meantime, your bump is swelling. Do you want help or not?"

I nearly decline. "All right."

He repositions his hand lower on my waist—*ripple, ripple*—and walks me forward. Though the movement intensifies the throb at my temple, I'm half grateful because it distracts me from all that inane rippling.

Finally we reach the single step, and Axel practically lifts me onto it. As he pulls the screen door open, a bowl of dog food catches my eye. "What happened to Errol?"

He nods over his shoulder. "There."

Sure enough, the big lug lies on the far side of the yard gnawing on a stick—probably the one that knocked me out. Something is very wrong about that.

"If it would make you feel more comfortable, he can join us inside," Axel says.

The king of dribble whose loyalty surely lies with this man? "I would hate to come between him and his stick."

A moment later we're inside the cottage, and memories unfold like crisp, clothesline-dried sheets that release the scent of sunshine when shaken out. As Axel leads me through the shelf-lined room stocked with canned and boxed food items, I remember the little girl I was the first time Mom and I accepted Uncle Obe's offer of a place to live—the Christmas he dressed up as Santa.

"Sit," Axel says, and I startle to find myself in the unpretentious kitchen where Mom and I made our first and last attempt at canning. We simply couldn't get the lids to pressurize.

I lower into the chair Axel has pulled out from the little breakfast table and look around. I haven't missed this place. After all, what is there to miss? A knotty, old kitchen table that creaked alarmingly when I leaned across it to share a dessert with Mom? An ancient refrigerator that's still humming and shuddering, the sounds of which probably wouldn't be as comforting now as when I was a child settling down for the night in a bed not my own? A monstrously ugly oven that burned more than it baked? Distorted windows that had only the view of the backyard to recommend them and through which Mom kept an eye on me? No, nothing to miss, especially considering my kitchen in L.A. And yet…

Axel returns and hands me ice wrapped in a kitchen towel. "Hold this to your head while I get some rubbing alcohol." He disappears through the narrow doorway that leads to the front half of the cottage.

I press the towel to my temple, and as the chill seeps through, the ache begins to ease, and I remember what led to my first stay at the cottage. That day at our house in town, I didn't know that the cause of my parents' first separation was another woman. All I knew was that it frightened me, particularly the tearful words Mom flung at my father, who merely looked annoyed. And increasingly so until

Mom saw me peering at them from where I hugged the doorframe. She smiled so brightly I thought I had imagined the whole thing, but when she hurried to me, tears were in her eyes.

Shortly, with suitcases in hand, we checked into a motel. Days later, Uncle Obe let us into the cottage. Despite my mother's sorrow that seemed to perch in every corner, with each successive stay I came to appreciate the cottage and estate grounds a little more.

"Let's get you cleaned up and take you to see a doctor."

Startled to find Axel once more beside me, I tilt my face up. "What?"

"You need to have your head looked at."

That's blunt. And I start to say so, but I see the gauze in his hand and catch the scent of alcohol. Oh. *That* kind of doctor. "That won't be necessary. I'm feeling better."

"You had that dazed look again."

"It's called thinking."

"Or concussion."

"I appreciate your concern, but I'm fine." Our fingertips brush as he relinquishes the alcohol-steeped gauze pad. *Ripple, ripple.* I'm going to have to do something about that. Starting with Grant, even if I have to go through his assistant to reach him.

"There it is again," Axel says.

"What?"

He crosses his arms over his chest. "The dazed look."

I sit straighter. "My head is perfectly fine. I'm just—" What? Bothered by his touch? Maybe something *is* wrong with my head. Why else would I be so affected by this ponytailed meddler?

"I'm driving to Asheville this afternoon to visit your uncle. You can go with me and have someone in the emergency room examine your head."

Perhaps that isn't such a bad idea. I really don't feel right.

"Are you going to clean the cut or should I?"

I jerk my arm up and pat at the cut that stings like the dickens.

Axel pulls out the chair opposite and settles into it. "So what can I do for you?"

"What do you mean?"

"If you didn't come up here to catch me in a compromising position, then…?"

I pat some more. "Well, I heard your voice and…" *Pat, pat.* The door! "Thank you for fixing the doorframe so quickly."

He smiles, but not the kind of smile you give away—the kind you keep to yourself. "You're welcome. Anything else?"

"Actually, yes. In case you haven't noticed, the mansion is a mess. Uncle Obe used to have a cleaning woman come in daily, but most of the rooms look as if they haven't been touched in years."

"Miss Victoria passed away a year ago."

I remember her, though she had about as much to say to me as my uncle did on the rare occasion we crossed paths. Of course, she *was* deaf.

"I've encouraged your uncle to find a replacement, but he hasn't."

It would be hard to replace Victoria, who posed little threat to Uncle Obe's privacy. "I'd like to find someone before he comes home. Any suggestions?"

He shrugs. "I'll ask around. Anything else?"

I squelch the impulse to bite my lip. "I'm uncomfortable with you having a key to the mansion."

Without sign of offense, he pulls a ring of keys from his pants and removes one. "On the condition that until your uncle returns, you let Errol in at night."

As much as I'd like to refuse, I say, "All right," and pluck the key from him.

Axel rises. "I'll give you a ride back to the big house."

I jump to my feet. "Oh, I can…" I slap a hand to the table to steady myself.

"You can't." His hand steadies me.

Little ripples. *Very* little ripples. I'm definitely on the mend, but not so near my destination that I can refuse his offer.

Shortly Axel putters the golf cart down the rise, and I sit beside him, my thigh glancing off his despite my attempt to maintain space between us.

He slows to negotiate the narrow garden path, then brakes near the back door. "Here you are. We'll leave for Asheville at one."

I exit the cart and turn back to tell him that I can drive myself but am struck by the unbalanced feeling of having stepped off a boat. All right, so I will ride with him.

With a whir, he turns the golf cart. "Don't lie down, in case it is a concussion."

I swing away, and my head throbs anew. "Thanks a lot, Axel." I can't believe he didn't apologize for knocking me out with that stupid stick. It wasn't intentional, and it was more my fault than his, but he should have said something.

Especially after you thanked him for helping you. I didn't, did I?

I enter the kitchen and close the door. As I turn the lock, my eye is once more drawn to the repaired doorframe—proof that if Axel wants in, he doesn't need a key. Just as Bart and Luc don't need a key, or anyone else for that matter.

Maybe letting Errol in at night isn't such a bad idea.

"Forgive me?"

"Of course, Grant. I know how busy you are." Although, really, how long does it take to make a call to check up on me?

"You're an angel, Piper." He chuckles. "Most of the women I've dated would have had a fit if I didn't return their calls within five minutes."

What if it had taken five *days*? Ooh, I'm not quite as understanding as he thinks. All things "Pickwick" considered, it would have been nice to have his support, even if only by phone.

"I really am going to have to ask you to marry me, you know."

He's said it so many times that its tingle factor has declined considerably. "Yes, you are, but—"

"—when the time is right."

I clench a smile. "Absolutely."

"Speaking of which, did I tell you that the timing of the new ad is perfect?"

Groaning under my breath, I rise from the sofa that I dropped to after the fifteen-minute hold I waited through to speak to him.

"We have Jacobs on the run. If he wants to stay in the race, he has a lot to answer for. You should have seen him backpedaling when the reporters cornered him yesterday."

I cross to the rolling ladder, climb to the shelf where I left the feather duster when Grant came on the line, and resume the task of making this corner of the mansion more habitable.

Grant continues without pause. As the dust flies amid the ticklish rays of the afternoon sun, I toss out the occasional "uh-huh," "right," and "good for you" to let him know I'm listening. And I am. Sort of. Fortunately, any pertinent developments in his campaign will be included in Celine's daily report.

"Now I know his daughter was over the age of consent when the nude pictures were taken—"

With a gasp, I tune back in to the voice coming across my earpiece.

"—but what does it say about how she was raised? Jacobs can spout family values all he likes, but this *is* a reflection of him and his parenting."

The feather duster quivers in my hand. Nude pictures…Jacobs's daughter…the Fourth of July parade…Piper Pickwick.

"I'm telling you, that kind of scandal does not sit well with conservative voters."

Feeling as if air is leaking out of me, I drop my chin to my chest. And yelp when my injured forehead hits a rung.

"Are you all right?"

"Yeah. Just…bumped into something."

"Well, as long as you're not bleeding."

Actually, I am, though just a little through the gauze I taped over the broken skin. "I'm fine."

"Good. So how's the weather in…what's the name of the town?"

"Pickwick."

"Right. I've heard of the Pickwicks. They were a fairly promi-
nent family at the turn of the century—about the time of the Van-
derbilts, I believe."

"Yes." And now is not the time to establish my connection to
them. Of course, if Grant ever gets past the thinking-of-asking-me-
to-marry-him stage, I will have to elaborate on my last name. But
by then he will have been reelected. Unless Janet Farr with the New
England accent *is* after me.

"My uncle went to college with one of them—until the guy got
kicked out."

Oh, Lord.

"Can't remember his name, but I think he was the eldest of the
four boys."

Uncle Jonah, Luc and Maggie's father.

"So who in Pickwick requires the services of the best image consultant in Los Angeles?" There's a smile in Grant's voice. "Wouldn't
be one of those Pickwicks, would it? If so, you might want to double your fee. I understand they're off the deep end."

I try to laugh. "Well, I'm sure your schedule is packed, so I'll let
you go."

"We'll talk again soon." A pop sounds across the line. "Kisses,
Piper. One on your cute little nose."

I wrinkle it. "Kisses back."

The line goes dead. And once more, it's just me and my deep-
end relatives.

11

W e're here."

The voice speaks over a vision of colorful bouncy balls that plummet from overcast skies and shoot back up after striking the pickled-corn pavement.

"Wake up, Piper."

I look around, but the disturbingly familiar voice has no body and the balls continue to shower around me. It strikes me then that none have come near enough to graze me. I stick out a hand. A blur of Blue speeds toward it and I hold my breath, but the ball comes to a screeching halt bare inches from my fingers and then swings wide and continues to the pavement. Its impact scatters bright yellow kernels, and it bounces back up, though with less force than the other balls. I compromised its momentum.

"Oops," I murmur when it stalls above my head.

It drops again. And blows a raspberry at me over its shoulder. I don't think that's possible…

When it grips my shoulder and shakes me, I swat at it, but it shakes me again. "I'm sorry," I mumble, "but you were in my air-space."

"Your airspace?" the ball says in a very masculine voice. "Come on, Piper, this is becoming a habit. And I don't care to be accused of slapping you again."

Hold it! The balls suddenly suspend around me like the skirts of my mother's polka-dot dress that I ran to when Maggie called me fat in front of her friends in first grade.

I open my eyes, and Axel's face is inches from mine, concern in his intensely Blue gaze. He does have incredible eyes, and I think I could get used to the mustache and goatee, but that long hair… Why, I'll bet Delilah felt the same way about Samson.

Axel draws back as abruptly as a child who has touched a hot burner.

What's his problem? I was just admiring—

Admiring? Hello! You are taken. Well, soon to be. Or later.

"You fell asleep."

I straighten in the passenger seat of Axel's top-down Jeep. I must have been exhausted to drift off with the air whipping at my hair. "I can't believe you let me fall asleep, especially since you're the one who's so worked up that I might have a concussion."

"I was somewhat occupied with driving, but I did wake you twice."

"I don't remember you awakening me."

"Then I won't take offense at being given the evil eye before you snorted back to sleep."

"I do not snort."

"You do." His mouth turns up. "I could hear it above the road noise."

How embarrassing.

"But I'll keep it between us."

As if I care to share my secrets with him! Now if he were Grant... I'm struck by how wrong it is that Axel knows about my snorting and Grant doesn't.

I pull the door handle and step out of the Jeep and into the hospital parking garage. "Let's see how my uncle is doing."

An hour and a half later, having been assured that the knee surgery went well and Uncle Obe would be out of recovery soon, I sit on an examining table as the elderly doctor who has poked at me for fifteen minutes jots something on my chart.

"Well?" I ask.

"Perhaps a slight concussion, Mrs. Wick—"

Mrs.? I glance at Axel where he stands nearby.

"—but I don't see any need to keep you under observation. However, as a precaution, I will ask your husband to wake you every two hours for a couple of nights."

"He's not my—"

"She's not my—"

"Oh." The doctor pushes his rimless glasses up his nose and looks at Axel. "Regardless, wake her every couple of hours."

He thinks we live together?

"I'm just a friend," Axel says, "but I'll arrange for someone to keep an eye on her."

Since when did he become my friend? And just who is he going to get to stay the night with me?

A while later, Axel and I leave the emergency room and enter the elevator.

"I told you I was fine." I attempt to keep space between us despite the press of the other occupants. "And as far as someone staying with me at night, that's overkill."

He nods.

So we understand each other. I feel better. That is, until we step into Uncle Obe's room and into the middle of a family gathering. I lurch back and come up against Axel.

"They don't bite," he says in my ear. "At least not in broad daylight."

I scan the faces of those whose eyes land on me. My red-headed, Easter egg–thievin' cousin Luc is here, and beside him is his mother, Adele, to whom Botox has been kind—in a stiff way. At the foot of the hospital bed, Bart and his mother, Belinda, perch on opposite sides of the mattress, and near Uncle Obe's head sits a girl with glasses poking out from dark hair that hangs around her face. She looks a bit like the one I saw entering church with Maggie yesterday.

"Piper." A drawn-looking, IV-connected Uncle Obe lifts his head from the pillow.

"Piper?" Aunt Adele zips her gaze down me and shakes her head. "My, you *have* changed."

"I'll say," Luc mutters.

"Yes," Aunt Belinda says.

Bart stands taller. "Told you."

"I'll take that as a compliment."

"Come in." Uncle Obe motions me forward. "You too, Axel."

I smile. "I'm sure the number of visitors you can receive is limited, so I'll come back later."

"Don't worry about the nurses," says a man I didn't notice until now. "We have an understanding." Past Aunt Adele's shoulder, he turns from the window, and for a moment I stare into my father's face. But it's the youngest of the brothers—Bartholomew, Bart and Bridget's father—who always bore such a striking resemblance to my father that the two could be momentarily mistaken for each other. Even though he has packed on twelve years, twice as many pounds, and there's silver among his red hair, the resemblance remains.

"You *have* changed." He shakes his head. "And here I thought my boy, Bart, was simply in a generous mood."

This is not going to work. "Uncle Obe, I think I should—"

"Do you know what I think?" says the girl in a honeyed drawl.

I wonder at the sparkle in eyes magnified by glasses. Who *is* she?

Her smile has Maggie written all over it despite a small gap between her front teeth. Is this her daughter? It follows, and yet other than the smile, she bears little resemblance to my cousin. Still, Maggie's daughter is nearly a teenager, and this girl can't be more than ten.

She lifts her chin. "I think you're lovely, that's what."

Nice kid, meaning it would be hard for her to be a close relation of Maggie's.

"And potentially inspiring," she adds.

Inspiring? *Potentially?*

Aunt Adele looks around Luc. "Now, Devyn—"

Devyn? This *is* Maggie's daughter. And that *was* her heading into church yesterday. And she *is* twelve—or soon to be.

"—it's kind of you to make Piper feel welcome, but remember what I told you about talking out of turn?"

"Sorry, Grandma. It's just nice to finally meet my long-lost relative."

"Piper, are you coming in or not?" Impatience battles fatigue in Uncle Obe's voice.

Axel nudges me, and as he follows me to the bed, Uncle Obe says, "Well, aren't you a nice-looking couple. And both of you single."

Axel stiffens, and while I read it as a sign that he doesn't like Uncle Obe's intimation either, I'm irked. Did he have to accompany me across the room as if we are, indeed, a couple?

"You're reaching, Uncle Obe," Luc drawls. "I hardly think my big-city cousin is about to fall for your Rambo *gardener.*"

So much for Uncle Obe's assurance that Pickwicks get better with age. Of course, he did allude to exceptions. I glance at Axel, who is staring at Luc, who is staring back. No love lost, but then Axel is thought to be behind the changes to Uncle Obe's will. And there was that altercation at the Easter egg hunt…

Devyn gives a heartfelt sigh. "True. Mom says that kind of stuff only happens in romance novels."

Uncle Obe smiles slightly. "Wait and see."

I lean near him. "How are you feeling?"

The tilt goes out of his mouth. "Fine."

"He's exhausted," Devyn says. "He was in surgery for an hour and a half and then moved to recovery for an hour. And though they let him return to his room, he's still feeling the effects of anesthesia. And he's hooked up to an IV for medication and a spirometer"—she eyes a machine beside the bed—"to keep his lungs free of postsurgery fluid. Nothing is 'fine' about that."

I stare at the plain little girl who has a remarkable head on her shoulders. Someone needs to tell my cousin that her baby was switched at birth.

Devyn lays a hand on Uncle Obe's head and pets his hair. "What you need is rest, Unc-Unc."

Unc-Unc? Of course, he is her *great*-uncle.

"You know me well, Devyn."

Does she? But that would mean Maggie has been spending time with him, which is as unbelievable as Bridget coming around. Strange.

Uncle Obe squints at my forehead. "Is that a bandage?"

I slide a hand beneath my bangs and touch the bandage. "I had a little accident, but I'm all right."

"Are you sure?"

"Yes, I had it checked a short while ago and was given a clean bill of health."

"What happened?" Bart asks.

Looking past Axel to my cousin and the others, I shrug. "It was a stick." I give Uncle Obe a grossly exaggerated wink that eases the lines on his brow. "A big one."

"Someone hit you with a stick?" Aunt Belinda chirps.

My lips twitch. "Sadly true."

Axel does that stiffening thing again. Making light of the matter at his expense—albeit temporary—may not be a good idea.

"Who would dare?" Uncle Bartholomew blusters, coming to stand over his wife's shoulder.

"I went up to the cottage to…" *Helloooo! What about the warning that you're always giving your clients—not to feed the vultures?* I keep my game face on in spite of the interest in Aunt Adele's and Luc's eyes. "I needed to talk to Axel, and when I came around the side of the cottage, he had just thrown a stick for Errol—"

"Errol?" Aunt Adele says.

"Artemis's dog," Bart supplies. "Real unfriendly."

Toward those who break into houses. "Anyway, I was in the line of fire." I touch the bandage.

"Is that right?" Luc runs a hand along his jaw. "I recall quite clearly that Axel has a good right hook."

"Still do," Axel says with a thrum in his voice, and suddenly I feel strangely safe beside the defender of little Piper Pickwick—certain that his big, capable hands would defend me again.

"Why, Axel Smith, are you threatening my boy?" Aunt Adele demands.

Uncle Bartholomew grunts. "Sounded like a threat to me."

"My godson would not strike a woman," Uncle Obe says. "And as long as your Easter egg–stealing days are behind you, Luc, there's no reason Axel should have to teach you another lesson."

Devyn's head swivels around. "You stole someone's Easter eggs, Uncle Luc?"

He has the grace to color—a little. "That's a matter of inter-pretation. Besides, I was just a kid."

Devyn sighs. "Kids can be unkind."

That didn't sound like an offhanded comment. It sounded like someone who has firsthand experience with "unkind" kids. But the daughter of Maggie the cheerleader?

"Fortunately, kids grow up." Uncle Obe lowers his lids, and when he lifts them again, it's only halfway. "For the most part."

Axel steps back from the bed. "Devyn is right; Obadiah needs to rest."

We murmur our good-byes and file out of the room. As the

door closes behind us, one of two nurses heading past mutters to the other, "Those Pickwicks."

I'm surprised when, rather than cringing at being lumped with the Pickwicks, my defenses rise.

"Well, don't you look like a bunch of vultures?" Bridget says as she comes around a corner. "Well, not you, Axel." Her eyes light amid the dreadlocks on her brow. "Or you, Devyn Divine."

The girl runs to her, and Bridget throws her arms wide.

Strange. Though Bridget and Maggie were more accepting of each other than they were of me, they were hardly close. *We Pickwicks get better with age,* Uncle Obe said.

"Where's Mom?" Keeping an arm around her aunt's waist, Devyn steps alongside Bridget, and they advance on us.

"She said to tell you she's sorry, but her auction is running overtime."

Auction? Does she have to sell off something to pay her bills?

"She'll meet us here later and asked me to keep you occupied until then." Bridget glances at us. "I'm assuming I'm too late to visit Uncle Obe."

As the two halt before us, Devyn says, "For now—too many visitors. The nurses really need to enforce the rules."

"Obviously." Bridget considers me briefly before turning to her parents. "Mom...Dad." Then to her brother. "Staying out of trouble, Bart?"

"You know me."

She grimaces. "That's reassuring."

Luc sidesteps the group. "I have cars to sell. Let's go, Mom."

As he takes Aunt Adele's arm and heads down the corridor, I look around. "I should go too. It was nice"—this is what lies are made of—"to see all of you." Well, I *did* enjoying meeting Devyn.

They murmur similar lies and murmur more when Axel walks from the group to follow me.

"You two drove in together?" Bridget says.

I am surprised by a glint that quickly fades from her eyes. Jealousy?

"Your cousin was in no condition to drive herself."

Axel makes it sound as if I were intoxicated! I open my mouth to object, but Devyn says, "She sustained a head injury, Aunt Bridge."

I raise a hand in parting, but Axel says, "Bridget, can I talk to you?"

There's that brilliant smile of hers again, and something trembles through me. Maybe it's just Pickwick, but that *felt* like jealousy.

With a swish of dreadlocks, my cousin, trailed by Devyn, follows him down the corridor where their exchange takes place in hushed voices.

"What's that about?" Uncle Bartholomew demands.

"Oh, stop," Belinda says. "Bridget's a grown woman."

"And *that's* a grown man. A highly objectionable grown man, even if Obadiah believes he's worthy of an inheritance."

"Why?" Yes, I awoke yesterday morning with egg—er, *snobbery*—all over my face, reluctant though it was, but nothing is reluctant about Uncle Bartholomew's "highly objectionable" or Luc's "Rambo gardener" comments.

As I hold my uncle's glowering gaze, Bart leans in. "Dad's concerned that Bridget will end up giving him another son-in-law who can't support his daughter in the manner to which he wants her to become accustomed."

"Of course I want the best for her," my uncle snaps.

"And since Uncle Obe's heart is no longer an issue," Bart continues, "it could be a long while before Axel comes into money."

"Or any of you." Bartholomew's heavy brow takes on extra weight. "And don't forget my fool of a brother is set on rightin' wrongs that have no business being righted." He takes a step toward me and in a raspy whisper says, "We're counting on you to make sure that doesn't happen."

I resent being the cure-all, but I set my face to keep my emotions in check. "All I can do is reason with him."

The baby of the four brothers stares hard at me, then sighs and glances at the door to Uncle Obe's room. "The alternative is…distressin'."

I can't be sure, but Bartholomew appears genuinely upset at the possibility of having his brother declared mentally incompetent.

He shakes his head. "But Luc is right. Better that than a bunch of no-goods cutting into the Pickwick inheritance."

No-goods. "Is that your only concern? The inheritance?"

He looks at me as if I've taken on the odor of ripe cheese. "What else is there?"

Aunt Belinda lays a hand on his arm. "I believe she's talking about the media—what happens if they find out about the changes to the will and the reason for them."

Bart nods. "Yeah, bad publicity."

My uncle rolls his big eyes. "So what's new?"

"Actually," his wife says, "it's been nice not to have our name blasted across the papers for a while. And I can't tell you how much more relaxing my salon experience is when gossips aren't stealing peeks at me while I'm under the dryer."

"Nothing to worry about, dear." Uncle Bartholomew's eyes pierce mine. "Providing our niece does her job."

Job? I don't recall the Pickwicks offering a retainer for my services.

"Ready to go?" Axel asks.

"Yes." I turn and look between him and Bridget, who can't possibly be that pretty in the midst of those ratty ropes of hair. What were they talking about?

Axel steps to the side, and as I pass between the two, Devyn crouches to tie her shoe.

She gives me another gapped smile. "It was nice to meet you." She tilts her head to the side. "Do you mind if I call you Miss Piper? Or do you prefer Miss Wick?"

She knows about my name change. Of course, it's probably been a topic of discussion since my return. "Miss Piper's good, and I enjoyed meeting you too."

She rises. "If everything works out, I'll see you tonight."

Tonight? If *what* works out? Ugh. Not a family get-together. If so, I have a Pickwick-proof excuse—work.

Five minutes later, Axel hands me into his Jeep. "So," I say as he slides in beside me, "Luc doesn't much like you."

"No."

"Beginning with the Easter egg hunt."

He backs out of the parking space and, as we head for the garage exit, says, "He can't put the incident behind him."

It was probably the first time someone bettered him. "Until recently, I didn't know what happened between you and Luc. I remembered there was a boy with Uncle Obe, but I didn't know it was you. I mean, you were almost bald."

"Buzz cut."

"Right. And now look at you. You have a ponytail, for goodness' sake."

He smiles. "After a lifetime in the military—between my father's service and mine—I needed a change."

"I guess so. Anyway, thank you for defending me that day."

"You're welcome." He brakes at the parking booth, then hands the attendant the ticket and a five-dollar bill. "Of course, nowadays I try to be more reasonable in dealing with injustice."

"No more punching a person's lights out?"

His smile broadens. "Only when absolutely necessary."

I smile back as we accelerate out of the parking garage.

"Unfortunately"—Axel raises his voice over the air rushing into the Jeep—"now the problem between your cousin and me is that he believes I have too much influence over your uncle."

"Do you?"

"Not in any premeditated way."

"In what way?"

"Being there when Obadiah needs to talk and unburden himself. Someone to pray with." Axel glances at me. "He has a lot of regrets, and not only his own."

Exactly how much does Axel know about the changes Uncle

Obe wants to make to his will? More specifically, is he aware of the reasons behind the new bequests—such as Trinity Templeton taking the fall for me?

I start to pick at my cuticles, but the movement draws Axel's attention and makes me cringe at the return of a bad habit I overcame years ago. "I, uh, understand that you've influenced my uncle's faith."

He doesn't answer until he brakes at a red light, and then he turns the full force of his gaze on me. "That's a bad thing?"

"No! That is, providing you don't have your own agenda." *And maybe you should have put that more delicately?* Concrete proof that the hands-on practice sessions with my clients is where they get their money's worth.

Axel's pupils expand, shoving all that incredible Blue to the outer edges. "I'm not the one with the agenda."

Nice comeback. Blessedly, I'm saved from responding by three bursts of a horn. The light has turned green.

Axel accelerates, and soon we enter the highway. "You're one of your uncle's regrets," he says, raising his voice over the wind and road noise.

"Did he tell you that?"

"He did. He's bothered by how you and your mother were treated by his family and that he didn't take more of a stand."

How much does this man know about me?

"He believes that had he intervened, you and your mother wouldn't have run away from Pickwick."

My back snaps straight. "We didn't run away." We…shook the

dust from our feet. "We had our reasons for leaving, and it was the right decision."

His eyes shift to my hands, making me aware that I'm picking my cuticles again. "So you like the big city?"

"It's where I work and live."

"In that order?"

That *was* a Freudian slip. If—rather, *when*—Grant and I marry, I'll leave L.A. and my partnership in the firm as happily as I left Pickwick. I set my jaw and focus on the rusted bumper that hangs askew on the beater truck ahead.

Axel shifts lanes, passes the truck, then shifts back. "Right or wrong, Obadiah believes that Pickwick is where you belong."

"There's nothing here for me."

"There's Maggie and Bridget."

"Excuse me?"

He intercepts my wide-eyed gaze. "People change, as you can attest to yourself."

Yes, I've changed, but Maggie and Bridget? More likely, they've simply become more sophisticated in their dealings with those who don't meet their standards. "Some do, but I have a hard time believing it of my cousins."

Axel looks back at the road. "Then forgiveness isn't in your nature."

I startle. "I've forgiven them. It's what I'm called to do as a Christian. But that doesn't mean boundaries shouldn't be put in place to protect myself from further harm." As I counsel many of my clients to do.

"I agree that you have to watch out for Luc and Bart, that that's where those boundaries come in handy, but Maggie and—"

"I appreciate your concern, Axel, but I'm not just a once-bitten, twice-shy kind of person. With the Pickwicks, it's more like ten times bitten, twenty times shy. When I was growing up, Pickwick was much smaller, and despite the soiled reputations my relatives wracked up—my father included—they pulled a lot of weight and people followed their lead, even while they talked about them behind their backs."

Axel is focused on the road, but I sense he's listening in an unhurried way I'm unaccustomed to. He isn't waiting for his turn to speak. He wants to hear from me. And for some reason, I want to share what I don't normally talk about.

"It wasn't just the rejection and unkind words that my mother and I had to endure. It was all the seeds the Pickwicks planted and watered." A sharp pain alerts me that I've picked a cuticle to the point of blood, and I curl my fingers into my palms. "That's a big chunk of a person's life, and until someone takes something that precious from you, you can't possibly understand where I'm coming from."

I see him release one hand from the steering wheel, but I don't follow it and am surprised when it closes over my fist. His hand is work hardened and strangely comforting. "I do understand."

He does? I stare into eyes that would be markedly different from Grant's even if they were the same color, but the sincerity in Axel's eyes is taken from me when he returns his attention to the road and his hand to the wheel, as if realizing he's overstepped the bounds.

He did. But I miss his hand on mine. I close my right hand over my left in an attempt to retain the warmth of his touch. The gesture is telling, but before I can correct it, Axel's gaze flicks to my hands, and I force myself to leave them, though all of me longs to guiltily snatch them apart.

"I'm sorry for what you and your mother went through. It was wrong, but the point is that you *went* through it. You're on the other side now, Piper, and you're not the only one there."

Is he saying Maggie and Bridget are on the other side with me? That doesn't seem possible, but I'm too tired to argue. "I'll have to take your word for that."

"I wish you would."

His sincerity baffles me. "You know I'm damage control, so why are you being so nice to me?"

His mouth crooks. "While I disagree with what you're here to do, it's obvious you care about your uncle."

It is? For some reason, his observation chokes me up.

"Also, I like to give people the benefit of the doubt."

I swallow. "Thank you."

"But also a warning." He looks directly at me. "I don't like being made a fool of."

Okay, not choked up anymore. Gritting my teeth, I turn my head and stare out the window.

A half hour later, my cell phone alerts me to a message. Guessing I was out of range when the call came in, I listen to Artemis explain that he can't meet with me today—he wants to take his new tractor for a spin. I grunt as I flip the phone closed.

"Bad news?" Axel asks.

"Could be better."

As I look away, a staccato ring rises between us, this time from Axel's phone. With a glance at the screen, he flips it open. "Hi, Maggie."

Why is she calling him?

"Can you do it?" A pause. "No." Another pause. "Bridget's busy, so that leaves you." He chuckles. "Me? That would look bad, and I don't think she'd go for it."

Are they talking about me?

"You're the better choice." He slides his gaze over me. "Don't worry; she'll behave."

They *are* talking about me!

He closes the phone. "Maggie has agreed to spend a couple of nights with you."

I catch my breath. "Why?"

"Doctor's orders. I asked Bridget, but she has other plans."

This is what the two discussed when he pulled her aside?

"Devyn was rather enthusiastic about getting to know you, so Maggie didn't stand a chance." His mouth curves. "Her daughter is persistent."

As is Axel. Though tempted to argue over the choice of babysitter, I resist. If a reluctant Maggie is willing to awaken me every couple of hours, the least I can do is be awakened. Besides, it's not as if there will be any chumming, late-night talks, or bonding. And Devyn will be there, and she's likable enough.

I shrug. "All right." *And?* "Thank you for making the arrangements." A while later, I thank him again as I climb out of his Jeep in front of the mansion.

"Maggie and Devyn will be over around seven."

"I'll be here." I turn to ascend the steps, but as he accelerates up the driveway, I look around and catch him watching me in the rearview mirror as I'm watching him.

"Not my type." But whosever type he is… Well, good for her.

12

"You're early." I stare at my cousin, who looks gorgeous, from her tousled red hair to her pink toenails visible in one-inch sandals that elevate her that extra inch to six feet. I suddenly feel insignificant, especially in bare feet and toenails in need of a repaint.

She smiles halfheartedly, obviously as uncomfortable with the arrangement as I am. As for Devyn, the soon-to-be-twelve-year-old steps forward and beams with all the teeth to which her bowed mouth has access. "The cavalry has arrived."

They have—complete with briefcase, suitcase, and a bulging backpack that makes the girl lean hard to one side, where it hangs from a thin shoulder.

I open the door wider. "Come in."

Devyn bounds forward, followed by her mother, who carries the suitcase and briefcase across the threshold with less enthusiasm.

I close the door. "It was nice of you to come."

Devyn loops an arm through Maggie's. "If you can't count on family, who can you count on?"

Too bad her mother didn't feel that way when I was growing up.

Something glances across Maggie's face, but she looks away and pats her daughter's arm. "This is going to be fun, hmm?"

"Bunches!" The girl slips free. "I'll pick out our room." She lopes off, and I hold my breath for fear the backpack will topple her, but she makes it down the hallway, up the stairs, and out of sight.

"Your daughter is sweet."

A relaxed smile cranks up Maggie's beauty rating. "And smart as a whip." She makes a face that would wreak havoc on anyone else's looks. "Not at all like me."

I don't know how to respond. Maggie was never self-deprecating. Her report card was littered with Cs, Ds, and Fs, but she always said it was because she was bored and had better things to do than study.

"How's the head?"

I touch the bandage beneath my bangs. "Good. I don't understand what all the fuss is about, but…"

She nods. "Look, I know you aren't thrilled about this, but Devyn was excited after meeting you at the hospital, and Axel assured me it's important, so…"

I'm relieved I'm not the only one at a loss for words. Still, it's unheard of for Maggie, who always had a lot to say, though usually with more finesse than Bridget, who burned bridges as if there were a glut of them.

"I appreciate that you disrupted your schedule to babysit me." I nod past her. "I'm going to make myself something to eat. Are you and Devyn hungry?"

"We already ate." She turns slightly aside, and I envy her long, toned calves beneath the hem of a straight skirt that rests on hips that show no evidence of having birthed a child. "We'll just settle in, and then I need to get to work."

I eye her briefcase. Is she a fashion designer? interior decorator?

"I'm an auctioneer."

I startle.

"I make my living selling other people's castoffs."

"So you work for a company like Sotheby's?"

She chuckles, and her Southern belle accent is present even in the disjointed sound. "Although I do occasionally bring high-end items to auction, most times it's a house, land, farm equipment, or the miscellaneous contents of a deceased person's home."

A memory of the one time I attended an auction rises with all the pain associated with losing our home to pay for delinquent taxes after my father deserted us to avoid imprisonment.

The man standing behind the podium in our front yard wears overalls and has salt-and-pepper whiskers and a yammering mouth that sends saliva flying. I stand frozen until Mom hurries me away. Within a month, we leave the cottage on the Pickwick estate and return home. The new owner, an investor, has rented it back to us, and my world returns to normal. Or as far as normal gets when you're a Pickwick who doesn't fit the mold.

I come back to the present to find Maggie staring at me. "Isn't that a male-dominated profession?"

"It is, especially in these parts, but I'm making headway, much to the frustration of my competition." She smiles. "I have a knack for getting top dollar."

More like sex appeal. And she probably isn't averse to using it to her advantage as she did in high school. "I'm glad you found your niche."

She shifts the cases. "I'd better see what accommodations Devyn has chosen." She crosses to the stairs with a stride born of confidence in all things female. Despite years of observation and practice,

I can't quite get my hips to do what hers do—sway, but not so much that it's obvious.

Resigned to feel frumpy while Maggie is here, I decide to go all the way—two slices of cheese on my grilled cheese sandwich rather than one. And maybe one of those little pecan pies Uncle Obe must have stocked up on before he landed in the hospital.

Errol lifts his big head from his paws when I enter the library two hours after I holed up in the kitchen to munch through my sandwich and make calls to clients.

"I hope you don't mind that I let Errol in." Devyn sets her book aside and leans down to ruffle his neck. "I went for a walk, and he was down at the pond with Axel. Axel said you wouldn't mind if I brought him in for the night."

I *did* agree to it. "That's fine." I turn to Maggie where she sits behind the enormous mahogany desk in front of the windows. "I just wanted to let you know—" What is that on her face? Can't be reading glasses. But they are. Rectangular, faintly blue lenses perch halfway down her nose that pair with my dazzling cousin about as well as ketchup with caviar.

"Yes?" She leaves the glasses in place rather than ashamedly whipping them off.

"I'm getting an early night and wanted to tell you so you can schedule my wake-ups. The doctor said every two hours."

She glances at her watch. "See you around eleven, then."

"Miss Piper, can I ask you something?"

"She needs to go to bed, Dev."

"Just one question, Mom." Devyn beckons me forward, and I cross to the sofa as she retrieves the book from beside her. "I looked at your senior picture in Mom's yearbook—"

Oh no. My graduating yearbook, which I had no reason to purchase for the memories it held of a life I was leaving behind.

"—and I felt a connection with you." She studies a page I don't dare look at too closely. "Well, with who you were. Not that I'm close to being a senior, but there's definitely a connection."

Out of the corner of my eye, I see Maggie rise. "Let's not bother Piper with—"

"Please, Mom." Devyn peers at her over the back of the sofa. "It's not a question you can answer."

At Maggie's hesitation, Devyn pats the sofa cushion. "I won't keep you long, Miss Piper."

Aware that I'm wearing my discomfort on my sleeve, I lower to the edge.

"You were a late bloomer." Devyn taps the picture of an eighteen-year-old Piper Pickwick whose smile is forced and face is framed by an ill-fated attempt to give body to her flat red hair. Compare that to the previous picture of Maggie whose easy beauty shines off the page, and you have a study in opposites.

"But bloom you did," Devyn says, "which is inspiring. You see, I think I'm a late bloomer, partly by choice, because I view hair and makeup as a waste of time better spent pursuing things like astronomy, books, and environmental awareness." She sighs. "Anyway, my question is: How did you handle the 'it' girls? Some can be quite mean, as I'm sure you know."

It's all I can do to keep from turning to Maggie where she stands behind the sofa. Has anyone told Devyn that her mother was not only one of the original "it" girls but commanded a legion of "mean" girls? Now her daughter is one of those ostracized for not being pretty or fashionable or rich enough. How ironic—

Not ironic. *Sad.* Regardless of who you are, a childhood is far too long a time to be made to feel like an outsider. And it's not really the scars that are the problem, as they imply healing. No, the problem lies with those hurts that simply scab over.

I look into Devyn's eyes. "Mostly, I stayed out of their way, tried to develop relationships with others outside the privileged circle, comforted myself with the knowledge there was life beyond middle and high school, and prayed." Which I was much better at when life was painfully uncertain.

"But I can't seem to stay out of their way. It goes against my nature. If I'm walking down a hallway and they're coming four abreast, why should I flatten myself against the lockers to let them pass? One of them can step aside. After all, I have as much right to the hallway as they do."

In principle, yes. In middle and high school, no. "What happens when you don't give right of way?"

"Standoff, which can be uncomfortable, but unless I'm running late for class, they fold every time." Devyn's mouth momentarily curves. "Of course, there are always the snide comments, the eye rolling—"

I remember, though I did my best not to provoke it. Ask Maggie.

She lays a hand on her daughter's shoulder. "You can visit with Piper more tomorrow."

Devyn wrinkles her nose, too long and sharp to have come from Maggie. "All right." But as I rise, she jumps up and steps over Errol to avoid disturbing him. "Can I walk you to your room, Miss Piper?"

"De-vyn," her mother drawls.

I look to my cousin, whose glasses are hooked on the neck of her blouse in line with the bit of cleavage that makes me feel flat. "I don't mind, Maggie."

She shrugs. "All right, but no late-night"—a secretive smile appears—"tête-à-têtes."

"Ah!" Devyn bounces onto her toes. "You used it."

What is she talking about? And what's with "tête-à-têtes"?

"Told you I would." Maggie checks her watch. "Now go, and be back in five minutes or I'm coming after you."

Devyn hurries me away, and as we start up the stairs, I have to ask, "What was that about—your mother using something?"

"The word *tête-à-tête*. She has one of those Daily Word calendars to help her improve her vocabulary. I think most of the words are useless since people don't talk like that, so she likes to prove me wrong by finding a use for one."

Maggie trying to improve her vocabulary… Not the Maggie I knew, which leads to the question of how she must feel when her daughter talks about the "it" and "mean" girls. Some people can't see themselves for what they are—or were—even when a mirror is held up, but something tells me Maggie isn't one of them. Something about the way the air stirred as she stood over us.

When we top the stairs and start along the second-story hallway, Devyn says, "My mom's pretty, isn't she?"

"Yes, she is."

She nods. "I'm sure I'll come into my own after a few awkward teenage years, and once I allocate time for hair and makeup, but I don't harbor illusions that I'll be as pretty as her. That's probably my father in me."

Intrigued by this odd little girl who only *looks* little, I stare at her as we near my bedroom.

She frowns. "I don't know who he is, but sometimes I miss him. If that makes sense."

Sometimes I missed my father, even when I was older and told myself I shouldn't. "I understand."

"Really?"

I halt before my bedroom. "Really."

She beams, and I long to point out that she has her mother's smile. "Well, I'd better let you get to bed."

I nod, but as I start to turn into the room, her thin arms wrap around my waist and she hugs me. "I know I'll enjoy getting to know you. And I hope you'll feel the same about me."

While the last thing I want is to have any emotional ties to Pickwick, I like her. "I'm sure I will." I stare at the mousey brown hair at the top of her head as I fight the impulse to hug her back—to give her what I longed for someone other than my mother to give me. *Then do it.* I close my eyes and put my arms around her little shoulders.

A contented sigh goes out of her, and then she releases me. "I'll remind Mom to wake you in a couple of hours. Probably after we come down off the roof."

"The roof?"

"Unc-Unc has a telescope up there. Mom promised we'd do some stargazing."

I almost wish they would invite me along.

"'Night, Miss Piper."

"Good night." I step into the bedroom and flick the light switch, only to wish I hadn't. The overhead light is not supposed to play favorites, but it's spotlighting my go-anywhere Bible, which hasn't moved an inch since I fulfilled my daily devotional time with the Scripture about shaking off the dust of a town that doesn't welcome a person.

"Okay, okay." I trudge forward and swipe the little book from the dresser. Sitting on the edge of the bed, I fan through the New Testament section in search of yellow. Whatever I took the time to highlight must have impacted me—and therefore is something I can easily sink my teeth into.

Ah! Mark 6:11: "And if any place will not welcome you or listen to you, shake the dust off your feet when you leave, as a testimony against them."

I blink. "Hmm. Another one of those 'dust-shaking' verses." Coincidence or divine counsel? I blow a breath up my face. Regardless, it's a swift reminder of my Get In, Get Out strategy. No matter how likable Devyn is, no matter how changed her mother seems to be, no matter how Blue Axel's eyes are, Pickwick is still one dusty place.

"Dusty!" And with that and a promise to make more of an effort the next time I tackle a daily devotional, I close the go-anywhere and get ready for bed.

Unfortunately, my sleep and dreams are interrupted every two hours by suddenly dependable Maggie, who makes me open my eyes and respond before returning to her own bed. Very aggravating, especially as my cousin is nearly as beautiful groggy and out of makeup as she is on full alert and not a pore out of place.

Now if she really has changed as Axel wants me to believe, what a combination…

13

*I*t's one thing to know the Pickwicks are out there, quite another to have them breach the walls. As I stand frozen in the kitchen doorway, an irritated-looking Maggie stares at her brother, Luc, and her mother, Adele, where they sit on the opposite side of the island in the light slanting through the windows.

"I appreciate that," Maggie says, "and in some ways I feel the same, but—"

"Miss Piper, you're up!"

Feeling the eyes of my cousins and aunt, I look down at the girl who has appeared alongside me in the doorway. "Good morning, Devyn."

She studies my face. "Rough night?"

"Too much interrupted sleep." I don't mean that accusingly, but that's how it comes out, spurred on by the invasion in Uncle Obe's kitchen.

"The good news is, you woke up alive." Luc slips off the barstool and strides toward us.

I narrow my lids at him. "That is good news."

He ruffles Devyn's hair. "So what do you think of my new commercial, kiddo?"

"It's good." She hands him a slipcased DVD. "You spoke clearly and not too fast, looked directly into the camera, didn't overdo the hand gestures, and the navy polo was an excellent choice."

She sounds a bit like me.

"However, I think you ought to reconsider the mustache, Uncle Luc."

He smoothes the whiskers beneath his nose. "Too much?"

"Too stereotypically 'used-car salesman,' meaning you'll have all the stigma and preconceived notions that come with that."

"But Tiffany will throw a fit if I shave it off."

The blond bombshell I saw him with at church?

"She says it makes me look distinguished."

Aunt Adele harrumphs. "You might want to point out to that wife of yours—number three, isn't it?—that the more trustworthiness you exude, the more cars you'll sell and the more money you can fork over for those designer clothes she's so fond of. I'm with Devyn—shave the thing off. It makes you look slimy."

He leans toward me in a conspiratorial manner. "A used-car dealership is not what Mom had in mind when she sent me to college."

"If you had stayed in college, rather than get kicked out just like your father, maybe you would have made something more of yourself," Aunt Adele says.

Luc tilts his head at me. "You're the expert on projecting the right image. What do you think of my mustache?" He strokes it. "Shave it?"

I could say something sarcastic in support of truth in advertising, but I won't. "I think Devyn's objections are valid."

"So if I were a client, you would advise me to get rid of it?"

"I would."

He thrusts the DVD at me. "Before you make your final determination, have a look at my new commercial."

On an empty stomach? "Er…"

He puts an arm around my shoulders and turns me out of the kitchen. "It'll only take a minute."

Stunned by the physical contact, I'm unable to summon a protest as he leads me away. Soon I find myself in the sitting room on a sofa facing the television.

"Wait for it." Luc steps back from the DVD player. "And… there!"

The name Pickwick Regal Motors flashes on the screen, followed by a closeup of a mustached Luc. Grateful his attention is fastened on the screen so I don't have to worry about my twitching lips, I watch as he sweeps a hand over the hood of a sporty red BMW and extols its virtues in a subdued twang and deeper-than-natural voice.

"This baby will go fast." His television persona strokes its gleaming fender. *"So hurry in to Pickwick Regal Motors and take her for a spin."* He crosses his arms over his chest, assuming a stance reminiscent of the Jolly Green Giant. *"I'm Luc Pickwick, and if I can't cut you a deal, no one can."* He points at the camera, smiles wide beneath the mustache, and winks. *"Come on down!"*

Luc, in the flesh, whips around. "So?"

There's a lot I could say, but as he only asked about the hair on his upper lip, I'll stick with that. "The mustache is too much."

Hope slides off his face. "Tiffany won't be happy."

I rise. "Perhaps break the news to her when you take her shopping for a new outfit."

He lights up. "Great idea."

I start to turn away, but he grabs my arm. "While I've got you here, we need to talk about the mess Uncle Obe will make of the Pickwick name if he starts changin' his will."

As delicately as possible, I extricate my arm. "That's why I'm here, to talk sense into him. And I'll do my best as soon as the timing is right—meaning when he's fully on the road to recovery."

He settles back on his heels. "Glad to hear it, although I was surprised when Artemis told me you agreed to help. I thought we'd seen the last of you."

"A call went out and I answered it." Grudgingly and with a good serving of self.

Luc gives a crooked little smile. "Can I be honest with you?"

I've always thought that an odd opener, begging the response, "No, please lie to me," but coming from Luc it works. "I'd appreciate it."

"I'm thinkin' you have something to hide, like most of us Pickwicks—something that Uncle Obe's will could drag out into the open."

Steady, girl. He doesn't know anything. But if he knows that Trinity Templeton stands to be one of Uncle Obe's heirs, he might suspect. Heat creeps up my face, and I think a happy thought: Grant leaning across the conference table, careful not to disrupt the papers spread across it, laying a hand atop mine, saying we make a great team, wondering aloud what the IQ of our children will be.

I feel better, though not as much as expected. I downplayed the hit to the head, but it would have been nice if Grant had checked on me last night.

"If your expression is anything to go by," Luc says, "I'd say you have as much to lose as the rest of us."

I flubbed that. "It's in all our best interests that a solution is found to satisfy Uncle Obe and the family. If there is some way to make restitution to those he believes the Pickwicks have wronged without him writing them into his will—"

Luc holds up a hand. "Restitution? This is about protecting the family name, but it's also about protecting our inheritance. If Uncle Obe starts throwing our money around, there won't be much left when he finally passes away."

I don't like this conversation, and I decide not to hide it behind strategic body language. "It's his money, Luc. If he wants to use it to help those who—"

He takes an aggressive step toward me. "You sound like Axel and Bridget!"

My first thought is to return aggression for aggression, but I'm struck by the second name. "Bridget sides with Uncle Obe?"

Disgust gurgles from his throat. "You know her and her big mouth—hangs it out there for any and all. Doesn't care what others think about our family." He jabs a finger at the windows overlooking the front of the house. "She's the one who exposed the truth about the great crop circle. And just when nearly every authority on the subject concluded it was genuine. Oh no, she had to own up to it, and you know why?"

Because it had served its purpose and she wanted to thumb her nose at those gullible enough to believe aliens were responsible?

"Because Buck Horton was cashing in on it, charging admission to the visitors who trampled his field and threatened the habitat of her little woodland buddies more than those big old harvesters."

Oh.

"She has a twisted sense of right and wrong, that Bridget. And she doesn't even attend church."

Meaning her sense of right and wrong should be discounted? The thought surprises me since I never expected to defend her, even if only in my head. "Regardless, it's Uncle Obe's right to do with his money as he sees fit."

"Providing he's competent to do so." There's my shifty-eyed cousin. "He's not right in the head. Everyone knows it, and if it means having him declared mentally incompetent, I will make it my mission. So you had better—"

Movement at the front windows draws his attention, and Axel's Jeep pulls into the front parking area next to what must be Luc's car—a black Corvette.

"Gotta go." Luc the aggressor is so suddenly gone, it's almost laughable. He steps away. "Think about what I said. It's in everyone's best interest, including Uncle Obe's, that we nix the changes to his will." Turning down the corridor toward the kitchen, I hear him call to his mother.

I open the front door as Axel reaches the landing.

He nods over his shoulder, and I catch sight of the rubber band that grips his hair at the nape of his neck. "I can guess who your visitor is."

"Too bad you weren't here to intercept him."

"And guard Piper, hmm?"

I'm going to ignore that. "I don't trust him on the property, and as Maggie must have buzzed him in, it's all the more reason why it wasn't a good idea for her to stay the night."

"You would have preferred that I stay?"

"No!"

"Then?"

I open and close my mouth and then wave him in. "Fortunately, Luc and his mother are leaving."

Axel walks past me. "That explains why Maggie let him in."

I close the door and step into the sitting room. "What explains it?"

"If Luc hadn't brought their mother along, Maggie probably would have turned him away, since she's well aware of the boundaries you talk about."

She is? "I'd hoped when I saw him going into church the other day, he might have changed some."

"He has, though I wouldn't measure that change against church attendance." Axel smiles. "Apparently Luc believes quite a few members of the congregation are in need of a good used vehicle."

I envision him passing business cards down the pews and wince. "You said he's changed. How?"

"He's supporting himself and by legal means."

I recall Luc's mustache and Jolly Green Giant stance. "As a used-car salesman." *Hellooo! Why don't you play that back and see how it sounds?*

A frown forms between Axel's eyes. "We can't all be high-profile image consultants." He looks down his attire—an olive green T-shirt and worn jeans that fit loosely and yet somehow emphasize his solid physique.

Reluctant snob or not, there is a side to me I don't like. Has it always been present, lying dormant due to the situation Mom and I found ourselves in? Waiting for the moment I could prove myself as good or better than those who were snobs to me?

I pinch the bridge of my nose. "I'm sorry. Clearly I have repressed feelings that are surfacing now that I've returned to Pickwick. I shouldn't have come home."

Home... Emotion lodges in my throat (must be approaching that time of month).

"Your uncle is glad you came," Axel says, "and I think you will be too once you settle in."

My emotions scurry for cover. "Settle in? I'm not going to be here that long."

"That's your decision. I just hope you'll stick around long enough to make sure Obe gets back on his feet. He's counting on you."

Guilt trip. "I'll help out however I can, but I do have a life outside of Pickwick."

He's thinking about challenging that. I can see it in his eyes, but Luc and Adele come to my rescue. Peripherally, I see the two head for the black Corvette, and when I face the windows, it's obvious Adele is having a hard time keeping up with her son. A rash of color has spread across her cheeks, hanks of bleached hair have escaped her French roll, and the heels of her designer pumps barely touch down.

Taking advantage of the moment of levity to avoid further talk of my stay in Pickwick, I say, "You have a curious effect on people, Obadiah Axel Smith."

He draws alongside me, and his arm brushes mine before he sidesteps.

A *very* curious effect. Wherefore art thou, Grant?

"I have noticed that." His tone is droll. "And that back doors seem to be the exit of choice."

I feel the tug of a smile as Luc bundles his mother into the low-slung car. "Maybe it's your military background."

Axel doesn't respond. From the muscle ticking in his jaw, it's obvious I said the wrong thing, but it stills and his eyes meet mine. "Or it could be the ponytail."

The smile tugs again, and I give in to it.

As Luc starts down the driveway, Axel reaches into his shirt pocket and removes a business card. "You asked about a cleaning service."

I pluck the sparkly pink card from his fingers. "CSI—Cinderella Sanitation Inc."

"It's a new business, but the owner has worked for another cleaning service. She's building her clientele, so she's more flexible and reasonably priced than others."

"I'll give her a call."

His gaze moves up my face. "How's the head?"

"Better. In fact, I don't see any reason to disrupt Maggie's and Devyn's lives further by asking them to stay another night."

"Doctor's orders."

"Yes, but—"

"You prefer that I pound on your door every two hours? Or throw pebbles at your window? Of course, if I can't wake you, I'll have to break down the door again."

"I think I'll stick with Maggie." I start to turn away. "Er, have you heard from Uncle Obe? I'd like to drive to Asheville to visit him later."

"He called this morning and sounded more like himself—on the cranky side." Axel's lips tilt upward. "He wants to come home, but his doctor won't release him until Thursday."

"Complications?"

"No, the doctor just wants your uncle's first few days of rehab to be closely monitored."

I look at the card and my sparkly fingertips. Uncle Obe is not coming home to a dusty roost. "I'll give our Cinderella a call."

Silence unrolls between us, the kind where something has been left unsaid. "Thank you, Axel. For the card and…uh…cutting short my visit with Luc."

Blue eyes crinkle at the corners, drawing attention to the permanent lines that evidence he's a man of the outdoors. "You're welcome."

Now what? "Well, I'm going to get something to eat before I start my day."

"Would you mind telling Devyn to meet me in the garden? She's conducting a study on earthworms and asked if she could help with the weeding."

I'll have to get a handle on the new Pickwick dynamics. "I'll tell her."

Ten minutes later, savoring toast spread with Uncle Obe's blackberry jam, I stand alongside Maggie, peering out the kitchen windows as Devyn drops to her knees beside Axel and digs in the dirt with her bare hands.

"Maggie?"

"Um-hmm?"

"When did you find out that Uncle Obe's heart condition was broken heart syndrome?"

"Friday. Why? Oh." She grimaces. "You overheard Seth and me at Cracker Barrel."

"Sorry."

She shrugs. "I should have corrected him about Uncle Obe's condition, but I was ticked off. He…well, I just want to be friends, and he says he's good with that, but then he lays guilt trips on me. You would think I'd learn."

"I guess there's no getting over you."

She raises her eyebrows. "I want what's best for Devyn, and while Seth is a decent guy, he's not what either of us needs."

We stare at each other until Devyn's laughter returns us to the garden. She's sitting on her heels, laughing with Axel, and then she's back to digging.

"Now Axel…," Maggie muses, "he would make a great dad."

For Devyn?

"He's good for her."

And Maggie? Though I have no reason to feel jealous, I do, as if she's taking Axel from me as she took Seth. But Axel isn't mine. And besides, I have Grant.

"Axel lets her talk and he listens—really listens. And no matter what he's doing when we come around, he either includes her or puts it aside and gives her his time."

Might Axel have a thing for Maggie?

"At last year's parent night at school, I came down with the flu. I asked Luc to take Devyn, but he was busy. My mom said she wasn't up to it, and Uncle Obe wasn't feeling well either. I was trying to fig-ure out how to break the news to Devyn when Axel called and of-fered to take her. She was thrilled. Of course, Seth wasn't happy when he found out." Maggie's mouth curves. "And neither were the single ladies in town when the grapevine worked its way around to them. Thought I was stealing him out from under their noses."

Was she? It's not as if she doesn't have experience with that kind of thing. "So you and Axel—?"

"No." She looks at me. "I like him as a friend. But even if I felt more than that, it takes two, and Axel is not interested in me."

He's in the minority then. "So…does he date?" Oh, I can't believe I asked that!

"Some, but not seriously. I sometimes wonder if he's self-conscious about—"

The window panes rattle, and Maggie and I jerk our chins around to find Devyn grinning at us from the other side. Axel has hoisted her up by the waist so she can wiggle a fat, slimy earthworm at us.

"Devyn!" Maggie jumps back.

Her daughter laughs, as does Axel, who winks at me as he lowers Devyn to the ground.

With a wave, they return to their weeding and earthworm studies.

"I know what you're thinking." Maggie steps back to my side. "How did a girly girl like me end up with a daughter like Devyn?"

Not what I was thinking, but it is funny. I don't mean to laugh, but when I clamp my lips on the sound, it comes out my nose.

She looks sharply at me.

I shake my head. "It's just that I was expecting a mini-Mag, not young Einstein."

She returns her gaze to the two outside. "So was I, and though it hasn't been easy, Devyn is my proof that God knows what He's doing."

I'm struck by her sincerity…by the softening around her eyes and mouth as she watches her daughter work beside Axel…by the fingers that reach for and close around a cross suspended from a delicate chain around her neck…and by how much closer to God she sounds than I feel. How did that happen? Adversity? That as my situation improved, I had less time for God? That as her situation worsened, she made time for Him?

Regardless, Uncle Obe may be right—some Pickwicks do get better with age.

The car that put-puts and shudders heavily as it reaches the crest of the driveway is the first indication that my world is about to wing further out of whack. The battered old VW Bug is an astonishing orange—not professionally painted by any means—sectioned by vertical green lines and topped by a stem and curling tendril. Cinderella's pumpkin-inspired coach. The second indication is the woman who swings her legs out of the car—begrimed ballet flats, seriously tattered dress and apron, and a kerchief tied over her dark brown shoulder-length hair. Disney's version of Cinderella. But this last is the clincher. As she ascends the stairs, a clipboard clasped to her chest, green eyes big and blinking, mouth stretched wide to affect a smile of confidence, my heart lurches.

Not Trinity Templeton! This is a conspiracy. A pin-Piper-down-and-make-her-squirm conspiracy. And Axel is going to hear about it!

I push up off the top step, where I was trying to reason with a temperamental television chef before he hung up on me. No sooner do I straighten than Trinity is beside me, shaking my hand so hard my head bobs.

"I can't believe you called me. I about pitched a fit when Gran told me you wanted me to clean the Pickwick mansion. And here I was thinkin' I might have to give up my dream and go back to workin' for Maid For You. It's a good thing I don't have a problem with bladder control, I was that excited. Why, I…" I don't realize I'm gaping until her lashes touch the expanse beneath her thick eyebrows and she drops my hand. "I mean…that is…" She smoothes her apron, grabs a handful of it, and closes her eyes.

Oh, dear, what am I in for?

Her shoulders rise with a breath and lips pucker as she slowly exhales. Five times she does this before her lids pop up like a pull-down blind with a tension problem. "I believe you'll be pleased with my services and pricing, Ms. Pickwick."

I don't correct the last name for fear of knocking her off kilter, especially considering what it took her to find her kilter.

She nods at the door. "Shall we?"

"Let's." *Lame, Piper.* I turn back. "It's nice to see you again, Trinity."

A struggle ensues, and then she's hugging me, her clipboard digging into my collarbone. "Why, I am full up on happiness. Don't you dare pinch me."

Wouldn't dream of it.

14

*D*evyn accompanied Maggie to her office in town, and I finally have Axel to myself.

"Either you're admiring my physique"—with a ripple of biceps, he lowers the long-handled pruning shears—"or you need to get something off your chest."

And here I thought he had only five senses. Though it's true I *was* admiring his physique (mostly at a subconscious level) and how effortlessly he shears off branches, I determinedly maintain my you-have-a-lot-to-answer-for stance.

He turns, peers at me through dark lenses, and winces. "Not my physique."

Close call. "It's about Trinity Templeton."

Puzzlement wanders onto his face, but I don't believe a single crease of it until he lowers his sunglasses and those Blue eyes settle on me.

Is it possible he's unaware that Trinity is the one behind the business card he gave me? Or that Uncle Obe wants to add her to his will? "You do know that Cinderella Sanitation is Trinity?"

He shrugs. "Sure."

Ignorant, my foot! "So?"

"So you asked me to find you a cleaning lady."

I toss up my hands. "You should have told me it was Trinity."

"Why?"

"Why?! As I'm sure you know, Uncle Obe intends to add Trinity to his will."

Understanding leaves no feature on Axel's face untouched. "I didn't know." He looks earnest.

"Really?"

Axel sets the pruning shears aside, and with three hitched strides he closes the distance between us. "Really."

Feeling the weight of my head in the nape of my neck, I gaze up at him. "I find that hard to believe. You are his confidant."

"I am, but we have an understanding."

Has he been chewing spearmint leaves? The scent is slight, but I can almost feel the coarse little leaf on my tongue as when I was young.

"As I told you before, he talks about his burdens, and I listen. Sometimes I have an idea who he's talking about, but I don't ask for names or details."

Should I believe him? And where on earth did he get eyes that gorgeous color?

"As far as advising him, I give my thoughts when asked and back them up with Scripture."

I'd like to believe him. Hmm. I hadn't noticed that gap between his front teeth, but then it's more like a crack than a gap.

To my surprise—and embarrassment—Axel's serious expression falters, and he takes a step back.

You are so fired, Piper Wick!

He crosses his arms over his chest in what appears to be a defensive move. To ward off an unwelcome advance? *Oh, Lord, I wasn't advancing on him. Was I? Ridiculous. I was just…admiring his minty breath and got a little sidetracked by those eyes.*

"With regards to Trinity," he says, "I knew she was struggling with her new business and heard that Bronson and Earla Biggs had hired her, so I stopped to talk to them on the way into town this morning."

Be cool. Nod. Look thoughtful. There—that flicker in his eyes? He's thinking he may have misread the situation.

"They said that, providing you don't get caught up in a conversation with her, she does a good job."

I know all about that. It took two hours to walk her through the rooms I wanted cleaned when it should have taken a half hour. Despite the need to have someone put the house in order, it was all I could do to accept her offer to get started today. But I made a dash for it when she bounded out to her car to retrieve her supplies.

"I assume you didn't hire her," Axel says.

"Actually, I did. She's having a go at it as we speak."

His arms remain crossed, but his defensive posture eases. "I'm glad to hear it."

"Unfortunately, it's going to be uncomfortable." At the realization that I spoke aloud, I tense.

His head tilts. "She's here to clean your uncle's home, not hold him at vacuum-point until he signs his name to the new will. In fact, I doubt she or any of the others he wants to add are aware of his plans."

Though relieved by his misinterpretation of my discomfort, I forbid myself to relax. That was too close.

"Or is it something else? While stories abound of Trinity's oddities, I have no idea how she was wronged by a Pickwick."

Time to go. "Well, I have work to do, and I don't want to keep you from yours."

"But I might take a stab at which Pickwick wronged her."

I don't falter, and when I call over my shoulder, "Thank you for finding me a housekeeper," there isn't a tremor in my voice. But I'm sure wobbly on the inside.

Grant. Right. If I can get hold of him—hear his voice and bask in feelings I know I have for him—I can knock out the dents Axel is putting in me. Easy.

Except for the getting hold of Grant part.

"I don't get it." I sit near the lower shelves in the pantry and consider the ceiling, which is mostly in shadow due to the little bit of light coming beneath the closed door. "I'm usually so in control."

"Um-hmm," Mom says.

"So on top of my emotions and image."

"Um-hmm."

"But I'm losing my grip."

"Um-hmm."

"I don't know what's wrong with me."

Mom sighs. "Why, there's nothin' wrong with you, Piper." Her drawl, which has mellowed since we left Pickwick, kicks in on my name. "It's simply easier to put on a face in a big city, especially when you don't have time to let people get close to you. Now those people in Pickwick know you, and you know them."

"Not all of them." I catch the sound of Trinity's humming from beyond the kitchen and lower my voice. "Not Axel Smith."

"What did you say?"

I cup my hand over the mouthpiece. "Axel Smith doesn't know me, and I don't know him."

"Why are you whisperin'?"

What would she say if I told her I hired Trinity to clean the mansion and that the only way to keep her from talking me up one side and down the other is to lie low—as in, on the pantry floor? It wouldn't be difficult to avoid her if she thoroughly cleaned one room before moving on to another, but she's constantly distracted by a particularly thick patch of dust, large cobwebs, or the husks of hapless spider victims. Always something more in need of cleaning.

"Sorry," I say, slightly louder. "Anyway, Axel is the hardest one to get anything past, and he's only a notch above a stranger."

"And yet he knows you."

"He *thinks* he does."

She chuckles. "Sometimes people just click."

"We don't click, Mom."

"But you click with Grant?"

Grant. And, no, I haven't been able to get hold of him. He's a busy man. "Grant and I are highly compatible."

"Then maybe you should talk to him. As compatible as you two are, he should be able to offer insight into what's going on and how to handle it."

She says it without sarcasm. Not that she needs any, as I have plenty—as in, *Right, I'd be happy to share my dilemma in all its Fourth of July glory with my conservative client-slash-boyfriend.* When *he calls me back.* But for twelve years, my mother has remained unaware of what I did that night, and I won't have her swooning now.

I clear my throat. "So tell me about—"

The humming is closer. I ease onto my stomach and look beneath the door. Begrimed ballet slippers. Are they skipping?

"You still there, Piper?"

"Mom, I have to go."

"You're whisperin' again."

Both slippers come down, one pivots toward the pantry, and the other follows.

"I'll call you later."

"All right, but make it after nine my time. Rufus is taking me out again."

"I'll do that." *Turn, slippers, turn!* "Bye." I end the call and press my palms to the floor to lever up—just as the door swings open.

Trinity's eyes bulge. "I thought you were a mouse."

Cinderella would.

"Gol, what are you doing in here?"

I scramble upright and turn my phone toward her. "I needed a quiet place to talk to my mother."

She tugs on the kerchief that has slipped sideways. "You'd certainly think that in a home this size, a body could find some place a bit more comfortable."

You'd think.

"And with better lighting. And that doesn't smell like a mess of pickles. Phew! Someone done broke a jar of somethin' in here." She puts her hands on her hips. "Between the smell, grime, and layers of dust—"

It always comes back to dust. In my case, *Pickwick* dust.

"—Cinderella certainly has her job cut out for her."

So do I. "I'll let you get to it."

Trinity moves aside but touches my shoulder as I pass. "I want you to know how much I appreciate this job, Piper. You're God's answer to my prayers."

The sincerity in her eyes makes me pause. No doubt she has been praying about her business, and being hired to clean the mansion has to be a godsend. "I'm glad it worked out for everyone."

She smiles, but only for a moment. "I should warn you that when it gets around I'm workin' for you, people are bound to discourage you. They'll say I'm not right in the head, my morals are warped, and I'm a shameless hussy."

I hope this isn't what it sounds like.

"All because I... Well, something they think I did years ago." She frowns. "Right after you left Pickwick, I believe."

Right before...

"Anyway, I give you my word I didn't do it."

I swallow. "I believe you."

Her eyes widen. "You do?"

"Yes, and I'm sure you will continue to do an outstanding job for my uncle."

She gives a little jump of excitement and then turns with a flourish of arms, as if casting magical cleaning dust. "Now I just have to decide if I should finish cleanin' the baseboards, vacuumin' the rugs, or polishin' the wood floors."

All works in progress.

She steps into the hall, but as I start to relax, she pops her head back in. "Of course there's this ghastly bathroom out here. I've cleaned the sink and faucets, but the toilet… I might have to take a razor blade to them nasty mineral deposits. They're as tight as stalagmites. Or is it stalactites?" She makes a face. "Your uncle should have hired me ages ago. Why, just look at this kitchen. I'll bet there's an inch of dust on them cabinets. And no tellin' what's in them." She gives a violent shudder.

How is it possible she was mistaken for me that night? Of course, it all happened so fast. I got in, stunned, and got out. *And left someone else holding the bag.*

"And those windows! I declare, you can hardly see outta them."

"Yeah, pretty bad." And after what she unwittingly revealed, I can hardly see out of my windows—a.k.a. conscience.

She gasps. "Well, hush my mouth! I'm keepin' you."

"I do need to make some calls."

I hold my breath for thirty seconds after she goes from sight, but as I release it, I hear Devyn's voice. She and her mom are back. "Hi, Trinity. Have you seen Miss Piper?"

"She's in the kitchen."

"Great! I want to show her the games we're going to play tonight."

Above the sound of her approach, Maggie calls, "Don't push, honey. She might have other plans."

I look to the back door, but as I calculate the chance of making it outside before Devyn corners me, Trinity says, "I found your cousin on the floor of the pantry. Said she was makin' phone calls, but I don't know. A bit odd, if you ask me."

Odd? It's not my fault the pantry was my best shot at privacy in a home overrun with magical cleaning dust.

"Miss Piper!" Devyn appears in the kitchen doorway with an armful of board games. "I had Mom stop by the house to pick up some games." She halts before me. "You took the bandage off. Is your head feeling better?"

I touch the tenderness. "It is."

She nods. "It doesn't look so bad. So do you like Cranium?"

I consider the box that features a cartoon brain. "I've never played it."

"There's also Apples to Apples, Scattergories, and Scrabble."

"Actually, I'm not much for games."

Disappointment transforms her face. "But they're the perfect way to spend an evening together. And since there are three of us, we can make it a girls' night." Her face lights. "I've never done that. It's usually just Mom and me."

I knew the feeling at her age. Not that I didn't have the odd friend—literally *and* otherwise—but time together outside of school or study was rare. Remembrance makes me ache for Maggie's polar opposite. "You've never had a sleepover?"

"Oh, I have, and Mom has encouraged me to connect with my peers outside of school." She sighs. "But I always end up in a corner with a book or outside poking under rocks. Believe me, that doesn't go over well, no matter how nice the girl is."

"And you think a girls' night will be different with me and your mom?"

"Absolutely. No talk of guys or clothes or hairstyles"—she hikes up her lip—"or painting each other's nails. For goodness' sake, I'm still highly receptive to learning, so why waste time on stuff like that? Now these games are fun, interactive, *and* educational."

I don't know who I feel sorrier for—the girl I was or the girl she is. Though she's also the odd girl out, it seems, by choice. On the other hand, I longed to fit in and be accepted. Only failing that did I turn to intellectual pursuits.

"What do you say, Miss Piper?"

"All right."

"Excellent. I'll set these out, and you pick the one you want to play first."

I start to follow her to the kitchen island, but Maggie's voice carries. "How is your grandmother, Trinity?"

That Maggie knows she has one surprises me.

"She's fine, thank you. Of course, there are days when she misses her knitting shop somethin' terrible."

The family business that Artemis said Trinity's grandparents didn't believe could be entrusted to her after that night. Ugh.

"It's unfortunate it closed," Maggie says.

"Yeah, but they couldn't keep it open without reliable help, and my grandparents didn't feel I… Well, I'm a much better cleaning lady, I guess."

Could Trinity have kept the shop afloat?

"Miss Piper, come see!"

As I cross to the island on legs that feel heavy, Devyn looks up from the boxes laid out in the shape of a pyramid. "So?"

I tap the Apples to Apples box.

"Wonderful. It's not as educational as the others, but it opens the door for discussion and will help us get to know one another better."

"I see you talked her into it," Maggie says.

We turn as she enters the kitchen.

Devyn nods. "She's very receptive."

Maggie shifts her focus to me. "I'm glad to hear it. Would you like to ride to Asheville with us to visit Uncle Obe?"

"Oh yes!" Devyn tugs my arm.

Reluctance raises its head, but I say, "Sounds like a plan."

"If I hadn't been there when she was born, I probably wouldn't believe Devyn was mine either."

Once more, my face is saying things it shouldn't, and Maggie has found me out, just as she did this morning when we watched her daughter scrabble in the dirt.

I look from where Devyn is asleep on the sofa to my cousin as she straightens from tucking a throw around her daughter. Even with so slight a smile and the wee hours fast approaching, she's a stunner.

Having spent half the day with her and Devyn, which included the drive to Asheville to visit Uncle Obe, Szechwan takeout, Apples to Apples, and talk of the progress in Pickwick, I feel a connection with my cousin. It's unsettling but prompts me to be frank when I would normally advise a change of subject. "As I said earlier, she isn't what I expected."

Maggie walks forward and, as we leave the library, says, "Thankfully, hmm?"

I'm unsettled further by a need to soften the blow she dealt herself. "I didn't know you well."

We take the long way around Errol where he's sprawled on the floor, and Maggie flips the light switch alongside the doorway. "That's the point."

I falter when we enter the dimly lit hallway, but my cousin's long-legged stride carries her to the staircase and up half a dozen steps before I begin my own ascent. Suddenly, she halts and swings around. "I'm sorry, Piper."

I stare at her. What am I supposed to say? That it's okay? It should be. After all, it has been years since she belittled and snubbed me, and I did forgive her. Or did I? It still hurts. Not terribly, but enough to feel a part of me.

Maggie drops her hands to her sides. "I don't know what else to say, except thank you for seeing Devyn as separate from me."

How did I get here? I didn't come to Pickwick for Maggie to make amends. Or to connect with her daughter. Or to be Trinity's godsend. Or to be rattled by Axel. Or to have doubts about Grant. What happened to Get In, Get Out?

"And thank you for humoring her. Despite her quest for all things intellectual, she needs to feel a part of something bigger than the two of us."

"It was fun. I'm glad we could spend time together."

Maggie's lips strain into a smile. "I'll see you in a couple of hours."

Another round of awakenings, after which she and Devyn will go home. Which is what I want, as I have lots to do to prepare for Uncle Obe's return, not the least of which is to corner Artemis, who has forgotten the importance of our meeting before I talk to Uncle Obe about his will.

"Good night, Piper."

"Good night."

As Maggie turns, I glimpse the release of her smile, and I know I shouldn't withhold what she was asking for in not so many words, but— *No "buts." Yes, it still hurts, and it will until you do something about it. So do what God calls you to do!*

"Maggie?"

She looks around.

"It's okay." I give a nervous laugh. "We're different people now. All grown up."

A vulnerability I don't recall her possessing softens her face. "Thank you." She inclines her head and continues up the stairs.

Shortly, I sit cross-legged on the pilled bedspread in my room, my iPhone beside me in anticipation of Celine's call, my go-anywhere Bible in my lap, my jaw slack. I did the fan-and-search-for-yellow again, and there was another "dust-shaking" verse: Acts 13:51: "So they shook the dust from their feet in protest against them and went to Iconium." Coincidence? I think not. More like divine counsel.

"Dusty," I whisper just as my iPhone rings.

Ten minutes later, Celine has brought me current on everything, including Janet Farr. "She hasn't called again."

Should I take that as a good sign? Just because she's disappeared back down the hole she stuck her head up out of doesn't mean I'm in the clear. In fact, I'm certain I'm not, which is all the more reason I need to light a fire under Artemis. Surely together we can find some way to convince Uncle Obe to leave his will alone.

"Are you doing all right?" Celine asks.

"Yes and no."

"What's the yes part?"

"My relatives aren't as bad as I remember. Well, some of them."

"That's good news. And the no part?"

"That would be my return to L.A. Everything is moving way too slowly here."

After a long moment, Celine says, "Maybe God's trying to tell you something and you're not listening."

Ha! I pick up the go-anywhere. "Actually, I'm hearing Him loud and clear."

"Oh?" Her pert nose is probably wrinkling and her eyebrows lowering.

"I've been trying to work in a daily devotional during my stay, and every time I open to the New Testament, I land on a verse about shaking the dust from your feet if a town doesn't welcome you—as in 'Get thee out of Pickwick, Piper Wick.' "

Celine chuckles. "You and your Pickwick dust."

I have mentioned it a few times. In fact, when Celine chose the New Testament as our book club pick several years back, I pointed out to the group how many times dust shaking was mentioned.

"Okay," Celine says, "so whenever you randomly open the Bible and point, your finger lands on one of those verses."

I scowl. "That would be too unbelievable."

"Then?"

"I fan through the pages, and when I see something I've high-lighted, it's always Jesus telling His disciples that when a town doesn't welcome them, they should shake its dust from their feet."

"Oh." This is the kind of "oh" without wrinkled nose and lowered eyebrows—drawn out with lips forming an O.

"What?" I wince at how defensive I sound.

"Do you have your Bible handy?"

"I do." What's this about?

"I'll bet you a hundred bucks those are the *only* verses you've
ever highlighted."

Are they? No, I'm certain scores of Scripture have impacted me
enough to warrant highlighting. "You're on." I turn to the New Testament portion. "Ah! Matthew 10:14—dust." Further proof God
wants me out of Pickwick. "Mark 6:11—dust." Last night's selec-
tion. "Luke 9:5—dust." The night before. "Luke 10:11—uh, dust."
Maybe I need to fan slower. "Acts 13:51—um…dust." Slower yet.
But no matter how slowly I fan through the twenty-some books,
that's it. And no highlighting in the Old Testament. Meaning it wasn't
divine counsel that led me to those scriptures. Not even coincidence.

I sink back on the bed. "Okay, so 'dust' Scripture is all I've high-
lighted in this little Bible—which by the way I probably haven't used
since book club—but I'm sure that isn't the case with my big Bible."

"Uh-huh. Face it, Piper, you're stuck on shaking the Pickwick
dust from your feet."

There are worse things. "Still, it applies."

"Only if you're out there spreading Jesus's message and being received with contempt—*that's* when you shake the dust from your
feet."

I sigh. "So what would you do if you were in my dusty feet?"
There, I asked it, meaning I have only myself to blame if I don't like
what she has to say.

"I would try to make peace with my relatives," she says softly. "And I'd pray that when I did leave, it would be in such a way that I didn't mind taking some of that dust with me."

She would let herself get close to those who hurt her…make herself vulnerable. That's Celine for you. "You're a bigger woman than I."

"Yeah, by a couple sizes, but I am starting that new yogurt diet tomorrow."

I come up off the bed coughing and spluttering. "That's not what I meant," I finally spit out, then hold my breath in hopes of laughter.

And she rolls it out—the real stuff, not the shallow laugh when her day is rough and she's just being nice. "Sorry. It was too good to pass up."

We talk a few more minutes. At the end she suggests that I take a more positive approach to my daily devotionals. I'll probably regret it, but I bite again, and she tells me to look up Matthew 5:9 and Romans 8:28.

"Thanks, Celine. Have a nice evening."

"Oh, I plan on it—a little online shopping to see what your hundred bucks will buy me."

I groan. "Must you rub it in?"

"Just a reminder for you to stop with the dust."

"Good night." I set my iPhone on the nightstand and reach to do the same with the little Bible, but curiosity stops me. "Matthew 5:9…" I crack the go-anywhere just enough to locate the verse: "Blessed are the peacemakers, for they will be called sons of God."

"I'm trying, Lord." And succeeding, even if only with Maggie.

Curiosity calls again, but I don't take the call. Romans 8:28 will have to wait.

I turn out the light and burrow into my pillow. But sleep is long in coming as my mind mulls over Matthew 5:9, Celine's advice, the curious case of Janet Farr, and the conscience-battering matter of Trinity. When I finally do sink into the deep, Maggie appears to awaken me, and I have to start all over again.

15

*D*oes your uncle know ya hired Trinity Templeton?" are the first words out of Artemis's mouth as he bustles past me.

Relieved that Trinity is out of earshot, I close the mansion's front door. "I mentioned it when Maggie and I visited him yesterday."

Brow beaded with the effort of climbing the steps, he turns his great bulk to me with a wobble worthy of the Weebles I played with as a little girl. "And did ya notice the terror on his face when ya *mentioned* it?"

"No."

"No startle? No widenin' of the eyes?" He wiggles his stubby fingers before his face. "No jaw droppin'?"

"I know what terror looks like, Artemis, and Uncle Obe was not terrified."

He glares at me. "Then he was out of it—probably off visitin' la-la land again."

"La-la land?"

"Why, I'm talkin' about—" His eyes bulge. "Ahem! A-hem!" He jerks a handkerchief from his breast pocket and pats his mouth. "It's just that your uncle is a strange one." He wipes the moisture from his brow. "But that ain't no call for puttin' a body away or makin' like they're mentally incompetent."

So there is something beyond strange about Uncle Obe. He was definitely "out of it" yesterday, but I assumed it was due to his intense physical therapy session prior to our arrival. Now, it seems, la-la land may be responsible, at least in part.

"All of us are strange to one degree or another." Artemis puffs along. "Even you, Piper Pickwick—pardon me, *Wick*—with all your education and big-city job. A lot of people would say ya was strange."

I lay a hand on his shoulder. "Artemis, what's going on with Uncle Obe?"

"I told ya, he's strange." He gestures for me to follow him. "Now let's strategize about how you're gonna convince him to let bygones be bygones."

An hour later, my time with Artemis interspersed with breaks to check on Trinity to get her back on task, I'm no nearer to the truth about Uncle Obe and my ears are ringing with Artemis's arguments against changes to the will. Most are legitimate, but he admits to having presented them to Uncle Obe to no effect. As his "favorite" niece, I'm expected to make him see reason.

"You know," I say as Artemis heaves up from the library desk, "if you tell me about my uncle's ventures into la-la land, it would make what you're asking of me easier. Does he have a psychological disorder?"

He snaps his briefcase closed and comes around the desk. "He's just strange."

"Is it dementia?"

His fleshy neck quivers. "Ya do what ya came home to do, young lady, and it won't matter, will it?"

"Proof is what Luc and Bart were after when they broke in here, isn't it? Something that shows Uncle Obe isn't in a state of mind to legally change his will."

His mouth pinches, making it appear cartoonish in such a large face. "Attorney-client privilege. And now I'm off to defend the rights of another client whose family is tryin' to stick him in a nursing home though he can take care of himself. Good day, Miss Pickwick—pardon me, *Wick*."

He walks out of the library. Not until he's outside on the front steps does he say another word, and only when his gaze lands on Trinity's pumpkin coach. "I don't know why ya hired that woman, especially knowin' she's one of the wrongs your uncle wants to right."

Considering how he frowns on the influence he believes Axel has over Uncle Obe, I decide not to mention how I came by Trinity. "She needed a job, and Uncle Obe needed a housekeeper."

He scowls. "Well, don't think he hasn't tried to find one. He advertises weekly."

"And no one answers his ad?"

"Of course they do, but Victoria spoiled your uncle for anyone else, her being deaf and all."

And Uncle Obe being intensely private.

He glowers. "Just don't let Trinity go botherin' him with all her yackin'. He's gonna need peace and quiet when he comes home tomorrow, and I'm countin' on ya to make sure he gets it." He wags a finger. "And to make him see sense about the will."

"I'll do my best."

"Good day."

As he drives away, I turn my eyes up. *Okay, Lord, so maybe Uncle*

Obe does have dementia or something equally devastating. What am I supposed to do? It would be the easiest way to put the will to rest and get back to L.A., but it feels like betrayal. Is it? If he isn't competent, he shouldn't be making further decisions about his will. The whole idea of righting Pickwick wrongs is probably just the dementia talking—or whatever sends him to la-la land. And yet, after his surgery, he seemed so lucid and present and in high spirits.

I groan. Until I can substantiate what Artemis let drop, it's neither here nor there, as my mother would say. Where should I start looking for proof of Uncle Obe's mental state? I step back inside and am struck by the mansion's emptiness despite the singing that travels down the hallway. At least Trinity is happy.

"So am I," I remind myself. After all, Maggie and Devyn left after breakfast, bringing an end to board games and middle-of-the-night awakenings. "Happy," I singsong and cross to the study where I consider the desk in the far corner.

It's smaller than the one in the library and has the look of use about it. As it seems the best place to begin the search for Uncle Obe's personal papers, I step forward. Of course, Luc and Bart might have thought the same and already combed through—

I halt. I have joined forces with those Easter egg–thievin', breaking-and-entering, night-vision-wearing scoundrels. Me! Piper Pick—

Ah! Wick! Wick! Wick!

Now that that's straightened out—no thanks to Artemis—what should I do about proof of Uncle Obe's mental state? If Artemis isn't going to tell me, what choice do I have but to search it out for myself?

Probably the same line of reasoning shared by Luc and Bart.

I'm not like them. Uncle Obe asked me to stay at the mansion, and I was given a key.

And permission to go through his papers?

"But if he has only one foot in reality," I address the ceiling, "then surely he—"

"Who ya talkin' to?"

I swing around. Trinity stands in the doorway, a wad of sheets under one arm, a duster in the opposite hand. I relax my splayed hands and shoulders. "Talking to myself. You know, working through a problem. Lots of people do it." Just in case she doesn't realize it's normal—to an extent.

She brightens. "I was doin' that myself, sayin', 'Trinity, you are so blessed to be making decent money workin' for yourself, settin' your own hours, doin' work that helps others. You ought to find a way to repay Piper for the opportunity.'"

While she's working behind the scenes to make certain Uncle Obe doesn't name you as a beneficiary. And keeping to the shadows so you can shoulder responsibility for her wrong.

"How is Uncle Obe's room shaping up?" I ask.

"Good, though every time I walk past the kitchen, it's a struggle not to throw myself into that mess. But I look away, and when that doesn't work, I count to ten."

"Great."

"It's smart of you to put your uncle downstairs, what with his knee surgery."

Actually, Uncle Obe's doctor called attention to the necessity of altering the sleeping arrangements. Thus, we appropriated the downstairs bedroom used by the live-in cook during the mansion's early years.

"Do you need help bringing down Uncle Obe's clothes and personal items?"

She shakes her head. "You just get on with whatever you were doin'."

I don't think I will. Before I stick my nose further into this mess, I need to think it through. And spend more time with Uncle Obe to get an idea of this la-la land. *And pray it through.* Yes, I need to do that. And my daily devotional, featuring Romans 8:28.

"I just wanted to let you know…" Trinity frowns. "Well, butter my brain, I've forgotten what I wanted to tell you."

I fight a smile. "If you remember what it was, I'll be in the library." Lots of clients to call—top of the list: my young Hollywood couple. According to the entertainment news show *Celebs Misbehaving Badly,* last night Cootchie pinned a restaurant hostess to the floor and wrote a bad word on her forehead with red lipstick.

"I'm off to the laundry room." Trinity turns. "See ya."

As I veer toward the library, I pull out my phone.

"It was *pink* lipstick!" Cootchie screeches. "And I didn't write it on her makeup-caked face. I wrote it across her skimpy top, like a scarlet letter. And, no, I couldn't have handled it differently. I did what any woman would do when another woman rubs up against her man. I took her down."

"All right, Cootchie, take a deep breath—"

"Do you know the difference between right and wrong, Piper?"

As in going through Uncle Obe's personal papers? Apparently, I do.

"I know the difference, so don't play devil's advocate for a woman who would have dragged my husband into the nearest closet if I hadn't been there. It was dead wrong, and I won't stand for it."

"I understand. So let's discuss how we can get your story in front of the public so they can decide for themselves." Even if she has to settle with the woman, the public needs to know what was behind the attack—and sympathize with her.

"Really?"

"Yes."

"Oh, Piper, I'm disappointed that we have to do this by phone, but it's a relief to know you're in my corner." She sighs. "You are so lucky to be on that side of the spotlight. No one watching your every move, no one telling you to do this or that, no one wanting you to be anything other than what you are, no worry about how the choices you make will affect your loved ones. Really, you have no idea what it's like."

Don't I? "Let's talk about how to put your best face forward, Cootchie."

She gasps with delight. "You just tell me what you want me to do, who you want me to be, and where you want me to go, and I'm there."

If she wasn't on the other side of the country, I might shake her.

Axel lets another Pickwick in. Stopped midstep by the sight of him and Bridget in the garden, I narrow my gaze. Though they are somewhat distorted by the grime on the kitchen windows, I can see from their serious faces, they're not discussing the weather. Is it Uncle Obe's will? According to Luc, Bridget sides with Axel in supporting my uncle. That still strikes me as odd, and I have to wonder if Bridget is playing a role written by Luc. She may be an environmentalist/ animal activist, but she's also a Pickwick. Of course, so is Maggie, and she's certainly improved.

"Blessed are the peacemakers..."

Axel looks past Bridget and points in the direction of the Bradford pear tree I climbed as a child. With a swish of her dreadlocks, she turns and props her hands on hips that are fit with a fanny pack. She says something, and Axel smiles, and then she gives a shout of laughter and pokes him in the ribs.

What's that about? Is Bridget romantically involved with Axel as I earlier thought Maggie might be? Not that I care, but if a relationship exists, it could have a bearing on the will and might explain the reason they both support Uncle Obe.

Axel looks around. As his gaze captures mine through the window, his laughter tapers off, and he raises a hand that causes Bridget to turn.

You are so stealthy, Piper. If you ever get tired of PR work, you can always become a PI.

Attempting to downplay any appearance of guilt, I smile, move to the door, and pull it open. "Bridget, I didn't know you were here."

She starts toward me. "Mixing business with pleasure."

I don't understand the "business" part, but I understand the "pleasure" part, and it doesn't sit well with me. Of course, she and Axel are probably highly compatible, especially in light of her dreadlocks and his ponytail-mustache-goatee thing. "Oh? You have business at the estate?"

"The usual." She halts before the step I stand on. "Mulch, weed killer, fertilizer…" She bobs her head. "And I brought a crape myrtle to replace the one that died down by the gate."

I'm lost, but she must work for a nursery. While a good fit for her tree-hugging tendencies, where it doesn't fit is that she's a Pickwick. Hauling mulch and manure ought to be beneath her. Of course, Maggie is an auctioneer, and Luc is a used-car salesman. *I'm* the one with the glamorous, high-income job. The tables have turned, and though there was a time I would have secretly welcomed it, guilt is more my speed.

Axel's appearance at Bridget's side snaps me out of my musing. I blink at my cousin, who stares expectantly at me. "I suppose you need to be paid." I head toward the kitchen to retrieve my checkbook.

"I put it on Uncle Obe's account," Bridget says.

"Oh." I turn back. "I guess he would have one with an estate this size."

The black nylon of my cousin's fanny pack undulates, and I remember a family gathering when my older cousin asked if I wanted to see what was in her picnic basket. Being ten or so and having heard that her father was indulging her taste in critters with exotic varieties like the sugar glider and the chameleon, I steeled myself for a four-legged creature. But there were no legs on the glistening baby boa. My scream was met by laughter and a new name—Scaredycat. No amount of coaxing by my mother could convince me to come out of the car, where I huddled on the floorboard.

The fanny pack stills, rustles, and stills again.

I point. "What's in there?"

Bridget pats it. "My pet. Wanna see?"

I've heard that before. I cross my arms over my chest. (There is a time and a place to appear defensive.) "Is it a *snake*?"

"Oh no, a fanny pack would be all wrong for a snake. Let me show you."

I don't care to see it, but a glance at Axel roots me. He's amused, but I am *not* going to run screaming for cover. Not this time.

She rubs the creature through the nylon. "Reggie? Come out and say 'hi.'"

More undulating, and then the unzipped flap rises and a pink, ratlike nose pops out. Four-legged, then. I can handle four-legged—as long as it stays outside where it belongs.

After a round of sniffing, the whole head appears, but it doesn't belong to an exotic animal. It belongs to one I haven't seen in ages. With beady little black eyes, it stares at me.

"You keep a rodent for a pet?"

Bridget's eyes flash. "She is not a rodent. She's an opossum, a marsupial."

A rodent to me, but why argue over our definitions of what constitutes vermin. "I don't know much about wildlife. Speaking of which, doesn't it belong in the wild?"

Bridget's face turns grim. "She's my baby now." She strokes its head. "Her mother was hit by a car. I pulled her and her siblings off their mama's back, but only Reggie survived, less a tail." She lifts the rodent and turns its backside to me.

Sure enough, there's something more than a stub, less than a tail. "So no napping upside down," I say, hoping to end the conversation on a light note.

Bridget scowls. "You don't know much about wildlife. Opossums' tails are prehensile and help them stabilize while climbing. They can only hang by them for very short periods of time."

I'm glad we cleared that up. "I didn't know."

"Most people don't." She returns Reggie to her fanny pack. "And now for the 'pleasure' part of my visit." Bridget sticks out a hand. "I'm here for my corn."

Pickled corn is the "pleasure" part? I glance at Axel who smiles. I was *so* hoping she would forget and that her jar would replace the one I broke. "I'll grab it for you."

I slip inside and am halfway to the pantry when the screen door whines. I look over my shoulder.

My cousin steps forward, seeing nothing wrong with bringing a rodent into someone else's home. "Axel said he would unload the rest of my delivery so we can visit."

I eye the rodent peering out of her fanny pack. *Peacemaker...* "Uh, do you think it's a good idea to bring Reggie inside?"

She tickles it under the chin. "She's not going anywhere. Are you, sweetums?"

And it's not my home. "Be right back."

When I return from the pantry, salivating at the juicy kernels of corn pressed against the sides of the glass jar, Bridget sits on a stool at the island. Thankfully, Reggie remains in the pouch Bridget has substituted for its mother's. Not that her "pet" could still fit in an opossum's pouch at ten or so inches and a couple of pounds.

"It could be a while," Bridget says. "That was a lot of mulch."

And something tells me that Axel is in no hurry. I need to have a talk with him.

"Hungry?" Bridget asks.

"A little."

"Then why don't you fry us some corn?"

The jar nearly slips from my fingers. She's offering to share her pickled corn with me? Surely this is a cruel joke.

Now is the time to embrace the wisdom of "Never look a gift horse in the mouth." "Sure." Before she realizes what she's done, I'm around the island and pulling a cast-iron pan from the cabinet below. Pickled corn at last! Five minutes later, it's sizzling in butter—the entire jar.

"That's a lot of corn," Bridget says.

I look down at the be-autiful kernels that waft their distinctive scent, tempting me to shovel a spoonful in my mouth. "We'll just have to make it an early dinner."

She shakes her head. "That stuff is better than good, but if you don't go easy, you'll end up with a tummy ache. Of course, we could invite Axel to join us. A guy his size can probably polish off half of that without any serious repercussions."

Half?! *I* was counting on that half, or at least a good portion of it.

She slides off the stool and crosses to the refrigerator. A moment later, her face is stuck in it, which means the rodent's is too. Yuck!

"Slim pickin's," she says, "but I think we can make a meal of it." She looks over her shoulder. "If you'd like, I'll pick up some groceries and drop them by in the morning so Uncle Obe will have healthy meals to get him back on his feet."

I'm surprised by the offer and sheepish, since I had every intention of restocking the refrigerator. "That would be nice. Thank you."

She glances at the stovetop. "Don't let that burn. Uncle Obe keeps a close eye on his inventory, so that's our only shot at enjoying my winnings."

I apply myself to the corn. Just in time.

"Eggs and country ham it is," Bridget announces.

She's no longer a vegetarian?

"Toss two pans on the stove, will you?"

As she turns from the refrigerator, I groan to see Reggie snuffling at the packages six inches from its pointed nose.

Bridget follows my gaze. "Gotcha." She places the food on the island and turns away. "Wouldn't want my baby getting popped by hot grease," she coos as she unfastens the fanny pack.

The only consideration is that her rodent could get burned? Gritting my teeth, I lower the heat on the corn and retrieve two more pans.

Bridget arranges the fanny pack on a chair near the back door and rubs Reggie between the ears. Prepared to remind her to scrub her hands, I'm relieved when she turns her flip-flops toward the sink and steam rises from the water as she washes.

Fifteen minutes later, with domestic efficiency that belies a Pickwick—myself included—Bridget slides over-easy eggs and country ham onto a platter. "Plate the corn and I'll call Axel in." She carries the platter to the eat-in side of the island.

I quell the temptation to sample the pickled corn while her back is turned, and when Axel tramps in a minute later, I'm salivating where I sit beside Bridget.

"Thank you for the invitation." He wipes his feet on the rug.

"Hurry up—it's getting cold." Bridget pats the seat beside her.

As Axel settles on it, she wags a finger at him. "If you want to pray, keep it to yourself."

He grins at her and then lowers his head.

"Same goes for you." Bridget turns to me. "Of course, I'm assuming you're still the churchgoing type."

To prove it, I close my eyes and drop my chin. Silently, I thank God for the meal, especially the pickled corn, and ask Him to heal Uncle Obe, and help me with the matter of the will. When I open my eyes, I'm disappointed to find I did so a moment before Axel. Now he has no idea I was praying. He probably thinks I was impatiently tapping my foot like Bridget. Well, at least I proved to *her* I'm churchgoing.

Is that what you were doing? Silly me, I thought you were talking to God.

"Something wrong?" Axel asks.

God knows. *Sorry, God.* "Uh, could you pass the pickled corn?"

Axel raises an eyebrow and looks to the bowl in front of me. Right where I put it. "Oh, sorry." I scoop up three spoonfuls and pass the bowl to Bridget.

She takes one spoonful—a good sign—before offering it to Axel, who will surely undo all the good she did.

He shakes his head. "I'll stick with eggs and ham."

A *very* good sign.

"Your uncle's corn is good, but I only like it occasionally." He forks two slices of ham onto his plate and three eggs. "In fact, I had to toss out half of one of the jars he gave me when it went bad before I could work up an appetite to finish it."

He tossed out pickled corn? *One* of the jars given to him? Might there be others? One is all I need to get Uncle Obe's inventory back up to where it belongs. Of course, two would be nice, as I could take one to Mom.

"I agree." Bridget passes the ham and eggs to me. "Love the stuff, but it can get old, and as I warned Piper, there's a price to pay if you overdo it."

After taking an egg and a small piece of ham, I plow the tines of my fork through the golden kernels. Coming out the other side fully loaded, I raise the fork.

My cell phone *bleepity-bleeps*. I nearly stuff the corn in my mouth, but it's probably a media contact returning one of the calls I sent out to secure air and print time for Cootchie. With staggering restraint, I lower the fork to my plate and pull the phone from my pocket.

Grant's number is on the screen, and I haven't even called him recently. So why the struggle between answering and letting him go to voice mail so I can eat my pickled corn?

"Are you going to answer that?" Bridget asks as the *bleepity-bleeping* continues.

With an apologetic smile, I hit the answer button as I hustle from the kitchen. "Hello?" I infuse my voice with questioning so I don't sound eager.

"We have a situation, Piper."

Well, "hello" to you too. As I step into the corridor, a thought strikes me, and I look around to find Bridget angled toward Axel, punctuating what she says with fork jabs in the space between them.

"Hold on," I tell Grant. "Uh, Bridget?"

She looks around.

"Just leave my plate. I'll be back."

"Sure."

"And don't throw away any leftovers." Namely, the corn.

Axel's knowing glance makes me blush.

I do an about-face and head for the privacy of the library. This is the business side of my relationship with Grant. I have no reason to take offense at the first words out of his mouth, no reason for him to treat me different from the way other clients treat me. Though some of them do treat me like family.

I lower to the sofa where Devyn crashed last night and raise the phone to my ear. "What's the situation?"

"An article in today's local paper suggests there could be more to my bachelor status than a desire to serve my constituents without hindrance."

Hindrance. Each time he applies the word to wife and children, I'm twinged. But one has to admire that he places his work above personal happiness. "The one who wrote the article, does he carry any weight?"

"It's a *she,* and I've never heard of her—name's Jane Farredy."

Did that just ring a bell? I'm sure I heard a tinkle.

"We have to cut this off at the jugular, Piper. If my constituents start questioning my sexuality, the election could get away from me."

"Of course." If only I were clearheaded enough to whip out a plan of action. *Must* figure out where I laid my PR hat.

"So here's what we'll do…"

Despite a spurt of indignation that Grant presumes to do *my* job, I'm relieved. Doubtless, his plan will need tweaking, but he's intelligent and levelheaded.

"Which means," Grant says, "you'll fly to Denver first thing in the morning."

What?!

"Great idea, don't you think?"

16

I draw a deep breath. "You want me to fly to Denver?"

"I need you here for photo ops. Handholding in the park, cuddling at the symphony, whispering over candlelit dinners. The kind of things respectable, highly heterosexual bachelors do."

If I weren't so shocked, I would laugh. The strategy, though, is good, even if it turns me into a prop. "I agree that something needs to be done, but I can't—"

"If that doesn't do the trick, we can always slip into a jewelry store, if you know what I mean."

I do, and it isn't remotely close to a marriage proposal. "I'm sorry, but I can't come to Denver. I'm in the middle of something."

"More important than me?"

Is it? It wasn't before I left L.A., but something more than my Fourth of July stunt holds me here.

"Piper…"

I'm not taken in by his cajoling tone. After all, I helped to perfect it when several journalists noted it had shades of condescension.

"Not only am I a well-paying client, but we have a personal relationship—one that has the potential to be more. Once the timing is right, of course."

I know that's what we have, and yet it suddenly seems clinical. "We'll work this out, but I can't leave Pickwick now."

Silence…and then, "That's it!"

"What?"

"I'll fly out to you."

Whoa! Grant in Pickwick?

"I'll have to rework my schedule and cancel engagements, but doing so at this crucial time in the campaign ought to satisfy the press that this talk of my sexual orientation is a bunch of hot air."

I grip the sofa arm. "Let's think this through."

"I have. It shouldn't take more than a day, two at the outside, and then you can get back to whatever you're doing there."

And abandon Uncle Obe? Based on my assurance that I would be here for him, his doctor agreed to release him to home rather than to a rehab facility. "I can't, Grant."

"Of course you can."

"No."

"Piper…"

"I'm sorry. I have to keep my commitment, and I can't do it if you're here."

"What commitment?"

I don't have an answer for him. *There's always the truth.* And eventually I will have to tell him—when the timing is right and before he slips a ring on my finger. I touch my left hand and imagine a wedding ring there, as I've often done since the day he wondered about the IQ of our children.

Piper Spangler, wife of U.S. Congressman Grant Spangler. For some reason, it lacks its previous luster. *Piper Spangler, U.S. Congressman Spangler's wife.* Still on the dull side. *U.S. Congressman Spangler's lovely wife, Piper.*

"Piper? Is there something you're not telling me?"

As much as I long to deny it, it would take my lies of omission to a new level.

"Are you really there on business?"

"No." At his sharp breath, I say, "Actually I am, but not company business. Family business."

"Family?"

I brace myself. "I should have told you, and I'm sorry I didn't, but"—I moisten my lips—"Pickwick is my hometown. And my last name."

"What?"

"*Wick* is derived from *Pickwick.*"

Empty air. But I know he's there, meaning he's gone into politician mode—carefully thinking through a response so he doesn't say something he'll regret, mentally checking his jaw and throat muscles so when he speaks he'll sound in control.

"You're one of *them*?"

I startle, more at the accusation that makes me sound like a disease than surprise that he isn't using the technique I drilled into him. "Yes, and I came home to help my uncle while he recovers from surgery and to address issues regarding his estate."

"You should have told me. I'm a public figure, and things like this…"

Headlines to pay. "I know." Just as I know he needs to be told all of it. Even if I can prevent Uncle Obe from raising suspicion about Pickwick responsibility for what Trinity didn't do, Grant needs to be prepared. "Grant—"

"You've turned me inside out, Piper. I don't know what to say."

So long? Farewell? Maybe it won't be necessary to tell him everything, after all.

"I need to think this through."

"I understand."

"I'm not saying we can't work it out."

He isn't? Then I *should* tell him everything. "Grant—"

"I'll call you later." He hangs up.

Oh no. I call him back and, after three tries, leave a message. "Grant, please call me. There are…other things I need to talk to you about."

I wait ten minutes, and when he doesn't return my call, I console myself with a reminder of what I left behind in the kitchen. Providing Axel isn't suddenly struck by a craving for pickled corn, I won't want for comfort food—practically a whole jar to myself. *That* puts a spring in my step, and I enter the kitchen to find that Bridget and Axel have cleared out.

But I'm not alone. Oh no, I have company. Of the rodent, pickled-corn-thievin' variety. I stare at the creature that is right on the island, right in front of the overturned bowl of pickled corn, right over my plate.

I open my mouth, and when a choked sound emerges, that *rodent* has the audacity to act put out. A kernel in one paw, it lifts its head, fixes beady eyes on me, and makes a sound between a hiss and a growl.

"You!" I lunge forward, but when I'm five feet and closing, Reggie keels over. Its upper body lands on the plate of ham and eggs, its lower half amid pickled corn that will never pass my lips. It looks dead—eyes closed, mouth gaping, and tongue lolling, the kernel lax in its paw.

Though it's been a while since I've seen an opossum "play possum," I recall that it will remain "dead," unresponsive to the most determined prodding. "Nature's mystery," my fifth-grade teacher said after explaining that the opossum's reaction to extreme fear is an involuntary comatose-like state and that resuscitation occurs once the body senses the danger is past. Which, in this critter's case, could be a long time.

"You are *very* much in danger, so lay there and suffer."

It opens an eye, and I startle back a step. It's not supposed to do that. I look again, but the eye is closed. Did I imagine it? I lean nearer, and after a minute the eye opens and snaps shut again. "Some opossum you are!"

Its nose twitches.

"I saw that!" I grab a fork and nudge the rodent with the handle.

It doesn't respond. *This* part it has down.

I nudge it again. "Get going."

The screen door creaks, and Bridget pauses in the doorway with Axel looking over her shoulder. "What are you doing to Reggie?"

I pull the fork back, and the rodent immediately comes to life and makes for the opposite side of the island.

Bridget hurries forward to scoop up her "pet."

"It got into the corn," I say between clenched teeth. "The *pickled* corn."

She tucks the rodent beneath her chin. "Poor thing. She must have woken up hungry. And you had to go and frighten her into playing possum."

"*I* frightened her? How do you think I felt when I found her in my dinner?"

Bridget bobs her head. "Wouldn't have happened if you didn't take calls in the middle of meals. Very rude, you know."

"So it's my fault?"

She makes a show of thinking. "I suppose I have to take some of the blame since I shouldn't have left her here while Axel and I finished unloading my delivery." She narrows her lids. "A mistake I will not repeat." She retrieves the fanny pack, then steps to the screen door, which Axel opens for her.

That's it? No "sorry"? "There's something very wrong with that critter," I call.

She sticks her head back inside. "Now you're just being ugly."

"It's true. It has no idea how to play possum. It kept peeking at me."

Bridget harrumphs. "She's unique."

I nearly point out that's another word for *defective* but close my mouth at Axel's bemused smile. Why am I behaving like a put-out teenager? At thirty years old and the voice of reason for my clients, I know better. And what happened to peacemaking?

Returning my focus to my cousin, I concede the battle. "You're right; she's unique. Thank you for coming all the way out here to make the delivery." I nearly extend the thanks to her offer to share her pickled corn, but it might sound sarcastic under the circumstances. Intentional or not...

Bridget settles Reggie in the crook of her arm. "Tell Uncle Obe I'll visit tomorrow when I bring the groceries." She looks at Axel. "Thanks for your help."

"Anytime."

She turns, and though I expect Axel to follow, he walks farther into the kitchen. "I'm sorry about your dinner."

I look around. "All that pickled corn. Wasted."

"You really like the stuff."

I grimace. "I do, but I guess it's not meant to be."

"Come up to the cottage. I'll fry some for you."

I step closer to him. "You have pickled corn?"

"Four or five jars left from those your uncle gave me last summer."

Four or five? And he's not a big fan of the stuff.

"If you're worried I might have an ulterior motive, you can bring your pistol."

Which I seem to have forgotten all about. Trying not to appear eager, I shrug. "When should I stop by?"

"I have some things to do before I call it a day, so give me an hour."

A whole hour. "All right, I'll see you at the cottage."

17

*A*ll is still as I traverse the path through the garden, the only movement that of clouds sliding across the sky upon which the scent of rain is carried. Rain that may or may not fall. I hope it does, since California rain is a distant cousin to Carolina rain, and it has been too long since I felt thunder radiate through me. Then there's the lightning…

As I start up the hill, I turn my attention to what is waiting for me. I smell it long before I reach the back door, and when Axel calls for me to enter, I practically float in on the pickled scent, banging the screen door in Errol's nose.

Axel stands at the stove with his back to me, and I falter when I see he's changed into a casual short-sleeved top and cargo shorts. But what grinds me to a halt is his right leg—rather, its absence. In its place is a prosthetic that makes no attempt to appear anything but. I knew he was injured, but I had no idea of the extent.

"Five more minutes," he says.

How did he lose his leg?

"Would you prefer to eat inside?"

Was it a grenade?

"Or outside?"

A mine?

"I can light candles to keep the bugs away."

Maybe a bullet?

He turns, presenting a frontal view. The prosthetic is high tech, and suddenly I remember what Maggie said—or *almost* said—when we watched him and Devyn through the kitchen windows. She said he didn't date seriously and thought it was because he was self-conscious about something. *This.*

"You didn't know." His tone shakes me free of my reverie.

I meet his gaze. "I knew you had been injured but didn't know you had lost a leg. I'm sorry."

His eyebrows rise.

"I mean, for staring."

He considers me and then nods over his shoulder at the frying pan. "So?"

"Outside is good, providing the rain holds off."

"I'll bring it out."

I nod. Soon, seated beneath a dogwood tree at a weathered wrought-iron table, I focus on the bowl Axel carries across the lawn for fear of staring at his prosthetic. It's fascinating, not only the mechanics of it, but the missing details of how he lost his leg.

Axel steps around Errol, where he lies on his side, then continues to the table with a hitch that is more pronounced. Or is it my awareness of the prosthetic that makes it so?

Determinedly I give my attention to the bowl Axel sets on the table. The kernels glisten, and I close my eyes and breathe in the scent. *Thank You, Lord, for this delicious treat. And thank You for Axel losing only a leg and not his life.*

He takes the chair to my right and his Blue eyes capture mine. "All yours." He nods at the bowl and pulls a lighter from his shirt pocket. "I only fried up half the jar, so you can take the rest with you when you leave."

I don't plan ahead for breakfast, but in this case, I'll make an exception. "Thank you, and thank you for making it."

As he lights the citron candles on the table, I lift the spoon and am tempted to look around to ensure there is no impediment to the corn making it to my mouth this time. Though I'm just shy of drooling, I pause. "You remember that I broke a jar? I didn't know it at the time, but Uncle Obe keeps an inventory of his pickled corn."

Axel smiles, and I know he knows what I'm about to say.

"So maybe I could buy a jar from you to bring his inventory back up."

He shrugs. "By the time my appetite for pickled corn returns, your uncle will have canned a new batch. So they're all yours. No charge."

Oh, happy day! Well, Grant notwithstanding, but I'm not going to think about him. I'm going to enjoy every bite of my pickled corn. The spoon goes in, the spoon comes out, depositing sweetly sour kernels that light up my taste buds.

"Good?"

Only when I open my eyes do I realize I closed them. "Um-hmm."

"Fried in a cast-iron pan, per your uncle's instructions."

Absolutely.

"Then Pickwick's not all bad?"

I don't mind Axel's amusement, especially as the sparkle accentuates his Blue eyes. "Certainly not the pickled corn." I scoop another mouthful.

"You seem to be getting along well with Maggie."

True.

"And it looks as if you and Bridget are connecting."

Now that's a stretch. "In case you misinterpreted that last encounter, I was upset to find her rodent in my food, and she was upset that I had a problem with it."

"Minor differences." He grins, and I'm startled by the combination of mustache, teeth, and goatee—a rakish combination that makes him dangerously appealing. "I think if you give Maggie and Bridget a chance, you'll find you have a lot in common."

Another stretch. I hold up a hand. "Give me five minutes to enjoy this, and *then* we'll talk."

The next half-dozen bites are wonderful, and I have to admit there must still be some of the South in me to enjoy pickled corn more than I enjoy the gourmet foods I'm acquainted with in my line of work. And that goes for two-hundred-dollar-an-ounce Russian caviar. Unfortunately, my awareness of Axel's regard and proximity begins to interfere with my indulgence. I must look like a child hunched over a bowl of ice cream lest anyone steal a bite. I lower the spoon. I'll heat up the rest later and finish it off to my heart's content—in private.

I consider Axel, who looks a bit menacing as the dark clouds and approaching night overtake the light. "Why are you pushing Maggie and Bridget on me?"

He clasps his hands on the table. "A family is a terrible thing to waste. I didn't have much of one growing up. There was my father and mother as we moved from military base to military base. Then just my father when my mother passed away."

"Your mother must have been young."

"She died from complications of a miscarriage when I was thirteen."

"I'm sorry."

He inclines his head. "I know your relations are difficult, especially Luc and Bart, but Maggie and Bridget are decent. Though they've been dealt difficult cards—Maggie single-handedly raising Devyn and Bridget losing her husband—they're holding up their heads as best they can. And with little support from their families."

"You're saying their parents aren't there for them? If my memory serves me right, they were spoiled rotten." *That sounded bitter.*

Axel stretches his legs out before him. "They hurt you."

"There was no love lost between us."

"Because they didn't accept you and your mother."

Talking about my relationship with my cousins was a bad idea. "You told me you don't ask for names or details when my uncle confides in you."

"I don't, but sometimes he drops a name, and other times it's obvious who he's talking about."

I lower my hands to my lap. "What else do you know about me?" Hopefully not my Fourth of July stunt.

"I know why you weren't accepted."

Thank you very much, Uncle Obe.

Of course, it was hardly a secret that despite my mother being far down the social ladder, my God-fearing grandfather forced his son to marry her after a backseat fling resulted in her pregnancy. The consensus was that Dory Fisk tricked the "catch of the county," and her father showing up at the Pickwick mansion with a shotgun only inflamed such talk. Not that my mother wasn't infatuated with Jeremiah Pickwick, but she didn't plan the pregnancy to catch him. She made a mistake and I was the result.

"It doesn't matter." Axel's voice is low and understanding. "It's in the past and some people do change for the better. Just as you're not the teenager who fled Pickwick twelve years ago, Maggie and Bridget are no longer the teenagers who were among the reasons you left."

Until Maggie spent two nights with me, I wouldn't have believed that, but this older "hard knocks" Maggie is more likable. Then there's Bridget, who has been more responsive since my return to Pickwick than in all the years I lived here, as evidenced by her sharing her winnings. Of course, there's that malfunctioning rodent of hers. But Bridget wasn't all that bad.

"See?" Axel crosses his arms over his chest. "They have changed."

And I am transparent. "I'm sure you're pleased that your plan to throw us together worked, somewhat."

He runs a thumb across his goateed jaw. "One of the best ways I've found to heal is to expose myself to what wounded me." His eyes shift as he searches the clouds. "The passage of time can be a good thing, especially when you're young. Once you mature and have been beat up by the world and learned that conflict is never just black or white, it's easier to see the other side of things." He drops his head farther back. "And to forgive and be forgiven."

To make peace…

Axel defers to the crickets in the undergrowth and frogs in the distance. A minute passes. When it seems as if another might, he meets my gaze. "Deep, huh?"

I'm grateful for the candlelight that keeps the falling darkness from his face, unlike that first night, when he nearly passed for a Neanderthal. "I know you were in the military, but was it as a shrink?"

He laughs. "I was just a good, old-fashioned soldier." I detect emphasis on the last syllable. Is it regret? bitterness? anger?

"There's the proof." He nods at the prosthetic leg thrust alongside the table toward me.

I take that as an invitation to look closely at it, and though there isn't enough light to see clearly, there's no mistaking it beside the muscular, flesh-covered leg. I start to reach forward.

"Go ahead. There's no feeling below the knee, other than the occasional phantom sensation."

I set my fingers on the cool metal and slide them down to where it narrows. I glance at Axel and, at his nod, continue to the ankle that thickens into the foot encased in a shoe.

"I'm sorry." I wince. That sounded like what you say to someone who is under the weather.

"So am I, but good has come of it."

"How's that?"

"I was a part-time believer—believing in God but not living in Him. I'd never really needed Him, always scraping by on my own. But on my second tour in Iraq, this happened. I called out, and God was waiting to hear from me. I should have died from all the blood loss, but here I am—almost in one piece."

I sit back. "Was it a roadside bomb?"

"Friendly fire."

I gasp. "I'm sorry." Oh! I said it again. And it sounded lamer than the first time.

"That was the hardest part—forgiving the young soldier who mistook me for the enemy."

I can imagine. Bad enough struggling to stay alive with the enemy gunning for you, but to have one of your own—I can do better than imagine, since I also fell victim to friendly fire. No, the verbal bullets shot by the Pickwicks weren't life threatening, but if Axel can let the past go, surely I can. Surely I can stop perseverating on shaking the Pickwick dust from my feet and put more effort into peacemaking.

Concern shadows Axel's face. "What is it?"

I nearly share my findings with him, but they seem petty compared to his prosthetic. "Nothing. So I'm guessing you were hospitalized a long time."

After a long moment, he says, "I was."

"Did your father help out?"

"He did. And my fiancée."

Where did *she* come from? "You're engaged?"

"I was."

I like *was*.

"Teddy stayed by my side through the surgeries and rehab and while I learned to walk again. She was supportive, but it was too hard on her."

"I'm s—" *Don't say it again!* "Thank you for sharing that."

He draws his legs back. "Considering how much I know about you, it seemed fair."

What isn't fair is that he still knows far more about me. "Tell me about your first name. You said it was given in honor of my uncle."

"Not a matter of ingratiation." Axel reminds me of my inappropriate remark.

"Sorry about that."

He nods. "Obadiah saved my father's life when they were roommates in college."

I sit straighter.

"My father was drawn to the military, but his family threatened to disown him if he enlisted. So he went to college to become something they approved of—a doctor. He hated it." Axel's face tightens. "One night he had too much to drink and got hold of a gun. Your uncle talked him out of suicide and convinced him to pursue a military career."

And yet, years later, Uncle Obe fell victim to his own family's demands.

I smile. "That's worth honoring a person for. So why Axel instead of Obadiah?"

He chuckles. " 'Obadiah' brings out the bully in boys. My father made me tough it out until I consistently came out on top, then he gave me a choice. I had earned 'Obadiah,' so I decided to stay with it. But then my mother passed away." His jaw shifts. "She always called me Axel."

As I seek to express the tugging of my heart, a streak of blue lights the heavens.

"It's going to rain," Axel says.

Though I sense this is his way of ending the discussion, I don't want it to end. "You said it was just your father and you after your mother passed away. What about relatives?"

He frowns, as if questioning my interest. "My mother was an only child, but her parents were active in our lives—at least, as active as they could be considering how often we moved. They've since passed away. As for my father's family, they disowned him as they said they would." Regret fills his voice but not bitterness.

"Where does your father live?"

"Phoenix."

"Do you get to see him much?"

"Not as often as I'd like since he's partial to the desert." He smiles wryly. "I think North Carolina with all its greenery reminds him too much of Vietnam."

"Then does Phoenix remind you too much of Iraq?" Oh! I can't believe I said that. *Way* too personal.

"There is that, but I've always been drawn to the mountains, and there's a lot to be said for four seasons."

I have missed them myself. "So you see yourself growing old here."

"I do—and growing my landscaping business and eventually having a family."

Nothing lofty like my goals, and yet somehow his sound more appealing.

A drop of rain snuffs out the citron candle, causing it to sizzle and smoke and Axel to stand. "I'll bag the pickled corn and walk you home."

As I watch him cross the yard, I hear the rumble and am unsettled at the thought of walking alongside him in the dark. Not because I didn't bring my gun, but because of Grant. If he can't reconcile that the woman he may one day ask to marry him is a Pickwick, this thing between Axel and me could lead to rebound.

When the screen door bangs behind Axel, I put my elbows on the table and cup my face in my hands. That's when the pickled corn returns to notice. Fortunately it's good cold, and I slide in the last mouthful just as several drops of rain hit my cheek.

"Ready?" Axel steps from the cottage with a large brown bag in one arm.

I jump up. When I near him, the light filtering through the cottage windows tempts my gaze to his prosthetic leg. And I nearly offer to carry the bag, which wouldn't have crossed my mind to do when the hitch in his stride was only that.

"Errol!" Axel commands.

Since this is the last night I have to put up with that piddling beast, I don't protest when he bounds past us. We descend the hill toward the tentatively moonlit garden, and the rain picks up, happily dotting me.

"Is there anything you need for your uncle's return home tomorrow?"

I shake my head. "Bridget said she would drop off groceries in the morning, so we should be covered." The paper bag crackles with his forward movement, and I chuckle. "Especially now that our supply of pickled corn is up."

"I'm glad I could help out."

I glance at him and catch his smile. Ooh, *frisson, frisson.* Which I have no business feeling. Why am I? Is it the night, all warm and moist among the wafting scents of the garden below? Or Axel's smile, that broad stretch of white that is just the other side of secretive? Maybe it's his deeply masculine voice. Could be his Blue eyes that, despite the dark, summon the increasingly familiar color from my memory—

My left foot slides on the moist grass, and I try to catch myself with my right, but it also goes out from under me. With a yelp I fall back, wincing in anticipation of hitting hard. And forgetting that Axel is at my side.

His hand clamps around my arm, pulling me up against him, like that first night when I fell from the gate. But this time I'm facing him, and there is nothing remotely Neanderthal about his face above mine. Or his mouth only a tiptoe away.

"Are you all right?"

That's what he asked the first time. Warmed by his breath, I nod.

He doesn't set me away, and I feel his gaze more than I see it. "Déjà vu, hmm?"

"Yeah."

"All that's missing is your gun."

And fear. What's trembling through me now is something very different. Hoping he doesn't feel it, I take a step back. "It's a good thing I don't need it."

He releases me. "And a good feeling, I imagine."

Too good. Pickwick may be uncomfortable, but it isn't frightening. Axel may be big and a far cry from sophisticated, but I'm safe with him. And it's time to change the subject. "Oh, look! You didn't drop the pickled corn."

The paper bag protests as he tightens his arm around it. "It's safe."

Of course it is. I turn and step forward, more gingerly this time.

"We'd better hurry, or we'll get soaked." I expect Axel to offer his arm, but thankfully, he doesn't. Not that he needs to because he remains close enough to catch me should I fall again. Another good feeling...

When the ground levels off, we enter the garden to the sound of softly pattering rain and the crunch of the pebbled path underfoot. Almost home free.

"Why the gun, Piper?"

Almost. Of all the trips down memory lane I don't care to take, that night tops the list. But as I open my mouth to politely tell him I don't care to talk about it, he says, "What happened in L.A.? Were you attacked?"

The concern in his voice is my undoing. I stare at the illuminated path. "Two years ago I was working late, and when I entered the parking garage, it was practically deserted. I was so absorbed in the day's events that I wasn't paying attention." I shiver hard. "But suddenly I knew someone was behind me, as if God Himself whispered it in my ear. When I turned, a man was facing me, and all I could think was to bring my knee up when he grabbed me. I hit him hard, but he fell on me. I fought him, and finally he snatched my purse and ran off."

"How badly were you hurt?"

I know what he's asking. It's the same thing the police wanted to know. I stop, and Axel halts just past me and turns.

"It wasn't only my purse he was after." I look up into his moist face. "But that's all he got—and bites and bruises and scratches. And possibly a broken thumb. At least, that's what it sounded like."

I hear relief in the breath that goes out of him. "Was he caught?"

"No." Meaning I may not have been his last victim. Trying to override my dark feelings, I make a conscious effort to brighten my voice. "But God was watching over me. I walked away with only a black eye, a bloodied nose, and bruised ribs."

His smile is slight. "And a whole new appreciation for guns."

"The working-late woman's best friend."

"And yet you stayed in L.A."

"My mother and I discussed moving to a smaller city, but shortly after the incident, I made partner at the PR firm. It was what I had been working so hard for."

"And you couldn't walk away," Axel says with understanding that surprises me.

"No. Also, my mother is happy in L.A. She has friends like she never had here, a job she enjoys, a church that makes her feel loved and needed, and most recently, a gentleman friend with whom she has a kissing acquaintance."

"That's important," Axel says softly.

What? All of it? Or just the kissing part? As I peer up at him, catching the slight rise and fall of his shoulders, I imagine what it would be like to—

"Let's get you out of the rain." He resumes his trek down the path.

I'm grateful for his sharp right turn, but as we walk past the berry and herb patches and rosebushes, the strength of his presence expands, as if we're touching. By the time we reach the back door, I'm afraid of Axel Smith. Not because he would ever hurt me, but because he's more dangerous to my virtue than any man I've ever been so near. Because *I* want to be nearer.

Errol ascends the steps and puts his nose to the screen door, and Axel passes the bag to me. "Enjoy." His fingers brush mine.

Nerve endings jangling, I hug my windfall. "Thank you for coming to my aid again."

"You're welcome." He starts to turn away…to go back to his cottage…to leave me alone…

"Axel?"

"Yes?"

Amid the falling rain, I pick out the puzzlement on his brow. "I…" I don't mean to look at the moisture on his upper lip. It just happens as I avert my eyes—a detour so to speak, complete with a rest stop that boasts a lookout point. And a scenic view.

"Piper?" Now *he's* looking at *my* mouth.

Dangerous.

His brow smoothes.

Very dangerous.

His head lowers.

Alert! Alert!

His breath is between us.

Dive! Dive!

His moist lips touch mine.

Stop, drop, and roll!

His mustache and goatee lightly chafe my skin.

Too late.

I've never been kissed in the rain, but Axel Smith is kissing me. *Really* kissing me. None of that quick corner-of-the-mouth stuff that Grant—

"No!" I jump back and nearly drop the bag of pickled corn when my calves connect with the lower step.

"No?" He fixes those memory-enhanced Blue eyes on mine.

"I'm taken." I hug the bag with all my might. "Sort of. I mean, yes. You know…"

He slides his hand down my rain-moistened upper arm, over the goose bumps, and across the palm of my left hand that he raises between us. "You're not married."

No wedding band. "No."

"Engaged?"

No engagement ring. "No. I mean…well, I am engaged…just not yet."

His mouth quivers. "You're engaged to be engaged?"

That sounds pitiful. I pull my hand free. "I'm in a relationship."

"A serious one?"

"Yes." It is, isn't it? Grant's constituents have certainly been positive about our dating, and Grant has been enthusiastic about their response. Too, he's the one who introduced the words *marriage* and *children,* albeit couched in *if.* Of course, that was before I confessed to being "one of them" and he ended our conversation, as if afraid he might catch "Pickwick" through the phone line.

"I apologize," Axel says. "That shouldn't have happened."

No, it shouldn't have. *And wouldn't have if you hadn't invited it.*

A damp Errol whines where he sits on his haunches looking from me to Axel.

"I anticipate having your uncle home from the hospital by noon tomorrow."

"You? But Uncle Obe made arrangements with Uncle Bartholomew."

"Apparently something came up."

Hardly surprising. "I can drive in and get him."

"I'm happy to do it. And I'll have an easier time getting him in and out of a vehicle."

True. "You really seem to care about my uncle."

"I do. See you tomorrow." He turns, and a flash of lightning illuminates his sandy hair from his crown to the rubber band at his nape.

I whip around and hurry up the stairs. Errol dances at the screen door, and I barely get it open before he shoves his big head between it and the doorframe and squeezes his wet body in ahead of me. "Some gentleman," I grumble as I bump the door wide enough to make it through with the pickled corn.

I deposit my armful on the island and peer at the jars. "Well, at least there's one bright spot to my day." A memory of dissent steps forward—Axel's kiss. I try to send it back, but it plays out. At half speed. Once more, I feel his breath against my mouth. His lips touch mine, lightly at first but with increasing pressure. My heart pounds against my ribs, and it's all I can do to keep my arms around the pickled corn when I want to wind them around his neck—

"Oh, stop!" I flap my hands, as if to shake the memory from my fingertips. But it's in my head, and all the squawking in the world is not going to dislodge it. Time to try a different tack.

"Grant," I say to the kitchen. "*U.S. Congressman* Grant Spangler. Smart, sophisticated, well-connected, *not* down-to-earth—"

Actually, down-to-earth is kind of nice. In an Axel Smith way…

18

T his is some welcome home." Uncle Obe smoothes the covers I pulled up over him after Axel helped him out of the wheelchair and into bed.

"It's good to have ya back where ya belong." Artemis pats his paunch.

"It sure is!" Trinity waves a duster, dispersing a cloud that causes Bridget to scowl. "I've cleaned and cleaned and—goodness!—this place needed it. Why, it's a full-time job. And let me tell you, it wasn't easy fittin' you in, Mr. Pickwick, but I did. Day in, day out, I've worked my fingers to the nubs, and only now am I glimpsing light at the end of the tunnel. But it's worth it. Yes sir. I can't thank you enough for allowin' me to shine as your new housekeeper." She waves the duster again. "Shine, shine!"

She's not going to break into song, is she?

Uncle Obe clears his throat. "Thank you, Trinity. I appreciate all you've done. I don't recall the hardwood…" He frowns hard. "…er, *floors* in the entryway shining so bright."

"That's a trade secret." She puts a hand alongside her mouth and whispers, "Furniture polish."

I gasp.

"*Furniture* polish?" Bridget's jaw drops.

"The floors do look mighty nice, Trin." Bart nods his approval. "Good job."

Trin? It sounds as if he knows her, rather than *of* her. And she was in my graduating class—three years of ahead of him. Hmm.

Bridget punches his shoulder. "You do *not* use furniture polish on hardwood floors. It's slick as spit."

"Ow." Bart rubs his arm. "I didn't know."

Trinity's face turns thoughtful. "So that's why I went down quicker 'an a duck on a June bug when I had to run to the bathroom. Whoosh! Right on my seater."

I wince. I should have done a better job supervising her, but there were so many calls to deal with this morning, not the least of which was one from a senior partner at the firm who wanted to know when I'm returning to L.A. And, more specifically, how I intend to handle the rumors about Grant's sexuality. He was not pleased with my response. Just like Grant, he couldn't get his mind around my refusal to fly to his aid, but unlike Grant, he has no idea of my connection to the Pickwicks.

"It's got to come off," Bridget says.

"Don't want Obe's feet flyin' out from under him," Artemis says, "especially in his delicate condition."

Bart shrugs. "Bummer."

"I'll help you, Trinity." Axel's voice causes my nerves to do the shimmy. For the first time since his return from Asheville, I look him full in the face. His Blue eyes shift to mine, and the kiss I've been trying to forget returns in 3-D.

"Thank you, Axel," I say.

Uncle Obe turns his head to gaze out the window. "I like

the…" He points at the panes. "…view. I might have to move here permanently."

"Oh!" Trinity trills. "I can help. I'll move the rest of your stuff down here—clothes, shoes, books, pictures, that big box of papers under your bed."

Uncle Obe goes a little gray. "Thank you, but it was only a thought. Once I'm able to negotiate the stairs, I'll return to my own bedroom."

She shrugs. "Just let me know if you change your mind, hear?"

He slides his gaze over the rest of us. "I thank you all for the welcome home. Now I need to rest up."

We file out of the room. As I bring up the rear, I pull the door closed and follow the others to the front of the house.

"It does look kind of slick." Bart stands on the edge of the rug that runs down the hallway as he stares at the hardwood floor.

Bridget grunts. "It is." She continues past him, following Artemis and Axel toward the front door.

"But it's so pretty." Trinity halts alongside Bart.

He smiles sympathetically. "It's a pity to have to remove the polish. Sure you aren't overreacting, Bridge?"

"I'm sure."

As I sidestep Bart and Trinity, I mentally steel myself for when it will be just Axel, Trinity, and me. Though I'm grateful for Axel's offer to help with the polish removal, it will make it harder to avoid him. And forget about that kiss.

"Whoa!" Bart yells, and we all turn as his rear hits the hardwood floor, and he slides into the baseboard. "I'm okay!"

Bridget growls. "I told you it was slick."

With the help of Trinity, who nearly goes down herself, he gets to his feet.

"What a ding-dong," Bridget mutters.

Ten minutes later, having thanked Bridget for the groceries and Artemis for the use of Errol (more, for taking Mrs. Bleeker's "big boy" home, which he didn't seem too happy about), I suppress a smile when Bart rubs his backside as he slides into the passenger seat of his sister's truck. Artemis and Errol in the sporty red Lexus follow Bridget and Bart down the driveway.

"Let's get that furniture polish up, Trinity." Axel turns back into the entryway.

"All right." However, she doesn't move from my side until both cars disappear from sight. "That Bart Pickwick is somethin' else. I just might have to go behind Granny's back and take him up on his offer of dinner and a movie."

Keep your eyes in your head! "Bart asked you out?"

"Oh, all the time, but he's younger than me, and Gran says if that isn't taboo enough, there's that little problem he had with devil's dust." She taps her nose.

He *did* fall into the drug crowd his first year in high school.

"And to top it off, he's a Pickwick." Her eyes nearly jump ship. "Oh, that wasn't me talkin', but Gran. I have nothing against the Pickwicks, and how could I as you've been so kind to hire me as your uncle's housekeeper in my time of need?"

Would she feel the same way if I told her that *my* actions led to her losing the chance to run the family business? That the things people say about her are *my* due?

She sinks her teeth into her bottom lip. "Forgive me?"

"Nothing to forgive. I understand completely."

"Whew! Well, I'd best see about that polish." She swings away. "Oh!" She turns in the doorway, beyond which I catch sight of Axel. "You knew about Bart and the devil's dust, didn't you?"

"I knew he had a drug problem."

"Yes, and it got bad, but that was after you left town and before your uncle sent him to that fancy rehab center in Minnesota."

Uncle Obe to the rescue again. Never imposing himself on anyone, but always there when needed.

"Fortunately, from all accounts, he has stayed clean, and he's kept this last job for more than a year now."

I'm glad to hear it, and not just in passing. Maybe there can be peace between Bart and me as well. "What does he do?"

"Why, he works at the print shop on the town square—designs logos and letterhead and whatnot on the computer. He's what you call a…"

"Graphic designer?"

"That's it!" Her chin bounces. "A right honorable profession, don't you think?" Before I can respond, she says, "Hmm, maybe I *will* go to dinner with him."

As she flounces off with a hum and a hop, it strikes me that she and Bart might be compatible.

Once again, my eyes fall on Axel, but I turn away.

So what now? I could sit around waiting for Grant to call. No. I could check in on Cootchie again. No, she said she would call me after today's interview. I could look up Romans 8:28. No, my hands are full enough with all this peacemaking. I could go for a run. Yes, I haven't done that since my first day here, and I need to clear my head so I can figure out how to approach Uncle Obe about his will. The clock is ticking.

"You make a mighty mean sandwich, Piper." Uncle Obe settles back against his pillows. "I'm only sorry I couldn't eat more."

Grateful to Bridget for her grocery run and for telling me of his fondness for ripe tomato, cheddar cheese, and mayonnaise on white bread, I lift the tray from his lap. "Half is good."

"You eat the other half, unless you already had, uh, dinner."

Not for the first time I notice the hide-and-seek some words play with him. "Actually, I haven't had dinner."

"Then don't let that tomato sandwich go to waste. You haven't forgotten how good they are, have you?"

My mouth did water as I was making it.

"Sit down."

I back into the chair beside his bed. "Thank you." Balancing the tray on my lap, I scoop up the sandwich and take a bite. It is good, though not as good as pickled corn.

"Told you so."

"Uh-huh." I take another bite.

"So you're gettin' along fine with Maggie and Bridget."

"I am."

He looks at his hands on the covers. "They turned out pretty good, and I'm particularly fond of Maggie's girl, Devyn. She reminds me of you as a girl. Kind. Studious."

That makes me feel good. I take another bite.

"A bit awkward. Something of a loner."

Not so good.

"Of course, she has her mom in her too. Yep. Inquisitive. Confident. Not afraid to speak up for herself."

That's where we differ. I was always too self-conscious. "I like her too." Promising myself that I won't forget tomato sandwiches when I return to L.A., I finish my dinner and set the tray on the floor. "Uncle Obe, I know you don't want to talk about your will, but we need to."

He frowns. "It is what it is and what it will be."

"But when you pass away, questions will be raised about the new beneficiaries. And the answers could hurt your family." As his mouth tightens, I lean toward him. "I know your intentions are good, but sometimes it's best to let the past lie."

He stares at me so hard it's all I can do not to make myself a smaller target. I've only ever known him to be irritated, but this is anger.

"We Pickwicks have done our share of hurtin' others, using our position and wealth to thumb our noses at the standards others are held to. We are no different or better than anyone else but demand special treatment." He sets his jaw. "If no one in our family is gonna take responsibility for the hurts we've caused, by God I will. And I mean *by God*. I've prayed about it, and Axel has given me fine insight. When I die, everything will be set right as right can be."

I touch his arm. "*When* you die." When it will be too late for his illegitimate children to make peace with him, whatever their hurts may be. "I understand you don't have enough liquid assets to make the kind of restitution you want, but—"

"Artemis has been talkin' to you! Why, I've a good mind to sue him for breach of attorney-client privilege."

"He's worried that you're making a serious mistake."

His eyes narrow. "Near all the Pickwicks are worried, which is why you finally came home and why you've stuck it out this long though your work is calling you back." He grunts. "All day long that…*phone* of yours rings. If not for my knee, I'd have hunted it down and flushed it."

The third time I was interrupted while making his sandwich, I was tempted to do just that.

"Admit it, Piper. You came because of Trinity."

I startle.

"Uh-huh. The one who's drivin' me nuts with all that Cinderella-ing." He grunts again. "Does she never stop and listen to the quiet? It's a beautiful sound, I tell you."

I shrug. "She's good at what she does." *When* she stays on task. "Uncle Obe, how did you know it was me at the Fourth of July parade?"

"Why, I was there."

"So was most everyone, but they think it was Trinity."

"That's because they don't know about your tush."

"My…tush?"

"You remember. You were maybe three, and I had a sweet little dog named…" His brow crumples. "What was her name? O…O…Oleander! In a mischievous mood you were, and you did the poor thing wrong by stealin' her steak bone. Got her so worked up she bit you—right back there."

I do remember, but not this version. There was a little dog, and she *was* named Oleander, as in the highly toxic plant. But I didn't steal her bone. Uncle Obe enlisted me to demonstrate she wouldn't bite if a child took her bone. He didn't know his "sweet" little dog very well.

"Anyway, the scar from that bite gave you away. I saw it when you passed by in your Lady Godiva getup."

There it is—my scandalous stunt spoken aloud. As for my getup, it consisted of a "borrowed" horse, a long blond wig, and undies cut down to a thong that I didn't have the nerve to go without.

"And Trinity took the fall for that ungodly display, lost the trust of her grandparents. And her future."

"I understand Trinity didn't deny the rumor."

He raises his eyebrows. "She's a fruit of a different stripe."

That's an expression I'm not familiar with, probably an Uncle Obe original.

"Regardless, it doesn't absolve the Pickwicks of wrongdoing."

My wrongdoing. "Until Artemis's call, I didn't know she had taken the blame."

"You know now."

And haven't done anything about it, though there is a strong likelihood that Spangler will never be my last name.

Uncle Obe sighs. "Don't go beatin' yourself up. It will all come right in the end—when I'm good and dead—and no one will know you're the one who pulled that harebrained stunt."

I shake my head. "Your will is going to cause people to take a close look at those things that you make restitution for. They'll find us in it." *Well, that was all about self-preservation.*

"You're sayin' I shouldn't do a thing?"

I hope my expression isn't as pained as I feel. "It *would* be easiest to seek God's forgiveness and let the past lie."

He looks down at his hands, and when he looks up, fatigue has closed in around his eyes. "I'm burdened, Piper. I've asked God to help me put all the madness behind me, but I feel Him movin' me to do this."

"Are you sure it's not Axel moving you?"

Anger returns to his eyes. "My conversations with Axel have opened doors to God I never thought to open, but it's God who's movin' me. Whether or not my family agrees, I'm doing the right thing—absolvin' them and my…self." His voice cracks.

I think I know why. "Is this really about a Lady Godiva ride, a statue at the bottom of the lake, cheating the Calhouns out of their land, etcetera?"

His shoulders drop. "Artemis told you about my kids, didn't he?"

"I'm sorry."

He rubs a hand across his face. "All right, this is about them too. About puttin' my inheritance before them and their mother. About not knowin' them when I should have." His eyes moisten. "I did them wrong—set them aside knowin' if my father found out about them, he would leave the family fortune to charity. In the end, he left everything to me, the one upstanding Pickwick boy." He shakes his head.

Remembering what Axel told me about how Uncle Obe convinced his father to throw off family expectations and enter the military, I understand his self-loathing. He couldn't take his own advice. "What happened to your kids and their mother?"

"Your grandfather lingered for years with the illness the doctor said would take him in six months. By the time he passed away, Anita had given up on me."

"Anita?"

His lips take a turn for the better. "The prettiest woman I ever knew, inside and out." He sighs. "But my father would not have approved, would have said she was entirely unsuitable as a wife."

"Why?"

"Part Hispanic. He was prejudiced that way."

"But Grandpa Gentry forced my dad to marry my mom, and he didn't approve of her."

Uncle Obe winces. "Though it's true your mother wasn't of the proper social standing, she was Caucasian. With his churching and deep convictions, I do believe he would have had me marry Anita to legitimize our children, but there would have been no money for any Pickwick when he passed away. All of us would have been cut out of the will."

He momentarily closes his eyes. "I enjoyed a privileged life, Piper, and I wasn't strong enough to face life without those privileges. And I knew my brothers couldn't make it either and would need help."

He has always been there to bail them out.

"That's why there isn't much liquidity in the estate and why restitution can't be made until everything is sold following my death. You understand?"

He's going to see Artemis in my answer, but there's no help for it. "I understand it would be painful for you to let go of the estate. What I don't understand is why you don't make things right with Anita and your children while you're living. Contact them, apologize, meet with them to see if anything can be salvaged."

"I told you, they gave up on me—got tired of waitin'. Antonio was three and Daisy was two the last time I saw them."

Antonio and Daisy… "It's never too late—"

"It was too late long ago. Anita left Asheville. The last time she wrote, she told me she was getting married and thought it best that we cease communication." He clears his throat. "Three months later, my father died—a month after she married. It hurt, but I honored her request."

He sags, and I have to clasp my hands to keep from putting my arms around him. "But that was thirty years ago. Your children are adults now; it's *their* decision. Surely they ought to have the chance to know their father."

He tenses. "You sound like Axel. And aren't you supposed to be tryin' to convince me to let the past lie? To keep further shame from the Pickwicks? If it comes out that I fathered Antonio and Daisy, it will mean more mud on the family name."

Piper Wick the image consultant heartily agrees, but Piper the niece aches for him and all the lost years. "This is different, Uncle Obe. They're your children."

Struggle twists his face. "I agreed to cease all communication, and I've kept my word despite being sorely tempted to break it."

"Is their mother still alive?"

He sags further. "I don't know. For ten years after they left Asheville, I had a private investigator check in on her and the children. As much as I resented her husband, he was good to them. And the report never changed, so I let them go. I have no idea what path their lives have taken."

"Then you'll go to the grave not knowing what became of them, hoping the money you leave them will make up for your absence from their lives?"

He shifts his gaze to the windows.

I wait, but he doesn't come back to me. "Are you all right?"

"You've given me a lot to ponder, Piper. Now I'd like to be left alone."

I stand. "Thank you for talking with me, Uncle Obe. Good night."

He continues to stare out the window, as if the life he was too weak to claim as his own is staring back at him from the other side...taunting him with what might have been.

Lord, please don't let that be me thirty years from now. Don't let me settle for something that is shiny today but will turn fluid tomorrow and slip through my fingers to leave me wanting.

"Grant!" I jump up from the edge of my mattress. "I can't believe I got through."

"Caller ID. I knew it was you."

So what does that say about when he doesn't answer? "You got my message?"

"I did, and it was annoyingly cryptic. You should have left a detailed message. It's bothered me all day."

Had you called me back, I could have cleared up everything. Reminding myself of the conclusion I drew earlier when I went for a run—that until he proposes *and* I accept, he is first a client—I hold my tongue.

"So what else do I need to know about your past before I decide whether or not a serious relationship with you is possible?"

Ooh! I pull my iPhone from my ear and clasp it against my

chest as I struggle to hold back words my partners would not approve of. *You are a professional. Act like one. Talk like one.* I return the phone to my ear.

"Are you there, Piper?"

"Yes, and what I had to tell you has no bearing on the matter at hand, which is putting that nasty rumor to rest."

After a long silence, he says, "Are you sure?"

"Yes."

"So what's the plan?"

"A simple one." I can't believe I'm about to say this. "You are going to go on a date and do all the things that respectable, highly heterosexual bachelors do." *His* words, not mine.

He quiets but finally says, "That does sound simple. I can do it."

"Good." For *him.* "Now all we need to do is find you a date."

"Actually, I met this woman at a fund-raiser last week. Gorgeous."

Well, I feel better.

"She has your hair color but longer, more feminine."

I grab a hank of red hair and pull it forward. I could grow it longer…

"I'd say she's about twenty-five. And connected—the daughter of a tire tycoon."

I'm afraid to ask. "Did you get her number?"

"No."

Okay, I do feel better, somewhat.

"But she shouldn't be hard to track down. I'll put my assistant on it. You're the best, Piper."

If "best" is defined by the rather obvious solution of him going on a date, anyone could do that. I can't believe I am being paid for this. "Thanks, Grant."

"I'll call you." He hangs up.

I set my phone on the dresser and look at my face in the mirror. Pretty, even if I did sweat off most of my makeup during my run. And while my red hair isn't long, it's feminine, the length a good fit for my face and figure.

Drawing on my inner image consultant, I point at my reflection. "U.S. Congressman Grant Spangler is your client, a well-paying client you cannot afford to lose. Remember that. If something more is meant to be, it will be. Now be cool."

I'm cool. Everything under control. However, a moment later I fall back on my bed and peer upward. "Is he part of Your plan for me or not, Lord?" And what about Axel?

19

My partners are getting antsy. It has been a week since Uncle Obe returned home and two weeks since I arrived in Pickwick, and I'm no nearer to settling the matter of the will. Whether I push to leave the will as written or try to convince my uncle to reconcile with his children, he sets his jaw and says he's thinking on it or gripes about Artemis picking this most inopportune time to take his wife on a cruise.

Still, Artemis calls every day to check on my progress and say how disappointed he is with my "glorified" PR skills. The same goes for Luc, except his calls come twice a day. Despite my bristling, I'm also disillusioned by my inability to accomplish what I'm here for. After all, my clients need me.

Last night, as I pulled the covers over my head, Cootchie called. It was nothing pressing—a little advice on how to handle the positive feedback from her interviews and a strong recommendation that she not talk with the seediest tabloid in the U.S. Still, she was upset at not being able to meet with me.

So today is the day. For the sake of my career and peace of mind (the memory of Axel's kiss is showing on four to eight screens daily depending on how often I have to avoid him), I am going to get an answer out of Uncle Obe.

"Ready?" I step into his bedroom and smile when he turns his thoughtful expression from the carved handle of his cane to me.

"More than ready." He pushes up off the mattress.

Suppressing the impulse to offer assistance, which he calls demeaning, I stand in the doorway as he transfers his weight to the cane. Though the physical therapist is pleased with his progress and supportive of his independence, I worry that my uncle is pushing too hard. As if he did have a massive heart attack and his days are numbered.

"See?" He works his way toward me, strain in his jaw despite the smile. "Gettin' better every day."

"You are." Ooh, I did it again—drawled the *a* and practically dropped the *r* from *are*. If I'm not careful, the time spent with Uncle Obe and Trinity will require emergency vocal rehab when I return to L.A.

Uncle Obe pauses. "Have you seen Axel this mornin'?"

Too much of him while he was putting handrails on the ramp he built to give Uncle Obe access to his garden. Not that I meant to watch him through the kitchen windows, but my working breakfast of making calls to East Coast clients placed me firmly in his orbit.

And goodness knows, that yogurt container was way too heavy to carry to another room.

"After he finished the ramp, he went into town." Which means Uncle Obe won't be able to enlist him as a shield against talk of the will, as he has done several times. Providing Trinity stays focused on the upstairs bedrooms, all is set for what I pray will be a productive discussion.

With a tremble in his cane arm, Uncle Obe halts before me.

"I've been looking forward to spendin' time in my garden. As long as you don't start in about the will, this will be my best day yet."

Sorry, Uncle Obe. I step back. "Your garden awaits."

He maneuvers the turn in the hallway. The going is slow, but we make it through the kitchen and outside onto the stoop. He rests a minute, drinking in the sight of his garden, then closes his eyes and pulls the scent in through his flared nostrils.

"Now I really am home," he murmurs, and my heart tugs at the depth of his content. "Give me a hand."

That surprises me, but I grip his forearm as he descends the ramp. At last he eases onto a garden chair at the table Axel set near the bottom of the ramp.

"Iced tea?" I ask.

He squints against the late morning sun. "That would be mighty nice, but don't skimp on the sugar like you did yesterday."

A true Southerner.

Shortly I return with two sweating glasses, one mixed with four teaspoons of sugar, the other with one. Not that I'm a sweet-tea drinker anymore, as I hate to waste my calories on drink, but I can indulge a little.

Uncle Obe thanks me as I set down his glass and lower myself to the chair next to his.

We drink in silence that I'm loath to trespass on, but I have to. "Uncle Obe—"

"Give any more thought to Axel?"

At least once a day he pumps me with Axel's virtues. "No. Not only will I be returning to L.A."—if I want to keep my position at the firm—"but Axel and I are hardly compatible."

"How's that?"

I will not be drawn into this discussion. It benefits no one—

But it could. When he tilts his head questioningly, I venture, "How about this: we can discuss Axel and me if we also discuss your will."

He sets his glass heavily on the table. "That's manipulative. Is that what they teach you out there in…in…Los Angeles?"

I sit back. "You need to make a decision, Uncle Obe." Hopefully, the one that's best for all concerned. *Meaning the Pickwicks, Piper notwithstanding.*

To my relief, he nods. "All right, but first we talk about you and Axel."

"What about us?"

"Us?" He brightens. "Now that's promising."

Patience. "I don't know why you think he and I are compatible."

"You don't like him?"

To deny it would be a lie. "I do, but not in *that* way."

"Why? Is it his leg? Does it put you off?"

The tip of my tongue flies to the spot behind my upper teeth, but I squelch the denial. Why *am* I not interested in Axel? After all, I'm attracted to him. Too, it appears that I'm no longer "spoken for," as evidenced by the public's enthusiasm for the tire tycoon's daughter who has been on Grant's arm at a half-dozen events. As further evidenced by a photo of them holding hands and kissing. Gone are the rumors about Grant's sexuality…

"Axel is one of the most admirable men I know," Uncle Obe says, "but some women might consider him less than a man with that prosthetic. Is that how you feel?"

It isn't. I hardly notice it or the hitch anymore. And it's hard to believe any woman deserving of him would be bothered by the loss of his leg. Axel could lose both legs and still exude more masculinity than most men. So why do I reject knowing him beyond his role as a gardener, especially now that Grant is slipping out of my future? Is it the distance between L.A. and Pickwick? that I've only known him two weeks? Is it that I've always imagined marriage to a man like Grant—white collar versus blue collar?

"You've put your niece on the spot, Obadiah," a terribly familiar voice says behind me. "That's not fair."

Oh no. What did Axel hear? Rather, what *didn't* he hear? My denial about considering him less than a man. But I was getting there.

"I thought you had gone into town," Uncle Obe says.

Turn around. Face him.

"I forgot something." I hear Axel advancing over the grass. "And I thought I would ask Piper if she wants me to bring lunch back to save her the cooking."

Slapping on a smile, I look around. "That's thoughtful, but I don't mind whipping up something."

His Blue eyes are merely blue today, and though I could blame it on the bright sunlight, it's me. And that I didn't deny what I meant to.

At three feet away, he halts and shifts his gaze to Uncle Obe. "I should be back in an hour or two."

"Drive carefully," Uncle Obe says.

Axel turns away.

Heart thudding, I look back at Uncle Obe, who seems oblivious to the terrible misunderstanding.

"Oh," Axel says, "Maggie and Devyn were coming up the drive a minute ago, so they're probably at the front door."

And there goes our discussion about the will.

"Thank you." Uncle Obe looks to me. "Why don't you ask them to join us out here?"

That's triumph in his eyes, but I'm not done with him. I rise and, a few minutes later, lead a disgruntled Maggie and Devyn into the garden. Fortunately, whatever disagreement they had on the drive over has been put on hold.

"Unc-Unc!" Devyn slips past me and goes into Uncle Obe's arms. "You're outside! I'm so glad."

"Me too." His eyes shine as she pulls back.

"Why, I'll bet you were going crazier than a run-over dog—" She claps a hand over her mouth. "I'm sorry. I forgot about Roy."

He appears momentarily stricken at the mention of the dog he hit with his golf cart. "It's all right, though I do miss that old dog comin' around."

"Excuse me." Maggie steps around me and descends the ramp. "We brought you some bestsellers to read." She hands him a paper bag.

Uncle Obe peeks inside. "That was kind of you."

As Maggie lowers into a chair, I remember my manners. "Can I get you some iced tea, Maggie? Devyn?"

"That would be nice." Maggie still looks bothered by what happened between her and her daughter, but she smiles. "Sweetened, please."

Devyn nods. "Sweetened for me too, thank you."

When I return with two glasses, Devyn is gone and Maggie is leaning toward Uncle Obe with urgency.

A shoulder to the screen door, I hesitate.

"Devyn's pushing me again," she says. "Wants to know who her father is and cites ridiculous research on the importance of a father in a teenage girl's life." She throws her hands up. "And she's not even a teenager."

Uncle Obe pats her knee. "In another year she will be, and don't forget she's mature for her age."

"That doesn't mean she needs to know who fathered her." She shakes her head. "I don't know what to do."

I know what *I* should do, and I would give them privacy if the parallel between Devyn and Uncle Obe's children hadn't smacked me in the face.

Maggie flops back in her chair. "I'm not ready to talk about it. And it's more complicated than anyone knows. Maybe when Devyn is an adult…"

"If she's asking to know who her father is, my advice is to tell her. The longer you put it off, the harder it will be to deal with and she'll have more resentment."

Does Uncle Obe realize what he's saying?

"I'll tell you what the Good Book says." He digs himself in deeper. " 'He who conceals his sins does not prosper, but whoever confesses and renounces them finds mercy.' "

I give an Artemis-worthy, "Ahem. A-hem."

Maggie's head snaps around, but it's Uncle Obe's gaze I fasten on as realization blooms on his face.

I descend the ramp and set the glasses on the table. "Where's Devyn?"

"She went to the herb garden to get spearmint for our tea," Maggie says.

As I return to my chair, Devyn appears with a sprig of leaves, and I nod when she asks if I would like some.

Over the next half hour, talk revolves around the books Maggie brought, the auction business, and Devyn's boredom with summer vacation. Uncle Obe looks anywhere but at me, and more than once he seems to drift out of the conversation. Hopefully, he's thinking about the parallel between Devyn wanting to know her father and his children wanting to know theirs.

Maggie stands. "We should go. Lots to do before tomorrow's auction."

"Thank you for dropping by," Uncle Obe says, "and for the books."

"You're welcome."

As Maggie and Devyn go around the side of the house, I turn to Uncle Obe and he raises his palm toward me. "I know what you're going to say, but it isn't necessary. I've made my decision."

He has?

"I do need to make amends to my children before I pass away, give them a chance to know me if that's what they want."

My heart feels toasty. "That's wonderful."

"As for my will"—he drains the last of his iced tea—"with the exception of adding Antonio and Daisy, as is their right, I'll leave it as is."

Then there won't be headlines to pay? The impulse to clap my hands is so strong I have to lock my fingers. *Thank You, Lord, for making him see the sense in letting the past lie. What's done is done, right?*

I sigh. With my Get In, Get Out strategy a success, I can leave Pickwick. And Bart, Luc, Bridget, Maggie…Devyn…Axel…

Well, I don't have to leave right away. There are loose ends to tie up, the loosest one being to get Uncle Obe firmly back on his feet.

"Piper?" He snaps his fingers in my face.

I startle. "I'm sorry?"

"What do you think?"

"Oh, you're definitely doing the right thing."

"Even though I'll have to sell the estate?"

I jerk. Did I miss something? "Sell the estate?"

"Well, how else am I going to come up with the money?"

"For what?"

"To make amends to all those people."

I thought we were past that. "What?"

He sighs. "I'm talking about those I was going to add to my will before you made me realize the importance of making amends to my children while I'm still around."

What have I done?

"So why stop there? I'll right the wrongs now, even if it means selling the estate and seeing it turned into a…" His face tenses. "You know, buildings…houses…"

"A development."

"Development," he snatches up the word. "Anyway, at least I'll have peace about our family's wrongs."

Then there *will* be headlines to pay. I lay a hand over his on the table. "But this is so sudden. Shouldn't you give it more thought?"

"You said I had to make a decision. *That's* my decision." He pulls his hand from under mine. "Thank you for helping me see the light."

I don't feel so well. *Pull yourself together. That's it. Now think!* Okay, I knew this could happen. It was always a possibility, just not the one I would have chosen. Fortunately, all is not lost—*if* it's handled correctly. "Then restitution it is, but I have to warn you that the family isn't going to take this well."

"I know that. But more than that, I know that 'in all things God works for the good of those who love Him.' " He smiles. "Romans 8:28."

I startle. Coincidence or divine counsel by way of Uncle Obe? Either way, it's a wake-up call to go beyond peacemaking—to take the bad of my past and to find the good of it in my present.

"You like that, hmm?" Uncle Obe asks.

"It's a keeper," I say and quickly shift back to first gear. "I have a proposal."

"Yes?"

"That we start selling off the estate and, where possible, make restitution in such a way that it appears to be philanthropy."

His eyebrows dive. "But it isn't."

"We'll know that, but—"

"Is this how you get your fancy clients out of trouble? With lies?"

Ouch. "I like to think of it more as...an alternate version."

I wish he wouldn't look at me like that.

"I'm disappointed in you, Piper Pickwick."

So is my conscience, but there are others to consider—and not just me. "Uncle Obe, if you insist on selling the estate, this way is best for all."

"All who?"

I go for his soft spot, which is also mine. "Devyn tops the list."

His gaze flickers.

"I understand she's part of the 'out' crowd at school. If we don't put a sp—" Ooh, not the right word to use.

"Put a spin on it?" Uncle Obe rumbles.

So he knows the jargon. "That is what we'd be doing. If we don't, this could be hard on her."

His jaw grinds, but finally he turns his palms up. "So how do you propose to make"—his lips press—"res-restitution to all those people under the guise of philanthropy?"

Guise. "Unfortunately, it won't work in all instances, but let's take the statue that was dumped in the lake years ago by one of the Pickwicks."

"That would be me."

I gape. "*You* did that?"

"It was a terrible likeness of your great-grandfather. Made him look all honorable and beneficent when he was nothing of the sort."

"I can't believe you did something like that."

"Neither could anyone else." He smiles. "Just like no one suspected you were Lady Godiva." He jacks up his eyebrows. "Call it teenage rebellion."

I can relate to that. "Anyway, you would simply fund a new statue for the betterment of the town." I shrug. "Your conscience is eased, the town is grateful, and the Pickwicks earn a mark in the plus column."

"To counteract all those minuses?"

I smile.

He frowns. "Sounds slick to me—like Luc."

Oh, Lord, to be likened to Luc... Luc who is bound to cause problems when he gets wind that Uncle Obe plans to liquidate. If he seeks to have Uncle Obe declared mentally incompetent— No, I can't worry about that.

"You said this philanthropy gig won't work for everything. So then what?"

"We make restitution with an apology."

"Pay the piper, hmm?"

I hate that expression.

Uncle Obe grunts. "That's kind of fitting."

No comment. "So what do you think of the plan?"

"You make it sound easy."

Hardly, especially as I'll be the one doing the orchestrating, which will further jeopardize my job. And, of course, if something *is* going on with my uncle's mind, I'll be in even deeper. What happened to Get In, Get Out?

"You sure this is best for all?"

I hear his plea—for me to find a way to accomplish this without being "slick"—but honesty in its purest form can get you hurt. *Sorry, Lord.* "Yes."

He sits back. The seconds and minutes tick by, and then he slaps the table. "It's gettin' mighty hot out here. I'm ready to go in."

Hating that I feel like the enemy, I stand.

"But before I do, would you cut some daisies for my room?"

Daisies are his favorite. Because of his daughter? I retrieve clippers from beside the back door and hurry to the glorious patch of white-and-yellow daisies. I'm careful about which flowers I cut to brighten his room since he's particular about not taking those in their prime. This time I'm too preoccupied to pay much attention.

"Pity," Uncle Obe says when I return. "They didn't get their day in the sun."

Though the daisies are unfurled, they're in the "first blush of beauty." "Sorry."

He starts toward the door. "By the way, Piper, did you ever find out if you're immune to poison ivy?"

A reminder of the day he suggested to my ten-year-old self that I touch the plant to determine my skin's reaction to its oils. "No idea."

"Well, you're about to."

"What?"

At the base of the ramp, he tugs a scrap of leafy vine from among the daisies. "This here is poison ivy. You might want to wash your hands."

20

Oh, please let me be immune. I probably won't be. The fiery, blistery rash will break out, and I will be downright miserable. In fact—

No. It's in my head. My skin is *not* crawling. I pull my arms from the sink of sudsy water I immersed them in after enlisting Trinity to see Uncle Obe back to bed. *No blisters. See?* But that doesn't mean they're not forming.

In your head! Then why is my skin prickling? I have to scratch—my palms, the backs of my hands, my lower arms. All the places that might have come in contact. Did I sniff the daisies? If I did…

I shake the water from my right hand and scratch my nose so hard I break the skin. Self-mutilation on top of blisters. Lovely.

So what is taking Trinity so long? At Uncle Obe's suggestion, I sent her to Axel's cottage for the lotion he uses to remove the oil when he comes in contact with poison ivy. That was fifteen minutes ago.

I check in on Uncle Obe. Satisfied he's asleep and his cell phone is near should he need to call me, I go in search of Trinity. Hurrying down the garden path, I glare at the daisies. Poison ivy! Axel has a lot to answer for.

Though I expect to hear Trinity trilling as I near the cottage, all is quiet. My other expectation—of finding her twirling as she wields her duster among Axel's effects—is also unfounded.

I scratch my left hand as I cross from the small kitchen into the living room. "Trinity?"

A resounding thud is followed by an "Ow!"

I turn down the short hallway toward the bedrooms. "Trinity, I'm dyin' here." Did I just drop a *g*? Was that a twang? "Did you find the lotion?" *Every* word perfectly enunciated.

She pops out of the room on the right and rubs the back of her head. "I didn't mean to snoop, but then I saw the box."

"What box?"

"*The* box!" She steps back inside.

I peer into the bedroom that Axel has transformed into an office. On the floor beside a neatly organized desk is a black-speckled box of folders. "What about it?"

"It was under your uncle's bed. It disappeared last week after he came home from the hospital. I figured he asked you to do something with it, but Axel must have stolen it." She shakes her head. "There are a lot of personal papers in there."

I thought she didn't mean to snoop. Regardless, if it is the same box, what is Axel doing with it? *Did* he steal it? No.

The first day Uncle Obe was home from the hospital, Trinity offered to move the rest of his personal effects downstairs, including a box of papers she found under his bed. Uncle Obe's face had gone a bit gray, and he had declined. He must have asked Axel to bring the box here. Why? "What kind of personal papers?"

"Come see."

I follow her to the desk and lower to my knees beside her, only to startle when she jumps up. "I forgot that I have to go to the bathroom—bad."

How do you forget that?

She hurries from the room, and I scan the folders: expenses, legal, checking account, assets, taxes, deeds and titles, insurance, stocks and bonds, medical—

"Medical." A moment later, the file is on my lap. The first document is a summary written by a Dr. Dyer three months ago, and it answers what Artemis wouldn't. Explaining the findings of the documents that follow, Dr. Dyer concludes that Uncle Obe has early onset dementia, defined as dementia that strikes before the age of sixty-five. For the most part, he is able to function on his own despite minor word retrieval problems. I suppose that's good news, but only in light of the bad news, which is that it's going to get worse before it *never* gets better.

I swallow a lump in my throat.

"I'm back!"

I snap the folder closed as Trinity drops to her knees on the other side of the box. "You okay, Piper?"

"Yes, fine." As inconspicuously as possible, I slide the folder onto the floor.

"Let me show you somethin'." She retrieves a folder from the chair behind the desk. "I know I shouldn't have snooped, but that curiosity thing—wondering why Axel took the box—got the better of me. You aren't goin' to fire me, are you?"

She shouldn't have looked, but then neither should I. "No."

She sits back on her heels. "That's a relief, 'cause I need this job if I'm goin' to get my business turnin' a profit."

I glance at the medical folder. "You didn't look through the whole box, did you?"

She opens her eyes wide. "Heavens, no!"

So glad she has some scruples.

"I mean, it's not as if I had time, right?"

Er…right. I gesture at the folder she holds. "What's in that?"

She taps the label that reads Last Will and Testament. "It has to do with your uncle's will. And I'm in it."

Holding my breath, I take it and open to a handwritten page that lists beneficiaries to be added to the will. Beside each name is a dollar amount, all of them revised several times as evidenced by strike outs. This has been on Uncle Obe's mind for a long time.

Trinity leans across the box and touches her name. "I don't know why he's addin' me to his will, but it's awful nice of him. And I certainly could use the money. Not that I want him to die, but it's a relief that some day Gran and I won't have to struggle so much. We've had some real hard years since the knitting shop closed."

The lump is back. I scan the list: Antonio and Daisy, Dorcas Stanley, the Biggses, the town of Pickwick, the IRS, the Calhouns—

Ugh. That's a big dollar amount. Though my uncle originally valued the land he believes my great-grandfather cheated the Calhouns out of at two hundred thousand, the most recent figure is seven hundred and fifty thousand. But then, Pickwick is in the midst of renewal.

A quick calculation reveals that my uncle wants to make restitution to the tune of two million dollars. I inwardly groan. If there were any doubt the estate would have to be sold, there's none now.

"Why do you think he wants to leave me fifty thousand dollars?" Trinity whistles. "Whew! You know how big that sounds? Fif…ty…thou…sand."

You could tell her. Take responsibility for your *wrongdoing.*

But she's so talkative that even if she agreed to keep it between us, she probably couldn't.

So? If it were made public, it would likely be yesterday's news before the day was out. It was a teenage indiscretion, and it's not as if you're Cootchie Lear.

What about Grant?

Come on, you're pretty much kaput.

It looks that way. So maybe I should just— Wait. Even if our relationship is strictly business, from a PR standpoint, it could reflect poorly on him to have been dating me. Strike Grant Spangler from my client list. No, my partners would not like that. Besides, what's the benefit of telling Trinity? Money is what she needs, and money is what she'll get—philanthropically speaking.

Whose money, did you say?

Closing the door of my conscience, I return my gaze to the medical folder. In Luc's hands, it could be the ammunition to prove Uncle Obe is mentally incompetent. But that's not going to happen if I have a say in it. I wish all this would go away, but I will help him make amends to those our family has hurt.

"Your uncle must think highly of my cleaning services."

I look at Trinity. Does she not realize these papers predate her work here? "I know he's appreciative of all you do."

She frowns. "Still…that's a lot of money for just doin' my job."

If not for the real reason Uncle Obe wants to make restitution, I would be relieved that she has enough sense to realize that. I close the folder and set it atop the medical folder.

Trinity wags a finger in the air. "Of course, he did say the other day that he was sorry the knitting shop had to close, but I can't see as he had anything to do with that."

That's too close for comfort. "Well, whatever the reason—"

"If it's anyone's fault, it's mine. When that rumor started that I made the Lady Godiva ride down Main Street, I should have gutted it then and there."

Oh, Lord.

She tilts her head at me. "You heard about that, didn't you? Or had you already left Pickwick?"

"It…happened right before my mother and I went to L.A."

"Like everybody else, you probably thought I did it, but you'd be wrong."

If jealousy is green, what color is guilt? My face is suddenly cold and prickly. "I don't see you doing something like that, Trinity. In fact, I'm certain you didn't."

Her eyes get big. "Really?"

"Yes, and I'm sorry that you took the blame." *How sorry are you?* "What I don't understand is why you didn't deny it."

With a sheepish shrug, she says, "All that attention."

"What?"

"It was like entering a pie-eatin' contest. You know, enjoyin' all them berries and peaches and buttery crusts and not havin' to be the one to make and bake them."

"What?"

"Uh-huh. Though I didn't deny the rumor, I could never do somethin' so nasty and wicked as ridin' buck naked through town. And in a parade, no less!"

On top of being confused, I feel like pond scum. "Trinity, you've lost me. You enjoyed the attention?"

"Well, yeah. The guys looked at me different. I mean, *really* looked. Like they'd never looked before."

I'll bet.

"If not for Grandpa—God rest his soul—puttin' his shotguns in the front windows of our house, I would have had me one date after another. But even better than havin' a slew of suitors was that the family business my grandparents wanted me to run"—she jams her fist against her chest—"put a stake through the whole idea. That musty old place with all those balls of yarn and them pokey knitting needles… It makes keeping house seem like executive work."

I lean toward her. "Then you weren't harmed by the rumor? It was a good thing?"

"Well, mostly. My grandparents were so heartbroken when the knitting shop went under that I suffered guilt somethin' terrible. After all, I'm pretty sharp, and I probably could have made a go of it."

Could she have?

"Then when Grandpa was on his deathbed, he forgave me for my godforsaken indiscretion and made me promise I would never again do such a thing to shame the family. That's when I told him and Gran it wasn't me." She sighs. "They didn't believe me, and next thing I knew they were prayin' for my salvation. Then"—she snaps her fingers—"Grandpa laid back, closed his eyes, and up and died."

Pond scum—the slimy green stuff.

She gasps. "Why, you could help me, Piper."

I could do better than help, but…

"You could tell my grandmother that you believe me, that I would never do somethin' like that."

"Me?" My voice breaks.

"She might listen to you, seein' as you're one of the few upstanding Pickwicks."

She has no idea,

"And what I wouldn't give not to have her prayin' over me for sins I didn't commit when her body is ready to pack up and go home."

It's the least you can do. "All right, I'll talk to her."

She clasps her hands as if to pray. "Thank you. You're a good friend. And God knows I could use one or two."

Pond scum.

"Of course, I could also use the money." She gives a blissful roll of her eyes. "Fifty thousand dollars. Why, one day I could have a half-dozen girls workin' for me and a whole fleet of pumpkin coaches."

Fifty thousand dollars won't go *that* far.

She grabs me and hugs me so tight my ribs creak. "This has been some day. Know what I'm goin' to do after work?" She jumps up. "I'm gonna get me one of them expensive ice creams where they mix in gummy bears and Oreo cookies on a marble slab."

Gummy bears and Oreo cookies?

"Normally I treat myself only once a month, and I've already had mine for the month—" She gasps. "That reminds me. When I was at the ice cream shop last week, a lady there was askin' about you."

A distant alarm goes off. "Someone who lives in Pickwick?"

"If she does, I haven't seen her before. She also had one of those accents like they got up north. You know where they say 'pok' for 'park,' like the Kennedys."

The alarm is no longer distant. "A New England accent?"

"I think so."

Could it be Janet Farr, or is this coincidence? *Lord, please let it be coincidence.* "Who was she asking about me?"

"Me. Said she'd heard I'd been hired on at the Pickwick mansion. Was real friendlylike. Even paid for my ice cream."

Not coincidence. "What did she ask about me?"

"Oh, like why did you leave Pickwick, why are you back, why did you change your name to Wick, are you datin' anyone. That kind of stuff."

I feel each beat of my heart. "What did you tell her?"

"Mostly that I didn't know, though I did say that your uncle had surgery and you were helpin' him to get back on his feet."

Fairly benign. "Have you seen her since?" At the shake of her head, I ask, "Did she mention her name?"

"Just her first: Jane." She frowns. "Or maybe it was Janet." She shrugs. "One or the other."

Actually, both. Janet Farr, who tried to get information out of Celine about me, and Jane Farredy, who wrote the article questioning Grant's sexuality, are undoubtedly the same. And she's in Pickwick—or *was.*

"So you wanna join me for an ice cream, Piper?"

I shake my head. "Thank you, but maybe another time. I need to talk to Axel."

Her eyes flick to the box. "You aren't goin' to press charges, are you?"

"No, I'm sure Uncle Obe asked him to bring the box here to keep an eye on it."

"You could be right." She flounces to the door.

"Trinity?"

"Yeah?"

"Let's keep the matter of my uncle's will just between us, hmm?"

Her face grows serious. "You can count on me."

Can I? Not that I think she would intentionally blab. "And if you run into Janet or Jane again, would you let me know?"

"I sure will."

"Also, I may be here awhile, so would you check on Uncle Obe in case he wakes up and needs something?"

"You bet."

I hear her break into song as she heads down the hill.

Janet Farr/Jane Farredy, what besides my connection to the Pick-wicks and my Southern roots are you trying to dig up? My scandalous Lady Godiva ride? Of course, now that Grant is dating someone else, maybe she's moved on. Yes, I'm going to hang my hat on that. I have to because my plate is too full as it is.

I retrieve the list of beneficiaries and focus on the dollar amount beside Trinity's name. At one point it was twenty-five thousand, then thirty, now fifty. How did Uncle Obe arrive at that number? More, how can I stand by and let him pay my debt?

Blowing a breath up my face, I look up. "Lord, this is going to hurt."

21

*A*xel's back. Unfortunately, as absorbed as I was in the contents of the box, I didn't hear him drive up.

I start to rise from the desk, but when the floor creaks a second time as he walks down the hallway, I fold my hands atop the folder that contains documentation of Uncle Obe's assets, one of which was more than a little eyeopening. When Axel heads into the bedroom across the hall, it's obvious he's unaware of my presence.

I draw a breath to announce myself, but he halts, turns, and locks eyes with me. And I feel as guilty as a thief with a hand stuck in a victim's pocket.

He scans his desk, the orderliness of which has been overturned. "I see."

I lift my chin. "So do I."

He steps into the room. "I'm surprised."

I wish his eyes were Blue. Though I knew it wouldn't look good if he found me here, adding to the bad impression made when I didn't refute that his prosthetic bothers me, I didn't want to turn my discovery into a game. Me and my high ideals.

"Of course"—his nostrils flare—"all that's missing are night-vision goggles."

That stings. "I am not like Bart or Luc."

"No." He pushes aside the scattered folders, places his palms on the desk, and leans in. "Where they failed, you succeeded. You're entirely different, Piper *Wick*."

I tense from the roots of my hair to my toes. *What would Piper advise?* That I measure my words. I point to the folders. "This is not what I came for."

He raises an eyebrow.

"I came for—" How could I forget? I jerk my hands up and examine my wrists and lower arms. Still no angry rash. Maybe I am immune. Wait! The itch is back.

I shove the chair back. "I need your lotion."

"What?"

I thrust my arms out to reveal skin ripe for ruin. "I got into poison ivy, which is *your* fault for not keeping that bloodsucker out of the daisies."

I almost feel sorry for Axel, who has to edit the accusation on his face to make room for confusion.

I come around the desk. "Uncle Obe said you have a lotion that removes the oils."

"It's in the kitchen. What happened to your nose?"

The scratch. "I think it brushed against the ivy when I sniffed the daisies. It started itching—" Like it is now. I rub it with the back of my hand. "Do you mind?"

Shortly I stand before the kitchen sink, rubbing the lotion into my hands, lower arms, and nose. "It's probably too late. It's been over two hours."

"As long as you catch it within the first few hours, it usually works." Axel reaches past me and turns on the faucet. "Okay, rinse."

"Shouldn't I leave it on awhile?"

"It only takes a couple of minutes."

To be certain, I rub another minute before sticking my hands under the cool water.

Axel hands me a towel, and as I pat my skin, he leans back against the counter. "Let's talk about what you were doing in my office."

I step to the small table and take a chair. When he remains standing, I grudgingly concede the advantage to him. "I didn't come looking for those papers. And, yes, I went through them." Should I mention Trinity found them? No, it's an unnecessary detail that would only muddy the water. "You know what's in there, don't you?"

"From what your uncle has shared with me, I have a good idea."

I press my shoulders back. "Who, besides you, knows of his dementia?"

"His pastor, Artemis, and now you."

"What about Maggie and Bridget?"

"I don't think their brothers have mentioned their suspicions to them."

I frown. "Where did their suspicions come from?"

"The medication your uncle started taking after his diagnosis. It slows the advance of the disease." He leans farther back and puts his prosthetic ankle over the other. "The day Obe called the family together to discuss his will and before they arrived, I was in his hospital room with him. The doctor asked if Obe was taking any medications. Shortly after your uncle gave him the name of the one for dementia, I stepped out of the room. And into Luc. My guess is he was there awhile."

Good ol' Luc.

"Are you going to tell Luc so he can try to take away your uncle's right to do with his money as he wishes, thereby preserving the family's inheritance *and* their secrets? Including yours?"

I can't believe he thinks so low of me. I stand. "Obviously I've made a bad impression on you. Though I don't like that my uncle's plan to make restitution could lead to embarrassing revelations, I would never take this to Luc." I raise my chin higher. "But even if he did get ahold of that box, I don't believe it can be proven that Uncle Obe is yet at a place where he's incapable of making sound decisions."

"Your cousin would try. If there's a hole he can crawl through, he will, and I don't want your uncle to be deluged with lawyers, tests, the media."

"Neither do I, which is why I've been looking over his assets."

Cynicism crimps Axel's mouth.

I scowl. "I'm not going to do anything to hurt him."

"I'd like to believe you."

"And I'd like to think you're part of the solution!"

"Which is?"

"I—" I roll my eyes. "I don't have it all worked out, but let me show you."

He follows me back to his office, where I open the assets folder. "Earlier today Uncle Obe and I discussed his son and daughter, and he decided to make things right with them before he passes away."

"Just like that?"

I look up and realize we're side by side. I should have felt that. I do now. "No, not *just like that.* Maggie and Devyn dropped by, and it was obvious they'd had a disagreement."

"They've been butting heads recently."

Who is this man? And how is he so plugged into my family? Er, the Pickwicks. "Then you know Devyn is pressuring my cousin to reveal who her father is."

"Yes."

"And you know this how?"

"They've shared their frustrations with me."

"Why?"

"I'm a good listener."

I recall his exchange with Bridget in the garden when I felt the creep of jealousy. "Are you Bridget's confidant as well?"

"To a lesser degree. She's shut herself up since her husband's death, but from time to time she likes to talk."

"Is that all?" I can't believe I said that.

Axel smiles. "You're asking if she and I are involved?"

"No!"

"Liar."

I throw my hands up. "Let's get back on track here."

"Sure, but to clear the air, Bridget and I are not involved."

I drop my chin for fear my relief will show, which could prove precarious now that Grant is no longer between us. "Anyway, Uncle Obe told Maggie that the longer she put off telling Devyn about her father, the more resentment there would be. Then he quoted Scripture about concealing sin. I think that's when he realized he needs to make peace with his children now."

"I hope he goes through with it. He's talked about contacting them, but he always concludes it's better to imagine they would be receptive to reconciliation than to have it disproved." Axel looks at the folders. "Tell me about your solution."

I open the one that contains the will. "The current will remains in effect." Feeling tension rise off him, I hurry on. "With two additions: Uncle Obe's son and daughter."

"What about those he wants to add as beneficiaries?"

"Just as he has decided to reconnect with Antonio and Daisy prior to his passing, he wants to make amends to the others now— Well, in the near future."

His tension eases slightly. "You do realize that means selling the estate."

"That's what I thought, but maybe not." I slide the list of assets in front of him. "A good deal of the restitution can be made without affecting his ability to remain in his home, at least for a while. There's not much liquidity, but he has assets separate from the mansion and acreage that can be sold for a decent amount, especially in Pickwick's current market."

I run a finger down the list and hesitate as I did when I first saw the name of the property at Promenade Place, where I grew up— the eyeopener. As the date of acquisition coincides with the date the bank auctioned it out from under my mom, it's obvious Uncle Obe was our knight in shining armor. And I wouldn't be surprised if we lived there rent-free during our last years in Pickwick.

"According to current market values, this house should sell for nearly two hundred thousand dollars. Then there's the old movie theater on the square. Last year, the pharmacy opposite it sold for three hundred and fifty thousand dollars—and it's half the square footage of the theater."

"That's where Maggie's auction house is located."

I look up. "In the theater?"

He nods. "I don't know the terms of the lease that Artemis drew up, but it could be a problem."

It could, and I certainly don't want to cause Maggie any problems. See—trying to keep the peace. "Well, there are other assets, so we may not have to rock that boat." Big "maybe" as the theater is a large chunk. I trail my finger past items that will bring in far less but add up nicely. "There's the antique farm equipment." I glance at Axel. "Presumably in the barn by the pond."

"Yes."

"Most of it won't bring much, but three of the tractors are highly sought-after collectibles." I turn the page. "There are the books in the library—some rare first-print editions that could easily go for thousands each. And these are only the ones Uncle Obe listed as assets. There are probably more."

"I assume you plan on enlisting Maggie's help. She's good at getting top dollar for other people's castoffs, and I believe your uncle would approve."

I hadn't considered that, but it would be nice to have an expert on board with a stake in getting the best for all concerned. Of course, if the theater does have to be sold, that could get sticky. I straighten. "I'll talk to her."

His brow remains bothered.

"I believe this will work, Axel."

"*If* your uncle really is willing and *if* Luc doesn't fight it. I doubt your cousin will like this any more than divvying up the estate when your uncle passes away."

"No, but if Uncle Obe has to defend against charges of mental incompetence, it's easier to prove he's in a right state of mind to make these decisions while he's living than after he passes away."

Axel's face is impassive for what seems ages, but then he says, "It would be good for him to finally have peace, even if it means negative publicity."

Headlines to pay. "Actually, that's where I come in." Why do I feel dirty? I'm just protecting the Pickwicks—and, all right, I *am* one of them. "Where possible, restitution will be made through acts of philanthropy."

"Your idea, I assume."

"Public opinion can be cruel, Axel."

"But disguising repentance as benevolence…" He shakes his head. "I don't think that's the kind of peace your uncle is looking for."

But it's still peace! I square my shoulders. "The end result is that he pays the debt he feels responsible for without exposing himself or his family to the ugliness of public opinion. That has to count for something."

"All right, but consider his children. If he does attempt a reconciliation, it will have more impact on them than if he merely writes them into his will. After all, the greatest healing is often found in a sincere apology."

I knew I wasn't going to like what he had to say. "But money isn't bad either." Though it sure sounds bad spoken aloud.

He pats his prosthetic leg, and I wince at what he believes I think of it. "The young soldier who shot me made all kinds of excuses—said there was too much dust and smoke to see clearly… Smith wasn't where he was supposed to be…the commands were garbled…" His brow creases. "It made me angry. And vengeful. But a few weeks later, he came to the hospital and told me it was his fault, and he'd been too scared to admit it. I didn't forgive him immediately. But every day I awoke a little lighter with remembrance of his apology and the tears in his eyes. Eventually, I forgave him."

My nose tingles and eyes sting, and for some reason my thoughts turn to Maggie's apology. No amount of money could have made me feel as light as I had at that moment.

"I'm not saying that monetary restitution shouldn't be made where it's due," Axel continues. "Only that often it's best to start with an apology."

And let the headlines hit the fan. "I appreciate that, and where possible"—rather, *unavoidable*—"apologies will be made."

"How does your uncle feel about this?"

No need to detail his initial reaction. "He agreed it's for the best."

As Axel stares at me, I begin to feel like a moth on a pin. Finally, he says, "Where is the list of beneficiaries?"

I pass it to him, and he frowns. "Trinity's name has been crossed out."

What was I thinking?

He looks up. "You did it?"

This must be how Reggie felt when I came after her. Unfortunately, I'm less adept at playing possum. "Yes."

"That's not your decision."

I beg to differ, but that would require an explanation. So either I reveal *I'm* the one who will be making restitution to Trinity, thereby exposing myself as the perpetrator of the Lady Godiva ride, or I clam up and appear to be cold and calculating. If it's not one bad impression, it's another—on top of his believing I think less of him because of his prosthetic. I shouldn't care, but I do.

I draw a deep breath. "It's not what it looks like. Trinity will receive restitution, but not from my uncle."

Axel's lids flicker. *"You?"*

"I'll be the one writing the check." And, yes, it will hurt.

He tilts his head questioningly, and it strikes me that if I tilted my head opposite and stepped in—

Why am I standing so near him? Warmth invades my cheeks, and I sidestep.

"Then you're taking responsibility for something you did that adversely affected her."

Something? He hasn't heard of the Lady Godiva ride? That's hard to believe, but maybe there are too many stories about Trinity for him to put a finger on one. "I am."

A bit of Blue returns to his eyes—meaning I've made good my bad impression?

"Commendable," he says.

Score!

"But is this one of those instances where, in lieu of an apology, philanthropy is meant to serve?"

Penalty. "You can only rock the boat so much before it starts taking on water, Axel."

"Which is a problem for those who can't swim, hmm?"

Of course I can swim, but that doesn't mean I shouldn't use a life preserver in choppy water.

He sighs. "I'm sorry. Though I think it's best to be straight with people, I'll have to trust that you know what you're doing."

I do, don't I? Trinity did enjoy the attention for a while, and it's not as if she wanted to run the family business—

The ring of my phone causes my conscience to take cover. "Excuse me." As Axel turns away, I clap my phone to my ear. "Piper Pick—uh, *Wick*." Aargh!

"Obadiah Wick—uh, *Pickwick*," my uncle grumbles. "For once I'm grateful that phone of yours is attached to you like a…um…you know…birth cord."

Umbilical. Panged by his word-retrieval difficulty, I watch Axel step into the hallway and head from sight. "Is everything all right, Uncle Obe?"

"She's singing one of her Cinderella songs again, and right down the hall—'Zip-a-dee-doo-dah' this, 'Zip-a-dee-doo-dah' that, then 'bluebird on her shoulder' this, 'bluebird on her shoulder' that."

Not a Cinderella song, but I don't correct him. I come around the desk. "I'm heading back now."

"Where are you?"

I hope he doesn't read too much into this. "At the cottage."

"Is Axel there?"

I step into the kitchen and catch sight of him through the window where he stands in the yard with his back to me. "He's outside."

"Is that right?" No doubt he thinks Axel and I were up to no-good.

"I came up to get the lotion, remember?"

"Of course I remember!" he snaps, as if in defense of the dementia I'm not supposed to know about. He clears his throat and says in a lighter tone, "That was a couple hours ago."

As it's better that he believes my prolonged absence is due to time spent getting to know Axel rather than his personal papers, I say, "Time flies when you're having…" Not *fun*. "…a good conversation. I'll head back now."

"No rush." He chuckles. "She's singing 'Bibbidi-Bobbidi-Boo' now."

Now *that* is a Cinderella song.

"Not that it's any better, but it's a change, so visit as long as you like."

Incorrigible. "I'll see you soon." I return the phone to my waistband as I walk outside. "My uncle is awake, and Trinity is singing again." I descend the stairs.

He steps forward and extends the bottle of lotion. "If the rash appears, wash again. If nothing else, it should lessen the severity."

"Thank you." Our fingers brush as I accept the bottle, and attraction hums through me. Did he feel that? I glance at him in time to catch the curve of his mouth before it flattens and his brow pinches. "Are you all right?"

He shifts his weight. "Just one of my phantom pains."

I touch his arm. "I'm sorry about what I said in the garden." I roll my eyes. "I mean, what I *didn't* say when Uncle Obe asked if your…prosthesis bothers me."

His eyes move from my hand on him to my face. "What didn't you say?"

I snatch my hand back, only to wonder where to put it. As the options are limited, I clasp it with the other around the bottle, but it feels awkward. No wonder my clients groan and complain about the tasks I breezily set for them. It takes a tremendous amount of preparation and practice, both of which I'm lacking.

"What I didn't say was that I hardly notice it anymore."

Disbelief crosses Axel's face, and I'm reminded of his fiancée's inability to reconcile herself to his loss of a limb. "It makes a lot of women uncomfortable."

"Not me," I say with an eagerness that surprises—and embarrasses—me. "I mean, yes, it came as a shock, as I had no idea your limp was anything more than that, but it isn't off-putting. In fact, I think you're…" This is not the direction I should be going.

"What?"

Oh well. "You're attractive, even with that whole"—I wave a hand at his lower face—"mustache-goatee-ponytail thing you have going on."

His skepticism remains in effect, though I do detect amusement.

"I mean it."

"Under the circumstances, you shouldn't." He smiles. "You are taken."

Reminded of the last time attraction drew me to him, when Grant and I were still "on," so to speak, I feel an urgent need to update him. "Actually, it's basically over between me and…the man I was dating."

Axel tilts his head. "Should I say I'm sorry?"

I almost laugh. "Would you mean it?"

"It depends on how heartbroken you are."

Why am I not? I *was* practically engaged. Or was I? "I'm recovering fine."

He glances at my mouth, which suddenly feels dry. And in need of kissing. Not good.

I hold up the lotion. "Thank you again."

Without giving him time to respond, I hurry around the side of the cottage. As I start down the hill, I'm struck by a need to look back. Not that he'll be there. He's in the backyard where I left him, or else he's gone inside the cottage. But…

I look around. There Axel is with his ponytail and blue-collar attire and unsophisticated, down-to-earth persona. Pickwick might not be such a bad place to live after all—

"Ah!" I jerk my head around in time to avoid a low-hanging branch. What has come over me? I am *not* in need of kissing! And Pickwick, even it didn't have any dust, would not be compatible with me.

Maybe I need a shrink.

22

*N*ow my partners are mad. This wasn't supposed to take more than a week, and yet here I am heading into week number four with the Fourth of July parade just around the corner. Though Uncle Obe is getting around better and the words that go AWOL have yet to affect him in any significant way that I can tell, he has come to depend on me to meet many of his personal needs—for care, meals, and even companionship.

Of course, he's also depending on me to help him make restitution to those wronged by the Pickwicks. I knew it would require time and effort to devise a workable plan but didn't count on his unwillingness to allow me to handle the details. And to add one headache to another, he still doesn't like the spin of philanthropy, although he grudgingly acknowledges its benefit with regard to protecting the family.

One instance where it won't work is the compensation of the employees of the textile mill who continued to work for Bridget's dad after he stopped paying them. Based on his assurance that paychecks were forthcoming, nearly a hundred employees worked a month without pay. Pay still due them, with interest. As it's no secret the employees were wronged by Uncle Bartholomew and there are too many to expect them not to talk should anonymous checks start appearing in their mailboxes, this has to be handled in a forthright manner. Thus, if you're going to open old wounds, do it with salve and bandage in hand (in this case, an apology and generous compensation). If the press gets ahold of it, it will either be too scandal deficient to report or end up as a human-interest piece.

Uncle Obe liked that. What he doesn't like is the spin I came up with to make good on the statue he dumped in Pickwick Lake. Not only does he say we ought to bypass the philanthropy angle, but he balked at announcing at next week's Fourth of July celebration his plan to fund and commission a new statue. (And, no, I am not happy that I will be in town for that.) Uncle Obe was adamant that we write a check and be done with it, but when I pointed out that he wouldn't have a say in what ended up in the town square, he became thoughtful and had a muttered conversation with himself as he clunked his cane around the library. When he returned to me, he said he had a sculptor in mind and asked for assurance that the choice would be his.

Surprised that he knew any artists, I reassured him. He hobbled off, calling over his shoulder that he needed to start his third draft of the letter to Antonio and Daisy and that he would get back to me.

I'm still waiting, though not for much longer since I need an answer by tomorrow in order to make arrangements with the event organizers. So today is the day I pry an answer out of him—*after* church.

As Axel helps Uncle Obe out of the Jeep, I make an effort not to pay him too much attention, which has become a problem. His eye catches mine, and I hurriedly lean into the space between the driver and passenger seat to gaze through the windshield at Church on the Square.

Since I returned to Pickwick, it has begun to feel as if every Sunday is a blank page. No matter how much I scribble on it with the pen of work, the pencil of Uncle Obe, or even the highlighter I've started applying to scriptures other than those that deal with dust, I don't want to be here. And if this wasn't my uncle's first day back and he hadn't asked me to attend, I wouldn't have come.

Not because the church is overrun by Pickwicks. Not because Pastor Thurgood retired several years ago. No, it's for fear that once I step into the sanctuary of my youth, I may reconnect with my hometown on a more meaningful level than is good for L.A.-bound Piper Wick. Then there's God's voice, which has always sounded clearest to me when I attend services. It shouldn't be that way, but it is, as if we're meeting one-on-one in the only place where He can get my full attention.

"I won't let anyone bite you."

I snap my head around.

Axel pushes the passenger seat forward and reaches a hand to me. I accept it, and he steadies me as I unfold from the backseat and step down beside him. *So* glad I wore the dressy capris I purchased at Le Roco Roco this past Friday, when Maggie talked me into going into town with her while Devyn and Uncle Obe hunkered over a chess game. The outing was surprisingly fun, in an alternate universe way.

Axel releases me, and disappointment is my middle name. *It is not! Your attraction for him is merely a wrinkle in the big scheme of things. Once you return to L.A., it will all iron out.* Unfortunately, the trips I'll be making to Pickwick to orchestrate the liquidation of Uncle Obe's assets will make it more difficult, but I will forget how Blue Axel's eyes are and how nice he kisses in the rain…

"We're late," Uncle Obe says.

Realizing I'm staring at Axel, I cross to where my uncle stands on the sidewalk, his cane planted on the cement.

"Bad wig," he says, looking past me.

"What?" I follow his gaze to the Pickwick Arms and catch sight of a blond woman just as she turns away. He's right. Her wig *is* bad, and not just because it sits crooked on her head. Kind of reminds me of—

No "kind of" about it. Recalling the picture on my desk in L.A., I see the woman behind Grant—the one who asked so many tough questions, wore a crooked blond wig, and had a New England accent…

Hello, Janet Farr/Jane Farredy. So you're still digging, are you? You really ought to keep up with current events since Grant and I are no more.

"We aren't gonna stand out here all day, are we?" Uncle Obe says when Axel joins us on the sidewalk.

"Let's go." I walk alongside my uncle as we head for the ramp at the church's side entrance. Axel follows us into the lobby, and the muffled sound of singing greets us. As does Uncle Obe's nearest neighbor and year-round Christmas light enthusiast, Bronson Biggs. Despite his name, which one would expect to belong to a hulk of a man, Bronson is little. And age, which has put a curl in his shoulders, makes him more so. Guessing he's barely five feet tall and a hundred and ten pounds on a "buffet" day, I return his smile.

"Piper Pickwick, it's mighty good to have you back." He clasps my hand. "I've been prayin' for you."

I blink. "You…have?"

"Yep, ever since your name popped up on the prayer chain."

I was on a prayer chain?

Uncle Obe touches my arm. "I called in a prayer request when you got into that poison ivy."

"Oh." I know I shouldn't wish he hadn't done it, but it makes me feel a part of this community that I am not a part of. "Thank you."

"So, no nasty rash?" Mr. Biggs says.

I turn up my hands. "Either I'm immune to poison ivy, or the lotion I used to remove the oil did its job."

His brow lowers. "Are you discountin' all the prayers I said for you?"

Oh dear. "I'm sorry, Mr. Biggs. I'm sure it was the prayers. So, how is Mrs. Biggs?"

His brow eases. "Mrs. Biggs is fine, though you'll find she's scarce as hen's teeth this morning." No sooner do I translate that to mean she's not here than he exclaims, "Teeth!" His parched, whiskered face jerks as if by puppet strings. "Why, that's funny."

That I cannot translate.

"Mrs. Biggs ain't here 'cause she couldn't find *her* teeth. Get it? Hen's teeth. Mrs. Biggs's teeth."

I glance at Axel, who certainly gets it with *his* show of teeth, then Uncle Obe, who can't have gotten it with his attention on the doors of the sanctuary.

I squeeze Mr. Biggs's hand. "That is funny."

He releases me. "I'd best seat you before Pastor Stanky starts pounding the podium."

Stinky? Surely he didn't call—?

Axel's breath in my ear makes me catch mine. "Stankowitz.

Damien Stankowitz. The older members had an issue with
Damien—"

No doubt due to the movie *The Omen*.

"—so they started calling him Stankowitz, which has become
Stanky."

As Mr. Biggs opens a door to the sanctuary, causing the singing
to pour out, I look up at Axel.

"With his blessing," he adds.

"I see." And I do a moment later when the congregation, num-
bering a hundred and fifty or so, lower to their seats, and a man in
his early forties strides to the podium.

As we traverse the center aisle, causing heads to turn, I catch a
wave. It's Devyn, where she peers past Maggie. Three pews ahead,
my eyes meet those of Martha, formerly of Martha's Meat and Three
Eatery. I recognize others, most of whom nod and smile.

Here come the warm fuzzies. I am no longer part of this community, and yet—

Trinity comes into view, looking as if she might burst at seeing
me here. The warm fuzzies take flying leaps when she jerks her head
toward the elderly, pinch-faced woman at her side. Ugh. I still
haven't talked to her grandmother, and every day Trinity asks me to
make good on my promise, but I haven't had time. Of course, neither do I look forward to the encounter for fear my support of
Trinity's innocence won't be enough and her grandmother will probe
as Trinity failed to do.

"Good morning, beloved ones of God!"

I turn my attention to the pastor just as his eyes light on Uncle

Obe. An instant later, he's bounding forward. "Why, Obadiah"—
he lays a hand on my uncle's shoulder—"it's good to have you back."

I expect Uncle Obe to shrink in the spotlight, but he's all grin
and chuckle. "Good to be back, Stanky. And thank you again for vis-
iting me while I was in the hospital."

"My pleasure." The man nods at Axel and looks to me. "You
must be Piper." He thrusts a hand forward. "Pastor Stankowitz—
Stanky, if you like."

Catching Luc's eye on the left, I'm struck by how strange this
man's behavior is. He ought to be preaching, not greeting the con-
spicuously late. I accept his handshake. "I'm sorry we're late."

"Not a problem." He looks to Mr. Biggs. "Thank you, Bronson."
Bronson ambles away.

"Well, come on down here." Pastor Stanky falls into step with
Uncle Obe as they head for what I hope isn't the front pew.

"You'll like him," Axel says, bending near. "He's spontaneous."

"What makes you think I like spontaneous?" I whisper back.

"You would if you tried."

His smile is catching, but as I give in to it, I feel Luc's gaze.
Though he shaved his mustache, he still has the shifty-eyed look,
especially when he narrows his lids at me. On the one hand, I'm
thankful he finally stopped badgering my voice mail; on the other,
I'm suspicious. Hoping he isn't up to anything, I look away and run
aground on Artemis's rumpled brow. He is not happy with my solution to the will dilemma, so any help he has given has been with
mutterings of, "Don't know why I bothered to call ya, Piper Pickwick—pardon me, *Wick*."

As Pastor Stanky returns to the podium, I seat myself beside Uncle Obe—in the front pew—and Axel settles on my opposite side. While the distance between us is respectable, I scoot nearer my uncle in an attempt to dislodge any eyes that might be boring into the back of my head.

Pastor Stanky jumps into today's sermon, and I look up in anticipation of the presentation of key ideas on a screen. Though Pickwick is in the midst of renewal, that doesn't extend to technology where Church on the Square is concerned. And I'm glad. This sermon is about spending money wisely and using it to do good, and Uncle Obe is all ears. When the pastor references 1 Timothy 6:18, which encourages Christians to be rich in good deeds and generous and willing to share, Uncle Obe murmurs, "Amen." When Proverbs 15:16 is cited, about it being better to have little with the fear of the Lord than great wealth with turmoil, Uncle Obe adds, "Amen to that too." And when the sermon concludes with Luke 6:38, which tells us that if we give, it will be given to us, Uncle Obe pats his Bible. "Better believe it."

Soon I stand with the others to sing the closing hymn, and then we all try to leave at once. Except Trinity, who goes against the tide to reach us where we bring up the rear. As she nears, I get a good look at her and am surprised by her transformation from Cinderella to Susie Churchgoer. Her dark brown hair is pulled back from her face with a tortoiseshell headband, and the hair that sweeps her shoulders has a curl to it as opposed to its usual kink. She's also wearing makeup, and the softly smudged eyeliner makes her green eyes pop. She looks pretty.

She halts before me, lifts my hand, and presses a piece of paper into it. "Don't forget now." Then she wiggles her way back through the crowd.

"What was that about?" Uncle Obe asks. While he was pleased when I told him *I* plan to make restitution to Trinity, I didn't tell him I agreed to talk to her grandmother on her behalf for fear he might try to convince me to ditch the philanthropy angle.

"Probably just a list of cleaning supplies that are running low." I feel Axel's gaze. Has he figured out yet which wrong I'm righting? I crane my neck to see past those ahead. "If you don't mind, I'll push on so I can beat the rush to the ladies' room." I slip away, but when I step into the ladies' room, there's a long line. As no one looks familiar, I unfold the paper.

Hi, Piper!
Great message, don't you think? Pastor Stanky knows how
to grab your attention. Anyway, you said you would tell my
grandmother that you don't believe I did you-know-what.
You still mean to, don't you? I would really appreciate it.
(She's in one of her moods today.)

So today is the day I pay a visit to Trinity's grandmother.

When I emerge from the ladies' room five minutes later, the foyer is empty, and through the wide-open double doors I see Pastor Stanky talking with a group of teenagers. Beyond him, two elderly couples have their heads together, likely discussing where they should enjoy their after-church lunch.

A hand claps my shoulder. "We need to talk."

I take offense at Luc's self-satisfied smile. *How am I supposed to make peace with someone like him, Lord?* I force a smile. "Uncle Obe is waitin' for me." Ack! I did it again—dropped a *g*!

"It won't take but a minute."

"I'm sorry, but—"

"Dementia."

The word stops my lips in their tracks. *He's guessing...looking for a reaction to see if he's in the right vicinity. I'd say a little confusion is in order.* "Why, Luc, I—?"

"I know all about Dr. Dyer and the diagnosis he made three months ago."

How did he find out? Not Artemis or Axel, and I can't believe Pastor Stanky said anything.

"Mentally incompetent, Piper. He has no business making changes to his will, and I'm going to see that he doesn't—with or without your help."

I fight my anger, not only because I know better, but because of my increased awareness of God in this place. "Without," I say.

He removes a card from his jacket. "This is the attorney I've retained, and first thing Monday morning, he's going to subpoena Uncle Obe's records and put together a case that will preserve our inheritance."

Peacemaking, my foot! Before I can talk myself down, I snatch the card from him, tear it up, and stuff the pieces into his pocket. "You will do no such thing. It's Uncle Obe's money, and he'll decide what to do with it."

He snorts. "You're delusional if you think I'm just going to—"

"I don't think. I know." *Step back; think this through.*

"Oh yeah?"

"Yeah." *You haven't thought it through. Take a breather, walk it off.* "If you push this, I can almost guarantee you won't see a dime." *You're not listening, are you?*

Luc sighs. "You live in your little 'do right' world, and I'll live in mine." He pats his pocket. "Tomorrow."

I catch his arm. "Let it go!"

He tugs to free himself, but I grip him harder.

Uh, remember Cootchie? "How are you going to explain your actions when the doctor says that Uncle Obe *is* competent to make decisions about his will?"

He thrusts his face close to mine. "We're talking *dementia*, Piper, as in 'out of his mind.' In...com...pe...tent."

"I don't believe he is. Not yet."

He rolls his eyes. "We'll see."

I don't let go, though he once more starts past me. "You don't know about Antonio and Daisy, do you?" *You have crossed the line.*

"Nope." He pries my fingers loose. "Dementia is all I need to know."

"They're his kids." *You are SO Cootchie!* "And they have more of a right to an inheritance than any of us." *Lord, please work this for the good of those who love You!*

Luc stiffens and, after a long moment, points a finger at me. "You're spinning, aren't you, spidey woman? Trying to manipulate me, convince me that black is white."

"No. Uncle Obe has a son and daughter near our age. If you push this, don't be surprised if he leaves everything to them."

His expression wavers. "If that's true, he can hardly do it if he's mentally incompetent."

I prop my hands on my hips. "Number one, I don't believe you can prove he's mentally incompetent. Number two, I don't think there's a judge who wouldn't allow his children the inheritance Uncle Obe wants them to have."

"You may be right, but only if they truly are his."

Recalling the day my uncle poured out his sad tale, I say, "They are his, and if necessary, a DNA test will prove it."

Luc stares at me for what seems minutes, but finally he lowers his nose from on high.

"So leave Uncle Obe his dignity or kiss it all good-bye."

He draws a strident breath. "I'll consult my attorney and let you know what I decide."

I can't expect more from him. "Do."

He turns back toward the doors as a long shadow falls across the threshold, followed by Axel.

"Well, if it isn't my uncle's gardener," my cousin drawls.

Axel looks at me. "Everything all right, Piper?"

"I—"

"Of course it is." Luc claps Axel's shoulder. "Or don't you know about my uncle's dementia?"

In a flash, Axel's face hardens. In another flash, Luc is gone. As I struggle for an explanation, he strides forward. "You told him."

"No! He found out."

"How?"

"I…don't know. Maybe he broke into your cottage—"

"The day you found the box, I moved it elsewhere to prevent something like this from happening."

"Something like what?"

"You know what." He walks away.

He thinks badly of me again—that I'm hatching something with Luc! Fine. I don't care. *Yes, you do.*

I follow him, pausing only to thank Pastor Stanky. Despite Axel's uneven stride, I don't catch up until he's opening the door of his Jeep. I hurry to the other side and halt at finding the passenger seat empty.

"Where's Uncle Obe?"

"He accepted an invitation to lunch and asked that I pick him up this afternoon." Axel inserts the key in the ignition.

I jump in and pull the door closed. "I didn't tell Luc." I jerk at the seat belt. "You have to believe me."

He reverses out of the parking space and puts the car into gear. "Why?"

"Because I wouldn't do that to my uncle." I grip his knee, only to snatch my hand away. It's his prosthetic leg. Not that it bothers me. It just seems like a violation, especially as I'm not sure it actually is his knee. Maybe that's prosthetic too? Afraid to look at him for what may be on his face, I say lamely, "You know I wouldn't."

"I didn't think you would." He stares at the road and doesn't speak again until we're clear of the Super Wal-Mart. "All right, but he does know, and he's going to cause problems." He glances at me. "What else does he know?"

"Nothing. I—" Oops. "He knows about Antonio and Daisy."

He draws a sharp breath. "You don't know how he found out about them either?"

Lord, why do I always wait to consult You after *the fact?* "That blame *is* mine."

He momentarily takes his eyes off the road. "*You* told him."

"Only to use as leverage to prevent him from trying to have Uncle Obe declared mentally incompetent. You know, 'Back off or he'll leave it all to his children.'"

He looks forward.

"He's retained an attorney, Axel."

"I'm sure he has."

Silence, and I wish it were due to the windy road. Finally, Axel looks at me. "What do you suggest we do?"

"You believe me?"

He looks back at the road, and that jaw muscle, which seems exclusive to alpha males, tics and tenses. "I've learned to forgive, but if you're making a fool of me…"

He leaves it at that, but then silence is a language all its own.

I moisten my lips. "I suggest that we wait and see if Luc takes the threat of disinheritance seriously."

"What are the chances of that?"

"Good. I think."

"Let's pray you're right." Axel gives me a smile, albeit forced.

A few minutes later the estate comes into sight, as does the snazzy sports car parked before the gate.

I frown. "Who's that?"

"We'll know soon enough." Axel brakes behind the other car, and it's apparent the driver has abandoned it.

"Rental car," Axel says, taking in the license plate.

"Where's the driver?"

He points to a place beyond the gate. "I would say that's him."

I peer up the driveway. And who should be coming down it but Grant? *Oh, Lord.*

23

Another gate climber," Axel says. "Someone you know?"

What is he doing here? "A…um…client."

"One who knows where your uncle lives?" Axel looks sidelong at me. "That sounds like more than a client."

And his suspicions are back in full. "Just a client." I open the door and slide out. As I step between the two vehicles, I hear my name called and look around to see Grant waving as he comes down the driveway.

The gate opens in response to the code I punch in, and I hurry toward Grant, who is as leanly attractive as ever. Though he has started to bald in a way that makes him appear more mature than his thirty-nine years (a plus in politics), it hasn't hurt his appeal. But then, he does have soulful eyes, great cheekbones, and a two-phase orthodontic smile.

"Piper!" Sunglasses obscure his eyes, and he beams as he nears. I slow but he doesn't, and suddenly his arms surround me (very un-clientlike), his face lowers (highly unclientlike), and his mouth comes in for a landing (exceedingly unclientlike).

I turn aside to break off the kiss. "Grant! What are you—?"

"I've missed you."

He never missed me this much before. What is going on? And

what must Axel think? *And please, Lord, don't let that undercover reporter be anywhere near.*

Grant starts to lower his head again, but I press a hand to his chest. "You're making no sense."

He removes his sunglasses and hooks them on the neck of his shirt. "Actually, I'm making more sense than I have in weeks."

"Not to me."

His brow develops a minor furrow, usually reserved to express concern for his constituents. "This doesn't feel right?"

I pull back, and he releases me. "What are you doin' here?"

He blinks. "Did you just drawl?"

Oh no.

"You sounded a bit Southern."

"Well, technically, I am." I wave a dismissing hand. "What happened with the tire tycoon's daughter?"

A flick of his eyebrows erases his frown. "We should have dug deeper into Penelope's past."

She has secrets too? Something worse than being a Pickwick? Of course, I never got around to telling him about Lady Godiva.

"At seventeen, she ran away with her boyfriend and joined a radical cult—the kind that uses firearms and bombs to get their point across. Fortunately, her father tracked her down and had her extricated."

My jaw slackens. "Extricated? Sounds dangerous."

He holds up a hand. "The press doesn't know. I uncovered it on my own."

Janet Farr/Jane Farredy, you are after the wrong story—thankfully. "How did you uncover it?"

"She told me. She didn't want to get any more serious until I knew about her past."

"That was honest of her." Though I had intended to tell him about the last piece of *my* past when I thought I was still in his future, this young woman has one up on me.

"It's too bad," Grant says almost to himself, and something like distress spasms across his face.

Maybe the kiss they shared in the park was more than a photo op.

He sighs. "In every other way she was perfect."

And he has to do what's best for his career and constituents. I just hope that Penelope didn't have strong feelings for him.

He sheds his melancholy with a shake of his shoulders. "We received good press as a couple and diced that rumor, but my numbers weren't much higher with Penelope than they were when I was seeing you."

I know all about those numbers because I've stayed on top of his publicity.

"So here I am." Grant spreads his arms wide.

I shift my jaw. "Have you forgotten that I'm a Pickwick?"

He lowers his arms. "That's problematic, but we can work around it. After all, one is hardly responsible for being born into a particular family. And it's not as if you have anything sordid to hide yourself."

Don't I?

A groan sounds, and I turn to see the gate opening. Though I don't recall hearing it close, it must have.

Axel steps through. "Would you mind moving your car? I need to get up the hill."

"Certainly," Grant says as I turn back the way I came. He comes alongside me. "Who is that?"

"My uncle's godson."

"And you were with him?"

I don't care for his accusing tone. "He gave me a ride home from church."

"Oh? Considering the state of the road I took out of town, my guess is that's considerably out of his way."

"He lives here on the estate."

He gives a "hmm" of judgmental proportion. "Living off his doddering old godfather, then."

Doddering? Okay, I'm offended. And what right does he have to pass judgment on Axel? He doesn't even know—! Neither did I, and yet I thought the same thing when Artemis told me about him.

"Probably sucking the old man dry," Grant murmurs as we near the gate.

I shoot him a dirty look. "No, he isn't. He's my uncle's gardener."

Grant opens his mouth, then shuts it as we've almost reached Axel, who is punching in the code to keep the gate from retracting. With a low whistle, Grant slides the sunglasses onto his face.

Axel's eyes have taken on that distinctly un-Blue cast. Doubtless, he saw the kiss that appears to make a lie of my claim that I'm no longer in a relationship. "Uh…this is Grant Spangler, and…"

Grant thrusts a hand at Axel. "U.S. Congressman Grant Spangler. Piper's fiancé."

What?! But I…we're not… Oh no, what does Axel think? And after what happened with Luc? This could be bad. *Lord, did You not see me at church today?*

With a flick of his gaze that is colder than I've ever felt, even when I was last dumbstruck and didn't deny that his prosthetic leg bothered me, Axel accepts Grant's handshake. "Axel Smith."

"The gardener." Grant releases him and slides his hands into his pants pockets. "That's one fine mow job. I'm always amazed at how you guys do it—all those nice diagonal rows."

I catch my breath. I've never known Grant to be demeaning to those whose collars are other than white, but I'm pretty sure that is what's going on.

I look to Axel, hoping to communicate with my eyes how sorry I am, but he's also staring at the majestic expanse of lawn.

"I suppose it comes naturally to some people," Axel says. "Perhaps you should give it a try. You might be a natural yourself."

"I don't mind getting my hands dirty when it's called for, but I'm more a suit-and-tie kind of guy. Best to leave stuff like this"—Grant pans a hand at the landscape—"to the professionals."

And I thought *I* was a snob. Still, if one didn't know the true color of Axel's eyes, they would never guess he's anything but congenial toward my "fiancé." And what is that about anyway?

"Well, sorry for blocking you," Grant says. "When no one responded to the intercom, I thought it might not be working, so I hopped the gate."

And from the looks of his outfit, he was more successful than I—no snags or rust marks.

Grant retrieves my hand. "Thank you for giving Piper a ride back. I'll take her up to the estate from here." As he pulls me toward the gate, I struggle to piece myself back to some semblance of Piper Pickwick—I mean, Wick!

"Hey!" Grant looks over his shoulder. "That gate isn't going to close on me, is it?" He pats the sports car's fender. "Wouldn't want to put a scratch on this beauty."

"It's set to remain open," Axel says, and I hear the hitch in his step as he follows.

A moment later Grant hands me into the car and closes the door. And I feel how a purse that has just been snatched would feel if it had feelings— Oh!

As Grant slides in, I jump out. "I left my purse in the Jeep. Be right back."

Axel is in his seat when I pull open the passenger door. "Axel, I—"

He holds up a hand. "I told you I don't like being made a fool of."

I lean farther in. "He's not my fiancé. He's my client, and though we did talk marriage, we never made it to the engagement stage."

"He's the one you were engaged to be engaged to?"

"*Were.* For the past two weeks, he's been dating someone else, which was going well until he learned of the woman's past and decided he and I are on again. We aren't."

"Why did he say you are?"

"I…" I shrug. "Maybe he's jealous of you?"

Axel glances at the sports car. "Does he have reason to be?"

What am I supposed to say? That I would have preferred that Grant's kiss was Axel's?

That is *the truth.*

But Grant is more in line with the man I've always imagined myself marrying.

Maybe you've been in the wrong line.

But the line to Axel leads to Pickwick.

So?

So?! I don't belong in Pickwick.

You belong in L.A.?

I...well...

"I shouldn't have asked such a hard question," Axel says tightly.

"No! It's just that Grant is a highly valued client, and if I lose him..." I splay my hands in a pitifully helpless gesture that would make Piper Wick cringe. "I'm already in hot water with my partners for being gone so long."

Axel nods. "And you can only rock the boat so much before it starts taking on water." He slides on his sunglasses. "Maybe you need to learn to swim, Piper."

"Axel—"

"Whether you're just compromising yourself or this is another of your PR schemes to make sure *I* don't rock the boat by telling your uncle my feelings about your philanthropy idea, I'm not swallowing it anymore. And if you and Luc are—"

"*Me and Luc?* I am not part of his schemes."

As Axel stares at me through dark lenses, a horn honks. He smiles tightly. "That would be your client."

I look in the rearview mirror to where Grant is watching us. "We'll talk later."

I start to close the door when Axel says, "Don't forget your purse."

I am *so* sideways. I snatch it from the floorboard, close the door, and return to the sports car. "Okay." I settle in beside Grant. "What's this about me bein' your fiancée?"

He points a finger at me. "You did it again."

"What?"

"That Southern thing—the sticky sweet drawl."

I nearly groan. "Grant, you told Axel I'm your fiancée."

He curls a hand around the gearshift and looks at me over the tops of his sunglasses. "It's why I'm here, Piper—to ask you to marry me."

24

*N*o?"

With an apologetic grimace, I shake my head.

Grant takes a step back. "Why? I mean, we talked about engagement...marriage...kids...and you always seemed hopeful."

That's embarrassing, but though my staggered pride begs me to prop it up with a disclaimer, I say, "I was hopeful, Grant, because you're a nice guy and successful and everything I imagined in my future husband."

He tosses his palms up. "So?"

I turn and cross the library to the windows overlooking the front of the mansion. "There has to be more than that." I peer over my shoulder. "And not just from me."

He looks forlorn against the backdrop of the ceiling-high bookshelves. "What do you mean?"

I lean back against the windowsill. "When you said you had broken it off with Penelope, you seemed distressed, as if you really cared about her."

He shifts his weight and glances away. "Come on, I only knew her a couple of weeks. And you know I dated her to stamp out that rumor which *you* were too busy to help with."

"You kissed her."

With perfectly executed strides, he crosses the library to my side. "Is that why you're rejecting my proposal? Jealousy?"

I tilt my head back. "Grant, you are one of the most conservative people I know, and that kiss…" I shrug. "Though I chalked it up to being a photo op, I don't think it was. I think you couldn't help yourself and that you feel for Penelope more than you've ever felt for me. And if you weren't in politics, I would run a distant second to her, regardless of what either of our pasts hold."

His brow spasms.

"There's that distress again." I eye his forehead.

He drags a hand across it. "Two weeks, Piper. That's nothing."

"Could be, but it could also be the beginning of *some*thing. Something that you don't have with me."

He makes a sound in his throat. "But maybe I could have it with you." He suddenly looks desperate, and I feel sorry for him despite the sting of his admission.

I give his arm a squeeze. "If you're going to settle for someone, don't settle for me. You don't love me, I don't love you, and while you may reconcile yourself to being married to a Pickwick, there's a bit more to my past than that."

He narrows his eyes. "You said there was something else you wanted to tell me. You never did."

I nod. "Unlike Penelope, who was honest with you before you got too involved."

He takes a step back, dislodging my hand from his arm. "What?"

Feeling leprous, I clasp my hands before me. "I was eighteen…" And so the story unfolds.

Grant grimaces in all the places where I expect him to, and when my condensed story winds down, he shakes his head. "You know where I stand on pornography."

That's a strong word. "What I did was wrong, but I don't see it as pornography."

"Call it what you will—porno, public nudity—it's still political suicide." He claps a hand to the back of his neck and turns away. "Man! Isn't there a single woman out there with a clean slate?"

I stomp my foot. "Grant!"

"What?"

"Are you telling me you've never made a mistake?"

He frowns. "Of course I've made mistakes."

"So there are things in your past you regret?"

"Yes, but normal things, like being suspended in high school for writing on the bathroom walls, losing my cool and cursing, a speeding ticket here and there, misfiling my taxes—the kind of stuff that makes you human. Not pornography and radical cults..." He throws his hands up. "My constituents won't tolerate that, even if it was teenage rebellion."

And to think I was excited to try my PR hand at politics. "They're not very forgiving, then."

He laughs wryly. "Politics isn't forgiving."

"And politics is all that matters?"

His gaze turns stern. "It's my life. As for forgiveness, I'd say you're as afraid of what this Trinity and the town will think of you if you own up to your Lady Godiva ride as I am of continuing to see Penelope."

I wish I hadn't told him about my plan to make restitution to Trinity.

"You have far less to lose than I do." He glances out the window. "Especially as you don't have to live in this backwoods place."

"It is *not* backwoods."

Grant gives a half laugh. "Come on, Piper. This isn't L.A.—or Denver, for that matter."

"That's a bad thing?"

He stares at me, and the deeper his frown goes, the more it seems he's looking at something totally foreign. Am I? I do feel a bit strange.

He shakes his head. "Nothing truly new happens here. This isn't real life. Small towns, particularly Southern ones, are like the youngest kids in large families—everything is hand-me-downs."

I scowl. "I'll have you know that Pickwick is one of the fastest-growing towns in North Carolina. They have Wi-Fi, for goodness' sake."

"A recent addition, I'm sure."

"Pickwick may be relatively small and shamelessly Southern, but it has plenty of *real* life in it. And it has things a big city doesn't."

"Like?"

"People who know each other, and not just because they work together or live in the same apartment building. And it has charm, safety, clean air, a town square—"

"Town square?"

I don't know why I added that. "Yes, a pretty one with a park in the middle."

He looks like he might laugh. "It must have been a real sacrifice to leave all this for the big city."

I blink at the realization of what I'm saying and what it sounds like. "No, I wanted to leave—had to. Things were different then. *I* was different, and so was my family. It's better now."

"You're not considering staying?"

"No!"

He smiles like he knows something I don't. "That sounded knee-jerk."

Which I've warned him about when answering reporters' questions. It makes a person sound defensive, as if he's eager to get a lie off his chest.

"I'm going back to L.A."

He nods. "And I'm going back to Denver."

Less a fiancée. And less a story for Janet Farr/Jane Farredy, which he needs to know about. I tell him about my discovery, watching as his face goes from grave to horrified and certain his association with my PR firm is about to end.

At the end of the telling, he shoves his hands in his pants pockets and, head down, paces the library. On the third time through, he suddenly stops. "Politics! Conniving, backstabbing, double-dealing, bloodsucking!" He grunts, and in the bunching of his shoulders, curling of his lips, and baring of his teeth, I see a bit of the alpha male. "It's getting old."

I take a step toward him. "You aren't thinking of quitting the race, are you?"

He startles, causing the alpha male to go back underground. "Of course not, but neither am I going to let it run my life—or ruin it."

I sigh. "I'm glad to hear that. You're good for Colorado, Grant." I draw a deep breath. "I suppose I should remove you from my client list."

I'm surprised by his hesitation but more surprised by the words that follow. "We'll finish the race together—regardless of what this Jane Farredy has to say about me or you."

Meaning less hot water for my partners to boil me in. "Thank you." I move forward and stick out a hand. "Now you had best get back to Colorado before she finds out you're here and reads too much into your visit."

He shakes my hand and releases it. "Good-bye, Piper." With that unbroken stride of his—unnaturally perfect, if you ask me—he crosses the library.

"Grant?"

He looks around.

"I shouldn't say this, but with regards to Penelope—"

"Yes." He nods sharply. "Far better I remain the single, eligible bachelor I was when I was first voted into office."

"Actually, I was going to say—"

"No, that is what the specialist I'm paying to help me get re-elected was going to say." He continues to the doorway, where he turns. "But after the election…once I'm settled back into office…" He smiles and disappears down the hallway.

So he isn't giving up on Penelope? Feeling a tingle in my chest, I turn to the windows and watch him drive away.

One down, many more to go, though what I'm going to do about Axel, I have no idea.

I try not to think about him. I set my mind to the tasks ahead, the greatest being to get Uncle Obe's estate in order so that pieces can be sold off, and the next being to keep my promise to Trinity.

I sigh. "No time like the present." I cross the library, determined to drive to the little house where Trinity still lives with her grandmother. But what if she isn't there? I don't want to face the old woman alone.

I retrieve my iPhone and dial Trinity's home.

"Hello?" an irritated voice demands.

"Can I speak to Trinity?"

"Ain't here. Out with that Pickwick boy, she is."

Oh no.

"Fool girl. I told her no, and what does she do when I lay me down for a nap? Jumps in his car and off they go before I can make it to the front door."

Bart? Trinity did mention he had asked her out. Infusing my voice with sympathy, I say, "That's Bart Pickwick for you, all right." I hold my breath.

"Yep, that boy's bad news. All them Pickwicks are bad news."

Now is probably not the time to clear Trinity of the Lady Godiva stunt. "If I were you, Mrs. Templeton, I would lie down and get some rest. No sense worrying yourself silly."

"Well, you aren't me, are you? Good-bye, Miss Busybody." She hangs up without bothering to find out who "Miss Busybody" is. Thankfully.

I mull over the puzzle piece of Bart. Bart and Trinity. Bart and Luc, both of whom broke into the mansion in search of…the proof in the box. Which Trinity knows about, though only the will. Or maybe she lied when she said she didn't look through the whole box. That would explain how Luc learned the details of Uncle Obe's dementia. Still, I can't see Trinity taking an active role in this. Did Bart take advantage of her naiveté?

Bridget is less than cordial when I call—something about being up to her elbows in manure—but whips off Bart's cell number before curtly telling me she has to go.

Bart answers on the second ring. "Bart Pickwick speaking."

"This is Piper. Can I speak to Trinity?"

"Sure."

"Piper?" Trinity screeches. "How did you know I was with Bart?"

"Your grandmother told me."

She gasps. "I was sure she was asleep. She's gonna be ill as a sore-tailed cat when I get home. But hey! You talked to her? Discussed you-know-what?" On that last, she lowers her voice, although probably not enough to exclude Bart from our exchange.

I grit my teeth. "There wasn't an opportunity."

"Ah," she groans.

"Too, I think you should be there when I talk to her."

"You're probably right. Well, I'd best get back to this ice cream sundae I'm sharin' with Bart. Thanks for calling."

"Trinity!"

"Yeah?"

"Would you mind excusing yourself from Bart so we can speak in private?"

"This sundae is meltin' awful fast."

"It will only take a minute."

"Hold on." She says something to Bart, and then I hear the click of her heels over tile. "What's up?"

I nearly ask, "What in the world are you doing with my cousin?" But there's a more pressing matter. "When you found Uncle Obe's box in Axel's office, you said you didn't go through the whole thing."

"I didn't."

"I assumed that meant you only looked in the file about the will."

"No, I glanced at a few others."

"Did you *glance* through the medical file?"

"I did." She gasps. "Oh my stars! You found out. I'm so sorry. I didn't want to say anything, disturbin' as it was to learn that your uncle is strugglin' with demons, all the more reason I was pleased to see him at service today, but—"

"Demons?"

"Yeah. I think the doctor called it *demon-ti-a*."

I draw a cleansing breath. "Actually, it's de*men*tia, and it has nothing to do with demons." Although a person so afflicted might disagree. "It's a disease that affects older people's memory and intellectual ability."

"Like Alzheimer's?"

How can she know about that and not this? "Yes."

"Well, no wonder when I ran into Bart here at the ice cream place last week, he about laughed when I offered my condolences. That rascal! And here I thought he was using humor to deal with the pain."

So Trinity told Bart, and Bart told Luc. "I'm assuming you also told Bart the name of the doctor who made the diagnosis."

"I may have, though I don't recall his name. Dr. Die maybe?"

Demontia for *dementia. Die* for *Dyer.*

"Piper, if I don't get back to my sundae, Bart is gonna scarf it all down. I'll talk to you tomorrow. Bye."

Time to pay my ponytailed gardener a visit.

"Why didn't you tell me it was Trinity who found the box?" Axel finally speaks.

I stare at where he's pulling weeds in the flower bed, as he was doing when I found him here. In all that time, he looked around once—when I first appeared—and his face was impassive. What is it now?

"It didn't seem important, since I thought the file for Uncle Obe's will was the only one she'd seen, specifically the list of new beneficiaries."

"Was that before or after you decided to personally make restitution and marked out her name?"

"Before."

He looks over his shoulder. "Does she know the reason your uncle wanted to add her to his will?"

Does Axel? Has he put two and two together? "No."

He returns to redistributing the dirt disturbed by the removal of weeds. "So what now?" Wiping his hands on his jeans, he stands. "And what are you going to do about this reporter who followed you to Pickwick?"

I curl my fingers into my palms to override the impulse to wipe the dirt from his jaw. "The reporter? Nothing. All she can say is that I'm a Pickwick and that for a while it appeared that Grant and I were thinking beyond a business relationship."

He raises an eyebrow. "Meaning you no longer are?"

"He's on his way back to Colorado."

He cants his head. "That was a quick visit."

"He *is* just my client, Axel, and he accepts that now."

I wish he looked like he believed me—that his blue eyes would be Blue. "As for Uncle Obe's will, we're going forward with the plan to sell his assets and make restitution."

"Under the guise of philanthropy."

Guise. I don't like that word. "Where possible."

"And hope Luc takes the threat of Antonio and Daisy seriously."

"I'm banking on it."

Axel wipes the moisture from his brow with a muscled forearm. "How much longer are you in Pickwick?"

"I've made arrangements to return to L.A. this coming Sunday." Speaking it aloud almost takes my breath away. It seems that this time when I leave, I won't mind taking some of the Pickwick dust with me, as Celine suggested. "But I will be back however often it takes to see this through."

"Your uncle will appreciate that."

Only my uncle?

Axel turns away. "It's time for me to pick up Obe."

That's it? "Thank you." I hope he'll look back, but then he's gone, and I miss his broad shoulders, rubber-banded hair, and even the hitch in his stride.

25

Any questions?" Uncle Obe peers at his family gathered in the library.

I'm proud of him. Everything is out in the open—Antonio and Daisy, his plan to contact them (if he ever gets past the rough-draft stage of the letter he's writing), the liquidation of the estate, the plan to make restitution, and his dementia.

Throughout the telling, Artemis stood in the doorway, shaking his head and wrinkling his cruise-tanned brow. I didn't achieve what he summoned me home to do, but I believe I did better. And the papers Uncle Obe had Artemis draw up this week empower me to see it through.

Devyn lifts her head from Uncle Obe's shoulder. "Oh, Unc-Unc, I'm sorry your mind is going south."

Exactly how he expressed it—going south like birds for the winter. Of course, Luc had to point out that *these* birds aren't returning. Ever.

"But it's great what you're doing." Devyn pats his jaw that I helped shave this morning in preparation for the Fourth of July celebration, where he'll announce his plans for a new statue.

"Well, I don't like it," says Adele. "What's done is done, and I say we move forward from here."

Luc's hand shoots up. "I agree." He glances at Bart.

Bart shrugs and flops a hand into the air. "Bygones be bygones."

His parents, Bartholomew and Belinda, also raise their hands, and the former says, "Amen to that."

I glance at Bridget, but her arms are crossed over her chest as she stands on the lower rung of the book ladder. And Maggie?

"I don't know, Uncle Obe," Maggie says. "I understand your reasoning and that it's the right thing to do, but I worry about…" Her gaze flicks to her daughter. "I believe Piper has the ability to make the best of a bad situation, but this could open a can of worms that some of us aren't prepared to deal with."

Devyn sits tall on the arm of Uncle Obe's chair. "If you're talking about me, I did just turn twelve, so I can handle it. In fact—" She whips her head around and pins Uncle Obe with her eyes. "I think you should forget about prettying it all up, no offense to Miss Piper. Come clean and be done with it."

"Devyn!" Adele screeches. "You have no idea what you're talking about, child. You shouldn't even be here."

The hurt that fastens onto the girl's face stirs resentment in me. *Be a peacemaker. Peace. Maker.*

"I think Devyn may be right," Axel says from somewhere behind me.

I momentarily close my eyes at the sound of his voice, which has been mostly absent for the past six days as we've avoided each other.

"This isn't a game," he continues. "It's life, and it ought to be accorded the respect it's due, beginning with honesty."

If only it were that easy…

Gasping like a fish on the rocks, Adele stares at him. I'm sure she's tempted to give him a verbal smack, but it's Maggie she turns on. "Do something about your daughter, Magdalene. Send her outside or sit her in front of a television while we discuss what is only fit for adults to discuss."

Maggie is ten feet from me, sitting beside her mother on the sofa, but I feel her anger. "If Devyn wants to stay, then—"

"Shouldn't this just be family, Obadiah?" Uncle Bartholomew glares at Axel.

Uncle Obe raises a hand to calm the seething masses. "As far as I'm concerned, Axel *is* family, and he's as welcome here as the rest of you—including my great-niece." He pats Devyn's shoulder.

There is gnashing of teeth, but no one else protests.

"So that's the plan," Uncle Obe concludes.

"Fine," Luc says. "Let's take a vote. All in favor of leaving the estate intact, raise your hand." He thrusts his into the air, as does Adele, Bartholomew, Belinda, and Bart, though the latter with what appears to be flagging enthusiasm.

Uncle Obe clears his throat. "I'm sorry if you misunderstand, Luc, but this is not a…a…" He squeezes his eyes closed. "…democracy. I'm simply doing you the courtesy of making you aware of what I *am* doing."

Luc's color brightens. "You're making a mistake. Now I don't want to have to—"

"And I don't want to have to threaten my own family." My uncle sits forward, causing Devyn to adjust her seat on the chair's arm. "But either you nip in the bud any thought of having me declared mentally incompetent, Lucas Lee Pickwick, or I'll write you out of my will."

"But if you aren't competent—"

"I am, as proven by tests run this week."

It's true. Though I didn't tell Uncle Obe about my run-in with Luc on Sunday, I strongly advised him to return to Dr. Dyer and undergo further testing as a precaution against any attempts to contest his mental competence now or later. He said he wanted to discuss it with Axel and would get back to me. To my surprise, that same day he agreed. The results arrived yesterday, and they showed a decline since the initial testing, but the doctor and his colleagues feel that Uncle Obe is still capable of making decisions about his affairs.

After much exchanging of glances between those who have grudgingly lowered their hands, Uncle Obe says, "Thank you all for coming. Now I need to get ready for the celebration."

Devyn slips off the chair arm, leans in, whispers something that makes him smile, and then hurries to where her mother is waiting. "I'll see you at the parade," she says to me as she and Maggie leave the library.

I still can't believe that the one thing I wanted to avoid will soon come to pass. "I'll see you there."

Bart is the last of my Pickwick relatives to exit the library, but no sooner does he leave than my uncle calls to him. He ducks his head back in. "Uncle Obe?"

"I have something for you." He motions my cousin forward.

Bart's face brightens as he hurries across the library. "I'm honored, Uncle." He halts before the desk and gives his shirt a tug, as if preparing to receive an award.

Uncle Obe opens a drawer and pulls out something I haven't

seen in weeks. "Funny thing"—he turns the binocular-eyed object in his hands—"but I found these here in the library last week."

Bart stiffens a moment before his shoulders slump, as if in preparation to receive a prison sentence.

Though I did put the night-vision goggles in the drawer, I didn't say anything to Uncle Obe about that night. Did Axel? I look around, and he shakes his head. Hmm. Words may elude my uncle from time to time, but he's definitely not in the dark.

"Don't know where they came from," he continues, "but they immediately made me think of you."

I hear Bart swallow, a gulp so cartoonish I would laugh if not that I feel for him.

"Here." Uncle Obe extends the goggles across the desk. "I know you like gadgets. Maybe you can find a use for them."

Bart takes the goggles from him. "Th-thank you, Uncle Obe."

"You're welcome."

Turning, Bart frowns at me. I shake my head, as does Axel. Suddenly animated, my cousin hurries from the library.

I look at Uncle Obe, who just smiles.

"I'll pick up Piper and you at six," Axel says.

"That'll be good." Uncle Obe nods.

Then it's just me and my uncle, but before I can ask about the goggles, he says, "He's a fine man. A pity you're going back to Los Angeles."

Despite the obvious tension between Axel and me, he's still trying to match us. "It is where I live, Uncle Obe."

"Yes, but this is *home*." Using his cane, he levers up and comes

around the desk. "And you're going to miss us more than you realize. But at least you'll be coming back from time to time."

And maybe not only when necessary.

Uncle Obe halts before me. "Do you think our meeting went
well?"

"I do, and if Luc and the others have an ounce of logic, they'll
back down."

He chuckles. "I've got them by their belt loops." He hooks an
arm through mine and we exit the library. "Have you spoken to
Trinity's grandmother yet?"

I didn't intend to tell him about that. However, when Trinity reminded me of my promise yesterday in hopes my support of her innocence would clear the way for her to attend the parade with her
grandmother's blessing, he overheard. Thus, I spilled on everything,
including the discovery of the box.

Once his anger resolved, he said my peace of mind would be
better served by simply telling the truth. I know he's right, but I also
know that the chances of Trinity and her grandmother keeping quiet
about my Lady Godiva ride are slim.

I shouldn't care what anyone thinks of me, especially since Janet
Farr/Jane Farredy has returned to Colorado, according to Grant, but
I do. And, of course, if my scandalous ride were to come to light, it
could still reflect poorly on Grant.

"Have you spoken to her?" Uncle Obe prompts.

"Not yet, but I'll talk to her tomorrow before I leave Pickwick."

"That's cutting it close. Of course, that probably suits you fine
should Mrs. Templeton not take kindly to your *opinion* about her
granddaughter's Lady Godiva impersonation."

Exactly.

We halt before Uncle Obe's bedroom, and when he looks at me, his eyes are intense beneath silvered eyebrows. "Peace of m-mind is what I'm looking for, Piper, especially as I don't have much looking forward to look forward to." He squeezes my forearm. "Though I'm willing to give this philanthropy idea a try, I can't help but think Devyn has it right."

Neither can I. I lay a hand over his and return the squeeze. "It will all work out." I only wish I believed God would work it for the good of those who love Him…

Uncle Obe stares at me and then chuckles. "That Devyn. She reminds me of you when you were a girl. No airs or pretensions. Just who you see is who you get."

Which is no longer true of me.

He nods. "Real. I like that."

I wish there were a place for that in my world, but being real is akin to exposing one's underbelly in a den of predators. You don't get out alive.

Which wouldn't be an issue if you stayed out of the den in the first place.

26

With the lowering sun casting shadows across the town square, I try not to think about the last time I joined a smaller crowd of Pickwickians for pre-parade Fourth of July festivities. Regardless, as Axel and I walk on either side of Uncle Obe, the memories come out to play. And it becomes hard to distinguish between the children of the present, who are running around their parents, and those of twelve years ago. The same goes for the music that rises from the garlanded pavilion where the high school band is pooling its patriotic talent. Then the smells of hot dogs, hamburgers, and lovely fried things make my mouth water, just as they did when I was eighteen and trying not to give in to temptation that might void the sacrifices of my senior year. But this time I don't feel invisible. In fact, I am very visible, as evidenced by looks, whispers, and behind-the-hand comments.

"That's her," an older woman's voice wends toward me. "Piper Pickwick. I was her ninth-grade social studies teacher."

Mrs. Harding?

"Now that's one Pickwick who never saw the inside of the principal's office—or the sheriff's. Made something of herself, I heard."

One of only two *supposedly* upstanding Pickwicks.

As we near the pavilion where Uncle Obe will announce his

funding of a new statue, I glance around at the block of granite that is all that remains of the old one. And standing a few feet from it are Maggie and Devyn, neither of whom appears as happy as Seth Peterson, who is between them. Remembering Maggie's exchange with him at Cracker Barrel, I feel for her. She really has changed. The cousin of my youth would have told him she wanted nothing to do with him, and in such a way that he would have slunk away.

"She works for some fancy public relations firm in Los Angeles," a man's voice reaches me. "Leastwise, that's what Bart is puttin' around."

"Speaking of Bart, isn't that him with that Templeton woman?"

Trinity made it to the parade? Her grandmother allowed it? Or did she sneak out again?

"Yeah, they've been seen together a time or two."

Once we're clear of the voices, to which Uncle Obe appears oblivious and Axel probably isn't, I peer over my shoulder. Trinity, once more transformed from awkward to pretty, stands beside Bart in the shade of a beautiful old magnolia tree. It's the same tree I stood beneath twelve years ago when I overhead one of Maggie's friends tell another that it was a good thing Maggie had had her baby because she was starting to look like me.

I glance from Trinity's glowing face to Bart's grin. Maybe he wasn't using Trinity to get information. Maybe he does like her. Of course, once he has to deal with her grandmother, he might decide she isn't the girl for him. But at least he doesn't have to worry about old Mrs. Templeton today. Thankfully, neither do I.

As we halt to the right of the pavilion, I catch sight of a small, fast-moving object heading for Trinity and Bart.

Oh no, thankful too soon.

"Would you mind taking me through my speech again, Piper?" Uncle Obe asks.

"Uh…" It *is* Trinity's grandmother, hands clenched, arms swinging, jaw thrust forward, cheeks splotched red.

This could be bad. And on a day when the Pickwicks should be regaining a measure of dignity for their contribution to the community.

I glance at my uncle patting his pockets in search of the note cards I made him, then at Axel looking toward the scene about to hit the fan. While Piper would advise me to stay clear, this is of my making. "I'll be back, Uncle Obe."

"But I need to go over my speech."

"I won't be long."

"I'll take you through it," Axel says.

I shoot him a smile of thanks. As I head for the magnolia tree, Trinity catches sight of me and waves me forward—oblivious to the approaching storm—and I hear the rumblings.

"Can you believe that Templeton girl is here?" a languorous drawl reaches me. "Why, she hasn't shown her face on the Fourth of July since that scandalous ride of hers."

"Don't remind me," says another woman, whose voice carries louder than the others'. "That was utterly tasteless!"

"And sinful."

Déjà vu rolls over me, though this time it's Trinity who is ridiculed, and wrongfully so. *I* was the one who "showed them all." When night started to fall and the parade commandeered Main Street to begin its trek to the community park for the fireworks display, Piper Pickwick burst onto the scene in all her Lady Godiva un-finery.

"What *I* can't believe is that Bart Pickwick is with her. Not that he's much better, mind you…" A flutter of laughter. "Actually, worse."

I look over my shoulder at the clutch of older women, most of whom I recognize as lifelong Pickwick residents.

The sixty-fiveish one in the middle gasps. "Is that her grand-mother?"

"Ooh," croons the blue-haired one, "this could be mighty juicy."

I jerk my chin around. Mrs. Templeton is nearly upon Pick-wick's quirky version of Romeo and Juliet. I nearly call out a warning, but it would come too late and cause more of a scene.

"Trinity Louisa!" Mrs. Templeton screeches, causing her grand-daughter to jump half a foot. Bart's reaction is identical, which would be comical if fear hadn't quickly displaced surprise on their faces.

The buzz gains momentum, and I groan. I'm about to enter the fray.

When I'm twenty feet away, Mrs. Templeton grabs Trinity's arm. "I done told you to stay away from that Pickwick boy."

Though her voice trembles, it carries well enough that a person doesn't have to be front row to hear.

Mrs. Templeton jabs a finger at Bart. "He's a good-for-nothin', and he'll make you good-for-nothin' if you don't stay away from him."

"But Gran—"

"Don't you 'But Gran' me, you rebellious child!"

To his credit, Bart tentatively moves forward. "Mrs. Templeton, we're just—"

"Don't you 'Mrs. Templeton, we're just' me, you ne'er-do-well, devil's dust–usin' scalawag."

I lunge forward and place myself between her and Bart. "Mrs. Templeton, everything's fine—"

She thrusts her face near mine. "Don't you 'Everything's fine' me, Missy Pickwick who done run off from her family."

Did the band just stop playing? Feeling eyes on my back—could be hundreds—I move closer. "Do you mind if we talk somewhere else?"

"Why? Am I embarrassin' you?"

"Gran!" Trinity steps nearer. "It's *me* you're embarrassing."

As further evidence, the word *indecent* is hissed from somewhere to our right, followed by, "Makin' a right spectacle of themselves."

The old woman's eyes blaze. "Me, hmm? You done already embarrassed yourself." She jerks her chin over her shoulder. "Who do you think them old biddies are jabberin' about? You. And not just 'cause you snuck off with this scoundrel. No, 'cause you're showin' your face here after what you did years ago, gettin' all naked and ridin' through town."

I could just puddle as I stand silently by while the blame for my wrongdoing tightens around Trinity. It's time to set the record straight—sans spin. *Lord, please work this for the good…*

"Gran, I told you—"

The old woman throws a hand up. One beat passes…two… then her rounded shoulders slump. "Child, this is what they call paying the piper."

Isn't that your cue? My inner image consultant urges me to pick a better time and place, but I ignore her. Allowing my voice to carry and the Southern drawl to have its way with me, I say, "Why, Mrs. Templeton, are you talkin' about the Lady Godiva ride—what, twelve years ago?"

Trinity catches her breath, no doubt hopeful I'm going to keep my word.

"What else would I be talkin' about, Missy Pickwick?"

Deep breath. "Well, that wasn't Trinity." I increase my volume further to ensure the celebrants don't miss the front row seats so graciously provided.

The old woman ducks her head back like a chicken. "How do you know that?"

"Yeah?" Bart chimes in.

My throat is dry, and the eyes on my back are boring through me. "I know it because *I* was the one on the horse."

Gasps all around, and Mrs. Templeton's jaw unhinges.

"The one whose wardrobe consisted of a blond wig and toenail polish—oh, and a thong, although I don't think anyone noticed."

A fresh round of gasps and Mrs. Templeton's jaw unhinges farther. She looks to her granddaughter. "Is it...true?"

Trinity appears confused. "Uh, yeah, Gran." She shoots me a frown. "That's what I've been tryin' to tell you for ages."

The elderly woman's body starts quivering, and she raises her hands to the sky. "Praise the Lord!"

Who would have guessed someone that old was in possession of all her teeth? In the next instant, they disappear.

"Should have known it was a Pickwick." She jabs a finger at me. "You folks have got some nerve."

"I'll say," Bart mutters, and I know he's thinking about the night I found him atop a ladder in the library.

I meet Mrs. Templeton's gaze. "I'm sorry."

"And well you should be." She snaps her head around, and though she narrows her eyes on our audience, as if tempted to give back what was given her and Trinity, she pinches her lips closed.

Steeling myself, I look around. We aren't the center of attention I feared we were, but we have drawn something of a crowd. Unfortunately, it's only a matter of minutes before the gossip about Lady Godiva à la Piper Pickwick makes the rounds of the park. Within hours, it will be all over town. I dread it, and yet until now I didn't realize how heavy the guilt has grown since Artemis's phone call. In fact, I feel pounds lighter—until I catch sight of Uncle Obe and Axel, who aren't at the pavilion where they should be. They're within earshot of my confession, meaning they followed me.

What bothers me is the distant smile on Uncle Obe's face, indicative of wheels turning. And then there's Axel, whose face is no more readable than it has been since my eventful Sunday. Now that he knows about my scandalous ride, is he more disillusioned? disgusted?

"Well," Mrs. Templeton says, "I gotta tell you that I'm feelin' mighty smug. Gonna have to do me some prayin' to get myself right."

"Gran, does this mean I can stay for the parade?"

"What? And chance you messin' up our good name now that we've finally cleared it?"

I so long to remind her that Trinity is thirty years old, but I've had my say and this is not my battle.

"Mrs. Templeton," Bart says. "I really am a changed man, and

I give you my word that I will watch out for Trinity and not let any ill befall her."

"You?" She's back in his face. "You devil's dust—usin'—"

Trinity stamps her foot. "Stop sayin' that!" She puts an arm through Bart's. "He's a fine man, and I'm not a child." Her chin bounces. "Now I don't mean to be disrespectful, Gran, but I'm stayin' for this here parade."

Mrs. Templeton's little body startles and her brow lowers. Another scene in the making… But she just stands there and brews, her nostrils quivering and the muscles at the corners of her mouth convulsing as she looks between us and the crowd. "All right, I'll allow that, but I'm serving as chaperon, you hear?"

Trinity is back to beaming. "Why, Gran, it would be ever so nice if you joined us."

"Well, it has been years since I saw fireworks up close."

Bart shrugs. "Can I buy you a snow cone, Mrs. Templeton?"

She looks him up and down. "It is mighty hot out here."

"Well, come on, then!" Trinity tugs Bart forward.

Mrs. Templeton glares at me and gives a *humph!* before following.

Keep your head up, advises my inner image consultant. So she's still talking to me?

As I prepare to face the music ("paying the piper" doesn't do it for me), Trinity breaks from Bart and heads back.

"What's wrong?" I ask.

She throws her arms around me. "That was so nice of you," she whispers in my ear, "but you didn't have to go so far as to take the blame."

I draw back and, keeping my voice low, say, "Trinity, I wasn't just being nice. I *was* Lady Godiva."

Her smile falters. "You were?" She gasps. "So that's how you knew it wasn't me."

"That's how I knew."

"I can't believe it. You were always such a nice girl."

I smile sheepishly. "Even nice girls make mistakes. And I acted on impulse."

"I do that a lot. Gran says that's where trouble lies."

I touch her arm. "I want you to know that it wasn't until I was called back to Pickwick that I learned you had taken the fall for me. I really am sorry, and sorrier that I didn't clear this up sooner."

She twists her lips to the side. "Better late than never."

Forgiveness. "This is the reason my uncle wanted to write you into his will. He knew I made the ride and felt it had affected you adversely."

"Oh. That does make more sense. I mean, after all, I've haven't been workin' for him long."

"And I'll be the one writing a check to help with your business."

She tilts her head to the side. "Don't that make even more sense!" She steps back. "Well, now I really could use a snow cone." She hurries away.

Ignoring the parade goers regarding me with different eyes, I cross toward Uncle Obe, who has been joined by Seth, Maggie, and Devyn. Axel is gone.

Is he distancing himself from the scandalous Piper Pickwick as I years ago distanced myself from my scandalous, disapproving relations? This is still a small town, and one in which he has chosen to put down roots.

"I can't believe *you* were Lady Godiva," Seth says as I halt before them. As endearing as ever.

I resist the temptation to search out Axel. "Afraid so."

Maggie blows a breath up her face. "That took some guts."

Devyn nods. "I bet you feel tons better, Miss Piper." She slides a look her mother's way. "Honesty *is* the best policy."

So she's still after Maggie to spill on her father. I feel for my cousin, and I'm not surprised when she turns to Seth and says in a falsely chipper voice, "You know, I think I will let you buy me a Coke."

Seth brightens like a string of lights after the one bulb that caused them all to go dark is replaced. "Wonderful!"

"Can I stay with Uncle Obe?" Devyn asks.

"Sure you can," Seth says, and annoyance flashes across Maggie's face as he draws her away.

The annoyance is duplicated on her daughter's face, and for a moment a strong resemblance exists between the two. "I'll just die if *he's* my dad," she mutters.

"You'll be pleased to know I won't be attending your funeral anytime soon," my uncle says.

Her eyes widen behind her glasses. "How do you know Mr. Peterson isn't my dad?"

Uncle Obe shrugs. "Some things you just know. Call it instinct." He jerks his chin, as if to put a period on that, and turns to me. "I'm proud of you, Piper."

"Thank you." Where is Axel?

"So"—he turns toward the pavilion—"do you agree with Devyn that honesty is the best policy? that the truth will set you free?"

Even without the proper amount of lubrication, those wheels of his have been hard at work. Still, beyond the worry of how this will play out, I feel freer. And it would be selfish of me to deny him the same. "Though it will be uncomfortable for a while, it's nice not to have it hanging over my head—or Trinity's."

As we near the pavilion, I check my watch. It's five minutes until the mayor's opening address, meaning Uncle Obe will soon be on-stage. "I don't imagine you and Axel had time to go over your note cards?" And by the way, where is he?

"Nope. First off, they aren't in my shirt pocket where I put them. Second, I don't think I'm going to need them. Do you?"

Keep breathing. "No."

He smiles. "I prayed this morning for the Lord to guide me through the day. And so He has—just as He guided you."

It was God, wasn't it? God who has been hard at work on me since I returned to Pickwick. And, finally, I did the right thing. "Yes, Uncle Obe."

He halts before the pavilion. "I'd better get up there and get this over with."

"Wait!" I open my purse and pull out a notepad. "I'll jot down a few things in case you…"

"Forget?" He gazes at me from beneath those bushy eyebrows. "It's lies and half truths that are hard to remember, Piper. I don't need notes for this."

I imagine him at the podium, struggling for elusive words be-neath the heat of embarrassment. "Yes, but to be on the safe side—"

"I am on the safe side, feet firmly planted." He looks at Devyn. "Come clean and be done with it, right?"

"Right. Just like Miss Piper did with Miss Trinity."

As I look between them, the band strikes up "God Bless America," signaling the commencement of the celebration.

"Now," my uncle says, "I'm going to get some of that peace for myself."

Devyn escorts him to the steps, and I hold my breath as he grips the rail with one hand, his cane with the other, and makes his way upward.

Lord, please grant him the peace he seeks, and help the rest of us Pickwicks to control ourselves. And, one more thing—don't let Axel think too badly of me.

27

*T*he mayor welcomes everyone to the Fourth of July celebration, causing applause and whooping and whistling. There follows a brief speech about our Founding Fathers and their break with England, a reminder about the mayor's bid for reelection, and then my uncle is introduced.

Despite the constraint of his recent surgery, Uncle Obe is surprisingly erect as he walks forward to shake the mayor's hand. When the podium is yielded to him, he looks around. "I'm honored to be here today, and I hope you will bear with me if my delivery is not as smooth as our...our..."

Mayor. The word is *mayor.*

"...as the leader of our fine town."

Good strategy.

"Since I'm not a politician, words don't come easy for me." He looks down. "But there's more to it than that."

He's not going to—?

"Ahem. A-hem!" Artemis stands to my left, attempting to waylay my uncle.

"You see, I was recently diagnosed with dementia."

As a murmur once more circulates through the crowd, Artemis

shakes his head and blots his brow with a monogrammed hand-kerchief. "That's takin' honesty a tad too far if ya ask me."

"So," Uncle Obe continues, "if I forget a word or two, I trust you'll understand." He winks at Devyn where she peers at him from the foot of the pavilion.

And I feel Axel's absence more deeply.

"Now, as the…mayor said, my family and I have good news. On that granite pedestal"—he points to the left—"there once stood a bronze statue commissioned by my grandfather. Forty-odd years ago it disappeared. Now I could tell you that out of the kindness of my heart I'm commissionin' a new one, but the truth is, I'm makin'…"

As I steel myself for more honesty, pain flashes across his features. "…amends for a wrong I personally committed."

The voices grow louder.

"It was a young and secretly rebellious Obadiah Pickwick who convinced his friends to help him pull down that statue and sink it in Pickwick Lake."

Artemis sidles up to me. "It's all your fault. Had to let the cat out of the Lady Godiva bag."

I note the prickly flush of red above his collar.

"Not the influence I was countin' on ya to have, Piper Pickwick."

For the first time, he doesn't correct my last name to *Wick*. And I don't mind.

Uncle Obe continues. "Though the Pickwicks have made a great number of contributions to this community, along the way we've wronged some of our neighbors. Thus, our family has decided to make things right. In the months and possibly years ahead, restitution will be made. Unfortunately, it may cause some of you to think harshly of our family, but I pray for your forgiveness. Thank you." He turns to the mayor, who appears to be in a state of confusion. My uncle clears his throat. "Now as soon as y'all wrap your heads around that, we can continue the celebration of our nation's birthday."

The mayor hastens forward, a tensely toothy smile on his face, and shakes Uncle Obe's hand. "Thank you for your, uh, generosity." Stiff chuckle. "And honesty." He looks to the crowd. "Let's give Obadiah Pickwick a hand."

The clapping starts small and uncertain but grows as my uncle heads for the steps.

"Image consultant!" More neck chafing from Artemis. "It's all hype and no bite, if ya ask me."

I start to defend myself, but there's nothing to defend. My job is to help a client present an image that appeals to his audience, but it only works if it's something the client aspires to. Uncle Obe aspired to something higher than what I devised, and it's for the best, even if there are headlines to pay.

"Luc will be having a fit, I tell ya. And wait till Adele hears about this—if she hasn't already."

"They'll get over it." The voice that comes between Artemis and me makes me catch my breath.

"Get over it?" Artemis drops back to glower at Axel. "This ain't gonna play well for the Pickwicks."

I venture a look at Axel, but his eyes are on Artemis.

"Nope." More chafing. "Gonna get rougher before it gets better."

"But it will get better." Uncle Obe appears before us with Devyn.

Artemis whips his head around, freeing up Axel to look my way, which he does. And his mouth curves. And his eyes are Blue.

"I don't know why ya pay me to look after your affairs, Obadiah Pickwick, if you're just gonna do what ya wanna do."

Uncle Obe shrugs. Devyn giggles. And out of the thinning crowd, Maggie emerges less one Seth Peterson. She looks from her daughter to her uncle. "A little warning would have been nice, Uncle Obe."

He turns his palms up. "When your cousin set such a fine example of doin' the right thing, I couldn't help myself. And it felt mighty good."

"Well, the two of you have certainly put our family under the microscope. Any more revelations we ought to know about?"

"You mean other than what we talked about this morning?" Uncle Obe says.

"Yes."

His eyes flick to Devyn. "There might be."

"What do you mean?" Maggie's raised voice causes the stragglers to turn.

"We'll talk later." Uncle Obe pats Devyn's shoulder. "Should we scout out a piece of sidewalk to watch the parade?"

Devyn bounces onto her toes. "How about the fountain in front of the bank? The mist will keep us cool."

"Sounds good to me." And off they go, with a tense Maggie and muttering Artemis in their wake.

Acutely aware that it's just me and Axel, I nearly jump when his arm brushes mine. In the gathering dusk, I look sidelong at him. "I suppose you're pleased by what happened here today."

He appears neither smug nor satisfied. "I believe it will give your uncle peace. And you."

His arm brushes mine again, and I swallow. "Are you sure you want to stand this close? Some of my past might rub off on you."

"I'm not worried."

"But you disappeared. You were by my uncle, and then you were gone."

"Your aunt Belinda swooned when she heard about the real identity of Lady Godiva. I helped Bartholomew get her to the car."

The gossips will love that. "Then you weren't put off to learn what I did twelve years ago?"

He smiles. "I figured that out a while back, Piper."

I look down. "Why didn't you say anything?"

"You were a teenager and you made a mistake. What is there to say?" His hand closes around my upper arm, and all my bodily functions threaten to shut down.

"You're holding your breath," he says in my ear.

I lift my chin to find his face inches from mine, mouth kissably close. Way too much temptation, especially under the circumstances. "I am going back to L.A."

"Are you?"

"Yes."

"Then you miss the 24/7 life? And feeling the need to carry a gun?"

I don't, but I can't tell him that, not with everything inside me straining toward him. "Look, L.A. has its problems, but every place does. What happened there could happen here…" I should not have said that. I backpedal into a bright smile. "I need to get back to my job."

"Do you?"

Do I?

"You could stay in Pickwick." He smiles. "It's tame—relatively."

"If you're not a Pickwick."

"You aren't."

I scoff. "I may have changed my last name, but—" *What? You're a Pickwick? That* is *what you were going to say.*

"You're Piper." Axel lifts my chin. "Above all, Piper."

Is he going to kiss me? I believe he is. And though I know I should pull back, this time there's no Grant. There's only Axel, and I kiss him back and slide my hands up around his neck and my fingers into the hair at his nape. Nice—until a finger catches on his rubber band.

"Ouch," he says against my mouth.

I tug my pinkie free. "Sorry." I step nearer and his arms encircle me, head angles, and lips press mine. No man has ever kissed me like Axel kisses me, and it has nothing to do with the rasp of whiskers above and below my lips. No, never *ever* been kissed like this. Not that I have loads of experience, but I have enough to know that his kiss is different.

And dangerous.

I won't let it go any further. I just want to enjoy it while it lasts. And make it last a nice long while. After all, once I leave Pickwick— *if* I leave Pickwick—

Oh no.

He lifts his head. "See, Pickwick isn't all bad."

Not with Axel in it. "Maybe I should explore my options a bit more."

"Maybe?"

I smile. "Definitely."

"Meaning that one day you might consider being engaged to be engaged to one Axel Smith?"

I catch my breath. "That's certainly a possibility."

He chuckles and taps a finger to my lips, as if pushing the Pause button. "We should join your family to watch the parade."

My family… "Yeah."

He steps back, slides a hand down my arm, and meshes his fingers with mine.

"I only hope Maggie is in a better mood," I say as we start across the park. "Axel, when she asked Uncle Obe if there are other revelations we ought to know about, he said there might be and gave Devyn a funny look. Do you know anything about that?"

"I believe he was referring to the artist he wants to commission for the statue."

I shrug. "So?"

"He told me the guy lived in Pickwick for a while and that he had a bit of a history with Maggie."

I nearly shrug again, but then I remember how enthused Uncle Obe became when I told him he could choose the artist. And didn't he say he had someone in mind? And what about the look he gave Devyn? And his certainty that Seth didn't father her?

I halt. "Oh no."

Axel turns to me. "What?"

"Did he mention the artist's name?"

"He may have."

"Does Thorpe sound familiar? Reece Thorpe?"

"That's it. What's this about?"

I sigh. "I think Uncle Obe is trying to give Devyn what she wants." As Axel's confusion deepens, I blurt out, "A father. Reece Thorpe was one of Maggie's boyfriends in high school. He's now a renowned artist who works mostly in sculpture."

"How do you know this?"

"Our firm publicized one of his showings after he hit it big several years ago. I didn't work with him, but I recognized him from publicity photos circulated around the office."

Axel whistles. "Never a dull moment. You said Thorpe was *one* of her boyfriends, meaning he may not be Devyn's father?"

I wrinkle my nose. "Maggie dated a lot of different guys, but I believe Reece's family left Pickwick shortly after the beginning of our senior year, so timing wise, it's likely that another of her boyfriends fathered Devyn."

Axel pulls me forward. "Let's just hope your uncle knows what he's doing."

As we exit the park, causing another stir as Pickwickians note our clasped hands, I stretch up and whisper in Axel's ear, "There's always L.A."

He laughs, and though I do have to return to L.A. tomorrow, I will be back—for Axel and, yes, my family. Convenient or not.

Readers Guide

1. Growing up in Pickwick, Piper was treated like an outsider by her extended family. Have you ever felt like an outsider in your family? Have you treated other family members as outsiders?

2. To justify her attitude toward and speedy exodus from Pickwick, Piper perseverates on Luke 9:5: "If people do not welcome you, shake the dust off your feet when you leave their town, as a testimony against them." However, Jesus was referring to those who refuse to receive His message. Have you ever misinterpreted or molded Scripture to fit your circumstances?

3. As Piper's life improved and her successful career demanded more of her time, her relationship with God slipped. In contrast, as Maggie's "charmed" life gave way to struggle, she drew nearer to God. How can you guard against being a "foul weather" follower?

4. Although Axel's faith is relatively new, it positively impacts Uncle Obe, a much older believer. What things can we learn from those whose faith has less mileage than our own?

5. Piper attempts to go beyond forgiving her relatives to making peace with them. Are there members of your family with whom you need to make peace? Are you willing to make the first move?

6. Despite her peacemaking efforts, Piper must set boundaries with the "toxic" members of her family. Do you have relatives

you consider "toxic"? What boundaries do you need to set? Is it possible to set boundaries that allow for full reconciliation in the future?

7. As a young man, Uncle Obe sacrificed love for monetary gain, and the consequences were far-reaching and heartbreaking. When have you taken the wrong path? What were the consequences?

8. In the end, Piper and her uncle are set free when they act on Proverbs 28:13: "He who conceals his sins does not prosper, but whoever confesses and renounces them finds mercy." Are mistakes in your past holding you captive? What would it take to apply this Scripture to your life?

Don't miss Maggie and Devyn's story—
Available summer 2010!

O ne thing that should have been estab-lished at the outset, and which will doubtless become apparent in short order, is that my mouth is my best asset. Unfortunately, sometimes it lands me in the debit column, which

DAILY WORD CALENDAR
for Highly Successful Career Women

[bow'dlerize *verb* to remove or change passages, as in a play or novel, due to objectional or vulgar matter]

Thursday, February 11

is why I find myself flattened against the outside wall of Fate and Connie's Metalworks, one hand to my mouth for fear of emitting another screech, the other to my heart in an attempt to settle it. But it wants out—bad. And once again, the dreadful feeling that I might swoon can't be blamed on a gut-squeezing con-traption. That blame lies with Reece Thorpe. In the flesh.

As I came around the corner, one glimpse of his profile was all it took to take me back thirteen years—and let rip a screech as I re-versed and slammed back against the wall of the building. But that's not the worst of it. No, that would be too merciful.

Praying my screech wasn't heard over the racket coming from the tin-and-cinderblock building—*You can at least do this for me, can't You, Lord?*—I draw a stiff breath and inch forward to peek around the corner.

That's the worst of it. With his hands in his jacket pockets and face to the sky, Reece stands over my daughter. God and I are definitely not on the same page…chapter…maybe even book.

Lying on her back on the scrubby grass where I left her to make snow angels while I met with Fate to discuss my new signs, she shades her eyes against the sun and swings her pointing hand to the right where the clouds have retreated. "Those are stratocumulus. You see the way they're formed, like pillows stacked on each other?"

"Yes."

With a strangled gasp, I once more apply myself to the wall—not because of the deep, spine-tingling inflection on that single word, but because the voice is as familiar now as it was thirteen years ago. As if I never stopped hearing it—

Ridiculous! Fanciful! You are no Disney princess, and Reece Thorpe is no tights-wearing prince.

You can say that again. He may have been more interested in art than chest-pounding, bone-crunching football, but he was all guy in a quietly assured way that made a girl take a second look, and a third, and a fourth—

Oh, stop! He's just someone I knew, dated, and…may have conceived a child with. *Lord, what have You done? Piper assured me she had convinced Uncle Obe to go with a female sculptor out of Florida, so what is Reece doing in Pickwick?*

I peel myself off the wall and put an eye around the corner of the building.

His head is still back, the soft waves of his black hair brushing the collar of the shirt beneath his jacket, arms crossed over his chest, lids narrowed at the clouds in the distance. "So no more snow, hmm?"

"This is it." Devyn pats the pitifully thin layer that started falling two hours ago and which caused the schools to let out early.

Reece turns his back to me, and I notice that his well-worn jeans fit him even better than they did in high school. He filled out nicely for someone who was already well filled out—just an observation.

And a waste of time that would be better spent extricating myself and Devyn from what threatens to become a mess. I look over my shoulder at the loading dock, which is the only way to get Fate and Connie's attention, as they don't employ office help and have no time for front door etiquette. As it would seem to be Reece's destination, I can't go back inside.

I swing my head around and consider my SUV parked thirty feet away. It sports a magnetic door sign that advertises Serendipity Auction Services—my business, the one that makes such good use of my mouth. *Hey, bidder, bidder!* Fortunately, the sign is only on the driver's side, where Reece can't see it. The passenger side sign recently departed for parts unknown. *Un*fortunately, I can't get to the vehicle without being seen. Of course, it's possible Reece wouldn't recognize me. *Oh, like you didn't recognize him? Note: You are nearly six feet tall. Further note: You are still an unapologetic redhead.*

"What about those clouds?" He nods at the balls of fluff creeping toward Pickwick.

Devyn rises onto her elbows, causing her hood to drop to her shoulders and the sunlight to play up the golden hairs among the brown. "Just passing through."

"Too bad."

"Yeah, it would be nice to have more snow, but…" She frowns and then, horror of horrors, whips her head around.

I slam back against the wall so hard my head bounces off it. That hurt! But worth the lump if Devyn didn't see me. Did she? *Please, God, this is such an easy prayer to answer the way I want it to be. What have You got to lose, hmm? Surely not as much as I do.*

Above the grind and screech that sounds from the building, I hear Devyn's voice again…then Reece's…back to Devyn…more Reece. What can they possibly have to talk about?

I drop to my haunches behind the straggly hedge that fronts the building and spy between the branches at my daughter who is speaking. Unfortunately, another of Fate and Connie's machines—high-pitched and whiny—has joined the din, and I can't hear what she says. Reece says something that makes her laugh, and then his mouth turns slightly up at the corners.

Is that my daughter's smile? No, she has my smile. Nothing at all slight about that. Still, I dart my gaze between the two, searching for a resemblance that probably doesn't exist. Her hair is brown; his is black. No cigar. If memory serves me correctly—and it does—his eyes are green, while hers are brown. Again, no cigar. What about noses? Maybe Devyn's is on the slightly big side because Reece's is? No, his has a bit of a bump halfway down the bridge, whereas Devyn's is smooth—thankfully! As for their chins—

My daughter extends a hand.

I clench my fingers around handfuls of snow, grass, and dirt. "Don't say it," I whisper. "Do not say it."

But she does, just as the whiny machine quiets. "I should introduce myself."

You should not! Vaguely aware of the chill snow against my palms, I stare hard at her profile, willing her to be suddenly capable of telepathy. *He's a stranger, and you know what I'm always telling you about strangers—*

"I'm Devyn Pickwick."

Obviously, we need to have a little talk, Devyn Pickwick! Were I not looking for the snag between the time Reece's hand came out of his pocket and the time it closed around my daughter's, I wouldn't have noticed his hesitation. But it's there. In a collective Pickwick sense? Or a *Maggie* Pickwick sense?

"Reece Thorpe." He returns his hand to his pocket. "I knew some of the Pickwicks when I lived here years ago."

Please, Dev, don't ask which ones.

"Oh! So you've moved back?"

Good girl.

"Actually, I'm here on business."

Uncle Obe and I also need to have a little talk, but first I have to get my daughter away from Reece. *It's me again, Dev. Cease and desist! Say you need to…uh… finish reading your psychology journal!*

"What kind of business?" she prompts.

How about you have to go to the bathroom. Bad!

"I've been commissioned by Obadiah Pickwick, who I would guess is your…great-uncle?"

She bounces her chin. So much for telepathy.

"He's commissioned me to sculpt a statue for the town square."

Her smile flip-flops. "I thought he was going to hire a lady sculptor."

I press my cold, raw hands together—hands that have grown oddly numb.

Reece shifts his lower jaw, causing something to appear in the left corner of his mouth. A toothpick? He clamps down on it and shrugs. "Must have changed his mind."

Devyn wrinkles her nose. "He does that."

He puts his head to the side, as if sizing up my daughter's face as he once sized up mine before setting it to paper with the deft strokes of a charcoal pencil. "I'm guessing you're either Luc's—"

Help me out here, Lord!

"—or Bart's—"

I can't say where the snowball came from, all cold and compact and reinforced with scratchy grass and pebbles, but the moment of contact is etched in my mind—a blur of white striking Reece upside the head, his grunt of surprise, and then his chin coming around.

Finding myself on my feet and wondering why my throwing arm feels strained, I run. Down the side of the building. Around the loading dock. Behind the building. Up the other side of the building with its obstacle course of ankle-breaking debris.

When I stick my head around the corner, my daughter is alone with her hands on her hips as she stares at the opposite corner that Reece must have gone around in pursuit of the snowball bandit. Time to go.

"Devyn!"

She turns and startles at the sight of me.

I don't look that bad, do I? Of course, my face feels flushed, there's moisture on my upper lip, and if my peripheral vision serves me right, there's something greasy on my pant leg. Great.

Thinking a happy thought in hopes of passing off my smile as genuine, I say, "See, that didn't take long." Though I control the impulse to make a run for the SUV, I feel the impatient jerk in my stride as I close the distance between us. "I've okayed the new signs, so we're good to go."

Her lids narrow. "Are you all right?"

"Whew!" I fan my face. "It was hot in there." It really was. All that metalworking generates a lot of heat. Now if only I had the feeling back in my hands. Discreetly wiping my wet palms on my pants, I draw even with Devyn. "Let's go." I turn her toward the SUV.

"But you look—" As I hurry her forward, she jerks her head around. "Why did you come around that side of the building?"

"You know that article you were reading about the differences between the brains of happy people and depressed people—"

She gasps. "You haven't been throwing snowballs, have you?"

"Doing what?" I open my eyes wide and innocent, the art of which I perfected during my elementary years.

Devyn scrunches her nose and shrugs. "This really weird thing happened."

"Oh?" I give her a little push toward the passenger door and flap my hand for her to get in.

"I was standing over there talking to this man," she says as I hurry around the grille of my SUV, "who, by the way, has been hired by—"

"Get in, Dev." I meet her gaze across the hood of the SUV. "You can tell me on the way home."

She frowns. "O…kay."

As I jerk open the door, I imagine a hot breath on the back of my neck and glance around. No Reece. Hopefully, he's caught up in a conversation with Fate and Connie, allowing me to make a clean getaway.

"Hurry," I say as Devyn slowly slides in beside me.

"Why?"

I shove the keys in the ignition. "We have lots to do."

"But I thought we were going home."

"We are." No sooner does she close the door then I reverse, crank the wheel, and accelerate out of the parking lot.

"Mom!" She clicks the seat belt in place. "What's the hurry?"

I check the rearview mirror. Still no Reece. "Well, there are your chores…" I turn onto High Holler Road. If I can just make it around the curve ahead, we'll be out of sight. "And while you're at them, I need to run over to Uncle Obe's." I take the curve, and though all four wheels stick, it's a close one.

Devyn grips the door handle. "You're acting strange."

Yeah, well, you may have just met your father for the first time—not likely, but possible—so I'm a little freaked out here. Thank goodness she *isn't* telepathic!

"Sorry." This smile feels almost natural. "It's just that this early school dismissal has thrown my day a little." I ease up on the gas. "So tell me about the man you were talking to." I slide her a stern look. "You know I don't like you talking to strangers."

She sits back. "His name is Reece Thorpe, and he's the sculptor that Unc-Unc hired to make the new statue. Anyway, we were standing there talking when a snowball came from out of nowhere and hit him in the head."

I shift my hands on the steering wheel, noting that feeling has returned to them. "I suppose someone was having fun with him." I chuckle. "It's not as if he was hurt, right? It *was* just a little snowball." Even if a bit hard and scratchy and pebbly...

Devyn nods. "He seemed fine, though annoyed. I told him it was probably Mr. Fate and Mr. Connie messing around. You know how they are."

Fortunately for me, they *are*. "So he went in search of the perpetrator?"

"Yep."

I shrug. "I'm sure they'll work it out."

"Uh-huh."

Is that it, then? Did I pull it off? I look sidelong at her, and my tension eases when I see her open the psychology journal she was earlier poring over. I did pull it off. *Thank You, Lord—*

Do you honestly think He had anything to do with you worming your way out of that one? It's called deception, Maggie. God does not do deception.

The tension returns. Though I'm not perfect and have to ask for forgiveness on a fairly regular basis, I pretty much broke myself of the everyday habit of deceit years ago, but I have the feeling it's back. And, under the circumstances, I have no idea how to make do without it. I can't tell Devyn the truth, not at her age. And, in my defense, it's not as if I came right out and lied. I skirted the issue, cut out the objectionable matter—

Ah! I *bowdlerized.* I sit straighter. Though my Daily Word cal-endar defines the word in terms of written work, with a little bend-ing, it fits. And with its high-flying pronunciation—long *o* and all that—it lends an air of legitimacy to my attempt to spare my daugh-ter the truth.

"Here's the article," she says.

"Hmm?"

She nods at the picture that features colorful brain scans. I should have known my earlier attempt to change the subject would come back to bite me. Boring, boring, boring.

"It says here that there are decided differences between the brain of a person who is not experiencing major strife and the brain of a person who is under great stress—"

That would be me.

"—and has been diagnosed as depressed."

No diagnosis yet. Hopefully it won't come to that. I point to the scan on the right. "That one's kind of pretty."

"It's also kind of depressed."

Figures.

"You want yours to look like this." She taps the left scan.

Does my brain look like that? If so, for how much longer? *Be proactive.* Right, as in find a way to get Reece Thorpe out of town. And out of my life. Again.

Girls you can relate to

Kate Meadows is a successful San Francisco artist looking for a nice, solid Christian man. So when not one, but two handsome bachelors enter her orbit in rapid succession, her head is spinning just a bit. The question now is, what kind of work will Kate do on herself...and who exactly is she trying to please?

Harriet Bisset used to be a rebel. And she has the tattoo to prove it. Join Harri on the spiritual journey of a preacher's kid turned rebel turned legalistic Christian who discovers the joy of trusting in God's security—and the fun to be had along the way.

Laugh, cry and identify with
Kate and Harriet

...available from your favorite bookstore or online retailer!

All she wants is a job. All she needs is religion.

How hard can it be?

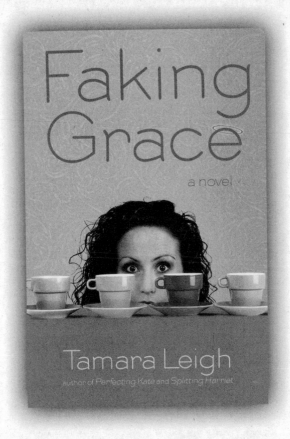

Maizy Grace Stewart dreams of a career as an investigative journalist, but her much-needed second job, Steeple Side Christian Resources, only hires committed Christians. Sure she can fake it with her Five-Step Program to Authentic Christian Faith, Maizy conjures up a plan that includes changing her first name to Grace, buying Jesus-themed accessories, and learning "Christian Speak." If only Jack Prentiss, the ministry's managing editor and blue-jean-wearing British hottie wasn't determined to prove her a fraud.